ALSO BY DENNIS McFARLAND

The Music Room

School for the Blind

A Face at the Window

Singing Boy

PRINCE EDWARD

Henry Holt and Company | New York

PRINCE EDWARD

DENNIS McFARLAND

Henry Holt and Company, LLC
Publishers since 1866
115 West 18th Street
New York, New York 10011

Henry Holt® is a registered trademark of
Henry Holt and Company, LLC.

Library of Congress Cataloging-in-Publication Data
McFarland, Dennis
    Prince Edward / Dennis McFarland.—1st ed.
    p.   cm.
    ISBN 0-8050-6833-3
    1. Virginia—Fiction.   I. Title.

PS3563.C3629P75 2004
813'.54—dc22   2003056698

Henry Holt books are available for special
promotions and premiums. For details contact:
Director, Special Markets.

First Edition 2004

Designed by Paula Russell Szafranski

Printed in the United States of America

1   3   5   7   9   10   8   6   4   2

For Michelle

PRINCE EDWARD

1

THE OLD COLORED WOMAN in the woods stopped speaking for such a long time, I thought maybe she'd had a stroke and died, in which case I would have got a good deal more from today's spying session than I'd wanted. I was in my usual spot, inside a rusty oil drum sideways on the ground, my heart thumping now at the prospect of Granny Mays's sudden death with me the only witness. I didn't know the precise medical meaning of a stroke, but I'd heard the word often enough, and something about it—*stroke,* a fatal-sounding noun if there ever was one—made me envision a person stung mute and stiff as a board, shot with a ray gun. I imagined a stroke to be the exact opposite of a fit, which I'd seen in two mad dogs and three different members of my family.

It was 1959, late summer in the lower part of Virginia known as Southside, where I grew up on a farm owned by my father's father, Cary T. Rome; noting the time of day, a little after one o'clock in the afternoon, I'd slipped into the woods about a quarter mile behind the tractor shed, taken up my hideaway inside the abandoned oil drum, and waited. Granny Mays, the old Negro woman who lived in Daddy Cary's tenant house with her son and grandson, had lately become a fascination to me—I'd found her to have a secret identity as an orator, and I believed myself the only agent in possession of this bit of intelligence. Four months earlier, in April, I'd turned ten, a milestone that had nurtured an already developing zeal for anything even faintly clandestine. Today, the August sun had warmed the woods and caused the sap to run in the trees, filling the air with the piney scent housewives seemed to want in their cleaning products and room deodorizers but which, in my opinion, had never been successfully reproduced in the laboratory. Midafternoon on a scorcher like this, I didn't typically worry about snakes, as they would be down at the creek cooling themselves on rocks or having a swim; but for some reason—maybe the way worry begets worry—I began to imagine a copperhead bellying into the oil drum with me, drawn by the barrel's reddish-brown camouflage. If Granny Mays didn't finish her speaking and move along soon, I would have to reveal myself, and though I had mixed feelings about revealing myself, I didn't want to do it today of all days: In the hip pocket of my dungarees was a deck of cards with pictures of people having sex, which I'd found in the attic of the Big House (Daddy Cary's house) half an hour earlier, and I knew that if Granny Mays were to see me now, she would detect guilt on my face.

Through the eye-size hole in the oil drum I viewed her: rigid, roughly the color of wet pine bark, and sitting stock-still in a ladder-back chair I'd dragged down here yesterday. The chair, which my mother was throwing out simply because it was old and scratched, had been my idea of an anonymous gift, a chance for Granny Mays to get off her feet when she came into the woods to do her speaking. I'd thought, rightly, that the old woman's broomstick arms and legs would be at home in it, but now I feared my thoughtfulness might have boomeranged. While I knew charitable acts were permitted between the races, as long as they flowed from white to black and not the other way, I wasn't sure about what amount of charity was acceptable and what would be too much. I didn't understand exactly where the line was drawn, though I certainly knew there was a line, and what if, even by accident, I had crossed it? What if Granny Mays had suffered a stroke precisely because she'd tried to do her speaking sitting down instead of standing up, and this was God's way of punishing me for overstepping the color line?

Scattered on the ground between her and me were the faded green hull of a 1939 Plymouth coupe with all the windows busted out, a set of bedsprings and a mattress, a ringer washer with a leg missing, a metal bread box with the lid hanging by one hinge, and a wide assortment of old cans, bottles, and rainwashed *Look* magazines. Nobody knew who'd left all this stuff here, or when, but my father had said it was the reason NO DUMPING signs had been put out on the road some years ago. Granny Mays was wearing the brown leather shoes she always wore, heavy and wide like men's shoes, and between the rungs of the chair I could see the knobs of her spine beneath her dress, which was cotton and floral as always, expertly fashioned from a feed sack on her black-and-gold Singer sewing machine. Her hair, what you could see of it, was silvery white, bound up in a cloth that matched the pink and crimson roses of her dress. You had the impression that her hair was wild and had to be bound that way to control it. My mother—one of the family members whom I'd seen have a fit (and more than once)—sometimes said of her own dyed-blond hair that it had a mind of its own. I'd seen her sit before a vanity mirror and beat her hair angrily with a brush and then finally give up and say, "Well, my hair's just got a mind of its own today, I guess." But she never wrapped it in a scarf like Granny Mays's. She wouldn't be caught dead with anything like a handkerchief on her head. She wouldn't wear a dress made from a feed sack either, though she wasn't above going to Newberry's and buying fabric that looked just like feed-sack material and then complaining about the cost. My mother, Diane Tutwiler Rome, had grown up in Richmond and hated nearly everything about her life, especially its country qualities, and she took pains to distinguish herself in small ways from the low class of people she was surrounded by. She also wouldn't put corn bread in a glass of buttermilk or peanuts in a bottle of Coca-Cola.

Inside the oil drum, I was struck by a comforting recollection. Some several weeks earlier, I'd found Granny Mays dozing in a rocker on the porch of the tenant house, and when the scrape of my shoe on the front step caused her to open her eyes, I said, "Sorry, Granny, I guess you must've nodded off."

"No, Mr. Ben, I was just stealing away," she said, in that voice of hers that was so surprising. She appeared frail and inconsequential, but her voice was deep, solid as a locomotive; it actually frightened some people when they first encountered it.

"Stealing away?" I asked, and she said, "Stealing away to Jesus, Mr. Ben," which didn't clear matters up entirely, but which was enough for me to get the general idea. I'd already begun spying on her in the woods by that time—I knew her to be a great deal more than met the eye—and I was ready for any amount of mystery, even religious mystery, with which I already had some experience.

Now I peeked through the hole again and thought maybe Granny Mays was stealing away to Jesus and hadn't had a stroke after all. Granted, I'd never seen her steal away to Jesus in this particular spot, this makeshift junkyard in the woods where she came to speak, but for a few seconds I convinced myself that it wasn't out of the question. Then to my simultaneous relief and horror, she turned in the ladder-back chair and stared from some twenty-five or thirty feet away straight into the peephole in the side of the oil drum. I ducked down quickly, careful not to make a sound, holding my breath, and after a minute I heard her say, "Well now, ain't the world just chock-full of a number of things. That old barrel over yonder got a eye in the middle of his brow just like the Cyclops from the storybooks."

I didn't move. I thought I heard thunder in the distance, though I could see perfectly well that the sun still shone. An abrupt blast of warm air swept the floor of the woods and drove a barrage of dry pine needles into the open end of the oil drum, prompting me to squeeze my eyes shut. Slowly, silently, I began to breathe again, and after another minute I heard Granny Mays say, "Amen, and now I'm gonna leave this off in my mind," which was the way she always ended her speaking. I think what she meant by this was that she hoped not to have to return to this place, because she would have said everything she had to say, once and for all. But of course she did return, day after day, who knew how many times? Too many to count, surely, and each time she would begin, "I come to speak on the daily hardships of my people, to say for my people, justice for my people," and she pretended that the trees were listening.

My grandfather's farm was a four-hundred-acre triangle of land formed by the dirt road we lived on, which was called Rome Road; the paved county road that intersected it at Rome's Corners; and the long squiggly hypotenuse of a stream that, as far as I can remember, was never referred to as anything but simply "the creek." I would one day discover on a map that it had a name, Beulah Lee's Creek, but I never learned who Beulah Lee was or how she came to have a wide meandering ditch of muddy water named for her. Three houses were situated on the land: the Big House, where my father had been born (as well as his two older brothers and two younger sisters) and where Daddy Cary now lived alone; our much smaller house, a quarter mile down the road toward the creek; and the tenant house, the four-room tarpaper shack where the Mayses lived. Each of these houses had sundry tales attached to it that were repeated in my youth, and of course each had its own particular atmosphere. The Big House was the oldest, alleged to have been built with Daddy Cary's own hands, out of lumber milled from his own trees; though I may have heard some version of this fact proclaimed a dozen times by my father's relatives, I never spoke the question it invariably raised in my mind: Did "own hands" refer to Daddy Cary's hired help or to the red, meaty, tobacco-stained, and versatile appendages joined to his wrists? The atmosphere of the Big House was historical: brick fireplaces in the bedrooms, feather mattresses and patchwork quilts on the beds, a cooking stove fueled by wood, interior walls of plain unpainted boards, and spooky walk-through closets between some of the rooms. Since my paternal grandmother had died of bone cancer when I was a baby, her absence—signified by a small sepia photograph in an oval frame on a wall of the kitchen—was all I had of her, and her spirit didn't much linger, certainly nothing like the odor of Daddy Cary's Dutch Masters cigars, which pervaded every cubic inch of the house, though it was two stories and six bedrooms. A screen porch, enshrouded and darkened by scuppernong vines, flanked the kitchen and living-room end of the Big House, and across the entire front of the house was a concrete porch with six wooden columns mounted on red-brick pedestals; no stick of furniture or any other thing inhabited this porch, and its unimpeded, tunnellike quality made you want to run the length of it, back and forth, whenever you saw it.

Our house, down the road, had been acquired dirt cheap by Daddy Cary when, some twenty-five years earlier, he annexed a small farm abutting his own. The house was modest and ugly, a one-story box with sand-colored asbestos siding and a front porch of jalousie windows, always gray with dust from the road. My father, who was still buying the house from Daddy Cary with low monthly installments, had added a new bedroom and bath to it before I was born, and its atmosphere was less physical than emotional—or maybe the emotional, which was sometimes like grand opera without music, simply overwhelmed the physical. Still, the house possessed two noteworthy details. The added-on rooms had necessitated a long hallway, which was paneled in knotty pine, and the grooves between the boards produced a neat rat-a-tat sound when you dragged your knuckles along the walls. And high in one corner of my bedroom, a bullet hole blossomed like a sudden blotch on the wall, a black cavity in the Sheetrock, surrounded by an irregular aureole of white; inside my closet, two corresponding holes indicated the bullet's trajectory through the closet as it exited the house. The original owner of the smaller farm had got drunk on white lightning one night and shot his wife, wounding her in the elbow such that she never regained full use of her arm.

When I was very young, I didn't know what the word *tenant* meant, and I thought in some vague way that the rundown shack where the Mayses lived was called the tenant house because of its tin roof. What was most interesting to me about the house was its method of arrival at the farm. Daddy Cary had bought it from a Cumberland County tobacco farmer in the early 1940s, jacked it up off its cinder blocks, loaded it onto a tractor trailer, driven it home, and plopped it right out in the middle of the cornfield. From time to time, I'd seen a house or half a house wobbling slowly down the highway, and the sight never failed to confound me with conflicting sensations. It was something like being very excited and having to hold still at the same time, and I compared this odd feeling to a dream I once had in which I swallowed a fish hook on a line, and my father had to draw it out of me painstakingly, so as not to snag it on something vital. Sometimes I imagined the tenant house going down the road on wheels, and for me that was its chief atmosphere, if a mental image combined with inexplicable feelings can be called atmosphere. In the summer, the long dirt drive to the tenant house cut through the high wheezing corn, and all but the gables and sagging line of its roof were invisible from the road. In the winter, it sat out in the barren field like a lonely game piece, marooned, not quite real except for the gray cords of smoke twilling up from its stovepipe into the sky.

Our immediate family ran the farm's egg business. My father had begun with the small henhouse and few white leghorns Daddy Cary kept for family eggs and created an enterprise that supplied a good deal of Prince Edward County, with retail deliveries to private homes and wholesale deliveries to food stores and bakeries. My father's name was Royalton C. Rome, and the C, like the T in his father's name, didn't stand for anything; it was simply Royalton C. My mother and Daddy Cary were the only ones who called him Royalton (pronouncing it "Roilton"); everybody else called him R.C., and the egg business was known as R. C. Egg Farm. (Secretly, I thought of the R. C. as standing for Rabid Chicken.) My father loved trotting out the egg as nature's most nearly perfect food, but my brother, my sister, and I were humiliated by having to reveal ourselves as chicken farmers. I thought this recurring moment of shame was connected to the abysmal stupidity of the animal who provided our livelihood. I knew far more than any child needed to know about the species, a universal symbol of cowardice, and I detested its crazy traits and habits. I believed the chicken flapped and darted about stunned and deranged because its eyes were placed on opposite sides of its head—it saw different views of the world from each eye and couldn't blend them into anything coherent—but I felt no sympathy, as I did for nearly every other breed of animal I'd known. Why had my father chosen this life for himself and for us? My mother contended that he sought in the egg business to earn Daddy Cary's admiration, which sadly never came. My father's siblings had long ago fled the farm and Daddy Cary's tyranny, but my father had remained, walking distance from the cold brutal man who seemed to dominate him with little more than an exercise of silence. Daddy Cary, by so constantly withholding his favor, had created in my father an unreasonable thirst for it. My aunts and uncles were around rarely and briefly, and I thought I noticed, even as a boy, a certain irony—that their scarcity had made Daddy Cary value them more than he did my father, who'd stayed close by; it was as if Daddy Cary respected these ordinary and wayward children for rejecting him outright, while my father had lost his respect for failing to.

When I think of 1959, an image comes to mind of my grandfather in overalls, standing in the middle of the dirt road outside the Big House; he has wet his thumb on his tongue and now holds it up to the air, a quizzical look on his face, and appears to be noting a curious change in the wind. I think this the feeble poetry of the subconscious, for though I may have actually seen my grandfather once stand in the road and test the wind this way, it certainly had nothing to do with the swell of change that was about to break over our lives. That year, the ongoing difficulties in the public schools concerning racial integration had come at long last to a head. It had been several years since the federal Supreme Court had decided *Brown v. Board of Education of Topeka*, and Negro students in our county who complained that their schools were inferior to the white schools had been one of the five plaintiffs in that famous case; as a result, our corner of the world had received some national attention, which a lot of white citizens resented to this day. Though Virginia had been legally obliged to desegregate its public schools for quite a while now, it had managed to delay the thing one way or another with a series of legislative maneuvers known as Massive Resistance. But lately, the state supreme court and the federal district courts had been steadily eating away at Massive Resistance, and Governor Almond, once a hero to men like my father, had caved in to the courts rather than go to jail. Locally, a kind of panic had begun to set in because some other counties in Virginia, as well as all over the South, were already starting to integrate.

According to men like my father (who belonged to the Defenders of State Sovereignty and Individual Liberties and to the Chamber of Commerce), the United States Supreme Court didn't understand our way of life if it thought we were going to send our children to school with niggers. That was how they put it privately. Publicly, they talked more palatable abstractions like states' rights and civic responsibility and quality education for all children, but what they meant, always, was that they flat-out opposed any form of mixing the races. Men like my father, who had the strongest feelings as well as power and influence—Defenders for the most part—were determined that such a fate wouldn't befall Prince Edward, no matter what any court said, no matter how many compromises more moderate minds might propose, and no matter how many outside agitators the NAACP sent down to stir things up. They were so determined that in June the county board of supervisors had made the extraordinary decision to cut off funding to the public schools, which meant that the schools would not reopen come September.

At first, some white folks (including my mother) had been upset by the prospect of the public schools closing, but with the help of J. Barrye Wall, Sr., owner and editor of the *Farmville Herald*, it had been turned into a kind of call to arms, our standing fast and not submitting to federal judges who would enslave us and dictate how we must live our lives. If we were to prevail against the forces that sought to destroy everything that had made Virginia great, a private school system had to be organized in place of the public one. Mr. Roy Pearson, a school board member who had once worked overseas for the Standard Oil Company, took charge of the effort. Now, all over the county, people were in a frenzy, making their contribution to the cause of establishing the new Foundation schools (named on behalf of the group who raised the money), mostly in church buildings. Donations of all sorts came from far and near, including 250 pounds of chalk from a man in Silver Springs, Florida. Some people, my father among them, were behaving as if it were the Civil War all over again. My father, like a lot of people in the county, was a good bit influenced by Mr. Wall, who maintained that integration would result in the destruction of both races and render the American people a mongrel nation. My father was not a religious man and attended church only at Christmas and Easter, but he claimed that the Negro's soul was as dear to God as the white man's and we whites had a sacred duty to "take good care of our niggers." However, like Barrye Wall he believed that integrating the schools would lead to the mixing of white and black blood, which was unnatural, a sin, and contrary to God's will. God wanted the races kept separate, which was why He'd put us on separate continents in the first place. My father, along with many of his Defender brothers, believed something else too, a theory that by today's lights seems paranoid and fanatical but which, in 1959, was a commonplace: that the Supreme Court's rulings on race were part of a Communist plot to divide and conquer America.

In the earlier stretches of this time, my grasp of these events was narrow and interior. I recall a slim but critical shift in my personality; I began forming and holding more and more opinions on an increasingly wide range of topics, from the scent of artificial pine to what was the best solution to my parents' violent and disastrous marriage. Forming an opinion and holding it inside seemed to make me count for something more than I had counted for before. I didn't distinguish between opinions and beliefs. One was as good as the other, and I mistakenly imagined that a storehouse of opinions could steer a person in times of uncertainty, like a travel guide to a foreign country. I suppose that growing older is always, among other things, a deepening acquaintance with human mischief, and mischief had lately begun to flourish in Prince Edward—which seemed to make the world spin faster and to demand more opinions of people, even of children. Everywhere I turned, folks were taking stands of one kind or another, and I wanted to be included, because I thought it my birthright. I hadn't yet discovered that what you believed true and fair, what you stood for, might serve as much to isolate you as to include you.

That August day when Granny Mays remarked about the Cyclopean eye in the oil drum, I felt, as I walked back home from the woods, that something in my breathing had changed and perhaps changed permanently; when the old woman had looked straight into my blinking eye behind the peephole, I'd caught my breath, and throughout the afternoon I couldn't seem to get enough air back into my lungs. That evening, while my sister Lainie and I set the table for supper, I tried to affect a mood of idle curiosity as I asked her if she was familiar with something called a Cyclops.

"Benny boy," Lainie said sadly, "don't you know anything?"

I did actually know a few things. Lainie was wrapping the paper napkins tight around the silverware the way they did it sometimes in restaurants, and I knew, for example, that our father would make fun of it when he came to the table. I knew that our brother Al, who was older than Lainie by two years, was coming to supper at our house to talk about the new football field he and the Jaycees were putting in next to the city dump, and he would get a good laugh out of my father's making fun of Lainie, and then she would start to cry and have to leave the kitchen. I knew all that.

In truth, it didn't take much to make Lainie cry these days, as she had serious cause for tears. Two months earlier, right out of high school, she'd married Claud Wayne Rivers, a big noise in the Air National Guard, and three weeks after the wedding, he was shipped off to Wiesbaden, Germany, for an indefinite period of time. (On top of everything that was going on in Virginia, there was the progress of the Cold War and the certain threat of nuclear holocaust.) Lainie had applied to Longwood College for Women, and been accepted, but then deferred her enrollment when she learned she was pregnant. She and Claud Wayne had planned to rent a place in town, close to the college and to the army surplus store where he worked as an assistant manager, but after these surprising developments—Lainie's pregnancy, Claud Wayne's sudden farewell—Lainie was still stuck living with us, six weeks along and a husband halfway around the world. Almost nothing had gone as she'd hoped, and really she hadn't hoped for all that much. Nobody would have described Claud Wayne as an obvious catch—he was boastful and lacked a sense of humor—but he was good-looking in a lanky sort of way, he could whistle louder than anyone else I knew, and according to Lainie he was a good dancer. Marrying him was meant to get Lainie off the chicken farm, a mere stepping-stone to a wider departure, for she'd decided some time ago that it was her fate to see the world; she'd intended to continue her twenty-hour-a-week job in town as a dentist's receptionist, take classes at Longwood, and ultimately lose the weight she needed to lose in order to seek employment as a stewardess on Eastern Airlines.

"It's from the *Odyssey*," she said to me now from across the red Formica table. "By an ancient Greek poet named Homer. Cyclops was a monster. You'll get it in the seventh grade."

"That's if there's a seventh grade to go to," my mother said, without turning around from the kitchen sink, where she was using a toothbrush to clean the silk from some ears of corn.

My sister said, "Don't worry, Mother. There'll be a seventh grade if Daddy has anything to do with it."

Lainie wasn't praising our father's efforts, but the opposite. She might not have freely chosen racial integration of the schools, but she believed it couldn't be stopped; she also believed that what was happening to the colored children of the county was cruel and foolish. What were the colored children to do without a public school to attend, and how could it possibly benefit the county to have a whole population of uneducated Negroes running around?

"A monster?" I said, not to be derailed from my primary interest. "What kind of monster?"

Lainie sighed, letting her shoulders drop, and looked at me hopelessly, as if I were a room that needed tidying. She was wearing light-blue pedal pushers and a yellow halter top, her brown hair pulled into a ponytail; she suffered dramatically in the heat, and—another disappointment—she and Claud Wayne had intended to put air-conditioning in their place in town. We had a powerful window unit in our living room, but that was where the eggs were kept cold after they were collected; you could go in there to cool off, but there was practically nowhere to sit, and there was always at least a hint of dirty egg odor.

Lainie came around the kitchen table and tapped the middle of my forehead three times with her index finger. "Not really a monster, Ben," she said. "A giant, with one giant eye. Right here."

Something about this moment made me recall the deck of pornographic playing cards I'd found in my grandfather's attic. The way Lainie stood in front of me, tapped my brow with her finger, and said *eye* made me shudder. I thought of my grandfather looking at me earlier that afternoon when I'd crawled out from inside the attic's storage space where he'd sent me to look for a certain straw hat; when I said I didn't find any hat, all he said was, "That so?" but there'd been a secret knowledge behind his eyes when he said it.

I was mostly inured to that sort of behavior; adults frequently made remarks accompanied by facial expressions that insinuated a hidden additional meaning. Not more than fifteen minutes ago, my father had come in from the henhouses, tracking mud on the linoleum, and my mother, gazing down at the sink drain, said, "You do that just to aggravate me, Royalton." She said it with such quiet resignation, devoid of any special desire, you might have doubted that anyone had definitely spoken.

My father, who was six feet tall and weighed 255 pounds, stomped back to the porch door; I heard the coils rattle inside the toaster on the kitchen counter. He kicked off his boots and said, "I guess you should've got yourself somebody like what your *mama* married."

Mother turned quickly from the sink, and I saw them exchange a deeply meaningful look. I was used to it. I'd noticed that adults rarely said all they knew, and they often seemed to suggest, with what they did say, that they were holding back a great amount of knowledge, even if they weren't. This dubious skill was apparently a cardinal attribute of being an adult. By the age of ten, I'd already heard enough about the cruelty of children, but no one ever mentioned the fact that with children, cruel or not, it was a lot easier to know where you stood. I'd also learned that there was status to be gained by acquiring and controlling more and more information and then holding as much as possible close to your chest. Meanwhile, all over the world, teachers, preachers, and scoutmasters exhorted children to tell the truth—it was even a Commandment—and from the way they stressed it, you would think they were actually afraid that children might grow up to become this rare and hideous spectacle, the adult who kept secrets. But of course children could see quite early that *everybody* grew into an adult who kept secrets. It was why people had to put their hand on the Bible in a courtroom and swear to tell the truth so help them God. It was why no song in the schoolyard had quite the voodoo of "I know a secret, and I'm not telling." It was why I had such a feeling of prosperity, of gaining status, crouched inside the rusty oil drum in the woods, as I listened to what Granny Mays had to say but couldn't say anywhere else for fear of being heard. When I thought of that deck of cards, where I'd hidden it inside my carton of Lincoln Logs on the top shelf of my closet; when I thought of those funny-looking people, the women with the broad hips and spit curls, the men with handlebar mustaches and their hair parted down the middle; when I thought of them in various stages of nakedness and what they were doing with each other in pairs and groups of three and four, I didn't recognize anything like sexual arousal—that hadn't yet arrived. But I felt something similar to what I felt eavesdropping on old Granny Mays in the woods: the force of knowledge, previously forbidden, now attained. I was beginning to acquire some important secrets—secrets to grow up with.

But none of that was what made me shudder when my sister tapped my forehead and said the word *eye*. Surely it was the image of a giant with a single organ of vision, large enough by implication to see things I wanted kept unseen, and considering that my grandfather was an enormous bullying man, it made sense that I might think of him then. It made sense that I might recall him standing on the bare wood floor of the attic, the blistering heat up there so close to the roof, the odd look he gave me as I climbed down out of the wall from the dark storage space beneath the rafters. I supposed I might shudder.

Lainie, looking rather sinister, now put a hand on each of my shoulders. She said, "What you should know, Ben, is that Cyclops and the other giants were all cannibals."

"Mary Eleanor Rome," my mother shouted from the sink, "that'll be just about enough of that!"

This made Lainie laugh and go kiss Mother on the cheek. It was our poor unhappy mother, at times as sweet as anybody, at times scary with overwrought emotions, now standing at the sink and applying discipline where she could, to insignificant matters: Apparently, she wanted no talk of cannibalism in her kitchen. At first she pulled away, as if she didn't want any of Lainie's kisses, but then she quickly kissed her right back and gave her a little shove.

The kitchen was the largest room in our house, spacious enough to accommodate all the usual appliances: the Formica table that seated six, and a white deep freeze where five-gallon cans of whole broken eggs were kept frozen until time for delivery to local bakeries. The deep freeze, about six feet long and four feet tall, opened from the top with a heavy coffinlike lid. If you climbed inside and let the lid accidentally shut, you would be trapped—in the cold, in the dark—and because of the freezer's weight, its insulated airtightness, and the hum of its motor, your screams for help would be in vain. Round the clock, this reminder of the nearness of death purred against the wall of the room in which we did most of our living. Mother had painted the kitchen walls neon white and the abundant woodwork black, both in high-gloss enamel, and recently the color aqua had cast a kind of spell over her. She returned home regularly with household items in that color—a mop bucket, a dish drainer, a dustpan, silverware trays—and even our modern unbreakable Melmac dishes were trimmed around the edges with bands of gold and aqua. (They looked horrible on the red Formica table, which Mother hoped someday soon to replace.) She was, about her kitchen, the way my brother Al was about his car; there appeared to be no end to the breadth of detailing she could bring to the room, and the walls and counters and windowsills were riddled with knickknacks and gadgets. A brass napkin holder, styled to look like praying hands, rested on the table, clutching the napkins so tight they tore when you tried to take one. A tin match dispenser hung on a cabinet door and held a full box of kitchen matches, dispensing them one at a time in a neat tray. On the countertop, a redheaded woodpecker perched on a little hollowed-out log where toothpicks were stored; when you wanted a toothpick, you pressed the woodpecker forward on its hinge, and its needle beak speared a single toothpick from the log. There were many decorative pot holders, and on the wall behind the stove hung two pot-holder *holders*, colorful ceramic figures of black children, a boy and a girl, their eyes impossibly white and wide, their puffy cheeks half buried in slices of watermelon; out of the rinds of the watermelon came little gold hooks for the pot holders.

I had imagined that you furnished a room and were done with it, and I recognized Mother's boundless decoration of the kitchen as a need to get something right that was always wrong. In the dry-goods store, coming upon vivid greenish-blue place mats, her face would suddenly glow, and she would say, "Oh, look . . . aqua!" She would finger the place mats hopefully, then remember the ugly red table at home and turn away, almost teary. In the simplest terms, I thought she wanted her kitchen "nice"; that was all. But I could tell that a current of disappointment flowed beneath all the decorating, and when I caught her, as I often did, slump-shouldered at the sink or stove, her head inclined in the attitude of a grieving angel on a tombstone, I knew that whatever was wrong with her life would not be corrected, nor would she be lifted up, by any color scheme.

What I made of the ceramic figures on the wall behind the kitchen range I'm not entirely sure. I was fond of the ornaments because they suggested a happy world in which children had huge portions of what they enjoyed eating, and I admired the meticulous painting of many seeds in the flesh of the melons and the way the children's crammed brown cheeks were stained with a blush of red I'd never seen in real life. But lately when my eye happened to fall on them I felt a vague uneasiness. I had a private idea that the children, as represented, belonged to a species of colored folk who were colored folk as we would have them be, as we wished them to be. I'd seen another manifestation of this at a country restaurant we sometimes went to called The Cotton Patch, where fried chicken and biscuits and homemade pickles were served by large Negro women wearing floor-length skirts and white cotton bandannas. "Like the old days," my father would say, obviously pleased, but I hadn't seen any old days, and I didn't quite believe in them.

I caught myself staring uneasily at the pot-holder holders that night Al came to supper and talked about the new football field he was helping to put in next to the city dump. He'd seemed nervous when he arrived, and I guessed it had to do with the dogs barking outside in their pen; it was his fault the dogs were making such a racket—they were happy see him—and he knew how much Daddy hated hearing them.

Daddy, as usual, sat in his chair and hid behind the *Farmville Herald* until Mother told him to put down the paper and eat. As he folded the *Herald* and let it drop to the floor, he said, in a kind of mock-pouting tone, "I was reading about Nikita Khrushchev," and Mother said she didn't care one iota about Nikita Khrushchev.

"He called the reporters at his press conference his *sputniks*,"

Daddy said, and giggled appreciatively, almost as if he admired the infamous Communist leader.

At that moment, the dogs quieted down—first the mutt, Bullet; then Lady, the collie—and I noticed that a visible change came over Al's face. He was sweating so profusely from the heat, and possibly from having been nervous about the dogs, that Mother gave him permission to eat in his undershirt, but Al, relaxed at last, pumped his eyebrows like Groucho Marx and said he was afraid Lainie might get too excited if he took his shirt off.

It turned out I was both right and wrong in my speculations about what would happen at supper. Daddy did make fun of the way Lainie had wrapped the silverware; he lifted the knife, fork, and spoon, which looked like a neat miniature mummy, rotated them this way and that, and said, "Now this here is got to be the work of Miss Priss." The Miss Priss epithet had been a long-standing emblem of war between him and Lainie. According to him, Lainie saw herself as too good for the rest of us, which, also according to him, she came by naturally, from her mother. (According to Mother, our father came by this attitude and name-calling naturally, for when they'd first married, Daddy Cary used to call *her* Miss Priss.) Lainie refused to work for Daddy on the egg farm, and he sometimes called Lainie the Queen, or Queenie, for this reason. Meanest of all, he sometimes called her Piggy or Fatty-grub, when Lainie was anything but fat yet always, as he knew, about five pounds over the maximum allowed for stewardesses on Eastern Airlines. Now, since all Lainie's future plans had fallen through and she was expecting a baby, his calling her any of those names had a kind of razor's edge. And Al did laugh, as I knew he would, but that wasn't what made Lainie cry and leave the kitchen. That came a bit later, after Mother had served the pineapple pudding, which she'd made because it was Al's favorite.

Al had begun talking about the new football field that was to replace the one at the public high school; apparently, a lot of people felt that if a serious private school system was to be established—and if people were to *believe* in it—it had to have a regulation football field, with lights. He told of how Thornton Thomas had donated a bulldozer to level the big lot next to the dump, of how Herring Hardware had donated grass seed and fertilizer, and how the Jaycees had been tilling and planting and watering night and day to get the new field ready in time for the fall season. When Daddy asked him where he thought they would get the lights and poles, he asked it with a sly-looking smile, as if he already knew the answer, and Al smiled back and said, "You'll see." Al was very pleased with himself and full of chatter, and Mother kept telling him to stop talking with his mouth full. He'd turned twenty the previous March and lived in a rented house in town with a pair of twins with whom he'd gone to Farmville High, Shelby and Frank O'Bannon. These boys, as well as Al, had jobs and girl-friends and cars of their own, but because they no longer lived with their families yet otherwise hadn't settled down, they'd earned a repu-tation for being wild; Mother referred to Al's housemates as "those heathens." Here was the kind of wild thing they were known for: Recently, they borrowed one of Daddy's trucks, drove somewhere late on a Saturday night, and then showed up Sunday morning with a flatbed full of ripe watermelons. They parked the truck in the middle of High Street and handed out free melons to anybody who passed by. The only one to say no-thank-you was Reverend Griffin, the heavyset preacher at the Negro Baptist church; he knew, like everybody else, that those watermelons had been stolen. It could be that Mr. Griffin, a member of the NAACP, suspected they came from a colored man's field, or it could be that he just didn't want any handouts from white rascals like Al and the O'Bannon twins.

My father was occasionally outspoken on the subject of Mr. Griffin and his "anti-white" views and called him a troublemaker, a rabble-rouser, and the ringleader of everything that was wrong in Prince Edward today. Daddy once said that a man named Vernon Johns had lit the torch of dissatisfaction among the coloreds in the county more than a decade ago, and no sooner had we rid ourselves of him when L. Francis Griffin came along to take it up again. He said that prior to this Vernon Johns telling the coloreds they ought to be unhappy about what they didn't have, they didn't know they were unhappy, and my mother said it was just like herself and a mink coat: She wasn't unhappy about *not* having one because she'd never known what it was *to* have one.

Mother scooped pudding out of a Pyrex bowl onto saucers and began passing them around, and when Lainie said she didn't want any dessert, Mother said, "Now remember, Lainie, you're supposed to be eating for two."

"What I hear," said Al, "she's sleeping and bawling her eyes out for two."

It was true that Lainie had been sleeping an extraordinary number of hours, at least during the daytime, which Mother said was natural during the early weeks of pregnancy; and Lainie had been doing a fair amount of crying late at night, when she should have been sleeping. But what upset Lainie now was that Mother had evidently been talking to Al about the situation, discussing with Al topics Lainie considered private. She stared a dagger at Mother from the opposite end of the table; then she turned to Al, who was on her left, and said, "You and your Jaycee buddies think you're such big shots. You think you're such heroes."

She was angry and on the verge of tears about Al's sleeping-and-crying remark, but she cloaked it in this other thing.

"I wonder what you think's going to happen to the colored children with the schools closed," she said. "I bet you haven't given any thought to that, have you."

"Well, no," said Al, "I can't say I have, Lainie. But tell me: Why would I?"

As if he wanted Daddy to appreciate his position, Al glanced over at him as he asked this question, smiling—which I thought was weak-looking and morally low. It pleased me that Daddy didn't visibly pay him any mind. Our father had a way of appearing completely deaf and blind to everything going on around him, especially if he was eating or dealing with a sick chicken, and that's what he did now, totally absorbed in his bowl of pudding. His black hair was still wet from the shower, and I noticed for the first time in my ten years how far his ears protruded from the sides of his head. He wore a white shirt with whiter stripes in the fabric, and he'd rolled the already short sleeves into two wide folds to expose the muscles in his upper arms. From time to time I thought him handsome, even harmless in a moment like this, as he ate pineapple pudding, apparently benign, apparently detached and composed, and I wanted very much to love him the way I imagined other boys might love and be loved by their fathers, but my mother had told me two years earlier—when I was eight—that he was possessed of the Devil, and this arresting little detail had lodged in my mind. I had to look away from him now, because all I could see were his enormous ears, like rats' ears, like bats' ears, and the few coarse black hairs growing out of each one.

Lainie said, "What do you think's going to happen to Bogart, for example?" and suddenly it seemed she was asking the whole table, indicting us all.

Bogart, whose name was actually Burghardt, was Granny Mays's ten-year-old grandson, the only child of Julius, Daddy Cary's hired hand. I'm not sure if white folks referred to him as Bogart in defiance against calling him an unfamiliar (and possibly highfalutin) name, or if it was a universal misunderstanding that went uncorrected; they also sometimes called him Bogie, but I called him Burghardt, his real name, since I knew he preferred it. He and I had spent quite a bit of time together over the summer because we'd reached an age where the two of us together could be trusted to do certain tasks unsupervised, like taking toilet brushes and cleaning the waterers in the henhouses, or marking cards for the cage birds. Burghardt was taller and stronger than I was, and off and on I had the feeling when we worked together that he was actually in charge and everybody knew it, but nobody would ever say so.

I felt reproached by Lainie's surprising question, or by the surprising way she'd aimed it at all of us. Even though I'd heard about the public schools not reopening in September, and even though I'd heard Granny Mays speak in the woods about Burghardt having no school to return to, I'd thought only one time, before that day, about how he might be affected; that one time I'd foolishly thought how lucky he was not to have to go to school anymore. I'd simply accepted it that I would be starting the fifth grade on schedule, probably in the new fellowship building at the Methodist church; I'd accepted it that colored people would not be able to do the same thing, to hold school in their churches, but now I realized I didn't know why.

Al said, "Old Julius's boy, Bogart? Why should I care what happens to Bogart?"

Al looked unsure of himself as he spoke, and glanced again at Daddy in that very low way. Then he turned back to Lainie and added, "That boy's nothing to me."

Now Lainie's eyes were brimming with tears, and honestly, I couldn't tell how much had to do with Burghardt and the abandoned colored children of Prince Edward and how much had to do with Mother betraying her confidence to Al about the sleeping during the day and the crying at night.

"Why can't the colored kids just have school in their churches like us?" I said, from what suddenly felt to me like a faraway place inside my thinking. It was unusual for me to move from thinking to speaking without an appraisal of the consequences.

"Because they're no-account, Ben, that's why," said Al. "Do you really think a buncha black no-accounts like the ones that live around these parts could get organized for something like a private school system?"

Lainie pushed her chair back from the table and deliberately made the legs screech on the linoleum, really loud. She sat like that for a few seconds, a good three feet away from the table, just staring at all of us with those brimming eyes. At last she looked at Al and said, "You make me sick. Do you know that you make me sick? I mean, actually, physically, ill."

Mother groaned—"Oh, Lainie"—but Lainie snapped, "Don't Oh-Lainie me!" and stalked out, slamming the door between the living room and the kitchen behind her. A burst of cold air entered the kitchen from the frigid living room, and then I became aware of how the skin on the backs of my thighs was stuck to the vinyl of the chair I was sitting in; this was often a problem when I wore short pants to supper in the summer, though there was something pleasant about peeling it slowly away when you stood.

Daddy was scraping the bottom of his bowl, getting the last bits of custard and meringue, evidently oblivious to Lainie's exit and all that precipitated it. The kitchen fell silent except for the purring of the deep freeze and the clinking and clanking of Daddy's spoon in the bowl. When he lifted his eyes, he saw Mother, Al, and me all staring at him. Mother averted her gaze and seemed to concentrate for a moment on the blue veins on the back of her own right hand, which rested on the tabletop alongside her dessert dish; she looked as if a number of things crossed her mind to say, but she rejected each one. At last she folded her paper napkin into a neat square, left the table without a word, and went to see after Lainie.

As soon as she was out of the room, my father heaved a great sigh, but it was not obviously connected to anything other than his having finished a satisfying meal. Al gripped the edge of the table with both hands and said, "Well, Benny, me and Daddy are gonna go help put up the lights at the new football field. You wanna come, or you wanna stay here with the girls and boo-hoo-hoo all night?"

2

THE SKY WAS NEARLY DARK, but the narrow road through the corn to the tenant house was darker still. The blades on the stalks nearest the road, glossy, lit-up, and plastic-looking in the headlights, slapped the truck fenders and the gates of the flatbed as we bumped through the field. If you closed your eyes, this noise sounded something like the crackling of a fire, and it mixed with the jagged roar of the truck engine, the exhaust fumes, and the nighttime heat in a way that was mildly sickening. We rode in Daddy's flatbed, the green Ford truck that was used for hauling chickens in coops and feed when it came in by rail. Al drove, and I sat in the middle, between him and Daddy. I had to keep my knees spread apart to accommodate the gearshift, which rose out of the floorboard on a long crooked spindle and had a black sphere at the top with a diagram of the shifting pattern. Each time Al changed gears, he'd say, "Watch it," as if I was too stupid to remember that he'd said the same thing two minutes before. He was nervous again, as he always was whenever Daddy was along for the ride. Nobody could drive anything, car, truck, or tractor, to suit Daddy; he would lean back in the seat and hang his arm out the window and get a look on his face, familiar and intimidating to all who knew him, that was utterly blank yet still managed to suggest he was waiting for somebody to make a mistake. Here, now, in the truck, it created an impression of his overseeing a driving test that Al would surely fail.

When we reached the small clearing where the house sat, yellow light was spilling from the open door and windows across the porch and dirt yard, both of which appeared to have been recently swept smooth. As we drew closer, I could spot through the screen door a single naked lightbulb hanging from the ceiling of the front room, the kind of yellow bulb I'd seen burning only outdoors, meant to repel bugs. Bolls of cotton had been used in several spots to plug up holes in the bulging screen of the door. Al brought the truck to a stop. We could hear radio music from inside the house, unmistakable harmonies I recognized as those of WFLO, the local station that played both black and white gospel records. Al summoned Julius to the porch in the traditional manner, two sharp blasts of the truck horn, and when Julius appeared, a very tall, featureless silhouette in the yellow rectangle of the door, he was wiping his chin with a napkin—we'd caught him in the middle of supper.

"Hop on, Julius," my father called out. "We got some work to do."

Without a word, Julius turned and went back inside the house, pausing to close the screen door carefully, silently, and I thought what a quiet person Julius was—a distinct part of him I'd never named before and an observation immediately confirmed by Burghardt's shooting from the house, straight to the rim of the porch, and letting the screen door slam behind him. Barefoot, he hung his toes off the edge of the porch floor and wrapped an arm around one of the weathered poles that supported the corrugated and rusty tin roof; he flattened a hand above his eyes to shield the glare of the headlights and craned his neck severely to one side, trying to peer into the cab. When

I leaned forward enough for him to see me, he jumped down from the porch, then sauntered slowly over, as if he'd been planning to walk in the direction of the truck even if we hadn't been there. He wore a white T-shirt with the sleeves torn off and some kind of blousy orange-colored shorts that looked to me like a pair of swim trunks that used to belong to Al. Burghardt stopped next to Daddy's window and peered up at us, his eyes moving back and forth between Daddy and me. Nobody said anything, but I could tell, though I couldn't see, that Daddy was giving Burghardt that blank sobering look of his.

From the house came the squeak of the screen door—Julius, ready to go—which meant Burghardt, short on time, had better say what he was thinking about saying. "Can I come?" he said, not quite able to keep disappointment out of his voice.

"Come where?" said Daddy.

Burghardt jammed both his hands into the pockets of his shorts and shrugged his shoulders. "I don't know," he said. "Wherever y'all going."

"You mean you don't care where it is?" Daddy asked.

"No, sir."

Julius was by now climbing onto the flatbed, and Daddy stuck his head out the window and called toward the back of the truck. "Hey, Julius, this boy of yours wants to come with us when he don't even know where we're going. What do you think of that?"

Julius hopped down from the bed of the truck and hurried over to where Burghardt stood. This was Julius Mays: very dark brown, lanky, with close-cropped hair and mustache and a broad, eager smile; a decidedly worried frown when he wasn't smiling; and a moment of uncertainty that passed briefly between the smile and the frown. He'd arrived at Burghardt's side looking worried but was now already smiling. He put a hand on Burghardt's shoulder, keeping his gaze fixed on Daddy. "Oh, Mr. Rome, that boy, he just likes to go," Julius said. "Always did."

Daddy said, "Well, I'll tell you what, Julius. Why don't you go on and tell him where we're going, and if he still wants to come, then I'll let him."

Julius's smile faltered slightly. He lowered his chin a fraction of an inch, as if he would bow his head but then thought better of it. I noticed that he began kneading Burghardt's shoulder with the hand that rested there. At last he said, "You know I don't know where we going, Mr. Rome."

Al started to cackle—this horrible, high-pitched monkey noise—and Daddy glanced over at him and chuckled too, sincerely, full of real pleasure and warmth. I stared into my lap, for though I didn't fully understand the purpose of this foolishness, I somehow sensed I would regret meeting Burghardt's eye right then.

His voice still soaked with laughter, Daddy said, "Well, Bogie, I suspect you better stay here and watch over your grandmama," and in another ten seconds, Al had the truck in reverse and was making his turnaround.

As we rattled and thumped into the cornfield, I looked out the window in the back of the cab. I saw Julius, squatting with his eyes closed in a corner of the flatbed, his arms draped over the middle rail in the gates; I saw the trembling cornstalks behind the truck, brown and dead-looking in the red glow of the taillights; I saw the tenant house with its yellow windows. But Burghardt had vanished, nowhere to be seen, and then we rounded a bend in the dirt lane.

Two or three times on the way to Farmville, Daddy told Al to slow down, no matter how slow Al was going, and, "Didn't I tell you to slow down?" no matter how much Al slowed down. Then he criticized the route Al was taking, and Al made the point that it was himself who'd attended Farmville High for three years, not Daddy, and that he ought to know how to get there. Eventually he said, "Why don't you just drive yourself?"

Daddy said, "Because I told *you* to drive, that's why," and Al down-shifted gears and said, "Watch it!" as if he was put out with *me*.

I'd assumed we were headed for the city dump, since that was where the new football field was going in, but when we reached the school and Al drove behind it and the athletic field came into view, I began to put together a few pieces of the puzzle. Lights and poles were needed for the new playing field out by the dump; the high school had lights and poles; the high school wasn't going to be using its lights and poles.

What I didn't understand then, but what Lainie would explain to me later, was why they'd chosen to conduct this operation at night: If the courts were going to allow the county supervisors to get away with not funding public education, it mustn't look as if any public facilities or equipment were being used for the private Foundation schools. This made absolutely no sense to me, since anybody could observe that the sudden absence of poles and lights at the public high school coincided with the sudden appearance of them at the new field, but when I experienced this kind of doubtfulness, I typically imagined that I'd missed something. The world couldn't possibly be as incomprehensible and full of contradictions as it seemed.

All around the athletic field, trucks and cars were parked with their headlights shining over the grass, and because they were necessarily parked behind the several sets of bleachers, a complicated network of shadows lay across the field. At first I wondered why the men didn't just turn on the field lights, but then I realized that they were planning to take the lights down and didn't want to get electrocuted in the process. When Al had pulled around to the end of one set of bleachers and aimed the truck's headlights into the field, two men carrying Jax beer cans passed in front of us and waved, lit up like zombies in a horror movie; their tremendously long shadows slunk behind them over the steel scaffolding of the bleachers. Al put the truck into neutral, raised the emergency brake, and left the engine running so as not to deplete the battery. Then he and Daddy got out, leaving both doors open, and without a word to either me or Julius in the back, walked away toward a bunch of men huddled on the other side of the field.

Through the windshield, I watched Julius running across the grass to catch up to them. As they approached the cluster of men on the other side, some of the men turned to greet them, hands were shaken, and then a discussion ensued regarding Julius's presence. It was a pantomime from my vantage, and obscured by the irregular fretwork of the bleachers, but there was sufficient pointing and gesturing for me to understand that some of the men objected to Julius's being there. I looked around and saw no evidence of any other colored man, and I wondered if maybe Daddy and Al hadn't known this was a whites-only event. But whatever Daddy said to the men, it must've satisfied them, for in another minute, somebody put a shovel into Julius's hands and he disappeared into the darkness behind the far bleachers.

Now I was left straddling the gearshift, not knowing what I was supposed to do and wishing already that I'd stayed home. I thought about Burghardt at the tenant house and how he'd wanted to come with us and I wished he had come, for then I would have some company. I thought about Julius—smiling, but with sadness in his eyes—saying to my father, "You know I don't know where we going, Mr. Rome," and how that had made Al and Daddy laugh. I felt sympathy for Julius, for though he was colored and I was white, I too was expected in most of my life to do what I was told and not to ask questions. Even more mystifying, we were expected to know what to do when we *weren't* told anything and *still* not to ask questions. In a very deep and general way, I knew I would never be smart enough, and it didn't even occur to me to ask the question: Smart enough for what? I knew only that I was fated to make stupid mistakes of one kind or another, and that at times like this—late at night, alone, sitting on the sidelines, useless and at loose ends in a world where everyone else seemed to know what they were supposed to be doing—I would inevitably and repeatedly make the error my father often appeared to be waiting for me to make. This business of knowing what was expected of you when no one had told you seemed an important element of what it was to be a man; and when you became a man, you would expect others to know what you expected of them without your having to tell them. I thought all this masculine silence created a lot of unnecessary confusion and terror in my own life as a boy, but I very much looked forward to the day when I would be on the other end of things: a man, confident, silent, confounding. At the same time, in my heart, I didn't believe I would live that long.

Soon I grew sullen, then drowsy. I'd drunk two glasses of ice tea with supper, and I was feeling it, so I decided I should find a place under the bleachers to pee. As soon as my feet touched the ground, a man I didn't know came from behind the flatbed and said "Boo!" and then squawked like a bird when he saw how much he'd scared me.

He smoked a big wet cigar like Daddy Cary's—I saw a Dutch Masters band still on it—and he took a long drag and blew a perfect smoke ring straight at my face. He was about my father's age, in his early forties, but wiry; he wore a red baseball cap with no letter on it, no shirt, and raggedy old blue jeans slung low around his hips and exposing an obscene trail of black hair running from his navel into his pants. I fanned the smoke from my face and started to walk away, but he whacked the back of my head with his baseball cap and said, "Wait a minute, son. Where you running off to so fast?"

I told him I was going over to the other side of the football field to find my daddy and my big brother. I said if I didn't get over there this minute, they were going to come find out why.

"Is that a fact?" he said. "Well, if I was you I wouldn't just walk off and leave this here truck running. Somebody's liable to hop up there behind that wheel and drive away easy as pie."

This menacing remark played precisely into my dilemma: Just because my father hadn't specifically said I should stay there and mind the truck, it didn't mean I wasn't expected to. I looked around at the

other cars and trucks nearby. Every one of them sat empty, and presumably their engines were running also. The man could've stolen any
of them, and surely, if he was in the market for a free vehicle, he would
prefer something sharper than an old Ford flatbed. In the car closest to
us, a blue-and-white '58 Bel Air, the radio was playing, while our truck
didn't even have a radio. I'd never heard of anybody's truck being stolen
in Prince Edward, but I'd often heard about the perils of meeting up
with an escaped convict or—possibly even worse—an escapee from
the state hospital for the insane. Not two months ago, a nineteen-year-
old patient had escaped from Western State up in Staunton and was
later found crouching by the edge of Highway 29, staring straight up
into the midday sun, stark naked, his clothes wadded at his feet into a
perfect ball. That seemed harmless enough, but I knew they weren't all
like that; some were dangerous. Country music of the twangy variety
my mother hated most blared from the Bel Air's radio. The man stuck
the cigar between his teeth, looked dead into my eyes, and hummed a
few bars along with the song, which didn't clearly distinguish him in
my mind as a criminal or a lunatic. He removed the cigar, smiled, and
said, "You don't need to look so worried, son. You go on over yonder
and find your daddy and your big brother, like you said. I'll stay here
and keep a close eye on your daddy's truck, what do you say?"

I immediately began climbing back into the cab, saying, "No, sir,
that's all right. I guess I better stay with it myself, but thank you all the
same."

I closed the door, locked it, and rolled up the window. I slid across
the seat and quickly did the same thing on the other side. I heard a
noise and felt the truck rock a little, and when I turned and looked
behind me, I saw that the man had jumped onto the truck bed. He
came right at me and pressed his face against the rear window, his lips
and nose and even one eye, which he kept open, flattened against it
horribly; his front teeth clicked against it, and when he pulled away,
laughing, there was stringy brown spit on the glass. I scrambled onto

the floorboard and lay flat on my stomach. My shoulder brushed against the accelerator, revving the engine for a second.

I don't know how long I stayed there in the dark, immobile on the floor of the truck, but it seemed an eternity. I could hear muffled noises from outside—distant male laughter and occasional war whoops, men yelling things to one another, but too faint for me to decipher any words—the rich *vroom* of a bulldozer or a backhoe, and the radio in the nearby car. The floorboard, vibrating steadily, was unpleasantly warm and gritty and smelled of motor oil, gasoline, and the less agreeable odors of what people had tracked in on their shoes. After a while I could begin to discern things under the seat: a pair of flares, a lug wrench and jack, a tin funnel, some old red rags, and two men's magazines of the type found in barber shops, *Gent* and *Cavalier*. I considered looking at the pictures of naked ladies, but I was afraid Al or my father would come back and catch me at it.

Soon I had to pee so bad my stomach ached. The gearshift seemed to press against my bladder, and shortly I was gripped by the kind of familiar distress in which no available course of action felt tolerable. I could stay put and possibly wet my pants; I could make a run for it across the football field and find Daddy or Al, revealing to everyone how scared I was; I could leave the truck, pee under the bleachers, and risk getting my throat slit by a homicidal maniac. Eventually, I must have dozed off, for the next thing I knew, I woke to the sound of applause and cheering, and I thought surely I was dreaming. Before I had time to recall my worries, I sat up, my eyes at dashboard level, and saw through the passenger-side window one of the tall creosote light poles angling slowly toward the ground as if it were on a giant hinge. The standard of floodlights that had once adorned the top of the pole had been removed. Cars and trucks had backed away, giving ample room behind the bleachers for the pole to fall. Somebody hollered "Tim-burrrr!" More cheers went up from the men, and the pole pitched down like a felled pine tree in slow motion; it met the ground with a padded thud, billowing into the air a white dust cloud that was caught in the many headlights and looked like a tremendous flower opening in the night. I thought I felt the earth shake, and then my father rapped his knuckles on the driver's-side window, startling me.

I knew I would have some explaining to do about why I was kneeling there on the floorboard with the doors locked and the windows rolled up, but when he yelled, "Unlock the door, Benbo!" I felt better immediately. First of all, he called me Benbo only when he was in a good mood; second, now I would be able to pee; and third, I'd already decided not to tell the truth about what had happened before. I would tell him the mosquitoes were bad, so I closed the doors and rolled up the windows; I felt myself getting sleepy and thought it better to lock the doors; and (most unlikely) I must've rolled off onto the floorboard in my sleep. The terrorizing encounter with the skinny shirtless man had degraded me, exactly the way I was degraded by one of my father's whippings, and I felt the same urge to hide it. I wanted it not to have happened, and through some trick of my mind I thought I could erase it by not *saying* it had happened. I was ashamed of how scared I'd been, cowering on the floorboard of the truck, and I was ashamed of finding myself in such a fix to begin with, as if, through some personal failing, I'd brought it on myself.

Because our truck had one of the longest beds, we took all the poles while others transported the separate light standards. Even still, the poles were so long, a near quarter of their length hung off the back of the truck, and we had to tie red rags to the ends of them as a warning to other drivers. I didn't think a dirty red rag dangling in the dark from the end of a black creosote pole was going to make much difference, but Al said it was the law. I worried about Julius riding back there with the poles—it seemed vaguely dangerous to me—but I checked on him through the rear window and saw that he'd laid the tailgates across the poles and arranged himself in a way that looked safe enough. Al, in high spirits behind the wheel, participated in a fair amount of horn-blowing with the other drivers en route to the dump. He'd stripped down to his undershirt and smelled of sweat and Old Spice; his hands were black from handling the poles and his hair soaking wet from a water faucet at the high school. Now and then he leaned out the window and glimpsed himself in the truck's big rearview mirror, taken with how he looked with slicked-back hair. Daddy folded his arms over his chest and kept his eyes closed except for when Al blew the horn. I expected him to criticize Al's driving or tell him to stop the horseplay, but he just looked across at Al each time Al blew the horn and then closed his eyes again, as if he couldn't be bothered.

Directly in front of us, a smaller flatbed truck carried two of the huge light standards from the athletic field, and two boys I recognized as Al's housemates, the O'Bannon twins, rode in back with them. They stood on the bed of the truck with their legs spread apart, playing a daredevil game of who could stay balanced longer without grabbing hold of anything, and Al repeatedly flashed his brights in their eyes, as if to make them lose their concentration and stumble.

At the new field, aluminum bleachers had already been erected. When Daddy asked Al where they'd come from, Al just grinned and said, "I'll never tell." Daddy, in a rare prophetic moment, said Al's thieving ways were going to land him in jail one day, but Al said iron bars did not a prison make. Daddy didn't know what to think of that and shook his head. I remembered that particular line of Al's because of the interesting inversion of its subject and verb and also because it fell into a category of occasional remarks that characterized him, a humorous (and usually corrupted) reaching for wisdom that often sur-prised people. If he got to the last piece of cake before you or called shotgun in Daddy Cary's Oldsmobile, he would say, "He who hesitates is lost, and you just lost." When he still lived with us, and Mother would tell him to turn down his radio, he would say, "But music hath charms to soothe the savage beast, Mother, and I'm a savage beast."

The men at the dump worked into the wee hours, and I slept through most of it in the cab of the truck—fitfully, given the heavy piece of equipment Thornton Thomas had brought along, for the drilling of new holes, and the grinding of a cement truck pouring new footings. I was sound asleep when the job was done and we left to go home. What I could vouch for personally was little more than what anyone who lived around Farmville could vouch for: By morning, there were eight craters at the high school's athletic field, and the Foundation school's new football field had lights.

Because the night was punctuated with periods of sleep, it had for me an especially dreamlike quality. Some of the boys around Al's age stuffed handfuls of grass seed down one another's pants, then threatened revenge and chased each other in and out of the bleachers. A station wagon full of girls showed up, driven by Al's beautiful raven-haired girlfriend, Jeannette Winters, and Al swaggered over to her open window, stuck his head all the way inside, and set off a carload of squeals. I recall the smell of beer on my father's breath and an up-close view of his beard coming in black and scratchy on his chin, cigarettes glowing in the dark like orange fireflies inside cars and trucks parked around the field, and music and screeching tires and laughter and cursing. I woke briefly in the truck cab and saw my father looking at me as he said to Al, "Little pitchers have big ears," a mysterious expression I'd heard before. I interpreted it as "Little pictures have big ears," for many country people pronounced the word *picture* as *pitcher*. I hadn't the slightest problem thinking of myself as a "little picture," for I imagined it was how I must look to grown-ups, and there was something intriguing about being considered two-dimensional—I had a fantastical idea I might turn myself sideways to danger and simply disappear. Instinctively, I understood the expression to mean I might be hearing something I shouldn't—not something I needed to be protected from, but something I might repeat where I shouldn't.

On the way home, I awakened on Rome Road when the truck bounded over the wooden bridge that spanned the creek. I was surprised to find my head pressed up against Al's rib cage—he'd put an arm around me and had been letting me sleep like that while Daddy drove the truck. I didn't let on that I was awake at first, as I wanted to get my bearings. I'd been dreaming about Burghardt Mays, and in the dream we'd been swimming together in a wide muddy river.

There was a problem of some kind in the dream, but I couldn't think what, and I wondered if it was simply that I was swimming in the same body of water with a colored person and was afraid of catching disease. Recently, Oatsie Montague, the Holiness woman who cooked and cleaned for Daddy Cary, had told me about a fatal blood disease called sickle cell that you could catch from "nigras," as they were its chief carriers. She lived on our road halfway between our house and the creek, and seeing Burghardt and me on our way to the creek one hot afternoon, she'd summoned me from her front porch swing. "Benjamin Rome," she called out, as if she meant to scold me, "bring yourself up here onto this porch for a minute." She was my mother's age but heavyset and pale-complexioned, with black hair worn in a bun and huge breasts that rested down near her waist—physical traits I'd come to associate with extremely religious white women. Apparently she feared that because Burghardt and I were walking together, I might be planning to risk my health by eating or drinking after him, for she mentioned these hazards specifically; she said that if I was to swim with him in the creek, to be sure I swam at a spot where the water moved swiftly and to keep Burghardt downstream.

Burghardt waited in the road, outside the gate, while she explained all this to me in hushed tones. When I returned to his side, I asked him if he'd ever heard of something called sickle cell, and he said no, but he'd seen the yellow hammer and sickle of the Russian flag. His grandmother had a book at home with color pictures of the flags of the world, and what was more, she had a whole bookcase full of books, forty-one of them in all, not counting the family Bible. This surprised me because we had so few books in our own house. Mother had thrown out all the trashy dime-store paperbacks Al used to read in the bathroom when he still lived with us, leaving us with only Lloyd C. Douglas's *The Robe*, Frank Yerby's *The Foxes of Harrow*, a Webster's dictionary, a King James version of the Bible, an RSV, and *The New Testament in Modern English* by J. B. Phillips. On the other hand, the news of Granny Mays's bookcase made sense to me; I'd thought that some of her speaking in the woods sounded as if it came from books. Burghardt and I fell into a conversation about Holy Rollers and how they didn't believe in wearing lipstick or smoking or dancing, and he wondered if the Holiness, like Catholics and Jehovah's Witnesses, claimed to be the only ones truly saved, and I said I didn't know for sure. I said my mother always called Oatsie Montague "poor old Oatsie Montague" on account of her having lost both her parents and her sister to cancer in a span of seven years, and how she, Oatsie, was now all that was left of the Farmville Montagues. I told him I'd attended all three of the Montague funerals, though I remembered only the last two.

In the dream of Burghardt and me swimming together, he'd appeared supernaturally clear, right down to the little dots of water on his high forehead and the sunshine glittering in his hair as he drifted along close beside me in the river. He looked over at me and smiled, a kind of lopsided grin he had in real life. Great oak trees with Spanish moss overhung the water. When I opened my eyes and found myself resting up against Al in the truck, I felt for a minute that I was still being pulled along by the strong current in the river.

The wooden bridge under the truck tires made a deep drumming noise. Bright pink light glowed in the whole sky overhead. I sat up straight and saw that Al was asleep too, though I couldn't think how, with the truck jouncing us around; Daddy barreled over the bridge, and I thought it good that Al slept, since he would have been petrified had he been awake. My mother was fond of saying that all the Rome men had a heavy foot on the accelerator, and long ago she'd declared a moratorium on riding in any car driven by Daddy Cary. One of Daddy Cary's favorite pastimes was to put people into his blue Oldsmobile and fly up and down our hilly dirt road so that they got butterflies in their stomach.

When Daddy noticed that I was awake, he glanced at me and turned the corners of his mouth down but didn't say anything. I guessed things had taken longer at the city dump than he'd thought they would, and now he was unhappy about getting home at such an hour with a whole day's work to face. I feared my mother would be angry about his keeping me out all night, and that it might cause a fight. I gently lifted Al's arm, heavy as a dead man's, from behind me. He didn't stir, though I saw his lips move for two or three seconds as if they were forming words.

When we passed Oatsie Montague's house, I furtively observed how my father's hands on the steering wheel were a wonderful golden-pink color in the light. I thought about how much there was in my mind, like this simple observation, that I could never tell him, because he wouldn't take it kindly, because he would belittle it the way he belittled things like reading (with the exception of poultry magazines and the *Herald*), any kind of artwork, singing, playing a musical instrument—interests he considered acceptable in girls, but sissified in a boy. He had a long list of things he considered sissified: church weddings, cooking, cleaning house, decorating for Christmas, collecting insects, and, most curiously, even looking up at the stars. I'd kept hidden from him anything that might be kin to these pursuits, simply because I didn't want him to think me a sissy, and that was before I knew all he meant to imply with the word, a vista revealed to me by a boy at school named Paisley Chatham. Paisley, a dirt-poor skin-and-bones third-grader whose mother had died when he was six, lived in a shanty on the Appomattox River with two younger brothers and his father, an odd-jobs man; Paisley's one gift in the world was that he could sing like an angel. On the Tuesday before Thanksgiving, he performed "We Gather Together" and "America the Beautiful" during the lunch period, and immediately afterward, he was cowering next to the trough urinal in the boys' bathroom as a sixth-grade bully named Urban Hall fired plugs of wet toilet paper at his face and snarled, "You sissy, you scabby little queer, I bet you suck your daddy's dick for him every night." There was no doubt in my mind—nor, I imagine, in the minds of the five other boys who stood idly by and witnessed the event—that what happened to Paisley was brought on by his beautiful singing in the lunchroom. After that, I hid from my father just about everything that mattered to me or interested me. Aside from farmwork and playing ball, nothing was safe. I knew that the lovely color of the sky and its happy effect on my father's hands were observations I should keep to myself.

Daddy pulled the truck into our driveway and cut the engine. The sudden silence awakened Al, who reached a hand into his pants and adjusted his private parts, then got out of the truck and made a bee-line for the high weeds and goldenrod at the edge of the woods. Since the dogs were familiar with the sound of Daddy's truck, they didn't bother to come out of their wooden kennel, for which I'm sure Al was grateful; had they seen him, they would have started barking. Al's white '55 Fairlane was parked close to the dog pen, its windows fogged with dew.

Inside the house, Daddy told me to get straight to bed, and then he disappeared into the old bathroom off the kitchen. Al came inside and took a package of cinnamon rolls from the bread box and a nearly full quart of milk from the refrigerator. I sat at the kitchen table and watched him stuff an entire roll into his mouth, then upturn the milk bottle to his lips, pump his Adam's apple five or six times, and polish the whole thing off. I'd felt hungry too, but watching Al made me decide to forgo any food.

He said, "Gotta go, sport," and left through the back porch, careful not to let the screen door slam. The dogs heard the deep rumble of Al's Fairlane and started to bark, but when they saw he was leaving rather than arriving, they soon settled down.

And then the whole place was quiet.

I passed through the frigid dark living room and down the pine-paneled hallway to my room, the room I once shared with Al but now had to myself. A seam in the floor, about six inches wide, bisected this room and marked the line where the new part of the house had been joined to the old. The walls were a pinkish-orange color my mother called salmon, and behind the double bed a pair of pictures hung that depicted bloodhounds dressed as humans sitting at a game table, smoking cigars and playing poker. Though the room had two windows, it got only a small amount of light since one window opened onto the jalousie porch and the other onto a tall camellia bush. Al and I had shared the iron double bed throughout his adolescence, our sleeping together marked with his routinely waking me by crying out in the night, having suffered another of his nightmares, which seemed most often to involve giant turtles.

Now I closed the door to the room, shut the venetian blinds, removed my shoes and socks, and climbed into bed without taking off my shorts and T-shirt; I covered myself with only the sheet. I was grateful that Mother and Lainie were still sleeping, and that Mother hadn't been waiting at the door to stage any sort of confrontation. Immediately, I began to think of the deck of pornographic playing cards hidden in my Lincoln Logs on my closet's uppermost shelf; I saw it in my mind's eye and grasped for the first time that it was actually only half a deck, which meant the other half existed somewhere yet to be discovered. The black-and-white photograph that came to mind most legibly was the one I'd seen first: A man in an old-fashioned shirt and tie sat in an ordinary wooden chair, his pants crumpled down around his ankles; a woman wearing nothing but a white garter belt and white stockings straddled his lap, her bare, graceful back to the camera, her hands gripping the man's shoulders. I'd seen this picture first because it had been lying face up on top of the deck, which itself rested right out in the open on the lid of a red and much-dented tackle box.

Suddenly, from down the hall, I heard the muffled trapped-animal strains of Lainie crying—for Lainie, the dawn of another day; then female voices, hers and Mother's, in a conversation that quickly became an argument. From what I could make out, Mother was again angry at Lainie for crying when she should have been sleeping. She told her to "stop this nonsense and hush," and, most confusing—since Lainie was surely in her own bed at that moment—I heard Mother say, "You made your bed, young lady, and like it or not you're gonna have to lie in it."

After two or three minutes, these sounds ceased as abruptly as they'd begun, though I thought uncertainly that I could still hear Lainie whimpering. A breeze rattled the blind in one of the windows, and I turned to see it swing a few inches into the room and back into place, bumping weakly against the sill; in that moment, the room had grown correspondingly brighter and then darker, which made me think dreamily of a large eye opening and closing. I rolled onto my side, away from the window, just in time to catch a figure come gliding silently through my bedroom door. I closed my eyes, but loosely enough to watch through my eyelashes as Mother moved toward the bed, wearing her quilted blue housecoat. The room was too dark for me to see her face, but soon I felt the bed sink on one side as she sat next to me on the mattress. I pretended to stir in my sleep, then writhed, much perturbed, until I was flat on my stomach, moaning myself back into the depths from which I'd been so rudely churned—an admirable performance entirely wasted on Mother, as she drew the sheet in a prim line across my shoulders and said, in a perfectly normal voice, "You didn't even take off your clothes, Ben."

"No, ma'am," I said, trying to sound sleepy, but sounding instead like someone in a hypnotic trance.

"Did Al go on back to his place?" she asked.

"Yes, ma'am."

"Well, where's your father?"

"He's in the old bathroom."

She sighed deeply, as if this disclosure had disappointed her incurably. She leaned down and laid her head on my back, right between my shoulder blades, and I grew sharply conscious of the rise and fall of my breathing.

Soon she said, softly but with some amount of bitterness, "I wonder if *anybody* knows what time it is."

I observed that the sound of her voice seemed to come through my body, rather than through my ears, and, at a loss to answer her remark, I kept quiet.

After another minute of silence, she lifted her head and said, "You go on to sleep now," as if I had other plans.

She patted me on the back, sighing again, and said, "I don't think anybody but me even *cares* what time it is."

She kissed me on the temple and left the bed and the room without another word. For a while, it felt as if I still bore the weight of her head on my back, and that its gentle pressure was urging me toward sleep.

I saw myself climbing down from the storage space where Daddy Cary had sent me to look for a certain straw hat, and then Daddy Cary's face floated up, huge, round, and chalky white behind my eyelids. The look he gave me as my feet touched the attic's wooden floor distinctly said he knew I'd found the playing cards.

Earlier—what now seemed ages ago—as I hid in the oil drum in the woods where Granny Mays came to do her speaking, I'd worried that if she spotted me she would sense my guilt. But a similar risk never crossed my mind with respect to Daddy Cary; he had no such intuitive powers. If he knew I'd found and taken the cards—which I now believed with all my heart he did—it was because he'd known from the outset that they were there, in the open, waiting to be found and taken. When he sent me up there, armed with his big silver flashlight, he'd fully intended me to find them.

3

WHEN I WAS TWO YEARS OLD, something happened in our county that was important both in a traditional historical sense and also in how it formed abiding feelings in a lot of white people. Contemporary events were hardly necessary to form abiding feelings in a lot of white people, for plenty of feelings abided already, based on long-ago occurrences; drawing links between history and the present day amounted to a kind of cultural pastime in Southside, Virginia, and politics chiefly determined whether this pastime fostered reason or folly. It's not far-fetched—as I begin to tell the story of Barbara Johns, a black teenager who orchestrated in 1951 a student strike at Prince Edward's Negro high school—to recall that just a little over a century earlier, in Southampton County (a mere seventy-five miles from us), Nat Turner and friends had run amok and slaughtered fifty-five white men, women, and children. If this connection appears the least bit theatrical, remember that the political organization to which my father and two thousand other businessmen and civic leaders belonged, and which was chartered as a direct result of the threat of integrated schools, was called the Defenders of State Sovereignty and Individual Liberties—and it turns out that the phrase "defenders of state sovereignty" appears on the Confederate monument that stands on High Street in front of the Farmville Methodist Church. The fears that arose in our neck of the woods in the fifties were in many people's minds the same as those over which the War Between the States had been fought. When I said that some folks, my father included, were acting in 1959 as if it was the Civil War all over again, I meant that in some way they *believed* it was the Civil War all over again.

Barbara Johns happened to be the niece of the infamous Vernon Johns, whom my father considered a hell-raiser and the primary author of discontent among Prince Edward's Negroes, so it made sense to him that something like student insurrection would rise out of such uppity ranks. What Barbara Johns did, her crime against nature, was simply to get fed up with the shabby conditions at Robert Russa Moton High, and in the spring of 1951 she organized a protest that resulted in nearly four hundred students staying out of school for two weeks. People had heard about Barbara's family long before the strike, however, and not only because of her outspoken Uncle Vernon. Her father, Robert, ran a general store in the Darlington Heights section of the county, outside Farmville. Though Darlington Heights was mainly Negro farms and the Johnses' clientele was mainly Negro farmers, many whites did business with them too. Previously, Robert Johns had served in the army, and Barbara's mother, Violet, had spent some time in such places as New York City and Washington, D.C., excursions believed to have accounted for some of the Johnses' unconventional social expectations. Word got around the county, for example, that Violet didn't like being called by her first name by every white Tom, Dick, and Harry who happened to come into the store; she would tell overly familiar white salesmen and customers that she thought only her personal friends called her by her Christian name—a mild enough complaint that didn't go over at all well and usually led to some heated verbal wrangling. Then there was the story of a white boy who went into the general store one afternoon when young Barbara was helping her parents and, in the manner of the day, called Mr. Johns "Uncle Robert." In response to a confused look that crossed Barbara's face, her mother explained, right there in front of the white boy, that, no, Barbara's father was not really the boy's uncle. These, apparently, were the kind of formative moments that contributed to Barbara's later teenage unrest, not only to her unhappiness with the way things were at Moton High but also to her determination to change them.

The Negro high school in Farmville had been built back in the 1920s, big enough to accommodate only 180 students and therefore overcrowded within a couple of years. By 1950, there were nearly 400 students crammed into the place, and sometimes two or three classes had to be taught at the same time in the school's auditorium; the auditorium connected one side of the school to the other, and the classes held there were often interrupted by students passing through. Other classes were sometimes held on buses, which were hand-me-downs from the white schools. Students had nowhere to store their textbooks (also hand-me-downs from the white schools), as there were no lockers. The toilets were insufficient and in disrepair, and the school lacked a cafeteria and any facility where athletes could change or shower. Faculty were paid one-third less than the white faculty across town, the highest-paid Negro teacher making less than the lowest paid white teacher. Moton parents had petitioned the school board for decades to do something about the poor congested conditions at the school, but the best they'd managed to come up with were three temporary structures made of plywood and tar paper—long, low things that resembled chicken houses. The roofs of the tar-paper shacks leaked when it rained, and in winter the only heat came from a wood stove, which the teacher constantly had to keep stoked; kids who sat near it sweltered, and those on the other side of the room shivered, wrapped in their winter coats. Students had to tramp in nasty weather between the buildings, from one class to the next, and colds were chronic and epidemic.

Barbara Johns served on the student council and participated in drama and chorus, activities that sometimes took her out of Prince Edward to other schools, where she saw just how bad Moton really was. She decided something had to be done and persuaded a few other student leaders to her way of thinking. They began meeting secretly to discuss their plight and possible solutions. Eventually they decided to stage a protest in April of '51.

On the appointed morning, somebody phoned Moton's principal, a well-liked man named Boyd Jones, and told him he'd better get over to the Greyhound station; a couple of Moton students were about to get into a scrape with the police. As soon as the principal took off, Barbara and her comrades went into action. She'd written out slips requesting students and teachers to go to the auditorium for an assembly at eleven o'clock; these slips were passed out to all the classrooms, and nobody thought anything of it; it was the usual way in which Principal Jones called an assembly. (Barbara was even able to sign the slips with a J., without technically committing forgery.) Once the teachers and students had gathered in the auditorium, the stage curtain rose to reveal, not Principal Jones but Barbara and her committee of organizers. The first thing Barbara did was to step to the microphone and ask all the teachers to please leave the auditorium. Naturally the teachers objected, but all except one eventually complied. One enterprising teacher went up onto the stage as if to take things in hand but was booed off it, and the teacher who refused to leave the assembly was carried out bodily. Barbara then outlined for the students Moton's deficiencies, with which they were all fully acquainted, and explained the committee's plan—that as of that moment they would go on strike and a demand for a new school would be carried to the county board of supervisors.

When Boyd Jones returned to the school from the wild goose chase he'd been sent on, he discovered the renegade assembly in the auditorium. He told the students to get back to their classrooms, but they didn't obey. Jones was caught in a bind, sympathetic to the students on the one hand, worried about his job on the other. Though the kids had been careful to avoid creating any appearance of the principal's being involved in the planning and execution of the strike, the white men who ran the county's school system would inevitably blame Principal Jones for what happened. Some of them believed he set the kids up to what they did, while others just believed he should have been able to prevent it, but in either case they would hold him accountable.

Barbara Johns and a few other student leaders attempted to make an appointment to see the superintendent of schools, Mr. McIlwaine, but he refused to meet with them that first day; he also refused to come to the school. When he did meet with them the next day, he was convinced that Principal Jones and other adult Negro leaders had put the students up to what they were doing; he believed the kids had been given questions to memorize. The students met also with the chairman of the school board, Maurice Large (who was physically small), who told them the same thing Mr. McIlwaine and Principal Jones had told them, to get back to their classes. They were given assurances that a new school for colored kids would be built, but no one could say when.

One adult from the community did not tell the students to get back to their classes, and that was the Reverend L. Francis Griffin, the Baptist preacher who was a member of the NAACP and the man my father later said was the ringleader of everything wrong in Prince Edward County. Mr. Griffin welcomed the strike, for he'd been trying for some time to get colored people in the county to do something to improve their lives. Once the NAACP got involved in the strike at Moton and the thing grew into the huge thing it eventually grew into, some people contended that Mr. Griffin had been behind the strike from the beginning, along with his old friend John Lancaster, the county's Negro agricultural agent. White folks simply weren't prepared to believe that colored kids could actually bring off such a thing by themselves. It was never clear exactly who initially contacted the NAACP, but the lawyers there always claimed that a female student phoned them from the high school and asked them to come down to Farmville, which they did.

The NAACP, in the persons of Oliver Hill and Spottswood Robinson, told the students two main things. First of all, they could lend them their support only with the approval of their parents; and second, they would have to change the nature of their demands. Recently, the NAACP had determined that the separate-but-equal approach to public education was a dead end; separate schools could never really be equal because separate was inherently unequal. They would support the Moton students if the Moton students would shift their aim. No longer would they be demanding a new Negro facility, they would be demanding an end to segregated schools. Eventually they filed suit with the school board, calling for such, which of course the school board rejected. They filed the same suit in federal court, and it was later joined to four other similar suits in what became the famous Supreme Court case *Brown v. Board of Education of Topeka*. The Moton kids were out of school for only two weeks, for once the parents gave their support and everybody more or less agreed to follow the NAACP's plan, it was no longer necessary for them to continue the strike.

Over the following summer, the school board decided not to renew Principal Jones's contract, and somehow, soon afterward, the county found the money with which to build the new Negro high school. It was completed just two years after the strike. Throughout this time, J. Barrye Wall, Sr., sounded the same note in the *Herald* again and again, that we didn't need any outside influences helping us solve our so-called race problems—indeed, we didn't even have a race problem before outside agitators came along. We were perfectly capable of handling our own affairs, and the beautiful new Negro school was proof of that. He would not be confused by any observation that the beautiful new school was the direct result of the student protest, while decades of peaceful petitioning by the Moton PTA had accomplished almost nothing. Even more ironical, by the time the county saw fit to build the new facility, it was no longer a satisfactory solution, though a new school had been precisely the original hope of Barbara Johns and the other striking students. Nobody had dreamed that they would end up in the United States Supreme Court as part of a larger movement to end segregation.

My learning of these events came in dribs and drabs over a period of years and then, much later, from some reading I did. But even from the start, my feelings were decidedly mixed on hearing about this terrible thing Barbara Johns and her friends had done at Moton High and the unfortunate outside interference and unwanted attention it had brought upon the good people of our county. I accepted without any question that it was a story about the worst kind of colored kids, the trouble they could get up to, the bedlam and pain they could cause. But the irresistible particulars—Barbara's shrewd *J.* on the call-to-assembly slips; the teacher bodily removed from the auditorium— stirred me to secret envy and admiration.

Some of my mixed feelings might have sprung also from the fact that Granny Mays was distantly related to the Johns of Prince Edward. Not long after the night we took down the lights at Farmville High, I rode with my father one morning over to the tenant house to look in on Julius and Burghardt, both of whom had come down with the flu. Granny Mays sat on the porch, not in her rocker but already busy at her sewing machine, powered by the fascinating foot treadle. Granny Mays, known throughout the county as a topnotch seamstress, sewed everything from shirts and dresses to drapes and slipcovers. If you found her at the machine, you wouldn't expect her to look up from her work, as she was not in the habit of doing so, no matter who might arrive on her porch step. It was understood that you might carry on a conversation with her, but you mustn't expect her to divert her focus from the path of the needle. My mother said this ability of hers, not to be distracted by anything, accounted for Granny Mays's impeccably straight seams. So that morning my father went on inside the house to talk to Julius—to find out when Julius thought he and Bogie would be back to work—while I waited in the dirt yard and fanned soldier flies from around my head.

After five minutes, Daddy returned to the porch through the squeaky screen door, stopped a few feet from Granny Mays, and silently studied her for a long moment. He chewed on the end of his thumb as he did this—all of his nails were bitten down to the quick, and sometimes you would even see him go after the cuticles with his tiny front teeth.

"Well, Ole Nezzie," he said, for that was what the grown-ups in my family called Granny Mays. "I guess you done heard plenty about all this commotion going on in the schools."

Granny Mays hunched an inch closer to the machine's presser foot, passing a long piece of bright red material under it without pause. "No, sir," she said, though I knew from my spying sessions in the woods that she knew a great deal of what was going on.

"Well, I reckon you have," Daddy said, "and I reckon you know who's to blame for it too."

"No, sir," Granny Mays said again.

The blue and purple morning glory vines that grew along the kite string tacked to the side of the tenant house stirred in a mild breeze. The *clackety-clack* of the sewing machine seemed to grow thumpier and more boisterous, a kind of bossy noise that might have made somebody less obstinate than my father shut up and move along.

"It's that kin of yours," Daddy said, "Miss High-and-Mighty Barbara Johns. That's the little she-devil who instigated all this pandemonium to begin with, back eight or nine years ago."

Granny Mays continued sewing until she reached the end of the red cloth, then slammed on the brakes and popped up the presser bar. She leaned back in her old metal folding chair and gazed at my father, squinting as if to see him in all his details. For my part, I stood in the dirt yard and held my breath, sure that some fascinating drama was about to transpire on the old sagging porch.

Daddy stared right back at Granny Mays and said, "You know I'm right, too."

The old woman's head, swaddled tight in a plain kerchief the color of yellow sunflowers, began to move slowly up and down, and I thought I saw her eyes shine with a little extra wet light. Whatever was traveling through her mind appeared to reach its destination at last, and she pulled her sewing loose from the machine, clipped the thread with a scissors, and calmly began folding the long piece of fabric in her lap, holding it up with both hands to shake out the wrinkles. When she was done with that, she gazed again at my father. "Yes, sir, Mr. Rome," she said at last, "you are right about that. Violet's Barbara is most certainly the cause of everything that's going on today. You are right as a man can be, Mr. Rome. Just as right as rain about that."

Daddy stood still a few seconds, looking for all the world completely stumped. Then—as if to assure himself that he had indeed just encountered genuine conformity with his own thinking—he nodded, one sharp punctuating jab of his chin in the old woman's direction, moved down off the porch, and told me to get back into the truck and let's go.

Surely the imagination sometimes rides roughshod over memory, but I believe that Granny Mays, during that August of 1959, stepped up the frequency and intensity of her speaking in the woods. Maybe I just went more often to hear her, but in any case my spying on her—which eventually I came to believe progressed with her full knowledge and consent—reflected my growing enchantment with spying in general. Earlier that summer, I'd joined the I-Spy Club, which advertised in the pages of *Superman* comic books. For a nominal fee, you received in the mail a membership card, a menagerie of spy paraphernalia—such as a magnifying glass, a penlight, a bottle of disappearing ink—and an introduction to primitive schemes for composing and deciphering coded messages. Undoubtedly, the I-Spy Club soothed some of my anxieties about the Cold War, converting one of its most famous properties into a game, but the club's existence and my membership in it officially confirmed the idea that you didn't have a real life until you had a secret life. Human affairs occurred on one plane, in plain sight, and then, most meaningfully, on another, normally unseen but vulnerable to spying. Throughout the spring and early summer, Granny Mays had stayed mostly optimistic in her speaking—she gave an upbeat spin to current events—and even after the board of supervisors made the decision to cut off funding to the public schools, she spoke as if she meant to convince the trees of a Divine wisdom at work. She spoke of God stirring things up so they could settle back down in "a more advantageous condition"; she talked about "clarifying the waters." Regularly, she expressed a view shared by many colored people that summer: that white folks wouldn't really go so far as to shut down the schools, and even if they did they wouldn't keep them shut for long. "There's simply too many good white folks," Granny Mays told the trees, "good Christian white folks in the county, to let such a thing pass." Again and again, she repeated a line I imagined came from a Negro spiritual: "A brighter morn awaits the human day."

But as September drew nearer, I detected a change. Her silences grew numerous and long and, tonally, she seemed less intent on reassuring the trees than pleading with them. "I come to speak on the daily hardships of my people," she would begin, but now with great fatigue in her voice, "to say for my people, justice for my people," and it sounded as if she referred specifically to her own family. That day when

Julius and Burghardt were down with the flu, she came to the woods later in the afternoon than usual; I'd been waiting at the junk heap a long time. She always hummed as she picked her way through the pines, and if I wasn't yet inside the oil drum, I would hear her approaching and quickly take up my station.

Once she'd situated herself in the old ladder-back chair, she said, "I come to speak on the daily hardships of my people, to say for my people, justice for my people," paused briefly, and added, "Looks like come September, my Burghardt got no school to attend."

It was to be her topic sentence, a concern she'd adopted on at least one previous occasion. Since I enjoyed the privilege of taking school for granted, I'd never thought it especially important. A person *had* to go to school, so it wasn't something to be valued. Actually, school was for me a daily reprieve from working on the chicken farm, but for nine months out of a year it was just there, unasked-for, apparently free, and I didn't perceive it as any kind of gift.

Granny Mays, all in yellow, fell immediately into one of her long silences. I'd decreed to myself that no matter how long she kept silent, I wouldn't worry about strokes, but I did think after a while that she'd dozed off, and I wondered if I might extract myself from the drum quietly enough to escape the woods undiscovered. I'd lost track of the hour, I had twice as much to do today without Burghardt to help, and I wanted to get back to the henhouses before Daddy or Al showed up and found me missing. To make matters worse, the sky had grown dark with rain clouds, and now I felt that kind of cool breeze stirring that generally preceded a thunderstorm; it carried the scent of rusty metal and rotting paper.

"Now I ask you," Granny Mays said suddenly, as if no silence had intervened. "Is that how it's to be? Can this be where we come after all we've tolerated? No school? A right good amount of sacrifice, a right good amount of work, and this is where we've come? Can this be how it is?"

Her voice rose higher and higher with this series of questions. Through the peephole I saw that she'd crossed her arms and lowered her head. She moved it side to side five or six times, but soon she lifted her chin and continued, more composed, almost in a confiding tone.

"You know I got little to leave him," she said, "a few old books. What I got to give him I got to give in this lifetime. Breakfast on the table, see he gets to school, gets his education. Look in that boy's eyes, there's a wonderful prospect, finally a learned man to take up the speaking. And I don't mean out in no piney woods neither, not under the veil like me. A smart man, a cultivated man to speak in the open. A brighter morn awaits the human day in my Burghardt. When every natural gift of earth shall be good works and words, that's it.

"Now why do you think I'm here in this place? Why am I here if it's not to put a breakfast on the table and see he gets to school every last day? What else is my appointed task? When you know he can't count on Julius, not with all Julius's legionary dreams and delusions. What else am I put here for if not to see my Burghardt gets himself finished up? That's where I hitched my star a whole decade ago, moved it from Julius to that baby when I first laid eyes on him. And no school come September, that can't be. Deprive my hopes of his schooling, that can't be. White folks, they try to ride into town on that horse, they're liable to get themselves thrown, you just watch and see if they don't."

She sat still as a statue in the chair. I recognized this last remark as a reference to a story she'd told out here some weeks earlier, a story in which a rich white girl required, before going out riding, that her horse be groomed meticulously. A slave girl her own age was set to the job, and she groomed the horse meticulously for hours. When the rich white girl came to the stable, she drew on a fine white glove and rubbed her hand down the horse's back. On inspecting the glove, she found it slightly soiled, and she had the slave girl beaten within an inch of her life. Later that day, while the rich white girl was out riding, the horse threw her and she was killed.

Granny Mays put herself in the story as the slave girl who got beaten, but I knew she meant it somehow other than as historical fact. At the story's conclusion she'd said, "And who was that slave girl? None other than myself." Simple arithmetic told me that Granny Mays wasn't old enough to have been a slave, and I imagined she meant it the way Jesus meant it on the Mount of Olives when he said, "I was hungry and you gave me no food, I was thirsty and you gave me nothing to drink." I'd also heard her use the phrase "under the veil" before, and my only idea about that was that maybe she meant to refer to her long-gone marriage to Julius's father, about which I knew nothing.

Soon I heard the tinny pop of raindrops on the oil drum and outside on the beat-up shell of the abandoned Plymouth coupe; in another minute the whole junkyard came alive with this thumping and chiming, and even the needles up in the trees began to whistle.

"Amen," Granny Mays said, loud over the racket, cutting her speaking short. "And now I'm gonna leave this off in my mind."

She surprised me by producing a big green umbrella from somewhere, stood, and sprung it open high over her head. I watched her bob away in the direction of Daddy Cary's cornfield, the scalloped green canopy floating above her like some living thing in flight. Granny Mays herself disappeared, reappeared, and disappeared again behind the trunks of the pines, which were already turning blotchy with rain. As soon as I could, I made a run for it.

"Probably," Lainie said, painting the last toenail on her right foot, "they were afraid he was there to spy on them."

She sat on her bed, on top of her shiny pink satin comforter. Even though it was only about seven in the evening, she'd taken a bath and changed into her pajamas already, white ones with blue piping. I'd pulled a chair as far to the other side of the room as I could get, because I hated the smell of nail polish and nail polish remover, both of which permeated the air. She'd stuffed cotton balls between each of her toes, to keep them spread apart, and as I stared at her feet, decorated with the white cotton puffs and fire-engine red enamel, I thought they looked as if they were dolled up for a party, independent of the rest of her, and this made me recall a show I'd seen on TV before our TV broke, in which a famous pianist's hands, severed from his body, continued playing after he himself had bled to death.

Now Lainie laughed and said, "I'm afraid they don't know old Julius very well, if that's what they thought."

"What do you mean?" I asked.

"I mean Julius would be more likely to spy *for* them than *on* them," she said.

"I don't get it," I said. "What would Julius have to spy about anyway?"

She reinserted the brush into the bottle, screwed the cap tight, placed the polish on her bedside table, and then rolled onto her back and began waving her feet in the air like a dying cockroach—presumably to speed up the drying process. From this ridiculous position, she said, "Ben, haven't you asked yourself why they had to go and take down the lights in the middle of the night?"

I said, "Because it was cooler at night, I guess."

"No," she said. "Not because it was cooler at night."

"Well, why then?"

"Because they took the lights from the public school and gave them to the private school, that's why. And the courts wouldn't like that, not even a little bit. If they're going to get away with closing the public schools, nobody better be seen giving public equipment or supplies to the Foundation schools."

"But what if they paid for them?"

"Well, I guarantee you that if they paid for them, which I doubt, they didn't pay very much."

We'd had only a few drops of rain in the afternoon, but quite a strong wind, which blew chicken feathers all the way out into the blackberry vines that grew along the side of the road; then the clouds had parted, and out came the sun, which was now setting, shooting deep orange light straight through Lainie's window. Her room was paneled in the same knotty pine as the hallway, and here and there sap had oozed from a knot and congealed, like a sticky blob of melted candy. I coveted Lainie's room, mostly because of its private entrance—a door in one corner that opened onto a little brick stoop at the side of the house, where she kept her black Willys parked under a pecan tree.

The last couple of months, she'd begun giving me secret driving lessons on the Willys; I'd proved to be a natural behind the wheel, though the bridge over the creek was still more than I was yet willing to brave. Now I suddenly found myself wondering when my next lesson would be, but I didn't want to ask, for I didn't really want to change the subject. I told Lainie I couldn't see any sense in what she'd said about the lights at the high school, because any moron could figure out where they'd come from.

"It's how things look that counts," she said, still waving her feet around. "It's what people actually see that counts, Ben, not what they may secretly know. If a colored person was to go to the courts and say something about the lights, the judge would ask him did he see it happen. The colored person might know what really happened, even the judge might know what really happened, but knowing isn't seeing. Somebody would have to come forward and say they saw it. Obviously, none of the men who did it are going to come forward, so the only one to worry about would be Julius. Only Julius is nobody to worry about."

"Why?" I said.

"Why what?"

"Why is Julius nobody to worry about?"

"Because Julius thinks white people hung the moon. He would never cross a white person, man or woman, not in a million years. Haven't you ever noticed how he bows and scrapes around Daddy and

Daddy Cary? Now, how about clearing out of here so I can write a letter."

"You writing a letter to Claud Wayne?"

"No, I'm writing a letter to Dwight D. Eisenhower," she said. "Who do you think? Of course I'm writing Claud Wayne."

I went down the hallway to my own room and closed the door. Mother was finishing up the supper dishes in the kitchen, and Daddy was most likely doing some paperwork on the back porch, which he used as his office and where he kept his big oak desk with its nine drawers. With the closed-off living room between us, my parents felt very far away, as if they lived in one wing and Lainie and I in another; at times like this, I would feel restless and disappointed if I heard the kitchen door open, signaling that one of them was invading our part of the house.

Whereas Lainie's room had been ablaze with the sunset, mine, on the opposite side of the hall, was gloomy. She'd given me much to think about—Julius as a spy; Julius's high regard for white people; knowing a thing being different from seeing a thing—and I began to see the goings-on in Prince Edward between Negroes and whites as another kind of cold war, complete with espionage. While I found all this intriguing, it was more than I could keep in mind; when I lay on my bed with my hands under my head, my thoughts were like water cascading endlessly over itself, and I kept hearing Granny Mays's deep surprising voice, repeating, "That can't be . . . that can't be . . . that can't be. . . ."

This was so unpleasant that I rose from the bed, went into the hallway, and knocked on Lainie's door. She said, "Enter," but I opened the door only a crack and continued to stand outside it, peering in. She was not, as I'd been led to believe, writing a letter, but sat instead at her vanity, brushing her hair. Though her back was to me, I could see her face in the oval mirror. When she caught my eye in the mirror, she stopped brushing and said, "What is it, Ben?"

"Nothing," I said.

She returned to brushing. "Fine," she said. "Feel free to knock on my door any time for no reason."

I moved into the room and sat on the edge of her bed. "You're not writing a letter," I said.

"No," she said. "I tried but I couldn't."

"What do you mean, you couldn't?"

She turned away from the mirror and looked at the real me. "Did you ever feel, really deeply, Ben, that you had nothing to say?"

"I guess," I said, shrugging.

"Well, multiply that by a hundred," she said.

"Nothing times a hundred is nothing," I said.

"Right," she said. "Precisely."

She laid down the brush and began putting her hair into a braid, so quickly and deftly it seemed almost supernatural. "Is something wrong, Ben?" she asked.

"I was wondering," I said. "Who was Granny Mays's husband? Who was Julius's father? Who was Burghardt's grandfather? And where is he? What happened to him?"

Lainie laughed, twisting and popping a rubber band over the end of the braid. "I don't have any idea," she said. "But did you ever wonder about Bogie's mother? We don't know anything about her either, who she was or what happened to her."

"I think she died," I said.

"Why do you think that?"

"Because he said something once about his daddy being a widow, and I told him that if it was a man you were supposed to say *widower*."

"Really?" Lainie said. "Well, all I know is that for as long as I can remember, it was just those three. Bogie was a baby when they came and was raised by Granny Mays. Why are you thinking about them?"

"I just am," I said. The possibility of telling her about the junkyard in the woods and Granny Mays's speaking didn't even cross my mind.

"Has Bogart said anything about what he's going to do when school doesn't start?"

"No," I said, which was true. "But I guess Granny Mays'll teach him out of her books."

"Granny Mays has books?"

"Forty-one of them," I said. "Plus a Bible."

"There's more to that old woman than meets the eye," Lainie said.

Now she took a hard look at herself in the mirror, visibly saddened by what she saw. Her shoulders dropped, and I supposed her mind wandered onto her troubles—her eyes clouded over, first with a kind of blankness, then with tears.

"What's wrong?" I said.

"I was just thinking," she said. "I guess me and Bogie have something in common."

"What?"

"No school," she said.

"Oh."

"Yeah," she said. "That's just what I say. Oh."

"Well, you can go to college after the baby's born," I said, and she turned from the mirror and gave me a very watery fish-eye.

"Ben darling," she said, in a movie-star voice, "you know not the first thing about which you speak."

I said nothing, because I knew she was right; the world of pregnancy and babies had been painstakingly withheld from me. It was impossible to grow up on a farm with animals and not learn a few things, and yet as recently as one afternoon last winter, when Al and I were delivering eggs on our retail route, he pointed to a very pregnant woman standing in her front yard, and said, "Look at that, Ben, that woman must've swallowed a watermelon seed." Two or three years earlier, when I'd asked my mother how people had babies, she'd said it happened when a man and a woman were married and really loved each other and prayed to God for a child—an explanation I accepted with bewilderment even then, for I couldn't believe my mother and father loved each other, and I surely couldn't believe my father prayed, especially not to have children.

Lainie stood and moved to the bed. She cleared away the spiral notebook she used for writing her letters to Claud Wayne and threw it onto the floor beneath her window. I noticed that the sun had now sunk below the horizon, and the sky had turned an amazing copper color; everything else—trees, bushes, power poles, and birds on wires—were two-dimensional silhouettes, solid black. Lainie went to the window and stared out forlornly, a spitting image of Mother. After a minute, she made the kind of remark she often made when she was feeling hopeless, a dismal estimation of the dangerous time in which we lived, under the threat of a Communist takeover and nuclear war. She said, "Oh, what difference does it make, if you really think about it, Ben. We're probably all going to be blown to bits anyway. It's only a matter of time."

In my own room again, I switched on my bedside lamp, went to the closet, took down the Lincoln Logs carton from the top shelf, removed the half deck of pornographic playing cards, sat cross-legged on the floor, and did a quick run-through. I found it difficult to dwell on any one picture; there was something frantic about my need to move immediately to the next card, the next image, and I actually felt breathless as I reached the last one. I'd also noticed that when I did this thing, which had become a kind of rushed ritual, I tended to lose my sense of time, and, hands shaking, I quickly returned the cards to the Lincoln Logs carton. Any contemplation of them could occur only after they were safely back in their hiding place. Before I found the cards, I'd had no clear pictures in my mind of sex between humans. From biological events on the farm, I knew about penises and vaginas and even understood, in a panicky kind of way, that the one was inserted into the other for the purposes of sex; I'd happened upon dogs, cattle, horses, and pigs idling away at their awkward stand-up sex, and I'd also encountered insects grotesquely bound to each other through the use of some nightmarish needlelike apparatus. Most positively, I understood that human sex involved nakedness, the kind of nakedness that insects and animals enjoyed at all times. It therefore surprised me to see, in the photographs, men and women performing sex with their clothes on and in only partial states of nakedness. An even bigger surprise than that—and the one I spent the most time contemplating—was the tangible, undeniable proof, in black and white, that a woman would sometimes take a man's penis into her mouth, which apparently gave the man immense pleasure. A version of what the bully Urban Hall had accused Paisley Chatham of in the boys' bathroom was true. Of course I'd observed before that penises resembled certain foods. My surprise resided in applying this new reality to actual known persons. I couldn't begin to imagine my mother taking my father's penis into her mouth, or even going anywhere near it; likewise, I couldn't begin to imagine Lainie doing that with Claud Wayne. Interestingly, I could conjure up Al's bosomy girlfriend, Jeannette, doing it for Al. I'd not spent much time around them together, but when I had, I'd noticed that she was constantly touching him, and she tried to kiss him so often that he would have to tell her to stop. This eagerness, which exceeded Al's own, translated to me as a kind of hunger; I could see her in my mind, hungry, going for Al's penis while he tried to fend her off.

I lay on the bed and pressed the back of my head so deeply into my pillow that I could see the pictures hanging on the wall above me, the cigar-smoking, poker-playing bloodhounds, and it appeared from this angle that some of the dogs were looking down at me. I recalled a story Oatsie Montague had once told me about a man she'd known who went crazy and couldn't enter any room that had any portraits in it, because he was convinced that the person in the portrait was staring at him and reading his mind. She told me the man eventually went totally blind, and no doctor could explain it. She said they called it "hysterical blindness," a term I remembered because of the way it combined two conditions already known to me and created something completely new.

Now I sat up, went to my dresser, and took a mental inventory of the objects on it: a comb, my clock radio, a model battleship, a model B-52, a yo-yo, a juice glass and the two silver dollars and three buffalo nickels it held, and an unopened pack of Juicy Fruit gum. I moved to the card table I used as a desk and did the same thing: a stack of comic books, a plastic tray that held pencils and pens, the glass-covered box that housed my insect collection, a jar of paste, a bottle of glue with rubber dispenser, a tube of airplane glue, several small bottles of enamel paint, a bottle of formaldehyde (used for killing insects), a flashlight, a ruler, a box of sparklers, and a dirty odd sock. I heard the sound of Lainie's car and quickly moved to the window. I parted the blinds just in time to see the Willys, brake lights aglow, round the corner of the house and bounce into the road, turning in the direction of the creek. I couldn't think where Lainie might be headed when she was already in her pajamas, but I also knew she sometimes took a drive to nowhere in particular, just to think. Still, I felt oddly abandoned in the moment. I watched, with something like dread, the car's head-lights quickly sweep the far shoulder of the road and the woods beyond, then settle with a bump onto the road and glide away. For a reason I couldn't possibly have supplied, I suddenly found myself pray-ing for God to please bring her back.

Bullet and Lady, outside in their pen, barked three or four times—I imagined they too were saying, Come back—and then all was quiet again. I turned away from the window, looked at the clock radio on my dresser, and made a mental note of the time: eight-thirteen. I'd lately begun noting the time, in case something bad happened and I should be questioned by the authorities about what I might have seen. This, like the spying, was key-witness preparation. When the terrible thing happened that was bound to happen, and when somebody launched an investigation, I would be right there at the center of it, possessing the critical piece of evidence. Someday somebody would ask me, "Which way did he go, son?" or, "Son, who was it?" and I was determined to be ready, in service of the truth, to point my finger.

Tonight, I didn't have to wait long for a terrible thing (if not *the* terrible thing) to happen; at eight-fourteen I heard the crash of something in the kitchen, something heavy and metal, like a large pot, followed immediately by the slamming of doors, first the one between the kitchen and the living room, then the one between the living room and the hall. Each of these opened and slammed shut twice, and then my mother was shouting in the hallway: "You're nothing but a black liar, and you've never been anything but a black liar!"

My father yelled, "And you don't know a goddamn thing!"

"I know you've ruined my life, I know that!" Mother shouted, her voice hoarse with fury, and then the door to their bedroom slammed shut, so loud and hard it actually rattled the blinds in my windows.

The fight raged on inside their room, but I could no longer make out whole sentences; now and then a single word pierced through the walls—*why . . . never . . . horseshit*—and I knew there was the potential for their quarrel to turn physical. At an earlier age, I climbed onto my father's back during their fights, hung on to him with one arm wrapped around his neck, and pounded him with the fist of my free hand until he slung me to the floor. Because he was big and my mother small, I assumed he would hurt her, and I meant to try to defend her. The screaming and crying and smashing of furniture throughout these episodes prevented me from seeing then what I later saw—that he never actually struck her but that he held her wrists in check as she continued trying to strike him, a pistonlike agitation of his arms that looked like hitting and that sometimes left bruises on my mother's wrists. Eventually I grasped the full anatomy of their fights—that two things were required for them to turn physical: my father's vulgar language and my mother's hurling something at him. I'd seen her throw a fly swatter, a *TV Guide*, an empty Coke bottle, a jar of cold cream, a twelve-volt flashlight battery, a head of lettuce, an ear of corn, a cauliflower, a package of frozen field peas, even a gob of uncooked hamburger meat.

Now I did the thing I normally did when a quarrel began. I took a pillow from my bed, went inside my closet, and closed the door, enveloping myself in complete darkness. There was an odor in the closet—something added to the paint to repel moths—that had an inexplicable power to calm me. I lay down on the floor in the dark, and using my toes, my head, and my two arms, I touched all four walls, which made me feel contained.

In what felt like less than a minute the door to my own room banged open, and I heard my father shouting, "Benjamin! Where the hell are you?"

Stunned, I sat up too quickly and hit my knee on the doorjamb. Next, the closet door flew open, and from under the hanging clothes I saw my father's legs and feet—he was barefoot, in gray trousers. I noticed an astonishing crop of black hair sprouting from the tops of his toes. His voice subdued, he said, "What in the—?" and stopped himself.

After a pause, he turned and walked away, back to the hallway. From the door, his head still invisible from my vantage, he said, "Get up out of there, son, and go see to your mother. Your sister's disappeared."

Then he was gone, back out through the living room.

I knew what was in store for me, for I'd seen it before. If a fight had been especially bad, as this one must have been, the result was another of my mother's fits, a spell of uncontrollable shaking she referred to as a "nervous rigor." What was most terrifying about the nervous rigors were her eyes, which were huge and thoroughly vacant, like a cow's.

At the end of the hallway, a menacing-looking trapezoid of light spilled from her room onto the floor and up the opposite wall. As I moved toward it, I could hear her rapid intakes of breath and the longer, scarier, ragged gasps for air. When I reached the door, I saw her: Head bowed, her hair hiding her face, she stood at the foot of the mahogany bed, both hands clenching one of the bedposts as if it were the thing convulsing and she meant to control it. Her arms and shoulders jerked forward and back, and her whole body heaved up and down, as if her knees kept collapsing under her. I watched silently as she tried to remove a hand from the bedpost—it flew out in a wobbly flutter—and she nearly fell to the floor; she caught the bedpost in the crook of her elbow, swinging around it like a woman swooning in a dramatic dance, then pulled herself up again. I thought there was a kind of fog in the room, paling details, muting colors. From the door, I said, "Mommy . . ." and she turned those empty eyes on me, without light, without recognition. I took one step forward.

She turned her head away and, still shaking, she grunted out two words over and over again, interspersed between gasps, which I eventually managed to comprehend: "Go," she said. "Away. Go. Away."

I took another step toward her, but she stomped the floor with her left foot, the one nearer me, which stopped me cold. "Close," she groaned. "Door. Close. Door."

I returned to the hallway and closed the door. I sat on the floor, resting my back against the wall opposite my mother's room. I was wearing khaki shorts, and the tile felt cool on the back of my legs. I slumped farther down the wall, so that my toes touched my mother's door. It was fairly dark in the hallway, as no one had ever switched on a light, but the door to my own room was still cracked, providing enough of a glow for me to see a loose thread that hung below the hem of the right leg of my shorts. I'd been told I shouldn't pull loose threads, for you risked doing more damage than good, but I grabbed it between my thumb and index finger and snapped it off.

———

Surely Lainie's voice came from deep within a dream. I had fallen asleep on the floor of the hall. Lainie was saying, "Come on, Ben . . . come with me."

She was holding my hand, and we walked clear through her bedroom, out the door of her private entrance, into the night. She opened the passenger door of the Willys, parked beneath the pecan tree, and told me to get in. She told me to scooch over, to make room for her, and she climbed in after me and closed the door. She said, "Come here, Ben," and took me in her arms.

She held me like that for a minute without a word, and didn't seem in the least surprised when I started to weep. "That's okay," she whispered, "that's okay . . . that's just fine."

"I didn't know what to do," I said.

"I know," Lainie whispered.

"I fell asleep."

"I know. It's okay, Ben."

"Where are they?" I asked her.

"They're all right, Ben. You know they're always all right."

"I'm sorry I fell asleep."

"Listen to me," she said quietly. "I want to tell you something. A secret. Now, this is true, Ben, so I want you to believe me. Before Claud Wayne was shipped off to Germany, you know we were going to get a place in town, close to the army surplus store and close to the college. We were going to have air-conditioning and a little yard with a picnic table. And it was always part of the plan, Ben, to have you come live with us when we got settled. I swear to you that this is true. I could never have dreamed of leaving you here alone, with them. It was always, always, a part of my plan."

Immediately, I thought they would never have permitted it—for starters, they needed me as a farmhand—but I wanted so much not to undo the possibility of what she'd told me, I kept my mouth shut and only nodded. The car smelled good, a combination of Windex and Lainie's perfume and the Jubilee cream she used to clean the dashboard. She truly loved the Willys, which she'd purchased two years ago with savings from her receptionist job; she'd bought pink terry-cloth seat covers for it, at great expense; daily, she checked its finish for dull spots and polished them away with a chamois cloth kept for that purpose in the glove compartment. I'd been, for some time now, vaguely worried about my sister. As I thought of how much she loved the car, I understood more nearly the nature of my worry—I feared that she'd become too sad to love anything. Even our mother, who hated so much about her life, loved the color aqua and Jesus and all kinds of flowers. Our father, considered hateful by most who knew him, loved food and beer, country music, and chicken farming. Al loved Jeannette and trashy novels and raising hell. I loved stories from history, especially those like David and Goliath, Davy Crockett and Santa Anna, Barbara Johns and the school board; I loved the dogs and comic books; I loved spying, collecting coins and insects, assembling models, and being alone. Lainie had many desires, but desiring wasn't the same as loving—desire bore on things you wanted but didn't have, and love bore on wanting something you already had. What did Lainie love? I didn't believe she loved her husband; I didn't believe she loved the baby that was growing inside her. I supposed, given what she'd just told me, that she loved me, but that felt slippery, because my own feelings were directly involved. So it was a great comfort to think about her loving the car, the old Willys in which we now sat, weirdly, late at night, not going anywhere.

4

WE HAD BOTH CAGE BIRDS and ground birds on our farm, as my father was of two minds about the two different schools of raising and keeping chickens for egg production. Ground birds ran free inside long wide houses with floors of wood shavings and laid their eggs in wooden roosts filled with shavings or hay. The buildings that housed ground birds were bigger, more complicated, and more expensive to construct than those that housed cage birds. Manure removal was an ordeal, since the entire floor of shavings had to be replaced periodically. Likewise, the roosts had to be regularly cleaned. And egg collecting was a slow process that most often involved reaching beneath a possessive and hostile hen. It wasn't possible to keep any kind of laying record of individual ground birds, but it was thought that they produced more and better eggs than cage birds because they were happier running "free."

On the other hand, the cage-bird approach had several advantages over the ground-bird approach, all of them conveniences to the farmer, once you'd got past the labor of making the cages. We made our own cages, from a bendable but rigid wire mesh that came on rolls about four feet wide. We cut it in thirty-foot lengths and bent it in five places to form the frame of the cages, then partitions were cut and placed ten inches apart, creating individual cells just big enough to allow a hen to turn around in. The cages were suspended, three feet above the ground, from the rafters on either side of a plain narrow building composed of creosote posts, two-by-fours, and asphalt roofing. A feed trough of galvanized tin was attached to the front side of the cages, and a smaller watering trough went on the back side. The floor of the cage was inclined toward the ground from back to front, so when the hen laid her egg, it rolled down toward the front of the cage, beneath the feeder, and was caught by a wire lip. The cage system had the benefits of quick and easy feeding (you simply walked the length of the building, sliding a bucket of feed along the rim of the feeder); quick and easy cleaning of the waterers (you simply walked on the back side of the cages, dragging a toilet brush the length of the watering trough); easy removal of manure (since manure piled up in ugly stalagmites directly beneath the hens); easy collection of eggs (you just carried a basket along the aisle between the cages and picked the eggs from the handy wire lip); and a record of each individual hen's laying history could be kept, since she was confined to her one spot.

In the cage houses, cards with little calendar grids were mounted above each cell. Before the eggs were collected late in the afternoon, someone would move down the aisle with a black crayon and indicate on the card whether or not a hen had laid an egg that day; if the hen had laid, you put an X in the present day's box, and if she hadn't you left the box blank; this was called "marking cards." Despite the backto-front incline of the cage floors, an egg would sometimes catch in the wire mesh and fail to roll all the way to the lip; before the eggs were collected in the afternoon, somebody would move along the aisle and pull down any eggs that had got stuck that way; this was called "pulling down eggs."

One Saturday afternoon in August—it was August 15, 1959, the day before Daddy Cary's sixty-fifth birthday—Burghardt and I were busy, at around two in the afternoon, marking cards and pulling down eggs in one of the long narrow chicken houses where we kept cage birds. It was a blistering-hot day in a string of blistering-hot days. Marking cards and pulling down eggs were two of our regular chores, and sometime later in the afternoon, either Al or Julius or Daddy would be along to pick up the eggs. Burghardt was already tall enough to mark the cards unaided by any kind of appliance, whereas I still had to place a bucket upside-down on the ground and stand on it to reach the cards. This of course made him faster at the job than I, but he would take his time making the little black X's on the cards to avoid getting so far ahead of me as to prevent conversation. That particular Saturday, we'd been moving along the aisles slower than usual because of the heat. Burghardt said it had to be 100 degrees in the shade, but I told him the thermometer mounted outside the back door of our house had read 94; I'd checked it when I'd gone back to the house for dinner.

"Is that thermometer in the shade?" he asked. He was wearing the sleeveless white T-shirt and baggy orange-colored shorts I'd seen him in all summer.

"Some of the time," I answered.

"Some of the time?" he said. "Was it in the shade when you looked at it?"

"No," I said, "I don't think so."

"Then you don't know for sure what temperature it is in the shade, do you," he said.

"Burghardt," I said, "if it was ninety-four in the sun, that means it would be *less* than ninety-four in the shade."

"Depends," he said.

"On what?"

"On what kind of shade you're talking about. There's deep shade and light shade, and there's indoor shade and outdoor shade."

I'd never thought about this before, varieties of shade, but I was engaged by another discovery: if I stretched my arm a little farther to the right, I could mark a total of five cards before having to move my bucket; up till now, I'd been marking four.

"It's shady in this henhouse," Burghardt went on, "but I bet it's hotter in here than it is outside in the sun."

"Look," I said to him. (I had to say "look" because our henhouse conversations were always conducted with our backs to each other.) "I can mark five cards without moving the bucket."

"That's good," he said.

When I twisted around to look at him, he'd already returned to marking cards. I figured I hadn't shown enough interest in his discussion of shade, so I moved the bucket along the aisle, mounted it again, and said, "You're probably right about the temperature. Probably is hotter in here than outside in the sun."

"You know I'm right," he said. "And I can tell you another thing. Ninety-four up at your house ain't the same as ninety-four at mine. You try sitting up under a tin roof sometime when it's ninety-four and you'll know what I mean."

We continued along the aisle, marking the cards and pulling down the eggs, and I told Burghardt that we had an air conditioner in our living room but that we seldom went in there because of the eggs. He said if he had an air conditioner in his house he wouldn't be sharing it with no eggs, and I explained that the eggs had to have the air-conditioning or they would go bad.

"Maybe that's what happened to some folks around these parts," he said. "Maybe it was the heat made them go bad."

He laughed after saying this, but I could tell it was the kind of laugh a person laughed when they wanted to make something seem funnier than it really was. He'd sounded a certain note or, more accurately, a certain chord: I knew he couldn't have been referring to any white person who might have gone bad, for it wouldn't have been possible for him to make such a remark, and yet I knew, too, that he had been referring to white persons, even if accidentally. In other words, the impossible had just occurred.

I sneaked another glance at him. He'd pulled his T-shirt up and was using it to wipe sweat from his brow, and I imagined that he could feel me looking at him. I also imagined that the hens were dancing in their cells more agitatedly than usual, and in the silence that fell between Burghardt and me, I became intensely aware of the metallic percussion these hundreds of yellow horned feet made on the wire mesh of the cages. In my mind I saw Lainie pushing her chair back from the kitchen table and staring at all of us, indicting us with her brimming eyes; I heard the horrible screak her chair made on the linoleum.

I moved my bucket farther along the aisle and took up my next position, pulling down a couple of eggs as I went, trying in every way to appear less interested than I really felt. At last, nonchalantly, I said, "Who do you mean, Burghardt?"

As much as five seconds elapsed. Then Burghardt said, "Nobody."

Of course I should have understood that it was the only answer he could give, and if I wanted him to say more, I would have to avoid putting him in the hot seat that way. So I said, "I guess you heard about the schools?"

It was the first time either of us had mentioned it, all summer long.

"I don't care about the schools," he said, in a tone that seemed to be asking, Now why are you bringing up that old boring subject?

"I wish I didn't have to go back," I said. "You're lucky, you know."

"I know I am," he said.

"You're so lucky," I repeated.

"I said I know it."

And that was all we said on the matter for about five more minutes.

Then, as if no time had passed, Burghardt added, "Granny says they probably won't really close anyway."

"Well, if they do," I said, "you'll be lucky."

"I know I will," he said. "Man, I gotta pee."

Quickly he was outside in the alley between the henhouses; from my perch on the upside-down bucket, I could see him running away in sunshine so bright it made me squint. He wasn't supposed to run anywhere near the henhouses, as the sudden motion scared the chickens, and we'd been warned repeatedly that scaring the chickens would make them lay bloody eggs. I didn't have any specific thoughts in that moment about having stumbled on a new form of lying, a new form of burying the truth into which two people could enter without even agreeing to, but I did feel a kind of inexplicable defiance, and I thought, almost angrily, that I didn't give a hoot if Burghardt ran between the henhouses and scared the damned chickens. I hoped they *did* lay bloody eggs. I watched him disappear around the end of the opposite building, out of sight. Then I did a little thing I'd never done before, simply because it had never occurred to me to do it. The hen directly in front of me hadn't produced an egg for the last four days—if she kept this up she would be in danger of getting culled—but I marked her card with a big black **X** anyway and bent down and moved a neighboring hen's egg into her spot. Each of the birds, the robbed and the falsely rewarded, stared at me with one horrible mustard-colored eye, then resumed their demented head twitching, as if they were visited by a dozen such sparkling distractions in every instant.

A while later, we were with Julius in the ground-bird house called House B. Burghardt and I had already finished cleaning the waterers and had hung up our toilet brushes to dry in the feed room, a wired-off enclosure where hundred-pound croaker sacks of feed were stored on wood pallets. You had to enter the house through the feed room, and we always banged around and made as much noise as possible going in, to scare away the rats the chicken feed attracted. It was frightening enough just hearing their scuffling noises under the pallets, but if you were unlucky enough to see one, it was a pitch-black blur, long as your arm, scurrying up the hogwire and onto an overhead rafter. In my opinion, the only thing more terrible than a rat underfoot was a rat overhead. Once, some years back, a rat had fallen from a henhouse rafter onto my brother Al, got inside his shirt, and bit him three times before he could shake it out. Even though Daddy said rabies shots were unnecessary, Mother and the family doctor made Al get them—twenty painful injections in the stomach—but Al said he would rather go for rabies shots every single day for the rest of his natural life than to ever have another rat inside his shirt. Afterward, he took to wearing his shirttails outside his pants, so any rat that might get inside his shirt would fall straight to the ground. He had officially become the most terrified of rats of anyone on the farm, and he made no attempt to hide it. Julius—who was technically Daddy Cary's hired hand but spent his afternoons with our chickens, mostly helping with the egg collecting—was probably the second most terrified. When he came to work in one of the ground-bird houses, he always brought a piece of pipe along, which Daddy allowed; he said the pipe was useless, as rats were way too fast to hit with any piece of pipe, but that it pacified Julius. He said they were mainly nocturnal, and if you wanted to kill one, you had to get down to the henhouse late at night with your shotgun and catch them in the beam of your flashlight, where they would freeze and stare right back at you with bright red rubies for eyes.

Now Julius had parked his pipe in a corner of the feed room and was performing at Burghardt's request the henhouse feat that awed us most: hypnotizing a chicken. He'd smoothed out a perfectly round patch on the house floor, captured a hen by her two legs, and placed her breast down on the ground. He stretched her legs behind her and stroked her full length, from comb to tail feathers. As he did this, he quietly crooned a deep-pitched undulation of sound in the back of his throat, and when he sensed that the hen's heart had stopped racing, when she'd ceased all twitching, he adjusted her head so the underside of her neck rested flat on the shavings. One hand still pressing gently on her back, he began etching with his finger a line that started at the tip of her beak and proceeded straight out away from her a distance of about a foot and a half. He traced this line over and over again with his index finger till it was a dark indentation in the shavings, a half inch deep. We had to remain absolutely still, as we'd been admonished to, so we wouldn't distract the hen; we sat Indian-style on the ground some six or seven feet away, and soon we heard Julius softly say, "There you go now, and bingo, bango, bongo," and he removed his hand from the hen, rose from his kneeling position, and backed slowly away. Burghardt and I stood up, and Julius eased into the space between us.

The chicken remained motionless, though entirely unrestrained, transfixed by the line in the shavings. Now Julius began speaking to us in a normal voice, to show that the hen was deep under and wouldn't be awakened by anything less than a direct assault. Though we'd seen him do it a dozen times, and we'd each tried it a dozen times ourselves, neither Burghardt nor I had ever been successful.

Julius was wearing a tan cotton work shirt with three gold plastic buttons I imagined came from Granny Mays's button jar; she had a big clear-glass cookie jar that must have held a thousand buttons, all shapes, sizes, and colors. Julius tugged on the straight hem of his shirt, then lifted his yellow baseball cap long enough to pass his fingers once across the top of his head, front to back. As if he meant to disclose his method once and for all, he said, "You see, now, she's just got to get herself transported, that's all it is to it."

We all three gaped at the hen—dead-appearing but for the rhythmic rise and fall of her breathing, and ridiculous, a pratfallen bird in a cartoon—and we gaped almost as if we ourselves were mesmerized.

"Uh-huh," Burghardt said. "Transported."

"She's got to know she's mine," Julius said, "all mine and nobody else's."

"Uh-huh," repeated Burghardt.

"Body and soul."

"Uh-huh."

"Safe from all alarms."

"Uh-huh."

"I'm the master, she the slave."

Burghardt cast his father a fish-eye. "You the master, all right," he said, and I wasn't sure if I detected a hint of sarcasm or not.

I'd noticed before that in contrast to me and my own father, Burghardt wasn't afraid of Julius, and sometimes it seemed they were more like brothers than father and son. I thought this might have been because they'd both been raised by Granny Mays. In this moment, staring at the hypnotized chicken who was Julius's slave, I thought of several of Granny Mays's remarks in the woods and suddenly added up something about the Mayses I'd not added up before: Just as in my own family nobody had to say certain things (like my mother would never leave my father but would always act as if she wanted to), nobody had to say that Burghardt was smarter than Julius and much more like the son Granny Mays wished Julius had been. It wasn't any brilliant analyzing on my part, just a longtime, completely obvious detail I'd not bothered to pay attention to till now.

In a tone so honest it made me think I'd surely imagined a hint of sarcasm before, Burghardt said, "You have got that chicken under a spell."

I thought of a fourth-grade spelling bee in which I'd misspelled *measles* M-E-E-S-I-L-S, simply because my mother, who'd tested me at home out of the practice booklet, failed to give me the word; she'd thought it so short and familiar she didn't need to test me on it, so I'd sailed right through *incontrovertible* and *sarcophagi* but had no idea how to spell the name of this common childhood disease.

From what must have seemed out of the blue, I said to Julius, "What do you reckon Burghardt's going to do about school come fall?"

Julius squatted right where he was, and Burghardt and I followed suit, the three of us focused on the still-immobile hen a few feet away. It meant some conversation was about to ensue, for when men talked, they often squatted like this and eyed some central thing nearby, not looking at each other.

Julius said, "We ain't worried about no schools, Mr. Ben. If you ask me, this is just what comes of people not being satisfied with what they already got. If you ask me, we had ourselves a perfectly fine colored school. And now, just because some folks thought it wasn't as good as the white one, we liable to have no school at all. If folks would just learn to keep they big mouths shut, everybody would be a lot better off. Now you tell me, am I right or am I wrong?"

Burghardt repeated what he'd said earlier: "Granny says they probably won't really close."

"She probably right," said Julius. "But if they do close, you're better off than most. You got a granny with books on a shelf, give you lessons out of them herself, right there at the kitchen table. We ain't worried about schools, Mr. Ben. We're lucky. Truth is, most people's lucky and just don't know it. Always peering over the fence to see who might have it better. White folks this and white folks that, when if it wasn't for white folks we wouldn't even be here in the first place. We would still be sitting in the mud somewhere over in Africa."

I glanced over at Burghardt and noticed that he'd shifted his eyes from the hypnotized chicken to the ground right in front of him, his face gone blank. He said, "But Granny says they brought them over here for slaves."

"And what if they did?" Julius said. "Least they had a house to live in and three square meals a day. Most everybody'll tell you how bad slavery was, but the way I see it, they was treated all right. Do you think a white man would mistreat the very person he depended on to plow his land and get his crops in? I don't believe he would."

Honestly, I hadn't given much thought to slavery until fairly recently, after I'd begun eavesdropping on Granny Mays in the woods. I knew it only as something that used to be but wasn't anymore, and I vaguely understood it as the primary bone of contention over which the War Between the States had been fought. But what I associated with that war—the beautiful Confederate flag, the statues all over the South of Robert E. Lee and other Confederate soldiers, the souvenir-shop rebel caps in cool slate blue, sized to fit children—signified a time of glory, of which people were proud. I wasn't inclined to think of the war as something terrible, and its connection to slavery wasn't recalled in any memorial statues I'd ever seen, or in the paperweights and pennants of any souvenir shop. Though I'd never before heard Julius's particular line of reasoning, I found it immediately appealing, persuasive, coming from a grown-up Negro man. The idea of slavery not having been nearly as bad as some people would have you believe fit nicely with a general notion I'd often heard expressed, that things used to be better than they were now. What it did not fit with, no matter how appealing, were the stories I'd heard Granny Mays tell in the woods, like the one in which the slave girl was beaten practically to death for failing to perfectly groom the white girl's horse.

Still, I wanted to support Julius's proposition, so I said, "If I had slaves on a hot day like this, I'd take Kool-Aid to them out in the fields."

It was all I could think to say, but it sounded much more foolish aloud than it had inside the privacy of my mind.

As if he wanted to make me feel better, Julius smiled and said, "I know you would, Mr. Ben. That's just the kind of thing I'm talking about."

I glanced again at Burghardt. This time he met my gaze with a kind of sleepy look I wasn't sure how to read. He said, "I'd take them ice cold bottles of Nu-Grape, a separate bottle for each man, woman, and child. I'd load them up in a wheelbarrow with crushed ice and go rolling through the pastures. And I'd have a handful of straws with me too, so if anybody wanted one they could have it."

"Just listen to you," Julius said. "If you had slaves."

We each returned our attention to the chicken, stationary on the ground in front of us, and Burghardt said quietly, "Well, I would."

"You got some ideas," Julius said, "I'll grant you that," and he jumped up and let out a whoop, flinging his long hands out before him, startling the hen into consciousness.

The heat inside the henhouse was suddenly unbearable, and I felt a trickle of sweat roll down my stomach, beneath my loose-hanging T-shirt. I watched the stunned chicken, on her feet now, shuddering, ruffling her feathers and craning her neck, trying to get her bearings. Julius cried, "Shoo! Shoo!" and the hen, recollecting her native state of terror-strickenness, tore off in the direction of the roosts at the center of the building, jerking her head this way and that, as if to say, What happened . . . what happened . . . what in the world just happened?

I stood and turned to Burghardt, who still squatted on the ground. He gave me that same fuzzy-sleepy look again. He was wearing a pair of black-cloth high-top tennis shoes, and the white rubber medallion on the ankle of one of them was half torn off and hanging. He reached down and ripped the medallion the rest of the way off, then threw it toward the feed room, where it bounced off the hog wire. He stood and said, "They didn't have Kool-Aid back in those days."

I didn't say anything, though I thought surely Nu-Grape soda hadn't been invented a hundred years ago either. Burghardt brushed away some shavings that had stuck to his bare knees, and I noticed the imprints they'd left behind, a kind of mosaic pattern that reminded me of the ferns that florists put in their flower arrangements.

Daddy Cary showed up a minute later. He entered the feed room wearing, as always, overalls and a long-sleeved plaid shirt buttoned at the cuffs and collar. Nobody could understand how he could dress that way in the summer. "It is *hot!*" he said. Behind the wire of the feed room, he looked like a big animal inside a cage, and I found this immensely satisfying. His size and appearance and manner were plenty to intimidate most people, especially children, but he also had a terrible habit of setting off firecrackers at odd times. He usually carried a few ladyfingers in his pockets and was apt to light one at any minute and toss it near a person's feet just for the sheer hell of it. I took solace in the knowledge that he wouldn't be setting off any firecrackers anywhere close to the chickens. As he came through the wire door, into the henhouse proper, Julius trotted over to hold the door for him and to latch it behind him, saying, "Yes, sir, Mr. Rome, truer words were never spoken. It is hot today for sure."

Daddy Cary stood with his hands in his overall pockets and looked around at the chickens. A big black paper wasp flew right over the top of his crew cut, its legs dangling so long and low I thought surely they must have grazed his hair. Then Daddy Cary looked at the three of us, as if he was noticing us for the first time, and said, "What y'all boys doing?"

We all had sense enough not to say that Julius had been hypnotizing a chicken for our pleasure. Julius said he was just about to start collecting the eggs there in House B, and I told him that Burghardt and I were on our way over to House C to finish up the waterers.

Daddy Cary picked something from his front tooth with the nail of his little finger and appeared to ponder the information we'd given him. "Julius," he said at last, "you can finish up the waterers for these boys, can't you?"

"Yes, sir, sure I can, Mr. Rome," said Julius, smiling broadly as if

Daddy Cary had paid him a compliment by even suggesting he was equal to this simple task.

"I think I better take these boys down to the creek," Daddy Cary said. "Let them get cooled off."

"I know they would like that," said Julius, still smiling. "I know they would." He looked at Burghardt and said, "What do you say to Mr. Rome, son?"

Burghardt gazed at Daddy Cary's shoes and said, "Thank you."

"Thank you, what?" said Julius.

"Thank you, Mr. Rome," said Burghardt.

"Thank you, Mr. Rome, what?" said Julius.

"Thank you, Mr. Rome, sir," said Burghardt.

"You're welcome, son," Daddy Cary said, almost with kindness, which surprised me. Then he turned and walked away without another word, out through both doors of the feed room.

"Well, go on," Julius said to us urgently, shooing us with his long hands the way he'd recently shooed the hypnotized chicken.

The sun outdoors was blinding, even this late in the afternoon. Daddy Cary lumbered along the alley between the buildings toward his Oldsmobile, parked at one end. Burghardt and I started to run after him but then remembered about scaring the chickens and fell into a brisk stride that was definitely not-running and that felt so peculiar it made us both laugh.

Daddy Cary already sat behind the wheel when we reached the Olds. Burghardt climbed into the back seat as I got in front. Daddy Cary had left the car running with the air conditioner on, and the shock of the cold air gave me goose bumps all along both my arms. I saw the fine hairs on my forearms standing at attention and I let out a very small giggle. As he put the car in gear, Daddy Cary looked over at me and said, "What's that you giggling about?"

"Nothing," I said. "I just thought of something funny."

"Well, what was it?"

"Oh, it wasn't really funny," I said.

He pulled the car up the hill that led to a wider lane along a fence, the Olds bouncing and squeaking as we went. "Hey, Bogie," he called to the back seat, glancing in his rearview mirror. "What do you think it means when a boy giggles like a little girl and then says it wasn't about nothing funny?"

I stared out the passenger window, at the barbed-wire fence alongside the car. After a brief silence, I heard Burghardt say, his voice full of misgivings, "I don't know, Mr. Rome."

"Well, I don't know either," Daddy Cary said, and laughed good-naturedly.

I had no name for the sinking dejection Daddy Cary could so quickly make me feel, but it was worse than any sickness I knew—shot through with self-loathing, since I would have been able to avoid it if only I weren't so stupid and forgetful; it was like puncturing your foot on a nail you already *knew* was there. When he'd appeared at the henhouse five minutes earlier and announced his intention to take Burghardt and me to swim, I'd foolishly let myself feel excited, putting my spirits in a higher place from which to fall. To make matters worse, I now recalled the pornographic playing cards I'd taken from the attic of the Big House, and because this was the first time I'd seen Daddy Cary since that day, it seemed his criticism of me was in some way attached to that. When, in the next moment, he reached across me, opened the glove compartment, removed his revolver, and laid it on the seat between us, I thought maybe he intended to shoot me for stealing the cards. I attempted the shaky strategy of making light of the situation. "What you bring your pistol for, Daddy Cary?" I asked, trying to keep my voice steady and relaxed.

We passed the cage houses, then Daddy's new egg room, a plain windowless building of white-painted cinder blocks where eggs were washed, candled, graded, weighed, and cartoned. Two of the egg-room workers, colored women from town, sat on a slab of concrete in front of the main door, smoking cigarettes. "Just look at them two," Daddy Cary said. "I reckon that's just the kind of trash your daddy would get to work for him, out there on their big black butts smoking Pall Malls."

We were about to turn onto Rome Road, and my own house came into view, across a field of tall weeds. I wanted nothing more than to be inside it, in my room. Daddy Cary stared straight through the windshield and still didn't answer my question about why he'd brought along the pistol.

Once we were on the road, I said, "Can we stop at the house and let me get my swim trunks?"

Without a word, he blew the horn as we passed the house, as he always did, and then stepped on the gas. We flew up and down the hilly road, and briefly I looked back at Burghardt to see if he was enjoying the butterflies in the stomach. He didn't see me look, for he was gripping the edge of the seat with both hands and had his eyes clenched shut. Behind him, out the back window, I saw brown dust clouds, discharged with great force from the rear end of the Oldsmobile like the exhaust of a rocket.

When we reached the creek, Daddy Cary slowed down and crossed the wooden bridge with its pleasant drumming of the planks under the tires. On the other side, he pulled off the road beneath an old oak tree, executed a U-turn so the car was aimed at the water, and cut the engine. He reached for his pistol and got out. I watched him move down the dry craggy slope toward the underside of the bridge. Burghardt, already out of the car, knocked on the window next to my right ear and shrugged his shoulders. I rolled down the window and told him I wouldn't be getting out of the car.

"Why not?" he asked.

"Because I think he's going to shoot me."

"Shoot you? Why would he shoot you?"

"I can't tell you."

"He's not going to shoot you," said Burghardt. "If he was going to shoot you, do you think he would've brought me along? That would make me an eyewitness."

I considered this argument, which seemed foolproof on its face, and immediately felt better. I opened the heavy door and climbed out, squinting even in the shade of the oak. Burghardt was clearly waiting for me to lead the way, so I started in the direction of the bridge where Daddy Cary had disappeared.

The creek, the color of a new clay flowerpot, rolled silently below a few overhanging trees, then entered the darkness beneath the bridge. Mostly, the surface of the water was smooth as glass—cloudy where the sun shone on it directly—but here and there, for no visible reason, little eddies formed and twirled away, or suddenly a long narrow ripple appeared like a giant underwater rope and then was swallowed up again. As Burghardt and I moved down the slope, the air grew cooler, and the silence of the moving water seemed to have some mysterious effect on time: I couldn't have said if Daddy Cary had disappeared beneath the bridge one minute earlier (as surely he must have) or if it was something that had happened more than an hour ago; I couldn't have said if I'd worried only today that he might shoot me for stealing or if it was something I'd worried about my whole life. The bridge spanned the creek at a height of about twelve feet, supported at either end by a wall made from enormous chiseled cubes of granite, stacked and cemented together. During the winter months, the water came right up to the walls as it passed under the bridge, but in summer you could walk beneath the bridge on a mud and gravel path about five feet wide. This is where we found Daddy Cary, sitting on a wooden crate, smoking a Dutch Masters. Bright lines of sunlight squeezed through the cracks in the bridge overhead, fell on the dark water, wigwagged on

Daddy Cary's genielike cigar smoke, and even segmented Daddy Cary himself in two places; one gash of light cut straight across his forehead, another across his knees. Those lines that fell on the water were reflected on the walls and underside of the bridge as a kind of eerie turbulence in the stone and wood.

Daddy Cary said, "Well, you boys hurry up and get your clothes off. I ain't got all afternoon. There's still chores to finish up."

Burghardt and I looked at each other, and I could tell that he was depending on me to say something. I'd been skinny-dipping in the creek before, with Al and with my father, but I hadn't done it for about three summers. I imagined I would be able to go skinny-dipping with Burghardt, since he was a boy my own age, but certainly not with Daddy Cary present. I thought Burghardt could simply take his shirt off and swim in his orange shorts, since they were actually swim trunks, and I was trying to figure out a way to suggest this when Daddy Cary said, "What's wrong with you two?"

Burghardt visibly quaked, and though I knew it was impossible that I should make myself naked in front of Daddy Cary, I began slowly lifting my T-shirt over my head. When I'd got it off and laid it on some gravel by the stone wall, I waited while Burghardt slowly removed his shirt and laid it next to mine. We eyed each other surreptitiously, and I sat on the ground and began unlacing my shoes. Burghardt sat beside me and began unlacing his. I got one shoe off, then removed my sock, carefully rolled it and placed it inside the shoe, then started on the other foot. Burghardt, because he was wearing no socks, had to dawdle even more than me, and when I happened to glance at Daddy Cary, I saw that he was scrutinizing us with his lips pursed around the circumference of his cigar. He removed the cigar and began to laugh, shaking his head.

In another thirty seconds Burghardt was down to his shorts, I was down to my dungarees, and I still didn't have a plan. I said to Daddy

Cary, "You know, Burghardt can just swim in those. They're really swim trunks."

"I'm not taking him back to his granny in wet clothes," Daddy Cary said. "Who in the world do you think's going to see you down here anyway?"

Neither of us dared utter the obvious answer, so we stood silent, and Daddy Cary narrowed his eyes at Burghardt and said, "You better *git* those shorts off, boy."

I couldn't tell how serious Daddy Cary's tone was—he'd used that confusing, ambiguous tone adults sometimes employed when they wanted you to think they were only pretending to be threatening. Burghardt looked at me one last time, then turned his back, stripped off the orange trunks, threw them to the ground, and dashed into the water. At its deepest, in the middle, the creek was about four feet, and that's where Burghardt headed. He drifted out from beneath the bridge, into the sunlight, dunked his head under and up again, wiping his eyes with his hands. He kept his back to Daddy Cary and me and gazed at the trees and sky overhead as if he'd entered his own world, as if he'd forgotten all about us.

Daddy Cary laughed again quietly, said, "That's the fastest I ever saw that boy move," then took a drag on the cigar and turned his attention on me. "I bet you never saw a nigger in his birthday suit before, did you," he said.

The question caught me off guard, but again, he'd said it in a tone so good-humored, I second-guessed my startled response. I answered, "No, sir," happy at least to dodge for another moment the question of my own nakedness.

He got up and walked to the water's edge, where he laid his pistol on the ground, returned to the wooden crate, and sat back down. "Hey, Bogie," he yelled. "How about coming over here and fetching me my gun."

Burghardt spun around in the water and looked at us. "Huh?" he called back, though I was sure he'd heard what Daddy Cary said.

"I said, how about coming over here and fetching me my gun. You see it laying right there by the water?"

"Yes, sir, I see it," Burghardt said, but still didn't budge. He spread both his hands out over the surface of the water as if he was trying to keep his balance.

"I can get it for you," I said, and started to move toward the water's edge.

Daddy Cary hooked one finger in the belt loop of my dungarees as I passed, pulling me backward. "If I wanted you to do it I would've told you to," he said. Then he called out, "Come on, Bogie, don't keep me waiting now."

I stood right beside Daddy Cary, and he kept his finger hooked inside my belt loop in an idle sort of way. Burghardt slowly glided through the creek toward us, emerging inch by inch from the water. When the water had dropped to a few inches below his navel, he knelt and continued to move forward on his knees; eventually he was prone in water only a few inches deep, at which point he quickly ran out onto the shore, grabbed the gun with one hand while covering his private parts with the other, and offered the pistol to Daddy Cary properly, holding it by the barrel.

But Daddy Cary just looked at the brown and silver revolver trembling in Burghardt's hand. He tilted his head side to side, examining it carefully. "Damn it if it didn't get some mud on the butt," he said.

Burghardt stared down at the pistol in his hand, pulled it toward himself briefly, then offered it again, saying, "Yes, sir, Mr. Rome, it did."

"Well, wipe it off for me, will you?" Daddy Cary said.

Burghardt quickly wiped the mud from the butt of the revolver. He returned his hand to his private parts, and offered the gun a third time. Daddy Cary accepted it, smiled warmly, and said, "Thank you, son, I appreciate it."

Burghardt ran back into the creek, swam to the middle, and floated out from under the bridge into the sunlight. This time he let himself drift a long ways downstream before stopping.

"Did you see that?" Daddy Cary said to me. "Black all over. Bet you didn't know that, did you."

"No, sir," I said.

"Black all over," he repeated. He took a drag on the cigar and blew a stream of smoke upward toward the wooden planks. "Now are you going to go swimming or not?" he asked.

"I don't really want to, Daddy Cary," I said.

"What do you mean, you don't want to?"

"I don't know," I said, shrugging. "I've guess I've cooled off enough already."

"You mean to tell me I brought you all the way down here to go swimming and you ain't going? You better be careful, 'cause you're just about to make me mad."

I turned my back to him and unbuckled my belt, unzipped my dungarees, and pulled them off. I was wearing yellow boxer shorts underneath, with little monkeys in red party hats. Still in my shorts, I walked toward the water.

From behind me I heard, "Don't you get them underpants wet, son."

I waded into the water, pretending I didn't hear him, and was up to an inch above my knees when I heard, "Did you hear what I said?"

Keeping my back to him, I said, "It doesn't matter if they get wet, Daddy Cary." I reached down and took hold of the hems of the boxer shorts, pulling them up higher so I could get into the water a few inches deeper without getting them wet, a few inches farther away from Daddy Cary. I looked downstream and saw Burghardt's head, which appeared to be floating on the surface of the creek.

"It does too matter," Daddy Cary said. "I'm not taking you back home in wet underpants. Now either get up here and get 'em off and go swimming or just get out and get dressed."

I fully imagined myself lifting my feet from the creek bed and letting the current take me away, down to where Burghardt was splashing around. What would the consequences be? I could even pretend that I'd tripped and fallen. But Daddy Cary said, "Come on up here, son," in a quiet sympathetic voice, and I walked out of the water. "Come over here, son, and let me talk to you," he said.

I stood before him, creek water trickling down my legs.

"Don't you want to go swimming?"

"Yes, sir, I do," I said. "I just don't want to take off my underwear."

"Well, I was going to let y'all fire my pistol off the bridge," he said. "But if you ain't going swimming I don't guess you get to fire the pistol."

I didn't know what to say to this, so I remained silent.

"Do you want Bogie to get to fire the pistol and not you?" he said.

"No, sir."

"Then get them underpants off and get on in that creek."

"I don't want to, Daddy Cary," I said.

"All right then," he said. "I guess that's the way it's going to be. Bogie's going to get to fire my pistol and you ain't. Do you know who you put me in the mind of when you act like this?"

"Yes, sir."

"Who?"

"My daddy," I said, and I had no idea how I knew this, except that it was the kind of thing people said.

"That's exactly right," he said. "Stubborn as a mule. Go on and get yourself dressed."

He stood up, called to Burghardt, and told him to meet us on the bridge. I began putting my clothes back on as Burghardt paddled upstream. Daddy Cary walked away without saying anything more.

From the water, Burghardt told me not to look, he was coming out.

When we were both dressed, he whispered, "What's he going to do now?"

"He's going to let you fire his pistol," I said.

Burghardt didn't believe me, but before he could say so, there was the report of a gunshot, and we both jumped and ran out from under the bridge, carrying our shoes in our hands. "Let's go," I said, and we quickly climbed the slope back up to where the car was parked.

We saw Daddy Cary standing in the middle of the bridge, legs spread, aiming down the length of his arm at some spot in the creek.

We dropped our shoes near the car and then stopped where the dirt road met the first wooden plank of the bridge and watched as he fired a second time into the water. He lowered the revolver, looked at us, and said, "Come on over here then."

He showed Burghardt how to hold the pistol with one hand and steady his wrist with the other and how to pull back the hammer with his thumb. "You ever done this before?" he asked him.

"No, sir," said Burghardt, "but I fired a twenty-two rifle one time."

"This is just the same as that," Daddy Cary said, "but with a little more kick. That's why I'm telling you to hold it with both hands like that. Okay, just aim it down there in the water and pull the trigger."

Burghardt fired the pistol, stumbled backward a step, and let out a shriek. Daddy Cary laughed and told him to go ahead and fire it again, which he did. Daddy Cary told him to fire it a third time, which he did, and each time Burghardt fired the revolver, Daddy Cary looked straight into my eyes.

At last he took the pistol away from Burghardt and said, "That's fun, ain't it?"

"Yes, sir," Burghardt said. "Thank you, Mr. Rome."

Daddy Cary looked again at me, put his cigar between his teeth, and squinted because of the smoke. "You're welcome, son," he said to Burghardt.

I didn't care. Or as Lainie might have said, I deeply, deeply, didn't care. I put my hands in my pockets, turned, and started walking, back toward the Oldsmobile under the big live oak tree. I liked the dry warmth of the wood on the soles of my feet, and I liked the way my shadow rippled over the planks of the bridge and seeped intermittently into the cracks. I thought about Daddy Cary saying that my father, like me, was stubborn as a mule. I imagined I had an incomplete understanding of the word—I suspected there was more to it than just a reluctance to do what you were told. I was glad Burghardt got to fire the revolver, especially since he probably wasn't going to have a school to go to in September. I was glad I didn't put my fingers in my ears, as I'd wanted to, each time he'd fired it. I was glad I didn't take off my underwear.

5

AFTER DADDY CARY dropped me at the house, he sped away in his customary cloud of dust. Burghardt waved good-bye from the rear seat, and something about how small and lost he looked, back there by himself, and the way Daddy Cary's dust cloud obscured him, made it feel like a farewell of unusual importance. As I climbed the stoop to the porch, it occurred to me that Burghardt might die before I saw him again, but I put the thought out of my mind. Inside the house, I encountered my mother and sister in the kitchen. From her station at the counter, Mother glimpsed me just long enough to identify me as her youngest child, returned to what she was doing, and said, "Hurry up, Benjamin, and get bathed and changed. I want to get supper over with early because I still have several hours' work to do."

She stood with her back to me, wearing a flowered apron, slicing tomatoes, and while I thought about hurrying up, she went on at length about all she still had to do in preparation for Daddy Cary's sixty-fifth birthday celebration tomorrow. She said she still had the potato salad and the ambrosia to make, and six dozen eggs to devil. She said poor old Oatsie Montague had been up at the Big House all afternoon frying chicken, and she didn't know how in the world the woman could fry chicken on a day like this when the mercury had surely hit ninety. She herself was about to die of heat prostration, and all she'd had to do was to boil some potatoes and eggs. She said that if she left everything till morning, she wouldn't be able to get it all done in time, since there was church services to get through as well, and she couldn't skip church, birthday celebration or no birthday celebration, because the alto section of the choir was missing three people and she was the only alto who was already familiar with the anthem they were doing, which was "In Calvary's Wake." My Uncle Dillon and my Aunt Bobbi were driving in for Daddy Cary's party tomorrow, and it would be just like Bobbi to show up early so she could stand around and criticize. Supper this evening was cold pot-roast sandwiches, bread-and-butter pickles, tomatoes, and potato chips, and if anybody wanted anything more than that, she was sorry, they would just have to find somewhere else to eat.

Lainie, who sat at the table, skimpily dressed in a halter and short shorts, was spreading mayonnaise on ten slices of white bread. Seeing the mayonnaise caused me to think of a story Al used to tell about the mysterious mayonnaise jar that replenished itself again and again overnight in the refrigerator, and when its owners finally emptied it to see what was what, they discovered a tiny green worm at the bottom with white pus coming from its eyes. Mother's rattling on, keeping me pinned there in the kitchen when she'd told me to hurry and bathe, and my recollection of the mayonnaise story made me woozy. I must have looked distressed, for Lainie lowered her head to the table dramatically—creating an angle that made her appear entirely naked—and said, "Mother, Mother, Mother, Mother, Mother," banging her brow on the Formica.

Mother, interrupted mid-sentence, turned from the counter and said, "What?" She wiped perspiration from her nose with the back of her hand and waited for Lainie to raise her head from the table. When Lainie did, Mother repeated, "What?"

"You just told Ben to hurry up, and now you're talking his ear off," Lainie said.

Mother twisted a bit farther, looked at me, then back at Lainie. She said, "Well, Lainie, I just want him to know what the plans are. Is there anything wrong with that?"

"No," Lainie said, "but let him go get cleaned up first."

It was the kind of thing Lainie would say ordinarily in a spirit of amusement and even helpfulness, but now she seemed serious, genuinely irritated. Obviously, something had been going on between them before I came in.

"Oh, well, yes, ma'am," Mother said, "just whatever you say, Miss Eleanor. You know, I sure am happy you're here to tell me what to do every minute, because I don't know how I would ever manage otherwise. Ben, you better do what your sister says, go on and get bathed. I don't know how I would manage my poor pitiful life, Lainie, without you around to keep me in line night and day. I just don't know how I would possibly manage."

I'd already started for the living room door. The second before I got it closed behind me, I heard Lainie say, "I don't either, Mother, I really don't."

I paused in the living room to soak up some of the frigid air. Mother's disappointment over her country life found its high note in the living room, this walk-in refrigerator for dirty eggs. Its beige walls and liver-colored asphalt floor tiles were always dark, since the drapes were permanently drawn for maximum cooling. A sectional sofa, black with gold thread, had been fitted like an L in one corner, and a kidney-shaped coffee table nestled flush into its crook; our RCA console television, which hadn't worked for months and which Daddy refused to pay to have repaired, stood between two windows, and above the sofa hung a reproduction of a painting of snapdragons in a Chinese urn. Every flat surface was occupied with red-wire baskets full of eggs: the floor, the coffee table, even the couch and the television. The hum and rattle of the huge window unit shut out all other sounds. I had a considerable appreciation for being alone, but there was something too-alone about being alone in the living room. The egg baskets gave it an invaded quality, and even the snapdragons looked deserted in the gloom. Because I'd come from the creek and ridden back to the house in Daddy Cary's air-conditioned Olds, I wasn't all that warm, but I made myself stand there for a minute because I liked the way the hot air in the hallway hit you once you'd thoroughly cooled down.

After my bath, I went to my bedroom and put on a clean pair of khaki shorts and a white T-shirt. I took down the Lincoln Logs from the closet shelf and pulled out the playing cards for a quick run-through. I sat on the floor at the foot of the bed and shuffled them. In my usual manner I went through, passing each card from top to bottom until the first one reappeared. Now, with each picture familiar, what I experienced was simple recognition—here was the one in which a woman stretched a black stocking away from her face, its toe clenched between her teeth; here a man nibbled a woman's breast as the baby Jesus did Mary's in religious paintings—but my heart still raced: the world fell away on all sides, and I sat for a whole minute in a very high place above it.

I heard the hall door open and shut with a sharp bite that meant my father coming in from a long hot day. Though there was little danger of his stopping at my door for any reason, I slid the cards under the bed just in case—a good thing, for in the next moment Al entered without knocking, stood over me, and said, "What are you doing sitting there on the floor, Ben?"

I shrugged. "I always sit on the floor."

"But what are you doing?"

"Just sitting on the floor," I said.

"But *why?*" he said.

"Are you taking notes or something?" I said.

It was a remark I'd learned from him, so I thought it would be effective.

"I might be," he said. "Mother wants you in the kitchen pronto."

"I'll go in a minute," I said, not moving from my spot.

Al squatted to my level, and I feared he could see under the bed. His face was caked with sweat and dust from the henhouses, and three or four wispy chicken feathers nested in his hair. He put a hand on my shoulder and spoke to me in a deep voice, an older man advising a youngster. "I think you better go now, son," he said. "Seems to me like she's on a short fuse this evening. I don't think it would take much to push her over the edge, if you know what I mean."

"Okay," I said, but I still didn't move.

Al scrutinized my face. "Are you all right?" he asked. "You look a little green around the gills."

"I'm fine," I said.

He stood, towering over me again. "Well, go on, then," he said. "And whatever you do, don't say anything about sandwiches being the only thing she's got for supper. If I was you, I would act like it was the best supper idea anybody ever had."

He moved to the closet and began poking around, rattling some empty wire coat hangers. "I can't believe you still play with Lincoln Logs," he said, noticing the open carton on the shelf. "I used to love those things," he added, then unbuttoned his work shirt, moved to my desk chair, sat down, and took off his shoes.

Most days, Al's work consisted of delivering eggs in the mornings and collecting the cage birds' eggs in the afternoons; he sometimes brought a change of clothes with him to the farm, and when he was done with work, he bathed and changed at our house and partook of whatever supper Mother had prepared. Apparently this was one of those times, and apparently he meant to spend a few minutes in his old room now. He looked at me and said, "Well, are you gonna sit there and watch me undress or do what I told you to do?"

I had no alternative but to go to the kitchen, leave the cards under the bed, and hope he wouldn't find them.

Al was at loose ends this Saturday evening because Jeannette had taken a trip to Harrisonburg for two or three days to be with relatives—somebody on her mother's side of the family was getting married. Shelby and Frank had made plans with their own girlfriends that didn't include Al. For supper, he took the fan out of the kitchen window and set it up on the deep freeze so it blew directly onto the table. I thought this a good idea, given the heat in the kitchen, but you had to hold on to your paper napkin every minute or it would go flying across the room. Al brought the *Herald* to the supper table despite Mother's idle protests, and I thought this, along with the fact that he sat in Daddy's chair, was an attempt somehow to stand in for Daddy, who was not present. He even read aloud to us certain interesting tidbits from the paper, as Daddy sometimes did, like the fact that we'd received about half the normal amount of rainfall during the month of July. Daddy, it turned out, had quit work early and gone into Farmville for a meeting of the Chamber of Commerce, a big deal, since there was to be a guest speaker from the Federal Bureau of Investigation. At the table, Al told us the FBI agent had come over from Roanoke, where he was on "special assignment."

"From what I understand," said Al, speaking from behind the newspaper the way Daddy often did, "he's to give a talk on the topic of increasing crime."

I immediately thought Al's phrasing had made it sound as if the FBI agent was to offer advice on how to increase crime, and Lainie said,

"You mean he's going to tell the Chamber of Commerce how they can increase crime in Farmville? Why would they want to do that?"

"Now, you know that's not what he's going to do, Lainie," Al said, lowering the newspaper and taking the exaggeratedly patient tone of a doctor on a mental ward.

"Well, that's what you said."

"No, I didn't," said Al, in the same tone. "Now, is that what I said, Mother?"

Mother said, "Of course it's not what you said, Al. Don't pay Lainie any mind this evening. She's not herself, and she hasn't been herself all day." Mother cupped her hand to the side of her mouth, leaned a few inches toward Al, sighed, and whispered, "It happens, you know."

"Oh, yes, it definitely happens," said Lainie bitterly.

"What happens?" I asked.

"You see, Ben," Lainie said, "what Mother is trying to say is that in her experience of life, which is *vast*, women, like all farm animals, get cranky and hard to be around when they're, as she so delicately puts it, *p.g.*"

I looked at Mother. I'd noticed that she appeared more frenzied than usual at the supper table this evening, and now I understood why: the fan was blowing directly into her face, which put her naturally curly hair in a constant state of motion and caused her to keep rapidly blinking her eyes.

She said, "That'll be enough, Lainie."

Al folded the rattling pages of the *Herald* into a large rectangle and held it up for us to see. "Look at that," he said. "Look at the size of that ad. And I bet you the space was donated, too."

BRING BOOKS the ad read, above a picture in which a teenage boy and girl had been made to look like bookends, leaning their backs up against three or four human-size tomes. The ad went on to say that August 17–21 had been designated Library Week and asked the public to contribute books to the libraries of the new private schools. It said

Prince Edward Academy needed two thousand volumes in order to receive accreditation from the state.

"Doesn't that look nice," Mother said.

"'Won't you give or lend your books to the Foundation schools?'" Al read aloud. "'Our needs. Reference books: *Webster's Dictionary*, abridged or unabridged. Encyclopedias: *Compton's* or *World Book*, *Americana* or *Britannica*. *World Almanac*, current or former years. *Information Please. Who's Who. Who's Who in America* or any good biographical collection. Encyclopedia: music, science, art. *Webster's Biographical Dictionary*. Science: any up-to-date science books. History: histories of United States and World. Fiction: classics or any good fiction for teenagers. Biography: individual biographies and collective biographies. Literature: American and world literature. Plays, essays, and poetry. Fine arts: music, sports, architecture—'"

"Since when did sports become a fine art?" Lainie said, but Al ignored her.

"'Sports, architecture, paintings,'" he continued. "'Useful arts: home economics, aviation, automobile, et cetera. Social science: government, etiquette, et—'"

"Etiquette's a social science?" Lainie said. "Who in the world wrote this thing?"

"'Et cetera,'" Al said, with emphasis. "'Religion: Bible and other books on religion, mythology.'"

He dropped the paper onto the floor beside his chair and took an enormous bite of his second sandwich.

Mother said, "By the way, Ben. I signed up to help out at the Presbyterian Church on Monday morning, and I want you to come with me. I already told your father I was going to need you."

"Help with what?" I asked.

"With receiving and organizing the library books," she said, as if I shouldn't have to ask. "That's where people are going to bring their donations, to the Presbyterian Church. I would ask Lainie, but she has to work at Dr. Shanks's in the afternoon and she'll be too tired to do both in her condition."

Lainie said, "You're totally obsessed, Mother, you know that, don't you?"

Mother, surprised, said, "I'm sure I don't know what you mean."

"You're obsessed with my pregnancy," Lainie said, "and I'm not even showing yet. Everything you do or think is planned around it. Can you even remember *life* before I got pregnant?"

"You're just feeling the heat," Mother said, blinking rapidly. "It's getting to me too, and I'm not even—"

"See what I mean?" Lainie said. "You can hardly speak a single sentence without coming back to me being pregnant. I'm so sick of it I could choke."

"Well," Al said, pushing his plate to one side, "I'm thinking about taking in a movie tonight myself."

"What movie?" I said, trying not to sound too eager.

"*Hercules* is playing at the State," he said.

"Oh, yeah," I said. "I kinda wanted to see that too."

Al told me I could come if it was all right with Mother, as long as I promised to behave myself and not squirm around too much.

Mother said of course I could go, smiling approvingly at Al. "Why don't y'all see if you can get Lainie to go with you," she added.

Lainie said, "I don't want to. *You* go."

"Oh, go on and go, Lainie," said Mother. "You know I can't, with all I've got to do tonight. Go on and go. It'll be nice and cool, and it would do you a world of good."

"You mean it would do me a world of good because I'm pregnant," Lainie said. "Thanks, but no thanks. I don't want to."

"Well, why not?" Mother said.

"Because if I've got nothing better to do on a Saturday night than to go to downtown Farmville, Virginia, and sit in the dark and watch Steve Reeves parade around half naked in a loincloth I might as well just shoot myself."

"Oh," said Mother. "Is that who's in it, Steve Reeves? Isn't he the one who played Tarzan on TV?"

Lainie looked at Mother, first as if she were the most ignorant person she'd ever seen, then her expression changed to one of pity, and her eyes filled with tears.

Al said, "Uh-oh, here we go again."

"Al, don't," Mother said, but Lainie had already turned her brimming eyes on him like two deadly crystals.

"Al," she said, "I've been meaning to ask you. Where did you get those shiny new hubcaps on your Ford?"

"I bought them off a man up in Scottsville," Al said. "What's it to you?"

"Really," Lainie said. "How much did you pay?"

"Ten dollars apiece," said Al. "That's four times ten equals forty."

"And what was the man's name?"

Al hesitated. "I don't remember the man's name, Lainie."

"Ha!" Lainie said, triumphantly. "I rest my case."

"Eleanor," Mother said hopelessly, "if you're not going to go to the movies, would you please please get out of this hot kitchen and go lie down." She reached across the table and touched Lainie's hand, adding, "You're just not yourself, sweetheart."

Lainie jerked her hand away as if she'd been stung. "I most certainly am myself," she said, not with passion but with tremendous defeat, as if being herself was precisely her inescapable doom. She rolled her eyes toward the ceiling, which caused the tears to spill out onto her cheeks. She'd taken only two or three bites of her pot-roast sandwich, and now she lifted what was left of it high above her plate and let it drop, laying bare the utter uselessness of the whole ordeal of food and eating. "I most certainly am myself," she repeated.

———

We rode into Farmville with all four windows of Al's white Fairlane down, and for most of the trip the noise precluded any conversation. When we turned onto the state road, Al winked at me, shouted, "Here you go, sport!" and passed me a stick of Juicy Fruit, a gesture not to be underestimated, since Juicy Fruit was one of his most closely guarded compulsions. I'd been thinking about Burghardt in the back seat of Daddy Cary's Oldsmobile, his waving good-bye, and how I'd thought I might not see him alive again. We passed a colored man walking along the side of the road in the dusk; he wore a kind of straw hat that was given out free to customers of a certain feed company, wide-brimmed and cherry red, and I noticed that the man placed his hand on top of it as we roared past him, lowering his head. I also noticed that he was built like Julius, tall and thin, and I thought of Burghardt at the creek and how Daddy Cary had tricked him into exposing his private parts. I recalled Daddy Cary's words—"See that . . . black all over . . . bet you didn't know that, did you?"—and though I'd answered no, in truth I'd never given the question a single thought. It had never occurred to me that the areas of a Negro's body usually covered by clothing might be a different color from those that were usually visible. I'd observed that Burghardt's palms and the soles of his feet were much lighter than the rest of him, a rosy tan, but these details posed only a passing interest when first observed; they were niceties about how Burghardt was made, noteworthy but unexceptional, like the dark blue veins on the underside of my own tongue, or the hairless milky skin on my dogs' bellies. Daddy Cary behaved at the creek as if his trickery had disclosed something marvelous, as if, had I not been shown otherwise, I would have imagined Negroes were "white" like us beneath their clothing. Now, in the car with Al—the thundering wind a kind of seclusion in which to entertain my more disagreeable thoughts—I understood that Daddy Cary's "black all over" referred specifically to Burghardt's penis, which struck me as especially odd, since I would have been as shocked to see a white penis on Burghardt as I would have been to see a black one on myself.

Still, the trip to the creek with Daddy Cary had caused me to consider Burghardt in a new way, as inhabiting a body different from mine, a distinction I hadn't previously paid much attention to, though I did have the impression that most white people in the world were preoccupied with the color of colored folks' skin, especially with the degree of its darkness.

"Look how dark that one is."

"That one's black as coal."

"Black as night."

"Black as ink."

Earlier in the summer, when I'd got very tanned from helping Al put up two miles of fence on the farm, my Sunday school teacher, a cheerful redheaded woman with varicose veins in her legs, had greeted me one Sunday morning with, "You get any darker, Benny Rome, and you're gonna look just like a little nigger boy."

While this kind of talk made me conscious of colored folks' skin—that it came, like my sister's pastel underwear, in assorted shades—I'd been made aware, through keeping almost daily company with Burghardt, of other differences between us that were surely more significant. He had no mother and couldn't be made to say anything about what exactly had happened to her. He lived in a house with books but no indoor plumbing. Aside from his Sunday-go-to-church outfits, sewn by his Granny Mays, his clothes were few and ragged. He was taller and stronger than me, and he could turn his eyelids inside out and make them stay that way. He wasn't afraid of his father. And yet, despite these important differences, was I not more like him than I was like Daddy Cary? Was Burghardt not more like me than he was like Granny Mays? Were we not all more like each other, white or colored, than any of us were like Russians? Everybody was different from everybody, that was the simple truth, and everybody was, I supposed, alike to varying extents.

I glanced over at Al, noted the complexion of his arms, and tried to think of what it resembled. The closest comparison I came up with was the light-brown hue of pecan meats, but even that didn't quite fit. The Juicy Fruit he'd given me was causing a pain in one of my molars, and I turned my head away from him, carefully removed the gum from my mouth, and dropped it out the window. I had a sense that I'd postponed at least one other matter in the back of my mind, and then I recalled Library Week and the fleeting disappointment I'd felt at the supper table about not having any books to contribute. I knew Mother wouldn't part with any of her three Bibles or the dictionary, and I doubted she'd want to give away either of the two novels, even if they were suitable for a school library, which they probably weren't. I suspected that was the main reason she'd volunteered to help at the Presbyterian Church; she meant to donate time in lieu of books.

About a mile from town, Al slammed on the brakes and said, "Goddammit," unusual since he rarely cursed in front of me, and even more rarely took the Lord's name in vain. A rust-brown jalopy pickup truck was wobbling along ahead of us, and because of all the hills and curves in the road, there wouldn't be many opportunities to pass. Al switched on the radio, fished around for something to listen to, and then switched it off, not really giving anything much of a chance. I imagined he'd felt an urge to fill the stillness in the car that had suddenly replaced the noise of the rushing wind. He looked at me and asked me what happened to my chewing gum.

"It was hurting my tooth," I said.

"You got a bad tooth?" he asked.

"I guess so," I said.

He craned his neck out his window to get a look up the road. He shook his head and said, "When was the last time you went to the dentist?"

"I don't know."

"You have to ask Mother to take you," he said. "She won't think of it if you don't ask her. Have you been brushing?"

I nodded, and since he hadn't said, "brushing every day," it wasn't a lie.

"Look at this," he said, and bared his teeth like a mad dog. "See how pretty that is? That's from taking care of them, brushing three times a day, up and down, not side to side. Two things girls really go crazy for—biceps and good teeth. Very important."

I nodded and touched my sore tooth with the tip of my tongue. "Is *The Robe* a book they might want in the new school library?" I asked him.

"*The Robe?*" he said. "Isn't that about Jesus?"

I shrugged and told him it was by Lloyd C. Douglas.

"Well, I think it's Jesus' robe it's referring to," he said, "so they'll probably get about a million copies of that one. What else have you got?"

I hadn't known this about *The Robe*, and I saw in my mind Jesus walking out of a river and slipping into a plaid bathrobe, held for him by John the Baptist. I couldn't recall the title *The Foxes of Harrow* because, as a title, it had never made any sense to me, so I shrugged again and said, "Some old purple book about foxes."

"Foxes?" Al said. "That might do. Probably they'd put it under science."

"I don't think it's science," I said. "Did you know Granny Mays has got forty-one books?"

Al turned and looked at me with real interest. "Who'd you hear that from?" he asked.

"Her grandson," I said. "Burghardt. Forty-one of them in a book-case."

Al glared at the old pickup truck ahead of us and bumped the horn three times with his fist, not actually blowing the horn but pretending to and clearly restraining himself. "Well, I only have one thing to say about that," he said. "Believe none of what you hear and half of what you see. What would an old nigger woman like Granny Mays be doing with books?"

After hearing Granny Mays speak in the woods, I thought "old nigger woman" insulted her intelligence. "You don't even know her," I said, surprised by how angry it sounded.

Al smiled, apparently amused by my reaction.

Defensively, I said, "She's smart."

This made Al smile more broadly, and he continued smiling as he returned his gaze to the road. We were coming into town on Third Street, and the jalopy truck stayed straight as Al veered to the right down Oak. It was getting dark now, but I could see that lawns and other grassy areas were brown from heat and lack of rain. There seemed to be more than the usual number of people milling about the sidewalks in town, and I figured it had to do with the temperature. Oak merged with High Street, and Longwood College and the handsome Rotunda on Ruffner Hall, my favorite building in Farmville, came into view. Al spotted a place for the car, pulled to the shoulder, and parked next to a huge old elm tree; we could easily walk from there down to the State Theatre on Main.

"Reach back there and roll up that window for me," Al said, cutting the engine.

I had to turn around and kneel in order to reach the crank for the rear window, and when I finished and sat back down, I found Al looking past me at Ruffner Hall. "Back in the Civil War days," he said, "the college girls huddled up in that building and watched, out the windows, our boys running scared down to Appomattox. I read about it in a brochure. Some of the rebel soldiers stopped to say good-bye to their girlfriends or their sisters, because they didn't know if they would ever see each other again. After the war was over, General Grant came up here and saw to it that the girls got back safely to their homes. I guess whatever else he was, he was a gentleman."

As Al spoke, I looked up at a second-floor window in Ruffner Hall. The back of my neck tingled, and for an instant I thought I saw a candle and the faces of three young women gazing out through the two lower panes. The window was actually dark, like all the windows, its panes utterly black. I figured I was tired near the end of a long day, and that I'd undergone a moment of what my mother called being "too suggestible," as when I sometimes felt sick because somebody else felt sick.

Al twisted the rearview mirror so he could admire himself in it and ran a comb through his hair. When he finished with his hair, he inspected a small bump below his right eye, then dropped the comb into his shirt pocket and straightened the mirror. I began to roll up my window, but he said, "Wait a minute, Benny."

"What?" I said, not looking straight at him but staring down at my knees, which sometimes looked to me like the rumpled faces of old men.

"What I don't understand," Al said, "is where an elderly colored woman like your Granny Mays would get forty-one books."

I wasn't sure what Al's shift in language indicated, but I appreciated it all the same. "Maybe they're hand-me-downs," I said. "Like some of Burghardt's clothes."

"I bet that's it," said Al. "Well, I don't doubt she's smart, Ben, just like you said. I'll let you in on a little secret if you promise not to tell anybody."

"Okay," I said.

"You don't know this about me," he said, "but I don't really have anything against colored folks."

"You don't?"

"No," he said. "I don't."

"You sure talk like you do," I said.

"Well, that's all it is, Ben," he said, "just talk. Mostly for Daddy's benefit, or to get Lainie's goat. All this Prince Edward Academy hulla-balloo, I couldn't care less about it. It's just what's happening, see, in a place where nothing ever happens. And I like to be in middle of things. I can't help it, I've always been that way. It's the sport of the thing for me. But I've never mistreated a colored man, woman, or child in my life, and that's a fact. And I don't give a damn where anybody goes to school neither. This'll all blow over in a few weeks, and me and Shelby and Frank will be back to running around and drinking beer, watching *Dragnet* and *Perry Mason* and twiddling our thumbs. Daddy and Mr. J. Barrye Wall, Sr., and all the rest of the big shots can tell the courts to go to hell if they want to. But believe me, it's the courts that'll have the last say. Because the courts is the law, and the law always has the last say. You wait and see."

"You mean the schools aren't going to close?" I said, thinking of Burghardt.

"Oh, sure, they'll close," said Al. "For a time, but not for long. They'll open back up and the colored kids'll go to school with the white kids and in a few years everybody'll be wondering what all the fuss was about. That's my prediction. Because, you see, this whole thing's not about schools, really."

"Not about schools?" I said.

He glanced over his shoulder, as if to make sure nobody would overhear what he was about to say. "You're too young to understand this," he said, "but I'm gonna explain it anyway. If they put colored kids into school with white kids, what do you think's gonna happen? There's bound to be some colored kid that'll do better than some white kid, and how's that gonna make the white kid feel? How's it gonna make his *folks* feel? They just wouldn't be able to stand it."

Briefly, I wondered how the white kid's parents would know, without seeing the colored kid's report card. But then I thought maybe Al referred not only to report cards but also to quizzes; I recalled that when a teacher graded quizzes and returned them to the pupils, she generally passed them out in an order from highest score to lowest. I also recalled an interesting observation I'd made on this subject: Boys who routinely endured the humiliation of being last to get their quizzes back were often first to be chosen for the baseball and football teams on the playground, and boys routinely humiliated by being chosen last on the playground were among the first to get their quizzes back. There were, of course, some exceptions to this pattern, and I myself tended to fall about square in the middle in both regards, average in every way.

"And here's another thing," Al said. "Some of the stupidest human beings I ever ran across were teachers of mine in school. I had this one, this civics teacher, Mrs. Dodge, who was so dumb she thought people who had the same first name might be related."

I didn't immediately grasp this idea, and when I looked at Al, he said, "Like she would think maybe you were related to Benjamin Franklin."

"Oh," I said. "And you might be related to Al Capone."

This remark gave Al pause. Al Capone was simply the first Al I thought of, and I hadn't meant to draw any connection between the famous gangster and my brother's reputation as a thief. He said, "Yeah. Anyway, if they integrate the schools, pretty soon they'll have to hire some colored teachers. And what do you think's gonna happen when some slow, lazy white kid comes home from school with a *D* or an *F* given to him by a colored teacher?"

I said I didn't know what would happen, because the thing that had entered my mind was too ridiculous to say aloud: Oatsie Montague, screaming and whooping, running back and forth from her porch to the road and back again, her hands in the air like a gospel singer—which is what she'd done when she got the news that her sister and last of kin had died of cancer.

"You ought to hear my buddies Frank and Shelby talk," said Al. "It's niggers this, and the NAACP that, morning, noon, and night, and you see, they're just scared of losing something precious to them, like everybody else. It's not about mixing the races, like Daddy would have you think. And it's not about states' rights, like the *Herald* would have you think. It's about having a whole race of people around that you can feel superior to. They don't want things to change, pure and simple, because the way things are makes everybody feel better about their own sorry lives. This is what nobody'll tell you, but it's the God's truth."

He smiled and arched his eyebrows, very pleased with himself, not only for having sole possession of the truth but for putting one over on everybody and keeping it to himself. I could think of nothing to say in response. I felt vaguely complimented by his choosing me. My big brother, it turned out, was just another person who was more than met the eye, different from what you might think.

"I have nothing against colored folks, Ben," he added. "And you don't need to convince me that some of them's smart. Hell, look at me. I grew up and became the thing I swore I'd never become—a chicken farmer. All this Jaycee three-ring circus Foundation School private school Choctaw bull . . . I'm just killing time the best way I know how to."

He tousled my hair. "So that's my secret. Now, don't forget you promised not to tell anybody."

"I won't," I said, though it wasn't a promise I would keep for very long.

"Come on," he said. "Let's go and watch Hercules whup the bad guys."

The State Theatre was crowded that night, as a lot of people had the same idea of seeking refuge from the heat. In the lobby I saw one girl and two boys I knew from fourth grade, and we exchanged the barely audible hellos that feel so difficult and awkward when you haven't run into someone all summer and you can't tell whether you're glad to see them or not. I was very happy to be seated in the cool dark of the theater once the lights went down, simply because I knew the next patch of time would be something that wasn't real life. (This was mostly the case for the first two-thirds of the movie, with minor intrusions.) Al sat on the end of a row so he could slump down in his seat and stretch one leg into the aisle, and I had to sit between him and a huge mountain of a man who wheezed when he breathed and dominated the armrest. Two rows in front of us and on the other side of the aisle sat three girls whom Al had said hello to in the lobby; throughout the movie, one of the girls, a blonde in a lime green sundress, kept turning around and smiling at Al, and each time she did it, the others would scold her in loud whispers.

I comprehended almost nothing about *Hercules*. I knew I might be in for a trial right off the bat, when it became apparent that the actors' lip movements didn't match the words they were speaking, a distraction that never went away for me and probably caused me to miss some things. I could tell there were deep themes in the story that sailed over my head, having to do with Hercules being part man and part god—he was unhappy being both—and this of course made me think of Jesus; I'd always pictured Jesus as very sorrowful, and I wondered if this might not have been a big part of his trouble too. The sibyl in the tale made a reference to Hercules' stubbornness, which caught my attention, but I wasn't able to determine its exact consequences. Since it would be several more years before I would learn in school of the famous twelve labors of Hercules, I didn't perceive any conflict about how loosely the movie drew on the actual myth or how freely it drew on other myths. The story, accurate or not, was too complicated for me to follow, but I thoroughly enjoyed what I'd come to enjoy—Herculean feats of strength: his bending a steel spear into something that resembled a giant bobby pin, his choking the life out of a man-eating lion, and, like Samson, his bare-handedly pulling down the pillars of a temple.

Real life's major intrusion occurred about two-thirds of the way through, when the Argonauts, on their quest for the Golden Fleece, encountered the Amazons: one of the beautiful black-haired Amazons reminded me of a woman in my pornographic playing cards, and I realized with horror that I'd never gone back to my room to put the cards away. I prayed that they would still be under my bed when I got home and even promised God that, if they were, I would show my gratitude by never looking at them again. Throughout the rest of the movie, I had to keep pushing aside a dreadful vision of my mother meeting me at the porch door, cards in hand, tears streaking her cheeks.

The very second THE END appeared on the screen, the girl in the green sundress dashed up the aisle, firing a smile at Al as she passed and causing him to jerk in his leg. We watched the credits for another minute, and I noticed that all the names, except for Steve Reeves, were Italian. The lights in the theater came on before the credits were over, and the vision of my mother, distraught at the porch door, all but consumed me.

Al glanced over and said, with genuine concern, "What's wrong, Benny?"

I shrugged and said, "Nothing, why?"

"Didn't you like it?"

"I loved it," I said. "Thank you very much for bringing me."

This sudden fit of overpoliteness flowed from my feeling of having been caught, as if the one could camouflage the other, and Al gave me the fishy look I deserved. "Come on," he said. "Let's go."

On the way out, I stopped to use the restroom, and when I returned to the lobby Al was talking with the blond girl in the sundress. Her hair, previously in a ponytail, was now miraculously in a French twist. She was a good half foot shorter than Al, and when she spoke to him she gazed up at his face with a kind of dazed adoration. The girl's two friends, neither of whom was nearly as pretty, stood about ten feet away, slouching with their arms crossed and feigning idle chat, but their eyes were glued to Al.

As I approached, Al pointed his index finger and pretended to shoot me, making a little gunshot sound through his teeth, which of course made me think again of Daddy Cary and the creek. The girl appeared surprised and utterly delighted by the sight of me. She smiled hugely, like Miss America, and said, "You must be *Ben!*"

I couldn't imagine what Al might have told her to make her greet me with such excitement and warmth. He introduced her simply as Rosemary, and when I said how-do-you-do, she leaned forward as if to get a closer look at me, causing, for an instant, a gold cross she wore around her neck to swing free and catch some of the red light from a nearby popcorn machine. Then she straightened up and seemed to sense the tiny fleck of pink iridescent lipstick on one of her front teeth; she appeared to suffer a passing moment of physical pain, then quickly rubbed the lipstick away with her index finger. She heaved an enormous sigh, smiling sadly at Al. She said, "Well . . ." and let her creamy-bronze shoulders drop a couple of inches.

Al bent his knees and whispered something in Rosemary's ear that made her eyes grow large. I thought I saw a very small fear in them, but immediately a smile returned to her face, and she looked at Al as if he'd challenged her in some way and she meant to accept.

She said, "Are you sure, Al? I don't want to be a . . . well, you know, I don't want to be a . . ."

She couldn't think of what it was she didn't want to be.

Al squinted at her. He kept squinting at her as he took his comb from his shirt pocket and began to run it through his hair.

———

When I awakened in the rear seat of the Fairlane, I vaguely recalled sulking about having been exiled to the back so Rosemary could ride up front. I was lying on my side, and from that vantage, I could see that Rosemary had slipped across the seat and sat right next to Al, in Jeannette's place. The car windows were down, so there was some wind noise, but I could tell from Al's moderate speed and the bumpiness of the ride that we were already on the dirt road that led to the farm.

Rosemary had her hand on the nape of Al's neck and when she began to move her fingers up and down, he said, "Quit it," using a businesslike tone I hadn't heard him use before.

After a brief pause, Rosemary began brushing his neck with her fingertips again, and he jerked his head to the side and said, "Quit it, I said."

She laughed but didn't remove her hand. "You don't like that?" she said. "I thought you did."

"How would you know what I like?" said Al.

She craned her neck so that she could speak directly into his ear. "Maybe a little birdie told me," she said, as if she was out of breath, and kissed him on the earlobe. Then she moved her hand away, and it disappeared from my view. After a short pause, she said, "There. Is that better? Is that what you like?"

Through the screen door on the back porch, I could see my father, wearing only his boxer shorts and undershirt, sitting at his desk and working with the adding machine, which made a kind of chomping sound that caused me think first of ocean waves and then of wolves. I would have to get past him, and I speculated that if Mother had found the pornographic cards under my bed, she would most likely have told him about it. Generally, if there was punishment to be doled out, she decreed and he enforced. But when I entered the house, he said only, "Hey, Benbo, how was the movie?"

"Good," I said.

He didn't turn to look at me. "Well, good," he said, preoccupied, and I moved on through, pausing in the doorway to remove my shoes and socks.

The kitchen, dark except for the small lamp over the stove, was oppressive in its quiet orderliness, the table and the counters wiped clean, the linoleum shiny and still damp from having been recently mopped. I heard the hum of the freezer and felt my heart in my chest. I stepped back to the porch door and asked my father if Mother had already gone to bed.

"She was pretty tired," he said, and rang up another sum on the adding machine. "She's got herself a big day tomorrow, you know." Suddenly he turned in his chair and looked at me, and I felt my ears burn. "Al didn't want to come in and raid the icebox like he usually does?"

"No, sir," I said, and began to wipe my cheek where Rosemary had kissed me good night through the open car window. "I think he was tired too," I added. "It's kind of late."

I concluded from the skeptical look on his face that my father hadn't found this a convincing answer, but apparently his interest in the subject didn't run deep. He returned to his paperwork without another word.

Just before I left the porch, he sneezed and blew a scrap of paper from the desk to the floor. I went to retrieve it for him, but he bent and snatched it up before I'd taken more than two steps. Not wanting him to catch me at this clumsy impasse, in which I'd made a foolish move to do an unnecessary thing, I tiptoed backward toward the kitchen door and slipped away.

———

The cards were not under my bed. I was sure Al hadn't found them, for he would have said something to me about it if he had. That left only one other possibility: Mother had come in to straighten my room or to put away some clean clothes or to generally snoop, and she'd found the cards. I lay awake in bed for a good long while, trying to contemplate my future. I imagined being whipped by my father as my mother stood watching. I imagined my mother, heartbroken, barging into my room and slapping my face. I imagined being made to go and have a talk with the minister of our church. This seemed a paltry list of outcomes, but I soon realized that nothing like this had ever happened before—I'd never stolen pornographic playing cards; I hadn't known such a thing existed to be stolen—so in truth I didn't know what to expect.

I drifted toward sleep that night thinking about the minister of our church, a balding, red-faced man in his sixties named Dr. Wells. I'd never seen the inside of his office, but I imagined it would have a leather chair with gold upholstery tacks. I imagined he would offer me a glass of ice water and send his secretary, Mrs. Busby, to fetch it from the church kitchen. I wondered if he would wear his black robe with the maroon velvet collar for our interview. Then a brand new idea came into my head: Dr. Wells would surely ask me where I'd found the cards, and I would have to say I'd found them in my grandfather's attic, because I wouldn't dare tell him a lie, not inside the walls of the church, and I was certain that Mother would rather die than to have Dr. Wells know that any member of our family kept playing cards in the attic with pictures of people having sex. Now, more than ever, I didn't know what to expect.

I heard the hallway door open and shut, my father on his way to bed. It was ungodly hot in my room and I was sweating though I lay in my underwear on top of the covers. I climbed out of bed, went to my window, and raised the venetian blind, hoping for some air. I knelt on the floor beside the window and recalled learning in fourth-grade science about the importance of air: that while a human could live three weeks without food and three days without water, he could live only a few minutes without air. Some night-flying insect, a beetle or a moth, banged against the screen and flew away into the dark. Moonlight shone on the waxy leaves of the tall camellia bush outside the window, though I couldn't see any moon in the sky. I didn't hear my door open, and I nearly jumped out of my skin when, behind me, my mother said, "What are you doing, Ben?"

Seeing that she'd startled me, she said, "Oh, I'm sorry, sweetheart. I tiptoed in because I thought you might already be asleep." There wasn't even a hint of distress in her voice—if anything, she sounded more at peace than usual. She stood behind me and rested her hands on my shoulders. "Looking at the moonlight?" she asked.

"Yes, ma'am," I said.

"Well, it surely is beautiful," she said. "And how was the movie?"

"Fine," I said.

"You enjoyed it?"

"Yes, ma'am."

"I'm glad," she said. "I hope you remembered to say thank you to Al."

"I did."

She heaved one of her famous sighs. I feared it might be the prelude to her broaching a difficult subject, but all she said was, "Well, I just wanted to make sure you got home all right." After a pause, she added, "I'll leave you to your moonlight," but she didn't remove her hands from my shoulders. Then, her voice faraway, she said, "You know, my daddy was always one to enjoy the moonlight."

I said, "What did Daddy mean that day when he said you should've married somebody like your mama married?"

Mother laughed quietly. "You know how he is, Ben. He thinks that just because a man helps his wife around the house a little bit, does some vacuuming or dries a dish, he must be a sissy."

"Oh," I said, secretly shocked, for until that minute I hadn't known that a grown man could ever be considered a sissy.

"I don't pay him a bit of attention when he talks like that," she said, which of course couldn't have been further from the truth. With that she kissed the top of my head, softly drummed her fingers once on my shoulders, told me get to bed soon, and left the room.

Here was an outcome I hadn't considered—that I would never see the missing cards and their dirty pictures again, their discovery and disappearance would simply never be mentioned, and life would go on as usual. I glanced at my clock radio on the dresser, which read seven minutes to twelve, and decided to wait at the window until one second past midnight, the tricky moment when tomorrow became today and today became yesterday.

6

WE'D HAD ONLY A LITTLE more than three inches of rain since June, and all over the county pastures were parched, dairymen had resorted to feeding hay, and tobacco farmers had begun harvesting early rather than letting crops burn up in the fields. Rome Road was so dry in front of the Big House that each time a new car arrived at Daddy Cary's party, guests milling about on the grass under the shade of the apple trees hurried back inside until the dust clouds settled. Since it was a Sunday, most had been to church earlier in the day and had kept on their best clothes. The flow of people in and out of the house filled the screen porch with flies, and Oatsie Montague said she might just as well have put the food table in the yard. Mother told her that if she'd done that, the food would be covered with dirt *and* flies, and Oatsie, wiping her hands on her apron for the tenth time in one minute, said she guessed Mother was right; at least people appeared to be having a good time and had plenty to eat, and that was what counted.

Of course nobody knew Daddy Cary's sixty-fifth birthday would be the last he would live to celebrate, but after he was dead, people would recall the party that hot August afternoon and evening as something special, despite the 95-degree weather and despite a fistfight that broke out between Frank and Shelby O'Bannon, who'd drunk too much beer and hadn't even been invited. Oatsie Montague nearly killed herself making the occasion what it was. With some assistance from Mother, she'd planned and organized the whole thing, from the invitations to the menu, prepared a good bit of the food herself, and baked and decorated three sheet cakes. She'd cut up and fried some twenty chickens, strung and boiled a bushel of beans, and driven all the way down to Drakes Branch and back for eight dozen ham biscuits from a woman who was known to make the best in the state. The only part that Daddy Cary took charge of himself was the fireworks display, in his own honor, after dark. For help, Oatsie brought along five women from her Holiness church, all versions of herself—plain, pale, heavy in varying proportions, big-breasted, and each wearing her hair in a bun at the nape of her neck. I overheard Lucille Mobley—a telephone operator who chain-smoked Winston cigarettes and who, in Lainie's opinion, was too old and overweight to wear her clothes so tight—remark to my mother, "Boy, that Oatsie Montague sure does knock herself out for him, don't she."

She'd said it in a rather bitter tone, and I wondered if it didn't have to do with the fact that she herself would soon be out of a job; come October, our area was converting to a dial system. Mother said, "Well, Lucille, who else does Oatsie have?" and the other woman said, "Oh, you're right, you're right, Diane, of course you're right, the poor thing."

Julius was on hand to keep the several galvanized washtubs replenished with crushed ice, bottled beer, and sodas. Every now and then he would lift a block of ice from Daddy Cary's deep freeze, slide it into a clean feed sack, and carry it out to the stone wall that divided the backyard from the barnyard; he placed the sack on a flat part of the wall and pounded it with the blunt side of a hatchet until the ice was crushed.

I observed that throughout this procedure Julius wore his most wor-ried-looking frown, but when he returned to the screen porch and poured the ice into a tub, he was smiling to beat the band. I also observed that somebody had found a ruby-red bow tie for him to put with his white dress shirt, and because he wasn't used to it, he kept touching it with the tips of his fingers.

I had no work to do at the party; I was, as Mother had stated after church services, free. I can't say how many people actually attended, but it was more than I'd ever seen at such a gathering, and my being free meant I could wander in and out of rooms or from one spot out-doors to the next, often unnoticed. When I did get noticed, it was gen-erally with passing interest, and I could linger or move along without its seeming to have any consequence, which fit nicely with my inclina-tion to spy and eavesdrop. I couldn't imagine that so many people cared about Daddy Cary or his birthday, for he was wholly unlikable, and I suspected it was the opportunity to socialize with one another and to enjoy Oatsie Montague's cooking that had brought them out. Daddy Cary spent almost the entire party on the green leather recliner in the living room, had his food and drink brought to him by one of Oatsie's Holiness women, and received short visits from guests who stopped in to wish him many happy returns.

A lot of the county's important men came, which occasioned a good amount of talk on the topic of the schools; J. Barrye Wall, Sr., edi-tor of the *Herald*, showed up late in the day and said a few words. I thought my father would be pleased to have such prestigious com-pany at the farm, but as the afternoon wore on he grew increasingly unhappy—he sank into a sour anxiousness that seemed to begin when he went into the living room to say happy birthday to Daddy Cary. A minute earlier, he'd found me leaning over the old well, across the road next to the smokehouse; on a bright day like today, you could see your perfect reflection in the well water's black round mirror some thirty feet below. My father walked up alongside me and said, "Come on inside with me, Benny, and say happy birthday to your granddaddy." I said, "Yes, sir," and wondered why he'd crossed the road to ask me when it would have been more like him to yell from the other side. As we headed toward the house, I thought with some pleasure that Daddy and I looked alike—we each wore a short-sleeved white dress shirt, black trousers, and a narrow black necktie, and we each had doused our hair with Vitalis and carefully parted it on the left.

We wove our way through the folks standing on the long front porch and then through those crowded inside the shady screen porch. A tall bony-looking man grabbed Daddy by the upper arm and pulled him close, then said in a quiet voice, "For crying out loud, R.C., can't you do something about the heat?"

For a second, my father looked alarmed, as if he thought the man serious, but then he grinned and said, "I'm working on it, Bob."

The man said, "Well, why don't you just speak to the management?"

"I'll do that," said Daddy, and a hint of the former edginess darkened his face.

"Who's your sidekick?" the man said, gazing down at me.

"This is my boy, Benny," Daddy said, and laid a hand on my shoulder; he pushed me forward an inch and said, "Shake hands with Mr. Crawford, son."

I didn't like the man's eyes when they first landed on me—there was a fire in them that reminded me of the lunatic who'd terrorized me that night behind the bleachers at Farmville High—but when he smiled, that nearly extinguished it. He grabbed my hand and pumped it up and down five times, saying, "Well, Benny, I'm very pleased to know you."

As we passed through the kitchen on our way to the living room, Daddy asked me if I had any idea who I'd just shaken hands with. I said I thought he was the Mr. Crawford who owned the dry cleaners in Farmville, and Daddy told me that was right but that he was also the first president of the Defenders of State Sovereignty and Individual Liberties. This meant nothing to me at the time, but I did think, for no logical reason, that Mr. Crawford's being a president of an organization with such a long name might account for the fire in his eyes; I noticed that when Daddy spoke this long name, he did it with the same lilting emphasis with which he said, of the egg, "Nature's most nearly perfect food."

In the enormous living room, with its walls of varnished wood and its two oval-shaped braided rugs, Lucille Mobley sat on the edge of the couch under a four-foot-square oil painting of a Saint Bernard, a work of art that had been in Daddy Cary's family for more than a hundred years, allegedly of Dutch heritage and worth a small fortune. Lucille was wearing a dress suit of the bright orange color usually seen only at Halloween, lipstick close to the same shade, and white high heels; on the floor next to her feet was a matching white handbag with a gold clasp that looked like the amputated claw of a large bird. A cigarette in one hand and a cocktail in the other, she sang out, "Well, hello, hello, hello, R.C., how in the world are you?" as if Daddy were her long-lost friend. "And Benjamin!" she cried. "Just look at you; how you have grown!" (Because Lucille had seen me earlier, when I'd overheard her exchange with Mother, it now seemed she was flabbergasted that I'd grown so much in the last hour.) "Come over here and sit down," she said, presumably to both Daddy and me, and slid to the end of the couch farther from Daddy Cary, who was relaxing nearby in his recliner.

Daddy Cary had the dark green chair tipped as far back as it would go, so what you first confronted of him were the barely scuffed soles of his cordovan dress shoes. Though people had been asked not to bring birthday gifts, a few wrapped and ribboned packages cluttered the floor between the couch and the recliner. On the other side of the chair was the ashtray on a brass stand we'd given Daddy Cary last Christmas, and in its amber-colored dish rested a shot glass of whiskey and a half gone but not forgotten cigar.

"We can't stay," Daddy said to Lucille. "We just come in to say happy birthday to the old man."

"Well, I guess he *is* an old man now," said Lucille, "though you would hardly know it, to hear him carry on."

"What's he been telling you?" Daddy asked her, eyeing her with an exaggerated suspiciousness.

"Oh, one thing and another," Lucille said. "All about how bad he is, mostly."

"He's bad, all right," said Daddy.

"I told him I thought it was high time he grew up, at his advanced age," said Lucille, "but he said if he hadn't *growed* up by now there wasn't any point in even thinking about it."

"Well, I guess that's true," Daddy said.

"Oh, R.C., don't say that—it most certainly is *not* true," said Lucille. "It's never too late to grow up."

"It is if you die first," Daddy said.

Lucille threw back her head and laughed as if that was the funniest thing she'd ever heard. I moved three or four steps backward and leaned against the cold metal woodstove in the middle of the room. It wasn't unusual for people to have conversations of this kind, about Daddy Cary, in front of Daddy Cary, as if he weren't present; I'd seen that before. But there was something off-putting about the way Daddy and Lucille Mobley seemed to be performing a skit, making up their lines as they went along, and about the way my father kept sneaking glances at Daddy Cary throughout.

Lucille patted the couch cushion next to her and said, "Why don't y'all sit down? It's a tiny bit cooler in here. I don't know why everybody wants to stand around out there on that hot screen porch with those horrible lizards running all over everywhere."

She'd shuddered on the word *lizards*, referring to the beautiful chameleons that inhabited the scuppernong vines and didn't in fact run all over everywhere but confined themselves to the outside of the screens. You were lucky if you got to see one.

"We can't stay," Daddy repeated. "I just brought Benny in to say happy birthday."

My father looked at Daddy Cary again, but Daddy Cary looked at me. I didn't recognize the moment as my cue to speak, if that was what it was, and Daddy Cary reached for his cigar. A sad expression overtook Lucille Mobley's face.

My father said, "Well, I'm gonna see if I can hunt myself up a cold beer," and then, to my astonishment, abruptly left the room.

Lucille smiled at me with heroic sympathy, slid back to the end of the couch closer to Daddy Cary, and whispered, plenty loud for me to hear, "He came in to wish you a happy birthday, Cary, and you didn't even look at him, not once."

Daddy Cary, studying the wet and tattered end of his cigar, said, "Where's that brother and sister of yours, son?"

Though he'd said *son*, it took me a moment to understand that he'd spoken to me. I stood up straight and answered, "Lainie's outside somewhere, and Al didn't get here yet."

"Well, I might have a buffalo nickel for you in my pocket," Daddy Cary said, "if you want to come over here and get it."

In truth, I didn't want to go over there and get it, but I thought it unreasonable of me not to, since I cherished buffalo nickels. When I moved within his reach, he spun me around by the arm so that I faced Lucille Mobley and said, "How old do you think this boy is, Lucille?"

Lucille leaned forward and stubbed out her cigarette in Daddy Cary's ashtray. She said, "I know how old he is, Cary. He's ten. He was born the same year as my niece Judy."

Just then two women wearing similar pink-flowered dresses came through the door; one of them held up a camera and snapped a picture, a flashbulb went off, and the two of them began to sing the birthday song. I recognized them as the wives of the Cheney brothers, tobacco farmers who bought corn and hay from Daddy Cary. When the singing was done Lucille broke into applause, and the Cheney wives laughed and stood awkwardly just inside the room. Daddy Cary, who hadn't in any way acknowledged the picture taking or the singing, reached his hand behind me, up between my legs, and gently squeezed my genitals. "Would y'all believe this boy is done messed in his pants?" he said.

The desertion of blood from my face caused me to look down, to see if the floor of the room had actually buckled beneath me, and I noticed with shame that my bare ankles were exposed as a result of his hiking up the crotch of my trousers. All the women laughed again, louder and more hysterically than before, and Lucille Mobley cried, "Cary T. Rome, you behave yourself! Benjamin, come over here, honey, and stand by me."

Daddy Cary didn't let go but continued a gentle pulsing with his fingers, his thumb pressing hard from behind, and I had to lift one of my feet from the floor and dismount his hand as if I were getting off a bicycle or a horse. He giggled quietly as I moved away.

"Come here, lamb," Lucille said, still laughing, and handed me her empty glass with a paper napkin wrapped around its base. "Do me a favor, sweetheart, and take this out to Oatsie Montague and tell her I'll have the same thing but with a little more ice this time."

As I walked away from the couch, I heard Lucille say, in a kind of mock-scolding tone, "You ought to be ashamed of yourself, Cary." In order to leave the room I had to walk between the two women still standing and smiling near the doorway, and I smelled the burnt plastic odor of the flashbulb.

I found Oatsie Montague in the kitchen and gave her the empty glass. I said, "Miss Mobley said could she please have another one of these."

Oatsie frowned and shook her head at the glass as if it were the sinner and not Lucille Mobley. She wiped her hands on her apron, and as she reached for the glass, she looked at me and said, "What's the matter, child? A person would think you was about to cry."

"Nothing," I said. "I just got some of Daddy Cary's cigar smoke in my eyes is all."

I went quickly through the back door into the dirt yard behind the house and saw Julius sitting on the stone wall. He was fanning himself with the kind of paper fan they gave out in some churches, a flat wooden stick stapled to a square of cardboard with a picture of Jesus. I sat next to him, hanging my feet and legs over the wall, and asked him where Burghardt was keeping himself today. I'd suddenly imagined inventing for myself an escape, an errand, maybe to the tenant house to deliver an important message.

"Somebody come and took his granny and him over to Rice for a barbecue," Julius said. "I don't expect they'll get back till past dark. I woulda went myself if Mr. Rome didn't need me today."

Julius and I sat in silence for a minute, and then he asked me if I'd wished Daddy Cary a happy birthday yet. I didn't answer right away, but watched my feet swinging to and fro. At last I said, "I don't care if he has a happy birthday or not."

Julius was in no clear way surprised by my response. He just kept fanning himself and, after another brief silence, said, "You oughtn't to be so chilly on him as all that. Didn't he take you swimming to the creek just yesterday?"

I said nothing, for not only did I lack the capacity for telling what had happened yesterday at the creek, I lacked the courage to speak what had come into my mind: the many occasions of Daddy Cary's cruelty to Julius—his flying into a rage over something Julius hadn't done to suit him, cursing and belittling him in front of Burghardt. Once, he'd gotten so angry at Julius for leaving the lights on overnight in the milking barn, he clamped his hands around Julius's neck and started choking him; I honestly believed he might have killed him if Daddy hadn't shown up and stopped it.

"I'll grant you there's a right much of mystery to the man," Julius said. "But we don't always have to understand a thing to respect it, now am I right or am I wrong?"

"I don't *care*," I said. "Stop talking about it."

"That's okay, that's okay," Julius said, nodding and fanning. After a moment he said, "You look mighty nice today, Mr. Ben. All dressed up and handsome." A moment later, he said, "Um-hm, just as handsome as can be."

I kept my head down, for despite all the desperate swallowing and blinking I was doing, tears had saturated my eyelashes. One of Daddy Cary's milk cows let out a long bellow from inside the barn. No doubt she was past due for her afternoon milking, but Julius said, with complete seriousness, by way of explanation, "She complaining she wants to come to the party."

After that, each time I saw my father, he appeared gloomier. He stood around holding a brown beer bottle, and I twice caught him staring from some distance at Robert Crawford and the small group of men Mr. Crawford was talking to. The men had gathered on the stretch of grass between the house and the road, right out in the sun, and it looked to me that Daddy wanted to join them but was having trouble figuring out how. When at last he did move forward and hung at the rim of the group, he remained silent, nodded his head each time Mr. Crawford spoke, and fidgeted with his necktie and belt buckle. I heard Mr. Crawford say to Mr. Pearson, the former Standard Oil man who was leading the crusade for the Foundation schools, "That's exactly it, Roy. You can't get anywhere trying to explain the real conspiracy to the average peanut farmer. Just tell him they're going to make his children go to school with niggers. Then you got yourself some emotional involvement, something you can work with." After this remark, Mr. Crawford seemed to notice Daddy for the first time, to his immediate right, and started to raise his beer bottle—which Daddy took as an invitation to toast the veracity of what Mr. Crawford had just said; he grinned ear to ear and clanked his own bottle against Mr. Crawford's, but Mr. Crawford laughed uneasily and asked Daddy if he would mind fetching him another cold beer.

"He's not out of sorts, Ben, he's getting drunk," Lainie said, when I'd joined her on a quilt she'd spread beneath the apple tree farthest away from the Big House. Though only yesterday she'd worn skimpy shorts and a halter, and though there'd been no visible change in her physically, she'd decided—in the night, apparently—that she was "too far along to continue to dress like a teenager," which probably meant she'd stepped on the bathroom scales and learned she'd gained half a pound. Today before church, she'd found in Mother's closet an ugly old summer smock the color of pea soup and put it on, and with her hair hanging straight down around her shoulders, she appeared to be atoning for something. When Mother saw her, Mother said she looked very nice, but Lainie laughed through her nose and said, "Yeah, right, Mother, thanks." Lainie brought her spiral notebook to the party and had been sitting on the quilt pretending to write a letter, but I could see now that all she'd done was to write *Sunday afternoon* in peacock blue ink at the top of a page, and then to draw flowers around each of the three big holes along the margin of the paper. Since it was nearly six o'clock, I pointed to the notebook and told her she was going to need to change *afternoon* to *evening*.

"Quit spying," she scolded, and flipped the notebook over. "It was the only way I could get Mother to stop coming over here every five minutes and telling me to 'get up off that quilt and *mix*.'" Lainie lowered her voice and said, "Daddy's not the only one who's getting drunk, Ben. Look over there at Bobbi."

Three trees away, our Aunt Bobbi, Daddy's youngest sister, stood talking with her husband, Dillon, and a man and woman I didn't know. She was the only one of Daddy Cary's children, besides Daddy, who'd come to the party. Mother had been a tad off in her prediction about Bobbi's arriving early so she could stand around and criticize; Bobbi had arrived late—not till around four, with Uncle Dillon and our five-and six-year-old cousins, Meg and Dee—but she'd done a fair amount of criticizing anyway. She sought Mother out and asked her if *all* the deviled eggs were coated with paprika, as she was sure Mother remembered that the girls were allergic to any kind of spices. Later, she said, "Oh, Diane, you don't skin the orange sections in your ambrosia? I don't blame you, it's such a lot of work." Mother would have liked to strangle her, but all she said was, "It's the plight of being only one person, Bobbi, and having only two hands." Aunt Bobbi was a mere five-three and, most confusingly, her reddish-brown hair was cut in a very short style that Mother and Lainie called a *bob*. Her husband, Dillon Halliday, a navy man stationed in Norfolk, was six feet two inches tall and had once been a finalist in the Mr. America contest. He was in the habit, any time he encountered a young child, of lifting the child by one ankle and one wrist and swinging him in circles, then depositing him back on earth just to watch him stagger around dizzy. When I first ran into Uncle Dillon today, I wasn't sure whether or not I'd reached a size and age that eliminated me from this treatment, and when he shook my hand rather than grabbing my wrist, I felt both relieved and let down.

"Look at her," Lainie repeated. "What do you think they could possibly be talking about?"

Aunt Bobbi had kicked off her shoes, making herself even shorter next to Uncle Dillon, and stood barefoot on the dying grass beneath the apple tree. She clutched a frosted Tom Collins glass in both her hands, close against her chest, and appeared to be following the conversation of her group with great sorrow.

"Something sad," I said to Lainie.

"Well, anyway, I guess she dispatched Meg and Dee in quick order," Lainie said.

"What do you mean?"

"I mean they weren't here ten minutes before she got one of Oatsie Montague's women to baby-sit. She's got her waiting on those girls hand and foot and playing checkers at the picnic table."

I asked Lainie who the people were that Aunt Bobbi and Uncle Dillon were talking to.

"I don't know," she said, "but I think the man's wearing a toupee. Did you see Al yet?"

"He's not here," I said.

"Oh, he's here all right," said Lainie, "and he brought the O'Bannon twins with him. Mother was fit to be tied."

"What did she say?"

"She asked him why he brought those heathens with him, and he said they were his friends and he *had* thought he would be welcome at his own grandfather's birthday party, but he could get back in his car and go if that was what she preferred. In a matter of about ten seconds he had her begging him to stay. Pleading with him to stay. Now he seems to have disappeared. He's a piece of work."

"Can I tell you a secret?" I said.

"About what?" she said.

"About Al, but you have to promise not to tell anybody."

"I can't think of anybody I would tell any secrets to about Al," she said. "Unless it was the police."

I told her what he'd said to me the night before, about his not really disliking colored people. I did what I thought was a good job of making Al's case, hoping it would improve him in Lainie's eyes. I reconstructed his idea of what was really going on in the public schools, about how white people wouldn't be able to tolerate a colored child doing better in the classroom than their own. I said that in Al's estimation, Daddy and men like Daddy wanted you to believe that the whole thing was about the danger of mixing white blood with Negro blood and us ending up a mongrel nation, but it was really about white folks needing a whole race of people to look down on, so they could feel better about their own sorry lives. I told her Al said he didn't really give a damn where anybody went to school and he just acted the way he acted to impress Daddy and to be a part of the only thing happening in a place where nothing ever happened.

Lainie listened attentively, outwardly unmoved, and when I finished, she said, "Okay, Ben, but consider this: Either Al is pretending to be something he's not to the world at large or he's pretending the same thing to you, and either way it makes him a hypocrite. You're familiar with that word, aren't you?"

I nodded but said I could never seem to remember how to spell it.

Late that night, bleary and too full of the party, I would learn from Webster's that *hypocrite* derived from a Greek word meaning to play a part on a stage—a curious discovery, since that was how life and people's behavior so often struck me.

An old pickup truck rattled by on the road, stirring up dust, but hardly anybody paid it any mind; dust had become by now one of the party's constitutional features. Dispirited about having broken, with no positive result, my promise to Al, I rose from the quilt and drifted in Aunt Bobbi's direction. As I drew nearer, I tried to determine without being too obvious whether or not the man standing next to her was wearing a toupee, as Lainie had suggested. I sat on the grass and leaned my back against the trunk of the apple tree, a weary traveler who'd found an arbitrary place in the shade to rest his bones. The man, who clearly did wear a toupee, caught me scrutinizing him but only smiled and returned his attention to what Uncle Dillon was saying. Uncle Dillon was saying that under communism you wouldn't be able to switch on the television set and watch just any program you wanted to. He said, "Why, in my own life here in the great state of Virginia, I can walk over to the shelf where I keep my phonograph records and choose any one of them I like. I can put it on the hi-fi and listen to it. Under communism, I wouldn't be able to do that."

The man in the toupee and his wife both nodded and said Uncle Dillon was a hundred percent right, and it seemed for a moment that those would be the last words on the subject. Then Bobbi, who had grown openly teary, spoke up. "There's one thing that nobody's said in this conversation," she remarked, and knocked back what was left in her Tom Collins glass.

Everybody turned and looked at her, with both expectation and profound concern.

"Before I would live under communism," Bobbi said, "I would take my children and go to God."

It took a few seconds for the others to grasp what she meant—that she would kill herself and little Meg and Dee rather than live under Communist rule. I recalled that last year in Asheville, North Carolina, a woman had done just that—killed herself and her two children with horse tranquilizers—but in her case, according to the note she left behind, it was because she felt she had too much housework and would never be able to get caught up.

After Aunt Bobbi's remark, a silence ensued, which she evidently interpreted to mean that she'd shocked people, for she added, "Well, I *would*," and Dillon put his arm around her, bent way down, and kissed the top of her head.

The other woman said, "I think I'm going to see how close we're getting to that birthday cake," and she and her husband excused themselves and wandered away toward the house.

As soon as they were gone, Aunt Bobbi took the damp napkin from around her glass and wiped her brow with it. She said, "What has that Holiness woman done with the girls, Dillon? I thought they were outside at the picnic table, but I don't see them now."

"That woman had to go home," Dillon said. "The girls asked me if they could play upstairs in the house, and I said I thought that would be fine as long as they didn't get into anything."

"You *what?*" said Bobbi. She reached up and planted one hand on his shoulder, steadying herself as she rammed her feet into her shoes. "I *told* you not to leave them in there, Dillon. Alone with him."

Uncle Dillon said, "They're not alone, Bobbi, there's about a hundred people—" but she was already trotting across the grass toward the house, out from under the apple trees, and threading her way through the many cars parked in the front yard. Uncle Dillon slapped an apple off a branch over his head, then stuffed his fists into the pockets of his white uniform pants and trudged after her.

I returned to Lainie's quilt, where I could see that she'd added the word *Dearest* to the page in the notebook; she sat holding the cap end of her fountain pen between her lips, pretending to think about what to say next. I lay on the quilt, put my hands behind my head, crossed my ankles, and stared up at a milky-white sky. I said, "He wasn't wearing a toupee."

Not moving her eyes from the page, Lainie said, "He wasn't? How could you tell?"

"I could just tell," I said. "I got a close look. You were wrong."

She gazed down at me and knitted her brow. "Benny," she said. "Are you mad at me?"

"No," I said, feigning surprise that she should ask such a question. "Why would I be?"

"I don't know," she said, suddenly glancing away, "but do you have any idea who that skinny little boy is standing out there in the middle of the road? He's glaring over here like he knows us."

I got onto my knees and shielded my eyes from the sun that was coming in across the cornfield at a low angle. "That's weird," I said. "I think that's Paisley Chatham."

"Who's Paisley Chatham?" asked Lainie.

"A kid from school," I said. "What would he be doing way out here?"

Paisley Chatham, the impoverished kid with the beautiful singing voice whom Urban Hall had persecuted last year in the boys' bathroom at school, began walking slowly toward us. I hadn't seen him since last spring when we got let out, and it now appeared that he'd lost some weight, if that was possible. Lainie said, "He's coming over here," and in another minute Paisley stopped at the edge of the quilt, barefoot, shirtless, and dirty from head to toe; his hair was sun-bleached and mussed, and a pair of plaid Bermuda shorts hung on his hips, cinched and gathered by a homemade leather belt. A housefly landed on the end of his nose, but before he shooed it he looked at it, which caused his eyes to cross and Lainie to laugh.

I said, "Hi, Paisley."

"Hey," he said, and looked at Lainie. "Is that your sister?"

"Yeah, this is Lainie," I said, and Lainie said hello.

"How old is she?" Paisley asked.

Lainie said, "You can speak to me directly, Paisley. I'm eighteen. How old are you?"

"I turned nine last month," Paisley answered. "Do you think I look it?"

Lainie smiled, clearly and immediately taken with Paisley. She said, "Nine is what I would have guessed. Wouldn't you like to sit down?"

Paisley said thank you and dropped to the ground, marionettelike, right where he was, just outside the scalloped border of the quilt. He sat Indian-style and began combing his hair with his fingers; satisfied that he'd neatened himself in this small way, he folded his hands in his lap and said, "My pa says I'm puny for my age. This is some big party, I guess."

I told him we were celebrating our grandfather's sixty-fifth birth-day, and he gazed over at the Big House and said, "Is this where y'all *live?*"

Lainie laughed again and explained that the Big House was Daddy Cary's and that we had our own much smaller house down the road. She asked Paisley where did he live.

"We got a little place on the river in town," he said.

"The Appomattox?" said Lainie. "That must be nice."

"It's not much," Paisley said, "just a shack, but if the water's real high in the river, sometimes you can hear it go tinkling by. And that's nice."

"I bet it is," said Lainie. "Are you thirsty? You must be thirsty."

Paisley put one hand to his throat and said, "Yes, ma'am."

Lainie asked me to go to the house and get all three of us a Coke, and as I started to stand up, she grabbed me by the wrist and tugged me down so she could whisper, "You better bring something for him to eat too."

Inside the screen porch, I made my way to the food table and loaded up a stiff paper plate with potato salad, two deviled eggs, some pickles, sliced tomatoes, three drumsticks, a wing, and a slice of watermelon. Oatsie Montague, who was looking more and more worn out, spotted me from the kitchen door, came over to the table, and asked if I had a tapeworm, for she knew I'd already eaten. I explained that I was making a plate for somebody else, and she said that was very thoughtful of me and it was too bad that all the corn and biscuits were gone but she supposed that was what people got for coming so late. She wrapped a napkin around a plastic knife and fork and stuck them into my shirt pocket. Julius pulled three cold bottles of Coke from one of his drink tubs and popped the caps off with a church key. He asked me how did I think I was going to carry three Co-Colas and that big plate of food too.

Just then, Dee's little sister Meg came tearing through the back door of the porch in a crisp pink pinafore, limping and crying and carrying one of her shiny black patent-leather Mary Janes in her hand. "Mommy mommy mommy mommy!" she wailed, and everybody at that end of the porch turned to see what the commotion was about. Aunt Bobbi emerged from the kitchen and the girl thrust the shoe into her mother's hand, upside down, so she could see the wad of chewing gum stuck to its sole. Bobbi told Meg to hush, that they could scrape that off in no time, and the little girl, in a new eruption of tears, pointed at Julius and cried, "Dee said it came out of that nigger man's mouth!"

"Hush now," Bobbi said, but couldn't quite keep herself from looking at Julius as she took the child by the shoulders and escorted her into the kitchen.

I turned back to Julius, who still held my three Cokes between his fingers. He smiled and said, "I'll bring these outside for you, Mr. Ben. Come on now, you lead the way."

We met Mother on the back stoop. "Was that one of Bobbi's girls I heard squalling?" she asked. "What happened?"

Mother had worn her string of cultured pearls to the party, an heirloom from her maternal grandmother. They were yellow with age, and I'd toyed with the idea of surprising her by purchasing some effervescent denture-whitening powder at the drugstore and using it on the pearls. I thought it might work.

"She just got some gum on her shoe," I said.

"Gum?" Mother said.

"Chewing gum," I said.

"That's all it was?" she said.

"Yes, ma'am," I said.

"Well, my goodness," she said, "Julius can take care of that for her. Julius, hand me those drinks and you go see what you can do."

Before Julius could make the transfer, there came a series of loud reports from the front porch, and this time the screaming we heard was that of adult women. Mother sighed and said, "That'll be Daddy Cary," and the three of us went quickly down the stoop and around the screen porch to the front of the house. Daddy Cary, standing near the middle of the long open porch, had just ignited a second string of ladyfingers and tossed it onto the concrete not more than a few feet from a cluster of guests. People were dispersing in every direction, covering their ears and forming a wide semicircle around Daddy Cary as the twelve new firecrackers rapidly twitched and popped and sent blue smoke into the air. There was a general uproar and my father came forward and implored Daddy Cary to cease and desist, but the old man pulled a single ladyfinger from his pocket, lit the fuse, and threw it at him; he then lit another and tossed it off the porch toward the section of people who'd retreated to the edge of the road. To my left, one of Mr. Crawford's buddies said, "That old man's three sheets to the wind," and Lucille Mobley came bustling up to Mother and said, "He's liable to hurt somebody, Diane. Can't anybody make him stop?"

"I imagine Bobbi Rome Halliday could," Mother said, and as if she'd conjured her, Aunt Bobbi opened the main door of the house, stepped onto the porch brandishing a red flyswatter, walked straight over to Daddy Cary, and told him that if he lit one more firecracker she would make him regret it for the rest of his life. He held a ladyfinger in one hand and an already-burning kitchen match in the other.

Aunt Bobbi said, "You blow that match out this instant or else." There was a solemn bullhorn quality to her voice—the promise of real consequences—and Daddy Cary looked at her suddenly as if he'd been given tragic news. He waggled the match out and returned the unlit firecracker to his pocket.

"I was just having some fun," he muttered, waving halfheartedly toward the road—an apology or a dismissal, it wasn't possible to tell. To Bobbi, he added, "On my own birthday, too."

Aunt Bobbi narrowed her eyes and held open the door for him. It really did look as if she were bullying a reluctant circus bear back into its cage, the flyswatter her trainer's whip. Daddy Cary moved into the house; Bobbi followed behind and shut the door. After about two seconds, the crowd broke into laughter and applause.

Lucille Mobley looked at Mother, her eyebrows very high, and Mother shrugged and said, "I don't know what to tell you, Lucille. She's always had some kind of mystifying power over him."

"Well, I guess it's a good thing she was here," said Lucille.

In the meantime, I'd noticed that Al had joined Lainie and Paisley

Chatham at Lainie's quilt. I whispered to Julius, "Come on," and we began walking away, toward the apple trees. We took three or four steps, and Mother called my name.

When I turned, I saw that she and Lucille Mobley were looking past me and Julius. "Who is that little ragamuffin that Lainie and Al are talking to out there on the quilt?" Mother asked, squinting.

I said it was Paisley Chatham.

"Paisley Chatham?" Mother said. "Is that the boy who can sing?"

"Oh, I've heard about that boy," Lucille said. "Look at the poor thing, he's nothing but skin and bones."

"I'm taking him this food," I said to Mother, thinking she would let me go now that she understood the urgency.

"That's a good idea," Lucille said, and Mother nodded in agreement, but I could see that her mind had wandered somewhere else, possibly to the smell of gunpowder that permeated the air.

On the way over to the quilt, Julius whispered to me, "I ain't chewed no chewing gum in ten years or more, Mr. Ben. Can't on account of my bad teeth. It pains me to chew gum."

Paisley Chatham's father had spent the day helping one of our neighboring farmers to assemble a new grain bin. He'd brought Paisley and Paisley's brothers along rather than leaving them alone at the river all day on a Sunday. On the way home, Paisley had sufficiently angered his father for Mr. Chatham to make Paisley get out of the truck and walk.

"But that's too far to walk," Lainie said. "You can't walk all the way to town."

She and Al and I had been watching in awe as Paisley tore into the plate of food. Al said, "Slow down there, little man, or you'll make yourself sick," but Paisley didn't seem to hear. I half expected him to run off with the food and crouch with his back to us, the way the dogs sometimes did when you threw them a table scrap.

He wiped his chin with his wrist. "I reckon he'll come back for me after he cools down," he said to Lainie, ripping another bite of chicken from a drumstick. "One time," he said, "Pa got so mad he didn't come back for me for two whole hours. That's the longest so far. I enjoy walking, though. You get to see some things up close that you don't even notice flying down the road in a truck."

Al laughed and asked Paisley what he'd done this evening to make his pa so mad.

"It wasn't something I did," said Paisley, "it was something I said."

"Well, what did you say?" asked Al.

"I inquired if he thought I might go back to school next year."

"Next year?" said Lainie. "You mean in September?"

"No," said Paisley. "I was talking about a year from September. Mickey and Sam get to go this year. Pa said the new private schools is gonna cost money, not free like the old ones, and he can't afford to pay the tuition for three of us. The most he can do is two, and even that's a stretch. We had to draw straws to see who went and who stayed home."

"Tuition?" I said.

"That's what they call it when you have to pay money to go to school," Paisley explained.

"How much is it?" I asked.

"Fifteen dollars apiece," said Paisley. His hands were greasy from the chicken, and when he wiped them on his shorts, Lainie passed him the paper napkin and told him to use that instead. He thanked her and said, "Can you tell me who made this potato salad?"

"That's Mother's," Lainie said.

"Well, I sure am enjoying it," he said. "I hope you'll tell her thank you for me."

"I will," said Lainie and then stared at Al with reproach in her eyes, which Al ignored.

Paisley took a swig of Coke and hiccuped.

Al said, "That doesn't seem like enough to make a boy get out of a truck and walk. Your pa must be easily provoked."

Paisley looked at Al thoughtfully, and I imagined he was worried that Al would think ill of his father. "Pa said that after breaking his back all day long in the hot sun, he'd like to drive home without me having to get up in his nose about something."

"You were just asking him a simple question," Lainie said.

Just then, Mother drove by in Daddy's white Impala, waving her hand at us out the window. Paisley was the only one to wave back, saying, "Who's that lady?" and I told him it was our mother.

"Darn it," Paisley said, "I coulda got a ride with her."

"Oh, she wouldn't be going into town," Lainie said. "But I wonder where she *is* going."

Paisley turned back to Al. "It's on account of Pa feels bad about not having the money," he said. "Besides, it worked out for the best. Mickey and Sam don't have talent like me. Pa says I'll always be able to sing for my supper, schooling or no."

Al chuckled again and said, "So you're a singer, are you?"

Paisley nodded and quickly stared down at the plate in his lap, as if he'd revealed this detail about himself by accident and now regretted it. I wondered if he knew I was among the several boys who'd witnessed Urban Hall's torturing him in the school bathroom last year; whenever I'd thought about it, I always felt guilty for not intervening in some way, though I couldn't imagine any viable course of action. Urban Hall was big, mean, and a sixth-grader; anything—a word of protest spoken to him or to a teacher—would have brought severe repercussions down on my own head.

We fell back into watching Paisley eat. After a minute I noticed that Lainie was now peering at Al as if from a great distance, with a kind of imperious expression on her face. At last she said, "So what do you think now, Mr. Big Shot?"

Al upturned a beer to his lips and looked at Lainie down the barrel of the bottle. "What do I think about what?" he said.

"I bet you never stopped to consider this little set of circumstances, did you," said Lainie.

"What set of circumstances?"

Lainie looked at Al as if he was dimwitted. "That it's not just colored kids that are to be left high and dry," she said. "But some white ones as well."

Before this, I hadn't heard about any tuition, and I hadn't actually given any thought to the question of how the private schools were to be paid for. Al glanced at me, hesitated a moment, then spoke in an apologetic tone. "I'm not involved in that end of things, Lainie, and neither is Daddy. That's school board business."

"School board business?" Lainie said. "You really don't understand anything, do you. This thing's been taken out of the school board's hands. That's the point: The school board doesn't have any say-so over private schools."

"Well, then it's Foundation business," said Al.

"Right, and that's the whole problem," Lainie said. "It's Foundation business. It's Defenders' business. It's the Jaycees' business. It's Barrye Wall's business and Roy Pearson's business and all the rest of the big wheels. Seems like it's everybody's business but the children's. I wonder how many of these fat cats running around waving the flag of Dixie even have children *in* school."

Al looked at Paisley, who was ravaging the watermelon, gripping the U-shaped slice with both hands, pink juice running down his forearms. Al said, "I honestly don't know, Lainie," and started to stand up. "I imagine there'll be provisions made for anybody who can't afford to pay."

"But you don't know that, do you," Lainie said.

"If you're talking about charity," said Paisley, looking up at Al, "Pa wouldn't take it in a million years. He won't take any kind of charity."

"Where are you going?" I asked Al, since he was about to walk away.

"I'm going to see where Frank and Shelby have got to. They've been gone almost an hour."

"Gone?" I said. "Gone where?"

"They're right over there," Lainie said with tremendous resignation. "Hobnobbing with the VIPs."

In the distance, I could see that Frank and Shelby O'Bannon had joined Mr. Crawford's group and that Mr. Crawford had a hand resting on one of their shoulders, Frank's or Shelby's, you couldn't tell from this distance. I noted that a roly-poly man with a pudgy face, who would turn out to be J. Barrye Wall, Sr., was now among them. I also noted that Daddy was not.

Al said to Paisley, "If your pa doesn't come for you, I'll give you a ride back into town when I go."

After Al left, I asked Lainie where Jeannette was; Al seemed down in the dumps, and I wondered if that mightn't be the root of the problem. Lainie said Jeannette hadn't returned from Harrisonburg yet, and before I could ask any more questions, Mother pulled up in Daddy's Impala, quite close to the quilt.

As Mother got out of the car, Lainie groaned. Absurdly, Mother began tiptoeing toward us, as if she were sneaking, and then sang out "Hi, you-all!" with the kind of artificial cheerfulness that meant she wanted something.

She stood at the edge of the quilt and said, "Well, where's your manners, Benjamin? Who's your friend here?"

Genuinely puzzled by her behavior, I said, "I just told you a few minutes ago. This is Paisley Chatham."

Paisley set his plate aside, quickly wiped his face and hands, but didn't stand up. Mother smiled faintly at me, disappointed with my answer, and said, "Well, hello, Paisley, I'm Benjamin's mother, Mrs. Rome. Can you be the Paisley Chatham I've heard about? The one with the lovely singing voice?"

I refrained from reminding her that this, too, was something she already knew.

Paisley said, "Yes, ma'am. Can you be the Mrs. Rome who made the delicious potato salad?"

Mother laughed and said she was the guilty culprit.

"I sure did enjoy it," Paisley said. He pointed to the spot on his plate where the potato salad had been. "As you can see."

Mother said she was delighted that he had liked it.

Because Mother remained standing and we three were sitting, we were obliged to gaze upward. I noted that Lainie had stretched out her legs and leaned back, propping herself in this position with her arms locked straight behind her, a skeptical audience for whatever performance Mother was launching.

Mother reached into the handbag that hung over her forearm and removed a folded chambray shirt. She bent down and placed it on the quilt next to Paisley, then beamed at him and said, "Well, I was wondering, Mr. Paisley Chatham, if you might consider singing a little something for us."

Lainie rolled her eyes and groaned again. Mother glared at her, then aimed a restored smile at Paisley.

"Mother," said Lainie. "He didn't come here to entertain."

"I know that, Lainie," said Mother. "I'm not asking him to entertain. I'm talking about one song."

Peering out over the expanse of lawn between us and the Big House, Paisley said, "Do you mean for me to sing a song for all *these* people?"

"You don't have to sing, Paisley," Lainie said. "Just say no."

"Would you please let the child make up his own mind, Mary Eleanor?" Mother said, maintaining a calm exterior. "It's not all that many," she said to Paisley. "A lot of people have already gone home."

Paisley peered again at the Big House. "Is there a piano in that house?" he asked.

"No, there's not," Mother said, "but I'm sure that anything a cappella would be more than suitable. And very much appreciated."

Paisley put a hand to his throat, the way he'd done earlier when Lainie asked him if he was thirsty. "If you don't mind too much, Mrs. Rome," he said, "I'd like you to let me take a rain check. My throat's been a little dry lately, what with all this dust."

"Oh, please don't say no, sweetheart," Mother said. "You don't want to hide your light under a bushel, now, do you?"

"Mother," Lainie said. "This isn't very hard to understand. He doesn't want to sing to a bunch a strangers, half of them drunk. Now leave him alone."

"I'm sorry, Mrs. Rome," said Paisley. "I do hope you'll let me take a rain check."

Mother sighed, all shoulders and air through her nostrils. "Well, all right," she said. "It wouldn't be polite to pressure anybody into anything."

"That's right," said Lainie.

She bent down to retrieve the shirt. "I guess I should've asked before I went all the way down to the house to get this shirt."

"That's right," Lainie repeated. "You should have."

"I'd just heard so much about that voice of his," she said. "I foolishly imagined that I might persuade him to sing for his supper this evening."

"He didn't ask for any supper," Lainie said, sitting up and growing fierce. "We offered it to him. Free of charge."

"Of course we did," Mother said. "I didn't mean to imply otherwise. I only—"

"Well, maybe I could sing just one," Paisley said softly.

"You won't do anything of the kind," said Lainie. "Paisley, you mustn't let Mother—"

"I did enjoy my supper," he said. "Pa says—"

"Sweetheart," Mother said, "Lainie's completely right, as usual. If you don't feel like singing, that's perfectly fine. I just thought I would ask. That's all I was doing, just asking. I want you to forget all about it now. Don't give it another thought."

She put the shirt back into her handbag and took one step toward the car.

"I'd just like to let my food settle for a few minutes," said Paisley. "If that's all right."

She turned and looked at him. "Are you absolutely sure, sweetheart?"

"Yes, ma'am."

She smiled and came forward, removing the shirt from the handbag. "Well, if you're absolutely sure," she said, and dropped the shirt back onto the quilt. "You just take your time and let me know whenever you're ready." She snapped the clasp on her handbag and looked around at all of us as if she'd come along to improve us in some way and was now pleased with a job well done. "Lainie," she said. "I do hope you've had something to eat."

Lainie didn't say a word but only looked at her.

Mother glanced over at the Impala and said, mostly to herself, "I guess I could just leave the car there, couldn't I," and walked away toward the house.

Lainie allowed her to get about ten steps away, then went after her. We couldn't hear what she said to her once she'd caught up, but whatever it was, it made Mother stop, face Lainie dumbstruck, then turn and keep walking. Lainie continued to harangue her the rest of the way to the house, but Mother acted as if she couldn't hear, only once waving her hand the way a person bats away a gnat or mosquito.

Paisley looked at me, shrugged his shoulders, and gave me a kind of *that's life* smile. After a moment, he said, "Don't hide your light under a bushel of *what*?"

"It's from that old song," I said. "I always thought it was a mistake and it was supposed to be Don't hide your light under a bush. Or maybe, Don't hide your light under one of those big bushel baskets."

"Then it ought to say Don't hide your light under a big bushel basket," he said.

I asked him what he was planning to sing, and he shrugged again, then gazed briefly toward the road. "I sure thought Pa would be coming back for me by now," he said.

"I bet he'll come along any minute," I said.

"Maybe," he said. "How many bedrooms does that house have anyway?"

"Six," I said.

The sun had sunk behind a stand of pines beyond the cornfield, and the sky was turning lilac; there were no longer any shadows in the road or the yard, and nighttime was already starting to pitch its tent under the apple trees. Paisley lifted the chambray shirt from the quilt, unfolded it, and held it up by the shoulders. I recognized it as one of Al's work shirts, which meant it would swallow him whole, and I wondered why Mother hadn't brought one of mine instead. He started pulling the shirt on, gingerly, as if the fabric might scratch his skin. Quietly, he said, "I sure wish I could hide my light under a bushel of *something*." He stared down at his hands as he began buttoning the shirt, which was going to hang below his shorts and look like a dress. "Your mother's pretty," he said. "And she smells good."

Reluctant to navigate the crowd and enter the house unaccompanied, Paisley asked if I would show him to the bathroom. He'd tucked the long tails of Al's shirt into his shorts, resulting in his looking less like a boy in a dress and more like a large, top-heavy, bony-legged, knobby-kneed bird. Our brief journey across the yard turned a few heads but caused no lingering interest. I showed him through the back door of the kitchen and down a long hallway, where we found the main bathroom occupied. I led him down another hallway, through two dim bedrooms with creaky linoleum and empty iron beds, through a dark closet that smelled of mothballs, to the extra bathroom at the end of the house, where I switched on a bulb that hung from the ceiling. He was especially pasty-looking under the light. I asked him if he thought he could find his way back, and he nodded, though not with any noticeable conviction. I said I would wait, but his pride got the better of him and he urged me away. I left him gaping about the small room with a wonderment that puzzled me before I understood what absorbed him so. It was the porcelain fixtures, the indoor plumbing.

When I returned to the screen porch, the food table had been cleared to make room for Oatsie Montague's three sheet cakes, each iced in butter-cream icing and festooned with yellow roses and a single white candle at the center. One of Oatsie's women stood dead on her feet behind the table, holding a cake knife but obviously without hope of ever actually serving the cake and going home. As I slowly skirted the table and pondered the cakes, another of the women moved next to the weary one and whispered, "Well, they finally found him."

"They did?" said the other. "Where 'bouts?"

"Upstairs. Sound asleep. Sprawled across a unmade bed."

"Now what does she say?"

"She says for you to go on home. She's gonna postpone the cake another half hour. Let him sleep awhile."

"Sleep it off, more like."

I wandered back through the kitchen and into the hallway, concerned about Paisley. When I had reached the little bathroom, a strip of light still gleamed at the bottom of the door. I returned to the nearest bedroom and sat on the iron bed, which squeaked under my weight and had a dank musty odor. The room was almost dark, with shades over two tall windows. I lay back, my toes touching the floor, and listened to the muffled and distant murmur of the party, which reminded me of the way henhouses sounded late at night. Now I sat up, drawn by a glowing keyhole in one of the room's three doors.

I crouched next to the door, which opened onto the generally unused end of the living room, and peeked through the keyhole. A desk lamp with a green glass shade had been switched on, and I could see the belly of a portly man standing at the desk and rooting through its drawers. When he bent forward to pull open the bottommost drawer, his head came into view and I saw that it belonged to J. Barrye Wall, Sr. He took a sheet of paper from the drawer, placed it on the desktop, and began to write with a yellow pencil. From the steady movement of his hand down the length of the page, I deduced that he was composing a list of some kind. There wasn't anything especially interesting about this—a man finding paper, writing something on it—but I had a premonition that if I continued watching, I would see him do something peculiar.

He appeared to read over what he'd written, and then he folded the sheet of paper three times and stuck it into his trousers pocket. He bent again to close the bottom drawer but suddenly paused; something inside it had caught his attention. From his bent-over position, he quickly glanced upward, into the body of the room, then reached into the drawer and lifted out an old-fashioned lipstick case that must have belonged to my grandmother. I'd seen one like it before—a small gold rectangular case, just the size of a lipstick, with a button that released a tiny pop-up mirror. Mr. Wall did this now, pressing the button that opened the mirror, and looked at himself in it. Then he quickly closed the case, pocketed it, and shut the desk drawer.

He took a couple of hasty steps in my direction—his brass belt buckle glinted light through the keyhole into my eye—so I scrambled away from the door, out of the room and into the next. This bedroom, with its iron double bed, mahogany dresser, and milk-glass sconces, was nearly identical to the first; its only significant difference was that in place of two windows, it had one window and a door to the outside, which I now yanked open. I pushed on the screen door and stepped onto a low concrete stoop overlooking the backyard, the stone wall, the milking barn, silo, and tractor shed, and the woods beyond. I'd just settled myself there, hanging my legs off the edge and trying to catch my breath, when I heard the screen door behind me.

For one second I hoped it would be Paisley, returning at last from the bathroom, but Barrye Wall stepped onto the stoop, right next to me, his oxblood loafers inches from the fingers of my left hand. Without a word he flipped open a silver cigarette lighter and began the ritual of rhythmic puffing and flame-flaring required to light a good-sized cigar; there was the satisfying metal chirp of the lighter cap opening and closing, the rasp of the striker wheel against the flint, and the transitory mixing of aromas, lighter fluid and tobacco. Once he had it going, he said, "Well, hello there, son."

"Hey," I said, and drew one foot onto the concrete and retied the shoelace. I meant to create an impression of my having some actual purpose there on the stoop.

With a fair amount of grunting and groaning he sat next to me, and I smelled the additional fragrance of bay rum. The yellow pencil I'd seen him use a minute before was now balanced behind his ear. After a moment, he said, "Having any fun?"

There was a warmth to his voice that made me tell the truth without thinking. "Not much," I said.

He winked at me and said, "Me neither. I guess you and me, we ain't much for parties, huh?"

"No, sir," I said. "I guess not."

"Are you a relative of Mr. Cary Rome's?"

"Yes, sir," I said. "I'm his grandson."

"Oh, you're R.C.'s boy," he said.

"Yes, sir."

"What's your name? I know you're not Al."

"No, sir," I said. "I'm Ben."

"How old are you?"

"I'm ten."

"That's easy to remember," he said. "Ben, who's ten."

"Yes, sir."

"Well, I'm pleased to meet you, Ben," he said, offering me his hand. "My name's Mr. Wall. Also easy to remember. Just think: Any time I'm in a room, there's five of us." I shook his hand with what must have been a quizzical look, for he added, "Four walls to the room, plus me, makes five."

"Oh," I said, and though I thought it genuinely amusing, I could only fake-laugh.

"What do you do for a living, Ben?" he asked me.

No one had ever asked me that question. I looked at him to see if he was serious.

"You haven't joined the workforce yet?" he said. "Well, what do you want to do? When you're older, I mean."

The air in the backyard had grown so dusky now that his cigar smoke was the brightest visible thing. I shrugged and said, "I don't know," deeply embarrassed by my answer.

"Don't want to take up farming?"

"No, sir," I said.

"It's a perfectly respectable profession," he said. "Fourteen signers of the Declaration of Independence were farmers."

I had no reply to this; I could see no connection between farming and signing an important document.

"Well, what are your interests?" he asked, after a moment.

"You mean what do I like to do?" I said.

"Yeah," he said. "What kinda things do you enjoy? What are your pursuits?"

I didn't need to review this roster to know that everything on it was suspect in one way (reading, drawing, collecting insects) or suspect in another (spying, eavesdropping, being alone), so I shrugged my shoulders again.

"Do you like to read?" he said, practically stunning me.

"Yes, sir," I said. "I like to read comic books."

"Comic books?" he said. "What can you learn from comic books?"

It hadn't occurred to me that the purpose of reading was to learn anything. I said, "I just like stories."

He looked away, out toward the barn, pressed his lips tightly together, and slowly nodded, as if he was digesting this information. "Well, there's all kinds of stories," he said at last. "Some of them useful, some of them not."

The idea that he might have swiped my dead grandmother's lipstick case emboldened me. I said, "What kind of stories do *you* like?"

"I'm a newspaper man myself," he said.

"I know," I said. "You're the editor of the *Herald*."

"Ah-h," he said, surprised and plainly not displeased. "I see my reputation has preceded me. But I meant it's newspaper stories that I like to read. Ask me how many papers I read a day."

"How many?" I said.

He leaned his face close to mine and looked straight into my eyes, as if he were casting a spell on me. "Five," he said. He straightened up and rocked backward in a way that made me think of Humpty-Dumpty.

"Five?" I said.

"Five," he said. "And two weekly newsmagazines. You see, Ben, those are the stories I'm interested in because they inform you. I'm only interested in what's happening. I can't think why anybody would waste their time reading anything else. When there's so much happening in the world, I can't think why anybody would feel the need to make things up. Why, right here in Prince Edward, there's enough going on to fill up a whole truckload of books. We're standing right smack-dab in the middle of history here."

I recognized this as a reference to the busy summer we'd had, getting ready to open the private Foundation schools and keep out the coloreds and, apparently, poor kids like Paisley Chatham. It seemed to me that he'd tricked me into confessing that I liked to read and then launched into a tirade about how I shouldn't be reading what I was reading. All I'd so far perceived about newspapers was that they purposely discouraged a person from reading them—with weirdly worded headlines like riddles to be solved; laborious sentences arranged in narrow columns that not only necessitated thousands of hyphenations but also sent you after a few paragraphs on a wild goose chase for the rest of the story; and all, in the end, only to leave your fingers smudged with black ink. I couldn't begin to imagine what kind of person read five of them a day, though it did seem to me that Mr. Wall considered himself better than most people, and surely better than me, for doing so. Even with my limited experience and education, I strongly suspected something else too: that he'd dismissed a lot more than my comic books into the rubbish bin of things not happening, of things made up. Still, I was intrigued by our standing "right smack-dab in the middle of history," for I was interested in stories from history—especially those in which lesser trumped greater—and I liked the notion that I might somehow figure in such a story. I thought I might vindicate myself in Mr. Wall's eyes by force of a close well-behaved relation, so I told him that my daddy read every issue of the *Herald*.

He nodded as if I'd underscored his very point. "That's why your daddy's as informed as he is," he said. "That's why he has a clear understanding of things."

I couldn't dispute, nor would I have wanted to dispute, my father's being informed, but I certainly didn't think him a person with a clear understanding of things. In my opinion, Daddy's choice of a life among the stupidest, stinkingest, and most disagreeable animals on earth eliminated him from that distinction.

Mr. Wall said that being informed and having a clear understanding of things were requirements of good citizenship. "That's where I come in," he said, "as the editor of a newspaper. You see, most people have good intentions, Ben, but they don't necessarily have what it takes to make the right decisions. It's not enough just to report the news. We have to help people to understand it, so they don't go wandering off down the wrong path."

I appreciated his speaking to me in this way, but I also thought it strange that he was sitting on a backyard stoop talking to a ten-year-old boy when there were scores of adults at hand. Something in his description of right decisions and wrong paths made me think of herding Daddy Cary's milk cows into the barn; from there, my mind leaped to a sprawling herd of cattle, driven across a plain by cowboys on horseback; and then I recalled Granny Mays saying something recently in the woods about the school closings—that if white folks tried to ride that horse into town, they would get thrown. Somehow this rambling little train of thought led me to a brand-new notion, that the decision to close the public schools was right for me but wrong for Burghardt. I sensed the weight of a general truth in this, and I said to Barrye Wall, "Do you think what's right for one person can be wrong for another?"

He didn't immediately answer, but stubbed out his cigar on the side of the stoop and pushed himself up from the concrete. Once standing, he said, "Sure it can," and tousled my hair; taken out on a whim, I was put back in my place.

In the small empty bathroom a grisly odor lingered—Paisley had been sick from gorging himself, just as Al forewarned. He must have taken a roundabout way back to the party, for he never passed my stoop, and the next I saw of him he was standing at the middle of the long front porch preparing to sing. Dusk had fully settled in, cooled the air, and bathed the house and lawn in a blue vapor. Out under the apple trees, Uncle Dillon and the little girls had fallen asleep on Lainie's quilt. The other guests who remained, forty or more, were clumped on the grass next to the road and straggled among the porch columns. Mother, or someone else, had deposited Paisley directly beneath the glass globe of the porch light, which shone straight onto the top of his head and cast spooky shadows down his face.

Lainie, who leaned against the column nearest Paisley, spotted me and motioned for me to come stand in front of her. She wrapped her arms around my waist from behind and drew me close, and though I felt myself color, I couldn't muster the heart to stage any kind of protest; I felt less babied than needed, and that her wanting my company was linked somehow to Paisley—barefoot, barelegged, stranded, railroaded, and draped in chambray. Mother, Lucille Mobley, and Aunt Bobbi stood shoulder to shoulder nearby, smiling and intent, as if they themselves were about to perform. At the dimmer end of the porch, where the concrete slab dropped two and a half feet to the ground, a man in a white shirt and black pants sat with his back to everything, resting his elbows on his knees. I looked up at Lainie and whispered, "Is that Daddy?" She sighed and lowered her chin to my shoulder, so I felt rather than saw her nod.

Paisley clasped his hands together at the waist and cleared his throat, and a general sibilation of women shushing men swelled and faded as he began to speak. "Nobody knows who wrote this," he said, "but some folks call this kinda song a sea chantey. It just means that sailors were the first to sing it. It probably got started on riverboats and then floated out to the ocean. The deep-sea sailors liked to sing it while they turned the giant wheels that hauled in the anchors." He made a large circular motion with his arms, in imitation of cranking a great capstan.

A peal of male laughter rose up behind us out by the road, but it didn't clearly have anything to do with Paisley. There was some neck craning and more shushing, and Paisley reached down and scratched his knee.

He refolded his hands and said, "It's about a trader who fell in love with a Indian chief's daughter. You most likely know it already, but it was what come to my mind to sing." He wiped his brow with the back of his wrist, swallowed twice, and licked his lips. He pulled on his earlobe and closed his eyes. There was quite a bit of foot-shuffling and some coughing and murmuring, but when Paisley got halfway through the second line of the song a real hush sank over the house and drifted clear through the apple orchard, across the road, and into the dark furrows and tunnels of the cornfield.

> *Shenandoah, I long to hear you,*
> *Away, you rolling river,*
> *O, Shenandoah, I long to hear you,*
> *Away, I'm bound away,*
> *'Cross the wide Missouri.*

> *Shenandoah, I love your daughter,*
> *Away, you rolling river,*
> *For her I've crossed the rolling water,*
> *Away, I'm bound away,*
> *'Cross the wide Missouri.*

Oatsie Montague came from around the corner of the screen porch and then was joined, one at a time, by the four remaining Holiness women. I wasn't surprised—I'd seen the cafeteria workers at school likewise emerge from the kitchen, Tuesday before Thanksgiving, and look at each other wide- and misty-eyed. Now Julius appeared behind the gauze of the porch door, somberly straightening his bow tie and cocking his head. Misters Crawford and Pearson, each wearing a straw fedora, removed their hats and held them in their hands. I saw J. Barrye Wall, Sr., move past the five tall and glowing windows of the living room, execute a brief business at Daddy Cary's desk, then move past them again from the opposite side. As Paisley reprised the first stanza, my Aunt Bobbi slipped her arm inside Mother's, and even my father, though never lifting his head, turned sideways to the porch, as if to better align his ear to the music. It was perfect, effortless singing, youthful and uncontemplated, and when Paisley was done wringing out the last *Missouri*, the only sound in the world was the tap-tap of a moth beating its chalky brains against the porch light.

During the applause, Julius pushed open the screen door and Daddy Cary stepped onto the porch. He gazed around the crowd delighted, as if the clapping—along with the freshly rediscovered party itself—were in his honor. Oatsie, whose raised voice was like a buzz saw, threw her hands into the air and shouted that ice cream and cake would be served on the screen porch. Lainie had begun to weep over the song, but it was immediately clear that she'd already moved on to weeping over other things. In the hubbub, she asked me to tell Mother that she was feeling tired and had gone home. "Are you all right?" I asked her, but she only hugged me and began to pick her way through the crowd. Paisley yanked at my shirtsleeve. When I turned toward him he stood stock-still and didn't speak. I said, "Come on, let's get first in line," and we took off for the food table.

Inside the screen porch, two buckets of homemade vanilla ice cream had been set out alongside the cakes, and two of Oatsie's helpers had taken up their stations, but so far there wasn't any serving going on. We each grabbed a plastic spoon from the table, and one of the Holiness women leaned forward and said, "Who wants a rose?"

I shook my head, but Paisley said, "I do."

She winked at him and said, "Well, honey, anybody who can sing like that ought to get just as many roses as he pleases."

Julius, who manned the drink tubs next to the table and was in accordance with this opinion, said, "It wouldn't've surprised me if the stars had fell right out of the sky," but the woman gave him a sideways look that said, Was anyone speaking to you?

At that moment, Al and the O'Bannon twins showed up at the tub and Julius nodded and said, "Mr. Al . . . Mr. Shelby . . . Mr. Frank," and asked them what he could get them. The O'Bannons were all red-heads, and the only way to tell the twins apart was that Frank had a small purple birthmark at his hairline above his left eye—which meant you had to be at least this close to know one from the other. Now they had identical goofy grins on their faces, and I couldn't help but note the contrast between them and Al, who stood with his hands in his pockets and appeared to be stuck with the O'Bannons against his will. Shelby said, "Well, if it ain't ole Julius . . . let me see, now, what *can* you get me?" They knew Julius by name from two previous summers when they'd worked for Daddy candling eggs in the egg room. "How you been keeping, anyway?" Shelby asked Julius.

Julius said, "I been just fine, Mr. Shelby, just fine."

"Still living in that little old house in the cornfield?"

"Yes, sir, I am," said Julius. "As long as Mr. Rome'll have us."

There was something behind this small talk I couldn't decipher, an unfriendliness beneath Shelby's friendly words, and I didn't like the way he and Frank were eyeing Julius. Normally, Julius would have been nothing more to them than a functionary, the nigger who handed them a free beer at a party, and they would have paid him as little mind as possible. I supposed, rightly, that they were drunk, but I wasn't sure that drunkenness accounted for all I sensed. The twins got new beers, Al said he didn't want anything, and as the three of them began to walk away, Frank—as if he was scolding Shelby for something—hit him hard on the back of the arm. Shelby wheeled around and curled his shoulder forward, trying to get a glimpse of the spot where he'd been frogged. I heard Al say, "Cut it out," and the twins moved on through the back door, which Al had pushed open for them.

Just as Al was about to step through the door himself, Mother emerged from the kitchen and called his name. He paused, and in another moment she was going with him onto the stoop. I said to

Paisley, "Wait here," and crept over to the screen at that end of the porch. When I'd situated myself as casually as possible under cover of the scuppernong vines, I heard Mother say, "For Pete's sake, Al, all I'm asking is for you to try."

"I don't want to try," Al said.

"Just see if he'll let you get him into the car," she said.

There was a silence of about five seconds, after which Mother said, "Please, Al. Before he makes a complete fool of himself."

Al said, "You know what I think, Mother?"

"No," she said.

"I think it's a good horse that pulls his own cart."

"I have no idea what that means," she said.

"It means that if you want him to go home, then you get him to go. I didn't marry him, and I don't care whether or not he makes a fool of himself."

"What is wrong with you, Albert Rome?"

"Nothing," he said, and I could tell from the sound of his voice that he'd started down the steps. "And don't call me Albert."

"Al," Mother called, "come back here this instant and tell me what's wrong with you."

Suddenly there was a terrible clanging noise that turned out to be Mr. Wall, rapping a case knife against a glass tumbler to get people's attention. Julius had set an empty washtub upside down on the floor for Mr. Wall to stand on, so he could be seen. I rejoined Paisley at the food table, and after a moment I saw Mother come back inside, clutching her pearls and biting her lower lip. People were filing onto the porch from all the doors, and it was beginning to feel like sardines. Mr. Wall, red-faced and profusely sweating, said in a loud voice, "Just don't nobody yell fire!" and everybody laughed.

Then Mother came over to me and urgently whispered, "Ben, do you know where Lainie is?"

"She's gone home," I answered.

"Gone home?" she said, as if I'd told her that Lainie had left the country.

"Yes, ma'am," I said. "She asked me to tell you she was tired."

Hopelessly, through tears, Mother said, "Oh."

When she'd walked away, droopy-shouldered, Paisley said, "Was she crying?"

"Yeah," I said. "A little."

"How come?"

"She gets blue sometimes," I said. "She worries too much about things."

Paisley pressed his lips together and slowly nodded. He knew just what I meant.

Mr. Wall clanged the knife on the glass again and said, "I've been asked to propose a toast tonight and I'm honored to do so." He beamed a searching gaze over the crowd and said, "Would somebody please go and bring the birthday boy out here? I imagine you'll find him in his recliner."

Mr. Wall set the glass and the case knife aside; he took a handkerchief from his hip pocket and wiped his face; he replaced this, then removed and unfolded a sheet of paper—the one I'd seen earlier through the keyhole—and looked it over. Daddy Cary appeared at the living room door, leaned against the doorjamb, and waved at Mr. Wall. "So glad you could join us, Cary," said Mr. Wall, prompting more laughter.

He continued to consult the sheet of paper now and again throughout his remarks. "Given where we find ourselves tonight," he began, "I thought it appropriate to share with you a true story I heard recently from jolly old England. There's a chicken farmer over there by the name of Smith who went to court to recover a sum of money he'd spent on sedatives for his chickens. It seems an airplane flew down low over his farm last year and caused quite a panic among his hens. The result was that egg production dropped drastically over the next two weeks. He tried treating the hens with tranquilizers, at considerable cost to himself, but it didn't improve their egg laying. In court, his lawyer told the judge that the hens had been—and I quote—'outrageously disturbed without warning.' This statement threw the judge into a quandary, which led to an indefinite adjournment of the case. The judge asked, 'How does counsel propose the chickens might have been warned? And what difference would it have made if they had been?'"

Amid tremendous laughter, Paisley and I looked at each other and shrugged our shoulders.

"Now," said Mr. Wall, "I know Cary won't mind if I say two or three words about something important to all of us and to our futures. Library Week begins tomorrow for the Foundation schools. The requirement for accreditation of the Prince Edward Academy is two thousand volumes. Librarians Candy Hartz and Kay Campbell will be receiving donations at the Farmville Presbyterian Church assembly room on Randolph Street. They'll be there from nine in the morning till one in the afternoon. Our efforts here in Prince Edward have caught the imagination of many people in Virginia. Seldom will you be called to a more worthy cause than this one, and I urge you all to give what you can.

"We've come a long way, but there's still a long way to go. The last week or so there's been some speculation that the public schools might remain open. The lawyers for the school board have said they believe segregated schools could operate for another year, but there's only one thing you need to know about that: No tax levy has been made for educational purposes and none's going to be made. There are no funds for the operation of public schools in Prince Edward County.

"What's to blame for this regrettable state of affairs? I'll tell you what: the unconstitutional decision of the U.S. Supreme Court and the ambitions of the NAACP. Come September, white people in Prince Edward will have no public schools. Negro people will have no public schools. This is the first time that Negroes have lost anything anywhere since the beginning of this drive by the NAACP to integrate the South. According to its own publications, the objectives of the NAACP don't stop with the integration of schools. They mean to see the forced integration of public and private housing. The registration and voting of Negroes in an attempt to control the South politically. Forced integration of hospitals and churches. Forced integration of all travel and public accommodations: hotels, restaurants, theaters, bars, and movie houses. Barber shops, skating rinks, and bowling alleys. Golf courses, parks, playgrounds, and swimming pools.

"Now all around us, folks are succumbing to those who would change our constitutional Republic by judicial fiat. But the good people of Prince Edward are not afraid to stand for their convictions. We have one primary purpose, to provide a sound education for our children, and we mustn't let anything or anybody divert us from it. As free people, we must stand for our sovereign rights, and we must stand steady!"

The crowd broke into applause—I had a feeling they'd been wanting to for some time now—but Mr. Wall cut them short by holding up his hands. "Well, you all know why we've gathered here tonight and enjoyed the splendid hospitality of Mr. Cary T. Rome and the fine gastronomical feats of a lady named Oatsie Montague. We're going to light the candles over here on these beautiful cakes and sing happy birthday to a man who exemplifies what dedication, determination, and the application of hard work can do. In a few short years, we've seen a handful of chickens and a family henhouse grow into one of the most successful business concerns in our county. I give you a man of few words but a man with a strong back and able hands. A man with a head on his shoulders. A family man. Cary, come on up here and blow out these candles."

Again the crowd broke into applause, again cut short, this time by the singing of the birthday song. Daddy Cary made his way toward the food table as Oatsie lit the candle on each cake. One of her helpers, evidently stirred by Mr. Wall, leaned down and said into her ear, "I reckon that man can speak, can't he!"

Julius was where he'd been throughout the speech, squatting next to one of his washtubs, creating work for himself, moving bottles around in the melting ice with exquisite care not to make a sound. Now he stood and joined in the singing.

I saw that Mother, whose long kitchen labors hadn't been mentioned in Mr. Wall's remarks, had moved to stand next to my father, whose life's achievements had been wrongly attributed to Daddy Cary. They both stood against the wall of the house, neither smiling nor singing, looking as if they'd suddenly found themselves among strangers. My father had been resting his head and back flat against the clapboard like a suspect in a police lineup, and now he pushed himself away from the wall and turned swiftly into the kitchen. Mother watched him go, and after a moment a door slammed, loud, inside the house. I recalled seeing Mother earlier that morning, immediately after church services, as she flew down the basement hall en route to the choir room, rushing to change and get home for the party preparations, her emerald green robe unzipped and sailing behind her.

Paisley and I stepped away from the table to make room for Daddy Cary. The singing over, the crowd at last unleashed an all-out barrage of cheering and whistling. When after a minute Mr. Wall held up his hands, he said, "Now I'm not telling anybody what to wish for, but if I was Mr. Rome, I'd wish for *rain!*" More laughter, and Daddy Cary blew out the three candles, followed by more applause.

The ice cream had turned to soup. The Holiness women ladled rather than scooped it out onto slices of cake. When Paisley and I had been served, we took our plates outdoors.

We slid open the hay door on the back end of the barn and ate our dessert cross-legged on the floor of the loft. From up there we could see a nearly full moon rising over the scalloped crown of the woods. We'd not switched on any light, for fear of giving away our whereabouts.

The whole barn was dark gray wood, rutted in the grain and shiny with age, and though the loft was still very warm, we sat close enough to the open door to feel the night air. Overhead, the four planes of the ceiling were peppered with the tips of hundreds of roofing nails and scores of dirt-dauber nests. From the stalls below, we heard the deep and intermittent thumping of hooves. Paisley set his empty plate aside, uttering, "Mm-mm-mm," then rolled onto his stomach and peeked through a crack in the floorboards. "I can see her tail swishing down there," he said. "Does she have a name?"

I told him Daddy Cary had bought both cows from a dairy farmer in Amelia County, and they'd come with names. The big one was called Dorothy Malone, named for another beautiful blonde, a movie star, and the smaller one was called Honey, because the dairy farmer had been fond of going out to his barn and telling his wife that he was on his way to "the land of milkin' Honey." I also told Paisley that Daddy Cary had been promising all summer long that he would teach me to milk, but he still hadn't done it. Paisley looked at me askance and said, "You want to learn how to milk?"

"No, not really," I said, "but it would give me a chance to get out of the henhouses once in a while."

He asked me if I'd ever been pecked by a chicken.

"I've been pecked so hard on the back of my hand it drew blood," I said.

He shook his head. "I would hate that," he said. "Do you think that was a true story, about that man giving tranquilizers to his chickens?"

I said I'd never heard of such a thing but I supposed it was possible, since we vaccinated our chickens under their wings for fowl pox, using little red two-pronged needles. I supposed you could substitute tranquilizers for vaccine. Paisley said he'd heard that turkeys were so stupid that if you left them outdoors in a rainstorm they'd drown themselves trying to drink the rain. I said I didn't know if that was true, but I did know that chickens were some of the stupidest creatures roaming the earth. I told him about the time two winters ago when there had been a cold snap and a power failure, and the brooders in the pullet house had gone off, and the idiotic chickens had piled up on top of one another to keep warm and smothered most of themselves to death. "We lost more than four hundred chickens," I said. "You should've seen it. It was like a big white mountain made of feathers in the corner of the henhouse, and only the chickens on the top still alive."

"What did you do with all those dead chickens?" he asked.

"There wasn't anything to do," I said. "We buried them in the woods."

This was not precisely true, but I wasn't sure about the legality of what we'd actually done: We'd dumped the chickens into a gully in the woods and let the buzzards have them.

The moon, rising quickly, was already lighting up the small pasture behind the barnyard and creeping over the bottom lip of the hay door. After some silence, Paisley said, "I don't think my pa's coming back for me this time."

I said he was lucky if he didn't, because Daddy Cary was going to be shooting off some fireworks pretty soon.

"Fireworks?" said Paisley. "I love fireworks. I love fireworks just about more than—"

"Shh-h-h," I said, for I thought I'd heard something below us, outside. We sat still and listened, and in a moment we heard what sounded like a jet of water striking the ground. We crawled quietly toward the open door and put our heads an inch over the edge. A man had come behind the barn to pee into the manure pit; we could see his back and shoulders and what looked like a moonlit arc of twine connecting him to the pit. We heard the man groan with relief, and then a deep voice from below prompted us to pull our heads in. "Oh, brother," we heard. "Have you got the right idea!"

"Yes, sir," said the first man. "That beer goes through you, don't it?"

There was the sound of a second jet of water joining the first, and then the man with the bass voice began to sing. "Oh, Shenandoah, I'm bound to wander, roll on, you mighty river. . . ."

Paisley looked at me and grinned, very pleased, in the moonlight.

"You're pretty good," said the first man, "but not near as good as that little girl that sang."

"That's wasn't no girl," said the second man. "That was a little sissy boy."

"Coulda fooled me," said the other.

Paisley stood, walked into the dark at the other end of the loft, and sat on a bale of hay. He rested his elbows on his knees and lowered his head, covering his ears with his hands. I crawled back to the hay door and saw that the men had gone. I began to slide shut the door, but when I had it halfway, one of the rusty wheels at the top popped off the rail. "Paisley," I said, "come over here and help me with this thing."

At my side again, he helped me lift the door and guide the wheel back onto the rail. When we got it shut, the loft was darker than ever, though moonlight sifting through the planks in the door fell in ribbons onto the floor. One of these ribbons struck Paisley across the face and neck. The long sleeves of Al's shirt had come undone and hung down below his hands. "Here," I said, "let me roll those up for you." He held out his arms, one at a time. I put my hand on his shoulder just for a second, to turn him toward the narrow stair well. "Now be careful," I said. "These steps can be slippery."

Downstairs, the barn was cooler and brighter, for the moon streamed through two high cobwebby windows on either side of the back door. Dorothy Malone rested her neck on the gate of her stall, drooping her huge head out into the feed passage; as we moved past her, she snorted through her enormous nostrils, which appeared wet and shiny in the moonlight. Paisley stopped for a moment to stroke her muzzle, and I waited for him at the front door. I lifted the wooden latch and pushed the door open for him. He paused next to me and wiped his hands on his shorts, smelled his palms, and wiped again. Without looking up, he said, "Why are you nice to me?"

I turned my back to him in order to close the barn door, and I let my hand rest for a moment over the latch. "I don't know," I said, for what I felt was simple but too complicated to express: I was confident now that he hadn't counted me among the boys who witnessed his humiliation last year at school; and I recognized his particular plight—that the thing best in him was also the thing that let him in for the most trouble.

We walked through the barnyard, climbed over the stone wall, and started up the hill toward the front of the house. As soon as the road came into view, we saw his father's old pickup truck idling in front of the smokehouse, dust still swirling in the cone-shaped beams of its headlights. Al, who was standing in the road next to the truck, spotted us, waved, and then whirled around and called through the passenger window, loud enough for us to hear, "Here he comes now." To my surprise, Jeannette stood next to Al, bare-shouldered and wearing a white blouse that seemed to be held up over her breasts with nothing but elastic. As we neared the truck, Paisley said under his breath, "Who is *that*?" I told him it was Al's girlfriend, and he offered the opinion that she looked like a movie actress.

At the truck, I saw Mr. Chatham smiling behind the steering wheel, and Paisley's little brothers, Mickey and Sam, sleepy in the middle of the seat. "Boy, I've been looking all over the countryside for you," Mr. Chatham said to Paisley, with a kind of false pleasantness. He looked at Al and said, "I can't seem to keep him from running off."

Al said, "Y'all want to stay for the fireworks? They ought to be starting any minute."

Mr. Chatham looked at Paisley and said, with the same pleasant tone, "Would you like to, son?"

Paisley said to Al, "No, thank you," and pressed his thumb on the big silver button that opened the truck door.

"Are you sure?" Mr. Chatham said. "We can if you want to."

For an answer, Paisley climbed onto the seat and pulled the door to. He stared straight ahead for a moment, then said, "Uh-oh," and began taking off the chambray shirt. He got it off quickly and passed it through the window to Al.

Mr. Chatham said, "Ready?" and Paisley nodded, almost imperceptibly. He never looked at me or at anyone else, but simply placed his bare arm on the ledge of the window and stared straight through the windshield.

We moved to the berm of the road and watched as the truck clattered down to the far end of the Big House, where there was a place to turn around. In ten seconds it came back toward us, tunneling through its own dust clouds. Jeannette fanned dust away from her face and rushed daintily toward the house with her arms crossed. Al looked at me and smiled; he appeared happier than I'd seen him all day. "Looking all over the countryside my eye," he said, then turned and followed Jeannette. When he caught up to her, he grabbed her by the hand and drew her into a long passionate kiss at the edge of the grass.

As the Chathams passed by, I looked for Paisley, but he was on the opposite side of the truck, out of sight. Down the road I could see the silhouette of his head in the rear window. Only one of the truck's taillights worked, a lurching red dot receding in the dust. Before it disappeared around the bend in the road, the truck let out an estimable backfire, causing me to shiver. Apparently, some people inside the house thought it was the start of the fireworks, for when I turned from the road, I saw that quite a few were pouring through the porch door.

I overheard more than one person on the screen porch complain about the hour and that the fireworks display hadn't yet begun. Many guests, including Mr. Wall, the Crawfords, and the Pearsons, had already gone home, and many of those who stayed were of the hard-drinking variety, sprawled on the rattan porch furniture. Of the Holiness women, only Oatsie Montague remained, and Julius was busy helping her and Mother and Aunt Bobbi clean up what it was possible to clean up. I feared I would be put to work cleaning too, but when Mother summoned me to the kitchen counter where she was loading leftovers into Tupperware containers, she kissed me on the forehead and asked if I would go upstairs and see if Uncle Dillon and the girls wanted to play dominoes. I asked her when the fireworks were going to start and she said my guess was as good as hers. She said that Daddy Cary had gone out to the tractor shed to "get ready" quite some time ago, but that I needn't worry, I would know when the fireworks began. "There's dominoes in that big desk in the living room," she said.

The huge Saint Bernard presided over the living room from his wall above the couch. The only human in the room was one of the Cheney brothers, slumped in a corner of the couch, asleep with his mouth open. I searched the drawers of the desk for the dominoes and found them in the bottom drawer, where I also found the old-fashioned lipstick case, borrowed and later replaced by J. Barrye Wall, Sr. I returned to the hallway and climbed the creaky stairs to the second floor.

Four bedrooms were arranged around a central dormered sitting room up there, and a lamp had been switched on in the the sitting room but nowhere else. There was no sign of Uncle Dillon or Meg and Dee. I gazed up the unbanistered stairway to the attic, but saw that the hatch was closed and bolted. I went into one of the rooms on the back of the house and sank into the deep feather mattress of a single bed. I stared at the slanted ceiling, which was marked by three brown blossoms of concentric water rings, left from the occasionally leaky roof. I was just thinking that it was much too hot to stay there on the mattress when I heard, as in a dream, what sounded like a crowd of men angrily shouting. I seemed to dream that the noise waked me in a sweat and that I moved to the bedroom window, lifted it, and looked down into Daddy Cary's dirt backyard. There—in a square of light, crisscrossed by sharp bars of shadow, like the muntins of a window sash—I saw two cutout copies of the same man, at war with himself, punching himself in the face; other men soon closed in on the two fighting duplicates and pulled them apart, and I saw bright red blood streaming down the chin of one of the fighters and dripping onto a white shirt. I thought it a very curious sight, and there was something familiar about the orange color of the fighters' hair. I returned to the bed and slept awhile longer, until I was awakened by a loud explosion followed by what sounded like a train whistle. Disoriented, I staggered into the sitting room and saw through its trio of windows trails of pink sparks descending from the sky.

On the lawn, Jeannette stretched out her arms to me. "Benny," she called, "sweetheart, come over here." I couldn't quite remember going down the stairs and out of the house, but there I was, standing near a patchwork quilt at the edge of the apple orchard and being tugged into a cozy perfumed nest between Al and Jeannette. Al said, "I was wondering what happened to you, sport," and Jeannette stroked my hair, which felt slightly wet, and said, "I think somebody's been sleeping."

Down a ways from the house, I saw that Daddy Cary had hauled a number of cinder blocks and an old wooden feed trough into the middle of the road, from which he was launching an array of Roman candles, stick rockets, mortars, and missiles. Now a rocket spewed into the air, leaving a bright tail of white and gold, then burst at maybe fifty feet into a chrysanthemum of green and yellow stars, whistles, and reports. Jeannette said, "Oh, isn't that beautiful! Sit up for a minute, sugar," and I realized that I'd been leaning my full weight against her. She wore large gold hoops on her ears, and I'd noticed that if you focused tightly on them you could see the colors of the fireworks reflected in the gold. She took a cigarette from her handbag, lit it, and then pulled me back. Softly, to Al, she said, "He's still asleep."

"No, I'm not," I said sleepily, just as an explosion from the road—a cherry bomb or something even stronger—sent a tin can flying into the air and rang in our ears.

Jeanette jumped and said, "God, I *hate* that!" and Al chuckled. She took a long drag on the cigarette, exhaled, and said, "You know, one of these days that old man's gonna blow himself up."

Another rocket, even higher, broke out a willow effect of red trails that slowly descended over the road, provoking *oohs* and *aahs* from the two dozen or so people gathered on the lawn. After the last of its sparks had died away, I saw how bright the night was, with the moon high over the house. I held out my hand and saw its perfect shadow on the quilt. In a confidential voice, Jeannette said, "Al, if you think you ought to, go ahead and go."

"I don't feel the least compulsion," he said. "They're big boys."

"No, they're not," Jeanette said. "They're big babies is what they are. They're childish as can be and never could hold their liquor, neither one of them. I didn't like the way that lip looked, though. I think it might've needed stitches."

"I'm not going to worry about it," said Al. "Hey, Ben. I think I see your little friend down the road there."

I turned and looked at Al as he pointed in the direction of the cornfield. "Who?" I said, wiping my eyes.

"Ain't that your little colored friend?"

"Why, Benny," said Jeannette, "do you have a colored friend?"

Under his breath, Al said, "Don't tease him about it. He's sensitive."

"I'm not teasing anybody."

I scanned the rows of corn, and at last I saw Burghardt, scrunched up inside one of the dark furrows with his arms wrapped around his legs, his chin resting on his knees. If it hadn't been for the moon, I never would have been able to see him. I stood up and said, absurdly, "Save my place," and walked away toward the cornfield. I heard Jeannette say, "I wasn't teasing anybody."

I crossed the road, walked back of the smokehouse, then entered the corn from the side of the field and came up on Burghardt from behind. I didn't scare him because he'd already seen me coming. He slid over to make room for me between the stalks. "Did you know it was a Chinese cook that discovered fireworks?" he said. "He mixed up charcoal and sulfur and something called saltpeter. Then they hollowed out pieces of bamboo and packed the powder inside to make rockets. I read about it in one of Granny's books. You think this thing's over already?"

"No," I said. "He's still out there with his box of matches."

Just then a row of five fountains gushed up sequentially ten feet or more from the road, two white, two green, and a red. "That's nice," said Burghardt. "Who's those girls in that window?"

From where we sat, we could see the living room windows, one of which framed the faces of Meg and Dee, watching from the lower panes with their fingers stuck in their ears. I told Burghardt they were my cousins from Norfolk.

"And who's that man over yonder?" he asked.

"Where?"

"Lying on top of that car like he's dead? Ain't that your daddy's car?"

There was indeed a man lying on top of my father's white Impala, parked by the apple tree where Mother had left it earlier in the evening—a big man, face down, his arms and legs splayed out as if he'd landed there after being pushed from an airplane. I was fairly certain that it was Daddy, but I said, "I don't have any idea. How was your barbecue?"

"It was good," said Burghardt, then winced at a succession of six or seven blasts from the road. "I just got back. Granny let me stay here and watch the show while she went on home. She said all that popping made her nervous as a cat. There was a woman at this picnic who could play the violin, and they had one of those old-timey pianos that can play itself. The only thing was, they had roasted a pig and I can't eat anything that's still looking at me or has ears on it. It was Granny's friends over to Rice, who have their own farm. Man, I wish we had our own farm. I wish my daddy—"

"What would you do with your own farm?" I asked.

"I would farm it," he said. "I'd raise me some sheep. Where did you get that necktie?"

I looked down at my tie, surprised to find it there, for I hadn't thought about it for four or five hours. "I'm not sure," I said. "I think Mother bought it at Davidson's. They were having a clearance sale."

"A Clarence sale?" Burghardt said. "What's a Clarence sale?"

"A *clearance* sale," I said. "When they discount everything, so they can move it out right away."

"Discount?" said Burghardt.

"You know," I said. "When they cut back on the price. It's called a discount."

"Oh, yeah," he said. "I remember that now. Whoa, look at that."

Daddy Cary had set off what was surely the grand finale, a rapid sequence of rockets and candles that exploded at fifty to a hundred feet in the air, with bursts of crackling stars with tails in white and gold and pink, and kept the air lit up and strewn with genies of smoke for almost a full minute. There was scattered applause from the lawn, and two men walked into the road and shook Daddy Cary's hand. Burghardt's mentioning sheep had made me think of the golden fleece, and I told him I'd been to the movies with Al the night before.

"Did you see *Hercules*?" he asked, and I said yes. "Damn," he said. "I wanted to see that. Tell me what happened."

Burghardt had never been to a movie in a theater, and I thought it unlikely that he would ever see *Hercules*, so I felt I had a free rein with the question. I said, "Well, he's part god and part man, see, so he's got magical powers and he can make people and animals and even buildings float clear up to the sky just by thinking about it."

"Magical powers?" Burghardt said. "I thought he was a strongman."

"He was," I said. "That too."

"Well, what's the part with the chain?" he asked. "I saw a poster of him slinging around a chain."

"That's where he's fighting off a whole army of buffalo with ice picks for horns," I said. "He spins the chain around over his head so fast it turns to butter."

"Butter?" said Burghardt. "What good does that do him?"

"I can't remember now," I said.

"Was they any colored folks in that movie?" he asked.

For a second, I thought he meant colored folks in the State Theatre, but since that was impossible, I said, "Three or four, friends of Hercules." Immediately, I felt I needed to somehow justify the lie, so I added, "They were sailors from the Greek islands."

"I bet your granddaddy spent a lot a money on all that fireworks," he said.

"Maybe," I said.

"You think he has a lot of money?"

"I guess." Suddenly thinking of Mr. Wall's speech, I said, "Have you ever been to a hotel?"

"No."

"What about a bowling alley?"

"No."

"What about a golf course?"

"No."

"Have you ever been to a bar?"

"'Course not."

"A skating rink?"

"No."

"I've never been to any of those things either," I said. "Have you ever—"

I stopped short, for I'd seen something that made me catch my breath—half a deck of playing cards, rubber-banded and lying on the ground next to Burghardt's haunches, apparently having fallen from the pocket of his shorts.

"What is that?" I said.

Burghardt scrambled to his feet as if I'd pointed to a rattlesnake. I grabbed the cards before he could, but he snatched them from my hand and stuck them into his pocket.

"What is that?" I repeated.

"Nothing," he said, and moved back between the rows of corn. "Just some old cards."

I followed him through the corn a distance of about thirty yards, where we reached the narrow lane that led to the tenant house. He started down the dirt lane in the moonlight, and I called to his back, "Where'd you get them?"

He stopped, turned, and faced me, keeping his hand in the pocket, clamped over the cards. "I didn't steal them," he said, "if that's what you think."

"Well, where'd you get them?" I said. "Tell me."

"I found them," he said, turned, and started walking again.

I ran to catch up with him, slapped his forearm, not hard, and said, "Where did you find them?"

He kept walking. "Somebody gave them to me," he said. "They're just old cards anyway."

"With pictures of naked people," I said, which stopped him in his tracks.

He took a long look at me. At last he said, "Are you gonna tell?"

"No," I said.

"You promise?"

"Yes," I said. "I promise."

He started walking again, faster, and I had to trot to keep up. Soon he stopped again. He pulled the cards from his pocket, popped the rubber band off, and shoved them into my hands. "Here," he said. "Look at them, then, if you want to see."

I quickly began rifling through the cards, which were quite clear in the moonlight, but he snatched them back before I was a third of the way through.

"There," he said. "You looked at them. If you tell, you're in trouble too."

He stretched the rubber band around the cards and returned them to his pocket. "Just remember that," he said. "You looked at them. If you tell, you're in trouble too. You looked at them."

I watched him tramp down the lane, break into a run, and disappear. His cards were not mine, not the ones gone missing from under my bed, but the other half I'd never seen, from the same deck. Now, abruptly alone, I looked at the sky, nearly starless and varnished slate blue by the moon. I looked at the ground and saw my shadow crumpled at my feet. Where I stood, the narrow rutted lane curved ahead of me and curved behind, giving no view of any destination. I was afraid to bolt and afraid not to. The corn towered on all sides, silent and glossy on its prop roots, and perfectly still.

7

THE FARMVILLE PRESBYTERIAN CHURCH—where donations of books for the Prince Edward Academy were to be collected, and where Mother and I served as volunteers that first Monday morning of Library Week—had a particular history with regard to school closings. There had been another time, four years earlier, in 1955, when the county supervisors, threatened with the prospect of having to integrate schools, elected not to fund public education. The idea of closing schools this way—by declining to fund them—most likely originated in Virginia with the Defenders of Sovereign States and Individual Liberties, and the Defenders' first president, Robert Crawford, was a prominent member of the Farmville Presbyterian Church.

After the U.S. Supreme Court had decided *Brown v. Board of Education* in May of 1954, it took another whole year to hand down its implementation decree, charging local governments to desegregate public schools "with all deliberate speed." Ordinary people like my mother—only modestly informed of current events and too busy answering the demands of domestic life to participate much in civic affairs—didn't imagine, when they heard about *Brown*, that it would actually apply to Prince Edwardians. We had our own way of doing things in Southside, and for all appearances there wasn't anything broken in our county that required a new law to fix it. There'd been that fuss some years ago at R. R. Moton, but in response we'd built an $800,000 Negro high school with all the modern amenities.

For another breed of person, however, *Brown v. Board of Education* sounded an alarm, a call to action. It wasn't quite five months after *Brown* that a state charter was granted to the Defenders, which already boasted two thousand members. By the time the Supreme Court handed down its implementation decree in 1955, the Defenders were not only a going concern, they'd already drawn themselves a picture of what resistance to the court's order should look like. With Mr. Wall's *Herald* at their disposal, they didn't have much trouble putting this same picture in the minds of most of Prince Edward's white folks. The Defenders' primary purpose was to maintain segregated schools—they published a report in '55, claiming that integration would lead to the "death of our Anglo-Saxon civilization"—and with the help of their lawyers they quickly made the brilliant observation that the Supreme Court hadn't said a word about a county's right not to fund public education; it said only that *where* there were public schools, the schools had to be integrated. In April of '55, a month before the court had even issued its implementation decree, a Defenders delegation approached the Board of Supervisors in Prince Edward and asked them to do that very thing—not to fund the schools. Since some of the supervisors were themselves Defenders, it didn't prove a difficult argument to win. At its official meeting in May, the board voted not to appropriate the money necessary to run the public schools. (When, at Daddy Cary's party, Lainie had said to Al that the whole thing had been taken out of the school board's hands, it was this strategy she referred to, in its most recent application: By cutting off funding, the supervisors made it impossible for any school board to comply with the Supreme Court's decree, even if it wanted to.) Immediately, the supervisors' decision raised a few troubling questions, the most pressing of which was, What would become of our white teachers? Our local Defenders arranged a mass meeting with the salient aim of dispelling such fears—but, less conspicuously, they also meant to gain support for closing the public schools and even to create an organization that would begin the business of setting up a private system.

Of course Mr. Crawford (and many others) believed that the conflict over the integration of schools was just one symptom of a much larger danger afoot in the nation, the Communist conspiracy to take over America. Nobody, from any walk of life, was immune to this menace, as its converts comprised not just agitators but teachers and churchmen. Though himself a Presbyterian and a churchgoer, Mr. Crawford believed that the southern white preacher was one of the biggest threats to maintaining segregated schools, and he wasn't afraid to say so publicly. Despite this feeling, the Defenders asked the white preachers of Prince Edward's churches to announce the forthcoming mass meeting that would take place on June 7, 1955, at Jarman Hall on the campus of Longwood College.

By then, even less civic-minded folks like my mother had got stirred up and worried. About fifteen hundred people poured into Jarman Hall, filling all the seats and milling about in the hallway outside the auditorium proper. Twelve speakers appeared on the podium, nearly all Defenders, though they aspired to appear that night in their non-Defender roles: as representatives of each of the white PTAs of the county; as a former school board chairman (Maurice Large, whom Barbara Johns had approached with her demands in 1951); as the mayor of Farmville (W. C. Fitzpatrick); and of course as the editor of an important newspaper (J. Barrye Wall, Sr.). Our current school board wasn't represented on the podium. Mr. Crawford wasn't among the speakers either, for though he lived in the county he was also the statewide president of the Defenders, and the organizers wanted to avoid an impression that the ideas presented were anything but local.

The evening had been shrewdly orchestrated. The Defenders intended to lay the groundwork for a private school system, but everything about the plan was dressed in the guise of guaranteeing the salaries of the county's white teachers, a cause that everyone could get behind. This enabled folks to set aside thinking directly about integration, and most were relieved that a committee of responsible citizens had taken the pains to design a solution to their worries. One after another, the speakers touted the importance of being prepared for the worst and ensuring that Prince Edward could hang on to its white teachers. Mayor Fitzpatrick made the premeditated motion that a private corporation be set up to guarantee the salaries of the white teachers. James Bash, the principal at Farmville High, responded with a number of troublesome questions on behalf of teachers: Who then would teachers be answering to? How might their duties change? If they were paid privately, would they still get credit for teaching experience that would be honored elsewhere? Would they have to forfeit their memberships in professional organizations? How could they continue to teach in publicly owned buildings while being paid privately? Bash ultimately declared himself a public school man and said, "I would be unable to accept a check from a private corporation of this kind." A dramatic moment came a few minutes later when Robert Gilmer, the football coach at Farmville High, stood up and said, "If some of you will feed me next year, you don't have to worry about giving me a dime to look after your children," a display of sacrifice and courage that was rewarded with a roar of applause. Other motions premeditated by the Defender organizers were made and seconded; opposing motions weren't recognized by the chairman. In the end, the vote of the mass meeting established the Prince Edward School Foundation, and pledges were garnered for a good percentage of the money needed to start up private schools.

People went home with a feeling that they'd contributed to something important. They went home thinking that—though the organizers had come prepared with ideas and suggestions—it was the ordinary citizens of Prince Edward who'd spoken with a nearly unanimous voice and helped to forge, with some amount of debate and spontaneity, a course of action. A few might have noticed that the pledge slips passed out in Jarman Hall weren't just scraps of paper found to hand but printed legal documents, and that the organization voted into existence at the meeting received its charter just two days afterward. Mr. Wall would report in the *Herald* that he'd counted only fifteen people who voted contrary to the majority, and one of them was a drunk who wandered the streets of Farmville the next day apologizing to anyone who would listen.

A little more than a month later, in July, a federal district court interpreted for Prince Edward the Supreme Court's decree and ruled that we could continue to operate segregated schools in September; the district court's three judges said we would have to desegregate eventually, but they didn't specify a date. Still, the Defenders had got what they wanted; the Prince Edward School Foundation had been established. It would hold on to its pledges and stand ready for that inevitable day (it was to come four years later) when the public schools would actually close.

Over the course of the Jarman Hall meeting, a handful of brave souls saw the Defenders' plan for what it was, an abandonment of public education, and dared to oppose it, sometimes enduring the boos and catcalls of the crowd. These men included Principal Bash and the Reverend James R. Kennedy, minister of the Farmville Presbyterian Church. They aired their opposition at a cost. Mr. Wall reported Principal Bash's renegade opinions in the *Herald*, along with a letter signed by high school teachers and staff members who endorsed and applauded the actions of the Jarman Hall meeting. Afterward, Principal Bash and his family were routinely snubbed in the street and in stores, and he tendered his resignation to the board as early as August, when it was already clear that he no longer enjoyed any authority at the school.

Rev. Kennedy took longer to arrive at his decision to leave Prince Edward, for he struggled considerably with his conscience. Lainie's husband was a member of the Presbyterian Church, and Lainie and I had once or twice attended services there with Claud Wayne before he shipped off to Germany. Its minister struck me as a kind, quiet man, very serious about faith and the Bible. Some people may not have cared for his contrary views, mildly expressed at the Jarman Hall meeting, but the real trouble began after Kennedy was quoted in an out-of-town newspaper as saying that he couldn't justify segregation on Christian principles. "You can't take the Gospel with its message of His love for everyone and defend enforced segregation," he said, a remark that more or less sealed his fate. To stand against segregation wouldn't have been popular with his congregants under any circumstances, but saying he opposed it on Christian grounds implied that those who thought otherwise were out of step with Jesus.

Somebody took it on themselves to make copies of the newspaper article and to circulate it around the county. Rev. Kennedy started receiving letters of criticism and unpleasant phone calls from all over, and some folks he'd counted as friends now treated him coldly. Mr. Crawford, a powerful influence among the congregation, believed that the minister, given his views, should find a new church. The struggle for Rev. Kennedy was that he wondered, given his views, if he oughtn't to stay; maybe it was his Christian duty, despite how unwelcome he'd been made to feel. In the end, when he decided to go, it was because he feared his staying might harm the church. "I love the church too much to see it divided," he said, and announced in the spring that he would be moving on as soon as his son graduated from high school in June.

His concern for the church was surely genuine, but he also described himself, after the almost year-long ordeal, as having fallen into a "run-down state of physical and mental exhaustion." And Lainie told me that the O'Bannon twins and some others had made it very hard at school for the Kennedys' son, who was subjected to unnecessary roughness at basketball practice, accompanied by snide remarks about his father. When, at the conclusion of the school year, the boy was overlooked by the Beta club even though he was fully qualified for it, his father blamed himself. After the Kennedys left the state, most of his congregation denied that the minister had been in any manner pressured. As proof, one woman pointed to the going-away present they'd given him, five hundred dollars and a sterling silver tea service.

When I set foot into the assembly hall of the Farmville Presbyterian Church three years later, that first morning of Library Week, I knew only the barest version of this complicated story that began with men scheming behind closed doors and culminated in the torment of a boy on a basketball court, which was that, a few years back, this church had run its minister out of town because he favored the racial integration of schools.

By one o'clock Monday afternoon, five hundred books, a full quarter of what was required for accreditation, had been donated and received at the church. For most people, this happy outcome would be what was noteworthy and memorable about the day. For me, it would be forever linked with something else altogether, a surprise visit, midmorning, by Granny Mays.

When I'd finally got to bed the night before, it seemed to me that Daddy Cary's birthday party had been such a large disruption in the river of life, it couldn't possibly resume its normal flow come morning. At breakfast, certain contradictions to this idea confounded me: Lainie, dressed as usual for the dentist's office, hurriedly ate half a piece of buttered toast and then began to search for the keys to the Willys;

Mother scolded her for not eating a better breakfast and wondered how in the world she expected to have a healthy baby; out the porch windows, I saw Daddy talking with the refrigeration man he'd hired to create cold storage in the egg room; in the distance beyond them, Al went bumping along the dirt lane that led to the henhouses, Julius and Burghardt in the back of the flatbed. So far, the only thing different about today was that Mother had waked me at eight o'clock, rather than Daddy waking me at six. In the car, on the way into town, Mother began to hum the tune to "The Church's One Foundation," and I thought surely I was still asleep and dreaming. The single piece of evidence that the party itself hadn't been a dream trembled now on the backseat of the Impala: a square foot of leftover birthday cake Mother was taking to Library Week.

The Presbyterian assembly hall on Randolph Street, which I gauged to be about as big as our whole house if you removed all our inside walls, smelled of fresh-brewed coffee when we arrived. Two long tables had been set up end to end just inside the main entrance, and to the right side, across the room, a pass-through window opened onto the church kitchen; on its stainless steel counter were an electric coffee urn, a tower of paper cups, and three round trays of butterscotch cookies. The polished hardwood floor of the hall squeaked with nearly every step, and its very high ceiling was sectioned off by five great beams; from the middle beam, a wagon wheel with electric lanterns hung down on brass chains. Two industrial floor fans whirred in opposite corners of the hall, pushing around warm air. A hundred or more brown metal folding chairs had been shoved against the rough ochre walls, and had it not been for a card table and some egg crates in the middle of the large room, you might have thought it the scene of a square dance about to take place.

At one minute past nine, Candy Hartz, a woman of about fifty, was already seated at one of the reception tables and making notes on some kind of form she'd clamped to a long clipboard. She wore thick glasses shaped like cat's eyes, which, along with her very small mouth, made her look something like a cat. Nearby, at the other table, Kay Campbell inspected two tall stacks of leather-bound encyclopedias, tapping the spine of each volume with the eraser end of a yellow pencil. Behind the reception tables, four or five crates rested on the floor, already filled with books and magazines. Immediately, the two librarians staged a small skirmish over who would explain our duties to Mother and me, which I thought Mrs. Campbell won on account of her being pretty and half Miss Hartz's age. She escorted us to the card table in the middle of the hall, pulled two folding chairs from beneath it, and invited us to sit. "It's very simple," she began, and as she went on to describe the day's procedures, I appreciated her directing her remarks equally to both Mother and me. Mrs. Campbell and Miss Hartz would receive all contributions at the tables by the assembly hall entrance and sort them into two categories, books given and books lent; she and Miss Hartz would also keep a record of everything, write the donor's name on a slip of paper, and put it inside each book. (Magazines were gifts only, and their donors needn't be noted.) As books accumulated at the reception tables, we would transfer them to this station, making sure to keep gifts separate from loans. We would be given nameplates, one of which was to be pasted into each book; then we would copy the name of the donor onto the nameplate, write *gift* or *loan* on each as appropriate, and place the processed books into cardboard egg crates, an ample supply of which we would find in the church kitchen. To my disappointment, Mrs. Campbell suggested Mother do the handwriting. She smiled at me and said, "Doesn't that sound like a good system? You can paste in the nameplates, and your mother can write in the names."

She pointed across the hall to the crates of books and magazines on the floor behind the reception tables. These, she explained, were early donations, left on the stoop of the assembly hall before she and Miss Hartz had arrived. We should get to these as time allowed. The majority of books in this group of early donations had no indication of the donor's identity. We should take these to be gifts, and Mother should write *Anonymous* on their nameplates.

Mrs. Campbell apologized for the rickety card table we'd been provided and then stepped back to the reception area for a moment. She returned with a packet of gummed nameplates, a good fountain pen for Mother, and a fully processed sample book for us to use as our guide. She looked at me and asked if I could spell *anonymous*, which was actually for Mother's benefit but cleverly avoided a potential moment of embarrassment. I said, "A-n-o-n-y-m-o-u-s," and Mrs. Campbell said, "That's perfectly correct." She then wanted to know if we had any other questions, though of course we hadn't yet asked any. Mother inquired as to whether we needed to put a separate nameplate in each volume of that set of encyclopedias sitting over there on the table.

Mrs. Campbell gave Mother a sad compassionate look, subtly implying that her question had been a stupid one but more obviously implying that volunteer work for a worthy cause such as this wasn't always going to be easy. All she said was, "Yes, ma'am, I'm afraid so."

Some cheerful donors had gathered now at the entrance, conversing more loudly than normal in order to be heard over the whirring of the fans, and their voices echoed in the large room. Mrs. Campbell quickly whispered to Mother and me, "Well, here we go!" shuddered with excitement, and started for her table. Her hair was the color of Lainie's, dark brown, and as she took up her position behind the table she ran her fingers through it and smoothed it behind her ears. She leaned forward ever so slightly, gazing toward the entrance, and called, "May I help someone, please?"

The prospect of having to lick the gummy backs of hundreds of nameplates daunted me at first, but Mother, showing mercy, found a sponge in the kitchen, set it in a saucer of tap water, and showed me how to drag the nameplate over the sponge to moisten the gum. We worked catercorner to each other at the card table, in silence except for her habitual *Hm-m-m* as she rotated a book I'd handed her, read its title, and concluded something secret about its donor. For my part, I found the job simpler if I ignored titles, donors, and everything else about the books; they were lifeless things to be stuck with a name-plate, lacking character or characters. I visited the reception tables periodically to retrieve books and brought them to our station in stacks steadied under my chin. Keeping gifts straight from loans was easy, as nearly all the books were gifts. Everyone dropping off donations was offered coffee and cookies, and occasionally somebody would stray our way and watch us at our task, which brought out Mother's shyness. She would smile, but quickly enough to discourage conversation, and even if it was someone she knew, she pretty much confined herself to "Just fine, and you?" Two women from our own church showed up around ten in the morning and said that Mother was an absolute saint for giving this way of her time. One said she wished *she* had that kind of time to give, and the other shook her head and said, "Me too, Carol Jean, I don't know where in the world Diane finds it." As the morning progressed, sunshine on the sills of the room's four tall windows grew ever more brilliant, and if I glanced at them even for a moment, their afterimages clouded my vision.

I believed I was first to notice Granny Mays standing outside the open door of the assembly hall. She wore an unadorned broad-brimmed straw hat that looked like a flying saucer, and the sun struck her such that a deep shadow fell over her face, blanking out all but a crescent of one cheek. She placed her hands on either side of the door-jamb and craned her neck, looking inside, one way and the other. Was it okay for her to enter? She spotted me and Mother and gathered the skirt of her dress in her fingers as if she was about to climb stairs; I rec-ognized the dress as one I'd seen her wear in the woods, with a pattern of roses. As she moved toward us gingerly, narrowly zigzagging, she appeared to be avoiding puddles on the floor only she could see. In another moment she stood before us, and Mother, alarmed, said, "Nezzie! What's happened?"

I too thought that only something bad could have brought Granny Mays to the church assembly hall this morning. Mother's question opened a gap in my mind, and my mind handily found a bad and fallow thing to fill it with: Burghardt's half deck of pornographic playing cards and my secret connection to it. At bedtime, I'd decided to neglect last night's troubling revelation in the cornfield. Neglected, it might go away in time, or I might find a suitable way to contemplate it. Vaguely, I'd speculated that maybe it didn't concern me, and there was nothing in it for me to fear. Now here was Granny Mays, turned up like an apparition, to lay it at my feet.

But she only stood still, mute as a wooden Indian. She listed to one side and the other, as if caught in the cross breezes of the huge electric fans. Mother told me to be quick and fetch another chair from the wall. Up till now, the twelve or fifteen people in the assembly hall had paid Granny Mays little or no mind, except to regard her briefly and then to dismiss her as a curiosity in a straw hat. But as I placed the folding chair next to Mother's and Granny Mays sat in it, people began to take an interest. Generally, Negroes didn't sit down in public places among white folks. They could shop in our stores but not go to the movie theater. They could buy food in our restaurants but not sit to eat it. Mother, aware of these taboos and conventions, would have deemed this occasion a medical variance—Granny Mays appeared to be on the verge of heat prostration. Dazed and silent in the chair, the old woman kept her eyes shut. Mother looked at me and whispered, "Ben, I'm afraid she's in a bad way. Go out to the kitchen and bring back a drink of water for her. You can take it from the sink but let it run until it's good and cool."

In the kitchen, I found a glass tumbler in the first cabinet I opened. A white-haired woman who was helping with the refreshments stood at the counter staring out the pass-through at Mother and Granny Mays. As I waited at the sink for the water to run cool, she said over her shoulder, "Is that y'all's maid?"

"Yes, ma'am," I said, then, judging myself to be technically inside church walls, I added, "Sort of."

"Sort of?" the woman said.

"Yes, ma'am," I answered, and started back into the hall with the filled tumbler.

I gave the water to Mother. She said, "Nezzie, can you hear me?" which I thought odd, but it made Granny Mays open her eyes.

She looked at Mother, then at me, and seemed to recognize us and her whereabouts anew. "Yessum," she said at last. "I can hear you just fine."

Mother said, "Here, Nezzie, drink this and tell me how you're feeling."

Granny Mays accepted the glass and lifted it to her lips. She lowered it without drinking and said, "Thank you, Miz Rome."

Now she took a good long drink, then another and another, until she'd emptied the glass. She returned it to Mother, who for some reason passed it on to me, and I placed it on the card table next to my sponge in its saucer.

"Now, Nezzie," Mother said, "tell me what's happened."

Granny Mays closed her eyes again, which provoked one of Mother's great sighs.

"Nezzie," she said, "has something happened or not?"

The old woman opened her eyes and said, "I reckon I'm feeling just about restored to myself now, thank you, Miz Rome."

She reached both hands up over her head, located a hat pin, slid it out through the straw, and removed the hat, under which she wore the usual kerchief; she held the hat in her lap and carefully replaced the pin. Now she fussed with the kerchief and tucked a fugitive thatch of silver hair back into place. "I got myself a ride in Jerome Sellars's panel truck," she said. "A right good part of the way. But I had to walk the rest and I bet you that's the longest walk I've had since the time I was fifteen years old and walked from Drakes Branch to Vincent Store. Dreaming about harp music and romantic love, eleven miles in all."

This didn't seem a cheerful memory—she'd delivered it with dead seriousness—or even idle reminiscing, but rather a calculated method to her recovery; she was using her voice to return herself to the world. She nodded, the outward sign of some resolve she'd reached in her thinking, and then gazed over at the reception tables, as if that was her next port of call. She found Miss Hartz gazing right back at her, which apparently she'd been doing for some time. Using the familiar word that applied to all Negro women of a certain age, Miss Hartz cried, "Can I help you, Granny?" and silenced every other voice in the assembly hall.

Granny Mays averted her eyes, pretending not to hear the woman, then said to me, quietly (for her voice had now returned to its usual strength and timbre), "Mr. Ben, I would be grateful to you for looking after my hat."

She passed it to me across the table, and I received it by the brim. The echoing murmur of voices had begun to rise again in the hall, and again Miss Hartz silenced everyone by crying, "I said, Can I help you, Granny?"

Granny Mays planted her hands on her knees and pushed herself up out of the chair. She moved in a straight line, looking down at her feet, and once she stood directly in front of Miss Hartz, she said, "I surely do hope you can."

Granny Mays didn't customarily bow and scrape around white folks, and the pitch and fiber of her voice seemed to announce this fact. Miss Hartz slid backward an inch in her chair, where she quickly recollected her God-given authority, and said, "Well, what is it, then?"

Pressed, Granny Mays looked straight through Candy Hartz, just as she'd looked straight through my father that day at the tenant house when he'd pressed her on the subject of Barbara Johns; it made me think of how you can hold a magnifying glass up to the sun and burn a hole in something. Granny Mays might have seen every important thing there was to see about Candy Hartz. She might have seen that she spent six dollars every week having her hair and nails done in a beauty parlor; that she was a crackerjack tatter and some samplers of her favorite sayings could be viewed in her sister-in-law's coffee shop on Third Street; that she considered herself an amateur historian and had published, at her own expense, a genealogy of families whose sons were killed or captured in the battle at Sailor's Creek; that she had complicated and troubling feelings for her only brother, Asa; that if she herself had ever married and given birth to children, she wouldn't have been so common as to give them plays on words like Candy Hartz and Asa Hartz for their lifelong names; that she was slowly losing her vision and seven years hence would be legally blind and substantially deprived of her two favorite pastimes, reading and tatting. Discomfited, Miss Hartz removed her glasses and rubbed her eyes.

Granny Mays turned her palms out to the woman and said, "All my books have gone missing, and it came to me that they might've turned up here this morning."

"Your books?" said Miss Hartz, replacing her eyeglasses.

Now everyone in the assembly hall, including Mrs. Campbell, directed their full attention to Miss Hartz and Granny Mays. The white-haired woman from the kitchen came out and moved close enough so as not to miss a syllable. At the card table, Mother said to herself, "I knew it had to be something."

"Yessum, my books," said Granny Mays.

"What books are you talking about, Granny?"

"I'm speaking of my own books," Granny Mays said. "I'm speaking of my books that stood like soldiers on their shelves yesterday afternoon when I drove over to Rice for a picnic."

"Over to Rice for a picnic? I'm afraid I don't understand."

"They were there when I left and gone when I came home last night."

Miss Hartz, genuinely perplexed, turned to Kay Campbell, which Mrs. Campbell took as a plea for help and scooted her chair within whispering distance. The librarians put their heads together for twenty seconds, after which Mrs. Campbell looked up at Granny Mays and said, "How many books have you lost, Granny?"

"There was forty-one of them, but—"

"Forty-one?" said Mrs. Campbell, astonished.

"Yessum," said Granny Mays. "Every last one gone except my mother's own Bible, but they none of them lost. Somebody came into my house when I was at the barbecue and took them right out of their shelves."

Mrs. Campbell said, "Well, what makes you think your books would've turned up here?"

"I saw where you were holding Library Week at this church," said Granny Mays. "It came to me that somebody might've brought my books over here to donate when they weren't theirs to donate. I walked all this way in the hot sun to reclaim them."

At that, Mother, no doubt uneasy about the direction things were taking, seized the straw hat from me and went over to the tables. "Excuse me, Candy," she said, "but this woman is Ole Nezzie Mays. I know her."

"Ole Nezzie Mays the seamstress?" said Miss Hartz, suddenly smiling. "I've heard of her."

"That's right," said Mother. "She lives on my father-in-law's farm."

"I knew that too," said Miss Hartz, "somewhere in the back of my mind. I might have figured that out when I saw her sitting down over there with you. I know three different people, right here in Farmville, who have her slipcovers on their couches. Why, I've heard of Ole Nezzie Mays since I was a young girl."

If Granny Mays was pleased by this testament to her fame, she didn't show it. She'd come a considerable distance on foot to carry out an urgent piece of business, and she wasn't going to be diverted by flattery.

"I just wanted you to know," Mother said to Miss Hartz, "that Nezzie's as honest as the day is long. I can vouch for it."

"I don't think anybody's doubting her honesty, Diane," Miss Hartz said, emphatically stunned by the notion. "We just don't know anything about her lost books, that's all."

"My books are not lost," said Granny Mays.

"Well, I'm sorry, Granny," Miss Hartz said, "but my definition of lost is what something is when you don't know where to find it."

This remark prompted some small amount of laughter in the room, but it was short-lived as Granny Mays said, "Somebody came into my house when I wasn't home and took my books. That's my definition of being robbed."

"Now you listen to me," said Miss Hartz, taking a tone she would have used with a naughty child. "If you think yourself the victim of a burglary, I suggest you take yourself over to the police station and report it."

Granny Mays might have given Miss Hartz another of her penetrating looks at that moment, but her eyes had fallen instead on one of the cardboard crates sitting on the floor behind the reception tables. Even before Miss Hartz had reached the end of her last sentence, Granny Mays had begun moving around the tables, so that the two librarians had to start swiveling in their chairs. As Granny Mays drew closer to the crates, I saw her face, which had brightened. She bent down and lifted a book from one of the crates, held it in her hands and petted it as if it were alive, then clutched it to her bosom and smiled. She fell to her knees beside the crate and began rummaging through the books inside it, then quickly moved to the next and the next, like a child overwhelmed at Christmas. From her kneeling position, she looked up at Miss Hartz and Mrs. Campbell, gratitude burning in her eyes. "I never had a single genuine doubt," she said. "All through that dark night, hope dwelled in my heart, all through. The Lord said, 'Get up and take the walk,' and I got myself up and took it." She moved her hands over the crates. "They're all here," she said. "I think it's every last one."

Miss Hartz whispered something to Mrs. Campbell, and Mrs. Campbell rose and went to the kitchen. Then Miss Hartz turned around in her chair and spoke to Mother. "Diane," she said, resigned to some universal sadness. "Do you think you could get her up off the floor?"

Mother called my name, motioned for me to come there, and when I reached her, she simply said, "Help me, Benny."

We moved around the tables and up behind Granny Mays. I could see in her hands an old brown and battered book, Volume *F* of *Compton's*. Mother said, "Come on now, Nezzie. Here. Take your hat."

Granny Mays upturned her head and looked at Mother, then at the straw hat. She replaced the book in the crate, accepted the hat from Mother's hands, and said, "Thank you kindly."

"Let me and Ben help you up now," Mother said, and Granny Mays nodded and again said, "Thank you kindly." We each took an arm and lifted her with little effort into a standing position. I watched Granny Mays as her eyes, sharp as fresh pencil points, roved the room, stopping at Mother, at me, at the crates on the floor, at the silent onlookers in the hall, again at the crates, and finally landed on Miss Hartz, at whom she beamed a warm apologetic smile. Granny Mays had seen her error: In a moment of joy, she'd overstepped an invisible line because she direly wanted something on the other side. Now she must do what she could to conjure an illusion, in which white women might give to her as charity what was already hers.

She turned the smile on Mother as well and moved back around to the front of the reception tables. She stood before Miss Hartz and held her hat in her hands, contrite.

Mrs. Campbell returned from the kitchen. Once she was seated, she turned to Miss Hartz and said, "Tom Horton's on his way. Said he wouldn't be two minutes."

Miss Hartz looked up at Granny Mays to see if she'd felt the impact of Mrs. Campbell's announcement. Granny Mays's face remained unchanged, but Mother quickly rounded the table and said, "Oh, Candy, was that really necessary?"

"We're just trying to get this thing sorted out, Diane," Miss Hartz said. "It's a little bit unusual. Someone intended us to have these materials for the academy's library. We can't just turn around and give them to anybody who shows up at the door and claims they were robbed. Kay and I both agree that it's a matter for the police."

I could see the word *police* register in Granny Mays's eyes, but she only straightened herself up and squared her shoulders. She said, "I know every last one by name. There's *Dusk to Dawn* and *Manners for Moderns* and *Two Plays by William Shake*—"

"You can just save that for Tom Horton," Miss Hartz said. "You needn't worry, Granny. We'll do whatever Tom tells us to do. I promise."

Tom Horton, who was Al's age and had played halfback for the high school, was now a junior officer with the Farmville Police. He arrived at the church in uniform, armed with his service revolver and a billy club dangling from his utility belt. Right between his shoulder blades, his blue shirt was marked with perspiration, a shape that looked exactly like a lightbulb. He'd come through the door with a worried look, and as Miss Hartz ran down the situation for him (Granny Mays silent throughout), the look faded and returned and faded again. He stood very tall and hooked his thumbs into his belt, then unhooked them, time and again, as if he wanted to appear at ease and in command when he wasn't at home with either of these conditions. Miss Hartz said someone who'd been unable to donate their books during the specified hours had left them on the assembly hall stoop before she and Kay Campbell arrived that morning. She said the donor, or donors, apparently meant to give the books anonymously since they'd left no indication of their identity. Then this old nigra woman, who was well-known in the county as a seamstress, had shown up a while ago claiming she'd been robbed and wanted her books back. Diane Rome, who was generously helping them out this morning, had vouched for the old woman's honesty, but everybody felt that the situation was unusual. Each and every book was valuable to the future of the private schools, as Tom knew—they needed two thousand volumes to be granted accreditation by the state authorities. The old woman had claimed that she'd been robbed of forty-one books. All anybody wanted to do was what was right, and herself and Kay had agreed that Tom or somebody else from the police station would be the best person to sort things out.

Mother jumped in and said she'd known the Mayses for some eight years and they lived quietly in her father-in-law's tenant house in his cornfield, they were clean as could be and had never caused a minute of trouble to anyone.

Tom Horton, tanned and handsome with a blond crew cut, smiled at Mother and the librarians and said they'd done exactly the right thing by calling him. Then, immediately, he turned to Granny Mays and gave her a severe look. "What's your Christian name, Granny?" he said.

"Inez," she answered. "Inez Awilda Washington Mays. Folks most call me Nezzie."

"Okay, Nezzie, come on around here and show me these books you claim belong to you."

They moved behind the tables and Granny Mays pointed to the egg crates on the floor. Tom Horton bent down and took a book randomly from one of them. He opened it to the title page and read aloud, "*Plane Geometry, Second Edition.* Why, this here's a textbook, Granny."

"Yes, sir," she said. "I put that red tape around the cover right there. Mended it myself."

"Is that right?" he said. "What would you be wanting with a textbook on plane geometry?"

"I've read a right much on any number of subjects," Granny Mays said. "My grandson Burghardt is coming along, and I thought to teach him some out of my books."

Tom Horton thumbed back to the front cover of the textbook. He looked at Granny and said, "So you can read, then."

"Yes, sir. Me and all my five sisters were taught to read by my father, whose father taught him."

Tom Horton turned the book around and held it up to her with the cover open. He said, "Well, read me what it says right there."

Granny Mays looked at the book only briefly and remained silent.

"Go on," he said. "What does that say right there?"

Granny Mays didn't look again at the book but said, "It says *Junior Wilkins*."

"Maybe I'm wrong, Granny," said Tom Horton, "but that tells me this book belongs to somebody named Junior Wilkins."

"No, sir," said Granny Mays. "It came to me by a friend of Mr. Wilkins's."

"I see." He passed the book into the hands of Miss Hartz, as if it was Exhibit A, entered into evidence in a courtroom trial. He lifted another from the crate, opened it, and said, "This looks like another textbook."

"Yes, sir," said Granny Mays. "English literature. Stories and poems, from—"

"Property of Susan W. Butterfield," said Tom Horton, holding out the book to her. "Now, who do you suppose that is?"

Granny Mays reached for the book with one hand, but he withdrew it and passed it to Miss Hartz. Granny Mays let her hand drop and said, "You see, most of these books are just castoffs."

"Castoffs?"

"I don't even know where most of them came from, Mr. Tom," she said, and the first note of distress crept into her voice. "I been collecting and studying in them over many years. My friends bring me books now and again 'cause they know I appreciate them. They're just castoffs."

"Well, do *any* of these books have your own name in them?" he asked.

"Didn't need to put my name in," she said. "They never left my home till last night, when somebody carried ever last forty-one of them off. They're mine all the same, name or no name."

"All right, Granny," said Tom Horton. "You strike me as an intelligent colored woman, so I'm going to try to use some logic on you here. If a person was looking to get hisself some free books, I don't think he'd go breaking into some nigger shack in a cornfield, do you?"

This observation caused one or two people in the assembly hall to laugh, but Tom Horton didn't acknowledge them. He said, "Can you tell me why it would even occur to anybody to go looking for books at your house?"

"No, sir, I can't," she said, "but I'm not lying about it."

"Now, nobody's accusing you of lying, Granny. Has anybody said you was lying?"

"No, sir."

"Okay, then, don't go putting words in my mouth. Now if somebody broke into your house, stole your books, and brought them over here to donate to the new school library, my guess would be it was some white rascals did it, wouldn't you think so?"

Granny Mays stood still, and I thought I saw something like panic cross her face. At last she said, "Didn't have to break in. You can walk straight on through, in the front and out the back."

"Well, be that as it may, Granny," he said, "I don't think colored folks is going to steal books from other colored folks and then give them to the white school's library. Now what do you think?"

Again, there was some laughter in the room, and again, Granny Mays stood perfectly still, searching her imagination for an acceptable response. She said, "I don't honestly know what to think. I wasn't home when it happened."

"Here's what I'm aiming at, Granny," he said. "How many white folks has visited your house over the years and had a chance to see these forty-one books of yours?"

Granny Mays looked up at the ceiling for a moment, then said, "Two."

"Two," said Tom Horton. "And who might those two be?"

"Mr. Cary Rome and Mr. R. C. Rome."

"Mr. Cary Rome and Mr. R. C. Rome," he repeated. "So in other words, you want me to believe that either Mr. Cary Rome or Mr. R. C. Rome burgled your house last night, stole your forty-one books, and brought them over here early this morning and left them on the steps of the Presbyterian Church."

Mother, unable to restrain herself, cried out, "Oh, Tom, Nezzie never said anything of the sort!"

He held his hand up to Mother, and stared straight into Granny Mays's eyes. "Is that what you want me to believe?" he said.

"No, sir," she said.

"No, sir?" he said. "Well, what other white man or woman knew you had these forty-one books?"

"None as I know of," she said.

"Well then, I don't see how it could've happened the way you say it did."

"I don't know either," she said, "but it happened all the same."

"Okay, Granny," he said. "I think we've taken up enough of everybody's time. If you want to come over to the station and fill out a report, that's your right. But I'm going to have to ask you to move on. You can't stay here depriving these ladies of their important work."

"You mean for me to move on without my books?"

Tom Horton didn't answer this question directly but said, "I'm happy to walk with you over to the station if you like."

She bowed her head and began to put her straw hat back on, carefully pinning it into place, which required Tom Horton to wait. Then she turned and began to move around the end of the reception tables. A half dozen new donors, gathered at the assembly hall entrance, stood whispering and watching. As Granny Mays slowly made her way toward the door, Miss Hartz and Mrs. Campbell put their heads together again, conferring in hushed voices. Mother came over to where I stood and said, "Go with her, Ben, and see if there's anything you can do."

The people at the entrance opened a path for Granny Mays, and just then Miss Hartz called out, "Excuse me, Granny."

Granny Mays stopped. The face she turned to Miss Hartz was void, as far as I could tell, of any feeling. By contrast, both Miss Hartz and Mrs. Campbell were on the verge of tears. Miss Hartz said, "Mrs. Campbell and I have talked it over, Granny. Under the circumstances? And considering how you've come all the way into town on such a hot day? Well, we'd be pleased for you to select one book from these over here on the floor, to take home. Any one of your choosing."

At Mother's urging, I'd moved next to Granny Mays, and I imagined I was the only one close enough to hear the rapid and labored rasp of her breathing. I noticed that her hands, at her sides, were clenched into fists and trembling. Under her breath, she muttered, "Mr. Ben . . . ?"

I thought she wanted me to answer Miss Hartz for her, but I couldn't think what to say. I don't know what instinct guided me at that moment, but I saw the concrete stoop outside the church building, blinding in the sun, and I simply went for it. Once there, I turned, squinting, and motioned for Granny Mays to follow. She looked specifically at my hand, appeared to recognize its signal, and strode toward me through the humans on either side; I supposed I'd only reminded her of something she already knew, of how a person walks out a door.

Now she'd found her marching feet, she went right past me, down the brick steps, and began to climb the long hill up Randolph, not pausing till she'd reached the top, where she crossed High Street and stopped at the edge of the Longwood campus, directly opposite the Confederate monument with its rebel flag and cannonballs. I was winded myself by the time I reached the intersection, and I watched as Granny Mays collapsed in the shade of the giant old elm where Al had parked his car two nights ago and explained to me his true feelings about colored folks. The minute Granny Mays had revealed in the assembly hall that she'd been robbed, I recalled my telling Al about her forty-one books. Had I imagined myself stepping forward and saying I knew who'd stolen the books? Yes. I didn't honestly think any judge or jury was going to send Al to jail for taking an old colored woman's books and giving them to the Foundation schools. But I couldn't be absolutely sure of that, and though I believed jail was where Al belonged, I didn't want to be the person who'd put his own brother behind bars.

Mother had told me to "see what I could do" for Granny Mays, and as I crossed High Street, I hadn't any notion of what that might be. I could have encouraged her to go to the police station with Tom Horton and fill out a crime report, but I was afraid a crime report might lead eventually to Al's arrest; it would be like him to leave his fingerprints all over everything at the tenant house. Granny Mays had sat on the dry brown grass between the sidewalk and the tree, turned toward the elm's wide and rutted trunk. I moved beside her and leaned down so I could see her face beneath the brim of her hat and also make my presence known. As her eyes were squeezed shut, I imagined she was stealing away, deep in silent prayer. But she tilted up her head and gave me a most grave look. "You run along, now, Mr. Ben," she said.

I stood still, thinking that running along wouldn't be what Mother expected of me, and Granny Mays lowered her head and said, "Go on, child, run along."

To the top of the hat, I said, "I know you're telling the truth, Granny."

The hat began to move side to side, and then her hands appeared. She plucked the pin from the hat, yanked the hat from her head, and threw it to the ground. To my horror, she tore away the kerchief as well—for an instant I saw her head engulfed by flames of silver-white—then pressed her hands hard against her mouth, one on top of the other, and uttered a terrible baying sound, smothered, like someone gagged or buried alive. A middle-aged Negro woman wearing gold sandals stopped on the nearby sidewalk and stared. A sudden gale swept down from the hill, drove dust into our faces, set the elm leaves hissing, and carried Granny Mays's hat and kerchief into the street. The Negro woman in the sandals went chasing after them, and I seized the moment to flee, taking off for the dark colonnades of Ruffner Hall.

I hid there for about ten minutes, squatting behind a brick column, and judged myself as harshly as I dared. Granted, I was a coward, ruled by fear as much as any pullet in the henhouse, but I was only a boy, about to start fifth grade—I'd had no experience with bearing witness against my own blood, and none consoling outraged old colored women. Still, I'd heard this old colored woman speak in the woods about justice, and I knew what great store she set by those books, how she'd hinged them to Burghardt's future. I should have stayed by her side, despite her telling me to go.

I got myself up and cut diagonally across the broad lawn, down the gentle slope toward the elm, but even from a distance I could see she was gone.

8

MOTHER ARRANGED with Candy Hartz for us to select one book on Granny Mays's behalf, for she was sure that the old woman would regret not having accepted the librarians' kind offer "once she got home and was feeling more like herself." She consulted me about which book to choose and I recommended the *F* volume of *Compton's*, because of its color plates displaying the flags of the world. Mother conducted herself with an artificial cheeriness the rest of our time at the church, and as we left, a little past one in the afternoon, she suggested we have a bite at my favorite eating place, Kelly's Main Street Diner, home of the bottomless cherry Coke, silver-dollar hamburgers, and shoestring potatoes. All I revealed to Mother about Granny Mays's departure from the assembly hall was that she'd sat down to rest under a shade tree up on High Street and instructed me to run along. I made no mention of any choked screams, and I couldn't determine whom I meant to protect with this omission, Granny Mays, Mother, or myself. As was often the case, Mother's behavior, rife with contradictions, confused me—I couldn't tell whether she'd believed Granny Mays's story about the stolen books, or if she thought the old woman, though honest, was suffering some kind of spell. When I considered Al's part in things, I knew I'd sooner get him into hot water with the law than with Mother, for at least the law wouldn't be mortally wounded by Al's transgressions.

We didn't arrive home until nearly two-thirty, and we found Daddy fuming in his desk chair on the porch, mad because Mother hadn't got back in time to make dinner. He and Al had had to fix their own sandwiches and ice tea, he said, and Mother said, Good, it wouldn't hurt either of them to learn their way around a kitchen. Daddy said he guessed that meant it wouldn't hurt her to learn her way around a henhouse, and she reminded him that she'd already learned her way around a henhouse, thank you, and she'd undergone two hernia operations for her reward. Daddy faced his desk again, putting his back to us, and said for me to go get my clothes changed.

I had about an hour before I needed to join Burghardt in the cage houses for marking cards and pulling down eggs. When I'd got into my work clothes (shorts and a T-shirt), I returned to the porch and asked Daddy if he knew where I might find Al.

Daddy was sorting through some receipts and writing down figures in an accountant's ledger. Without looking up, he said, "What do you want with Al?"

"I just had something to ask him," I said.

Preoccupied with his work, Daddy didn't answer for about ten full seconds. Then he said, "Al went down to the Big House after dinner."

"The Big House?" I said. "What's he doing down there?"

After another pause, he turned and glared at me over the top of his reading glasses. Dark circles cupped his eyes, and the furrows in his brow seemed deeper than usual. "Your granddaddy couldn't get his tractor to start this morning," he said. "Now get on out of here and stop asking me questions."

Blackberries grew along both sides of the road, but, coated with dirt, they were brown and whiskery, warmed by the sun and thoroughly unappetizing. The whole countryside seemed to loll under a peculiar stillness, as if the heat had struck it dumb. High overhead, the sun had bleached the sky to ash and faded most everything in sight. Soon I encountered a decaying-animal smell, and I imagined a rat, a blue jay, a possum, rotting beneath the tangled vines. I moved slowly down the road and thought about my father's asking me what I wanted with Al. It now occurred to me that my response, an intentional evasion, was actually the truth slipping out; I supposed I wanted to ask Al the most recurring query of my life so far: *why?* And yet, as I pondered the actual asking, I saw I wasn't the least bit interested in any answer he might supply. That kind of *why?* was just righteous indignation masquerading as something else. I pictured Al conveniently tethered to a post at Daddy Cary's tractor shed, waiting for me to horsewhip him; he would beg for mercy, which eventually I would grant, but in a pitying, disgusted manner. Over the woods beyond the cornfield, a buzzard circled—the miniature event in an otherwise static world—-and for a moment I saw Al dead on the ground, the huge stinking bird roosted on his face and digging at his eyes. Evidently this gruesome vision pushed me past some boundary of decency in my imagination, for I quickly wanted to withdraw it. The idea of Al dead brought to mind flames of eternal damnation, and now I was grateful to be startled by a piece of flattened black hose lying in the road that looked like a snake but wasn't. I picked it up and hurled it whistling through the air into the corn.

Soon an oak cast a saw-toothed shadow over my path, and I found that if I stood in its shade, and looked skyward through the leaves and branches, the tree became a perfectly flat thing against the sky, a lacy pattern cut from black paper. I came to a string of shrubby plum trees, where I picked a single ripe plum, wiped the dust off it with my T-shirt, and then continued polishing until it glowed a deep yellow. I held it up

between my thumb and forefinger so I could study it against the sky—
tiny translucent dots a deeper yellow beneath the skin; here and there
a small ragged flaw, a powdery tan—and soon it was a golden planet,
apparently stationary but actually barreling through the universe.
Then a damselfly found the plum (the brightest thing in the landscape), lit for one second, and glided away. I continued along the road,
and when I'd finished eating the plum I spit the pit over a barbed-wire
fence, into some weeds. A bumblebee orbited my head, whirred past
my ears, and then was gone, returned for one more revolution, and was
gone again. A pleasant drowsiness overcame me, and when at last I
rounded a bend and the Big House came into view, it took me a
minute to recall my mission and locate my former anger.

I'd expected to see Al's Fairlane parked at the house, but Daddy
Cary's Olds was the only car there, in its usual spot close to the screen
porch. I went through the backyard, down the four steps at the stone
wall, and past the milking barn. I found the old green John Deere in
the tractor shed, where the odor of oil and gasoline was unusually
strong; the hood of the tractor felt hot. A croaker sack had been draped
over the driver's seat, and on the burlap lay a couple of dirty rags, vise
grips, and a socket wrench, but no sign of Al.

From the direction of the barn I heard the crash of something
metal. I went immediately to the barn door and lifted the latch. The
instant I detected the smell of cigar smoke mingled with the aromas of
hay, urine, and manure, I knew and regretted my mistake.

"Get in quick and close the door," he said, from somewhere inside.

When I shut the door behind me, restoring the barn to darkness,
I could hardly see a thing, but soon I made out the feed passage and,
at the farthest stall, Dorothy Malone, her head lowered to a manger
of hay.

"Come over real quiet like," he said, but I stayed where I was.

"Daddy Cary," I called, "have you see Al?"

No answer. I took one step forward and said, "Daddy Cary?"

Still no answer. Finally I moved right up to the gate of the stall and stood next to the manger. I could see him back in the darkest part of the stall, low to the floor on a milking stool. One side of his face rested against the protruding belly of the cow as he reached beneath her and wiped the udder with a wet rag. Between his teeth he clenched the stub of a cigar, no longer lit but still reeking.

"Daddy Cary?" I said. "I'm looking for Al."

"Well, why in the world would you come looking for him in here?" he said.

It was the typical Daddy Cary question, designed to make me feel like a moron, and at the moment I didn't need much persuading. Around this time of day, I was sure to find Daddy Cary in the barn for the afternoon milking. All I'd needed to do to have avoided him was to stop for one second outside the door and *think*.

"Daddy told me Al came down here after dinner," I said. "Have you seen him?"

"Maybe so and maybe not," he said. "Climb on over here. You been wanting to learn, ain't you?"

"I can't right now," I said. "I'm expected up at the egg farm in a few minutes. I better be going."

"Well, now, wait just a minute," he said. "I thought I told you to climb on over here."

"Daddy Cary," I said, "I can't right now."

"Is it something wrong with your hearing, boy? Them chickens ain't going nowhere."

Daddy Cary had fashioned the crude stalls himself. Permanent posts had been anchored into the concrete slab of the floor, between which removable gates were seated into a groove in the floor at the bottom; the gates fit flush against the posts and were held in place at the top with a crossbar, a simple length of two-by-four that rested in metal hooks that were screwed into the posts at either end. When you needed to let the cow out of her stall, you lifted the crossbar, set it aside, and pulled the gate out of its bottom groove—a tedious ordeal necessitated by Daddy Cary's refusal to spend the money for hinges. Now I made sure the crossbar was secure and climbed the gate, turned at the top, and descended the other side. Dorothy Malone lifted her head and snorted, but once I was inside the stall she went back to tearing at the hay in the manger. In the next stall, Honey, awaiting her turn for hay and milking, issued a low complaint but not with much heart. Daddy Cary said, "Slide me that pail over here and come stand right up close."

In another minute the barn filled with a seesawing racket of shrill spurts drumming the bottom of the pail, the pitch of one note slightly higher than the next. Soon I saw that the method of my learning was to stand silently and watch, the length and breadth of his teaching simply to milk the cow, declaring at the onset, "Just like this, you see . . . it's all they is to it."

When the pail was a third full, I mustered the courage to say, "Daddy Cary, do you know where Al is?"

"Your brother's drove into town for spark plugs," he answered begrudgingly. "Are you paying attention?"

"Yes, sir," I said, "but I think I better be going. Daddy's expecting me to—"

A jet of warm milk hit me square in the face, shooting up my nose and splattering my eyes. I recoiled, bent into a corner of the stall, and pulled my T-shirt up over my face. I was wiping my eyes and spluttering into the shirt when I felt his hand between my legs. I leaped deeper into the corner of the stall, out of reach, and said, "Don't, Daddy Cary."

I continued wiping at my eyes, sideways to him now. I heard no more milking noises, and I could see peripherally that he'd pivoted on the stool to face me.

"Don't?" he said, his voice high with schoolboy mischief. "Don't what?"

I said nothing, but finished clearing the milk from my eyes.

He said, "I know you ain't gonna tell me you don't like it."

"I don't," I said, dropping my T-shirt.

"Aw, you're just ashamed to say so."

"Can I go now?" I said.

"Well, I ain't holding you, am I?"

In order to avoid having to get past him, I started to climb the divider gate into the next stall. Halfway up one side I heard him say, "You think I'm gonna grab you or something?"

"No, sir," I said, and kept climbing, "I just felt like going this way."

"You better *git* down off there," he said, fierce enough to make me freeze.

I'd reached the next-to-the-highest rung of the divider, one foot on one side and one on the other. "I really got to go, Daddy Cary."

"What are you so scared of?" he said. "You think I'm mad about them cards you took from my attic?"

This caught me by surprise, and I supposed that just being near him made me stupid. Stupidly, I said, "What cards?"

"The ones I ain't gonna tell your mama about," he said. He leaned back on the stool and reached into the pocket of his overalls, then held out his hand toward me, a silver dollar resting in his open palm. "Is this your silver dollar?" he said.

"No, sir."

"Well, you can have it if you want it," he said. "I got me a whole drawer full up to the house."

"No, thank you, Daddy Cary, I've really got to—"

Suddenly, he was on his feet, kicking the stool to one side, slamming it hard against the divider gate. Both cows danced briefly in their stalls. I faltered for a second at the top of the gate and then felt his hand slip inside the hem of my shorts—the barn rotated onto its side, a bright light struck my eyes, and I had a sharp sensation of flight. My feet hit the concrete floor and I was wedged into the corner of the stall, his full weight against me as he squatted and bored his shoulder into the middle of my back, his hands probing and tugging inside my shorts. I bit into the soft wood of the divider.

"You don't know it," he whispered against the back of my neck, his breath raspy and rank with cigar. "Don't nobody know it. But I can be sweet too."

I managed to pull my mouth away from the wood, though the rest of me stayed pinned and paralyzed, and inside my body, I heard the sound of my own voice. "Please stop," it said, then what had been only heat and pressure between my legs turned liquid and cool and traveled down one thigh to my knee.

He jerked his hands away. "Holy Jesus, son!" he cried, shrinking back from me and wiping his palms on his overalls. "Holy Jesus, what in the world?"

I wouldn't look directly at him, but I knew he'd sat on the milking stool again and was staring at me.

"Come over here, son," he said.

I didn't move or speak.

"Come on," he said softly, and I could tell he'd stretched one arm toward me.

My voice said, "No, sir."

"I ain't gonna hurt you," he said.

"No, sir."

"Well, dry yourself off then," he said, and the rag he'd used to wipe Dorothy Malone's udder landed at my feet. As I bent for it, I saw a dark stain on the cement between my feet. I began to rub my leg with the rag, below the hem of my shorts, which were fairly saturated on both sides. My voice said, "Can I go now, Daddy Cary?"

"You don't want everybody to see how you pissed all over yourself, do you?" he said.

"No, sir."

"Well, come on out here and let me scoot you down with the hose," he said. "I reckon if anybody asks you, you can just say you was hot and I scooted you down with the hose."

"Yes, sir."

He stood and heaved himself over the gate into the feed passage. After a pause I followed, but some darkness enveloped me, I lost a few minutes, and next I was standing ten feet away with my arms crossed over my chest and allowing him to soak me with water from a hose. The cows watched silently from their stalls. He closed the nozzle and dropped the hose to the floor. Swollen and kelly green, it twitched once or twice before settling, and I recognized it now as the thing used for cleaning out the manure gutters. Drenched, I went for the door, but he made me remove my hand from the latch and face him while he reassured me that I didn't need to be worried about anything. He promised not to tell my mama and daddy about what I'd done. He said he didn't want to get me in trouble with them, and besides, it was liable to kill my mama if she was to find out about what kind of boy I was. He said he himself was broad-minded, but he didn't think my daddy would understand. Throughout, a horsefly banged repeatedly against the inside of one of the small four-paned windows high on the back wall of the barn.

When he'd finished reassuring me, I asked him again if I could go, and he said, "All right, but what do you say?"

At first I had no idea what he meant by this question, but then I understood that he was prompting me to thank him. Not only did this seem entirely plausible to me, it felt far and away the easiest thing required of me since I entered the barn. I said, "Thank you, Daddy Cary."

He said, "That's all right, son," and I was out the door, nearly blinded by the light of day.

Directly ahead I saw the stone wall that marked the edge of the barnyard. Past that and tiered up three feet higher was the dirt yard behind the Big House; beyond that and to one side, the slope of dying lawn that stopped at the road. Against the dark green backdrop of the cornfield, Al was climbing out of his Fairlane, a small paper sack in one hand. He slammed the car door and began walking toward me, but I'd already started running. I bounded up the stone steps and had reached full speed by the time we collided near the corner of the screen porch and I torpedoed my head into his stomach and flailed at him with my fists, crying, "You're nothing but a damned hypocrite! Why'd you have to do it, you damned hypocrite!"

The paper sack went flying as he managed to catch me by the wrists. He hooked one of his legs behind me, in the bend of my knees, and pushed me over it, onto my back, and loomed over me; still grasping my wrists, he controlled me as best he could, using my arms like levers on a difficult machine. I tried to kick him from this position, but he quickly swung around so that he stood at my head, a shift that caused him to make an X of my forearms, and he gazed at me through one of its triangles, his face inverted from my vantage. "Calm down, Benny," he said. "Just calm down."

When at last I quit struggling, he moved to one side, uncrossing my arms but not releasing my wrists, and stooped next to me. "Look at you," he said, with an alarming tenderness. "You're soaking wet."

I resolved never to let him or anyone else see me cry, not ever again. I willed my lower lip to cease trembling and tried in vain to tear my wrists from his grip. He matched my strength exactly, exerting the precise amount of counterforce needed to stop our four hands, inert a few inches above my heart. I strained my neck forward, lifting my head from the ground. Al blinked, once, slowly, and I saw the pupils of his eyes contract.

Quietly, I said, "You're a hypocrite and a thief."

"Now listen to me," he said, pushing down hard on my wrists till they were pinned against my stomach. "I didn't do it, Benny, and that's the God's truth. I didn't do it."

———

When Al had returned from the auto parts store, he'd stopped by our house for a cold drink. Mother had given him a thumbnail sketch of that morning's events at the Presbyterian Church, and he knew instantly that I would think he'd stolen Granny Mays's books. He was glad when he spotted me coming out of Daddy Cary's barn, for he was anxious to explain that his only crime had been to mention the fact of Granny Mays's books to those two ne'er-do-wells he lived with, Frank and Shelby O'Bannon. The twins had disappeared for a while last evening during Daddy Cary's birthday party, and when they came back, Al had a feeling they'd been up to no good. Then, when he heard from Mother about this morning's episode in the Presbyterian assembly hall, he put two and two together.

"What did you say to Mother?" I asked him.

He was pulling the Fairlane into our driveway, where he came to a halt and popped the gearshift into reverse. In a minute he would have to return to the tractor shed and install the new spark plugs, but he'd given me a ride back to the egg farm as a peace offering. "I didn't say anything," he answered. "The fewer people know about this the better. I might not like what those boys did, but they're still my friends."

The dogs had started barking the second they'd seen the car and were now both up on their hind legs. Lady stayed put and barked, resting her paws on the wire of the pen, while Bullet, always the more agitated, leaped against the wire, sprang backward to the ground, executed a turn, and leaped against it again. Daddy threw open the porch door and yelled that we'd better make those goddamned dogs shut up before he had to come out there and shut them up himself.

Without a word, I quickly left the car, so Al could drive back to the Big House and the dogs would quiet down. But Al turned off the engine and followed me to the pen, where we knelt by the wire and petted the dogs and let them lick our fingers. After a minute, Al said, "Besides, Benny, I got to take some responsibility for what happened too, don't you think?"

I still didn't respond, for I could feel my silence eating at him and I didn't mind the feeling. Lady put her nose through a pane in the wire and Al rapped three times on the top of it with his knuckles, producing a satisfying hollow sound. "You know, Benny," Al said, "if you stop and think about it, you and me are both to blame. Granted, it wouldn't've happened if I hadn't told Frank and Shelby about that old colored woman's books. But I wouldn't've known to tell them if you hadn't told me first."

A few minutes earlier on the lawn of the Big House, when he'd first said, "I didn't do it," I'd eagerly believed him—at that moment, fleeing the barn, I would have snatched at the flimsiest shred of good news. As I'd sprinted toward him from the barnyard, headlong toward collision, I'd felt a certain exhilaration, but it was the exhilaration of pure loneliness. Now I detected some fancy dancing in his argument, with its equal indictment of us both, but mostly I was relieved to find myself put into the same boat with him, even in this unfortunate way. I knew he wouldn't just come out and say it, but he wanted more from me than continued cordial relations; he'd parked the car and followed me over to pet the dogs because he wanted me to keep quiet about the O'Bannon twins.

I turned to him and said, "Okay."

He smiled and winked, and while I valued the smile more than the wink, with Al, it was a package deal. "I figured you'd be mad," he said, "but not as mad as all that."

In my mind, I heard Daddy Cary's milking stool slap against the stall gate and I must have visibly shuddered, for Al pinched the still-wet sleeve of my T-shirt and said, "Now tell me truly, Ben, how'd you get so soaked?"

"I got overheated walking to the Big House," I said. "So Daddy Cary cooled me off with the hose."

Al squinted at me. He said, "That's not the whole story, now is it?"

I stood and went to the outdoor faucet on the side of the house, where I filled a bucket and brought it back to the pen. The dogs had an old dishpan for a water bowl, and I poured fresh water into it from outside the fence. They turned and watched me do this, but neither would leave Al's affection long enough to come over and drink. Al moved around the corner of the pen to where I stood, so the dogs followed him from inside the wire and ended up having a drink after all.

Al said, "I bet I can guess what really happened."

I felt my heart inside my chest, and when I looked down at my shirt, flush against my skin, I could actually see a pulse there, just to the left of my breastbone. I stared at the dogs, and they lifted their heads from the dishpan and stared back.

"I think you went looking for me inside the barn and Daddy Cary caught you by surprise," said Al. "I think he was in there cleaning the stalls and just started shooting you with the hose without even asking if you wanted him to. Which is just like something he'd do. Now tell me how close I am to the truth, Benny."

I kept my head lowered but took a deep breath and nodded.

"One of these days," Al said, "somebody's gonna give as good as he gets with that old man. I just hope I'm around to see it." He made a fist and socked me gently on the arm. "Well," he said, "better make haste while the sun shines."

As he swaggered back to the car, he pulled his work shirt over his head, wiped his face with it, and tossed it onto the seat through the window. His dark shoulders and arms were shiny with sweat; he idly lifted one arm, turned his head, and sniffed at his armpit, checking for physical flaws but apparently finding none. Once he'd got behind the wheel, he put his head out and called, "Hot, ain't it?"

The dogs trotted over to the other side of the pen and stood at attention, watching him go. They each looked at me as if to say, *Do something, make him stay*, and then returned their gaze to the departing Fairlane; for quite some time, they continued to stare in silence at the empty driveway.

With little or no success, I tried applying Al's logic to Burghardt and me. If Burghardt hadn't told me about his grandmother's forty-one volumes in a bookcase, I wouldn't have told Al, Al wouldn't have told the O'Bannon twins, and Granny Mays would still have her books. So didn't that make Burghardt partly to blame? I couldn't help but notice that this reasoning didn't give me the we're-in-the-same-boat feeling I'd got with Al. As I'd climbed into that boat with Al, I'd failed to notice right away that Frank and Shelby O'Bannon were there as well; this thing that had been drawing me happily into the grown-up world—my expanding mass of secret knowledge—was expanding a bit too rapidly for my own good.

When I reached the first of the cage houses and saw Burghardt about halfway down the aisle, already marking cards and pulling down eggs on the right-hand side, I feared for the first time that he might recall his having told me about Granny Mays's books; that he might suspect me of having told someone else, who then stole the books; or even that I might have stolen them myself. This fear—or some ragged version of it—was confirmed when he turned and looked straight at me but didn't wave hello.

I found my black crayon and bucket in the feed room and started up the left-hand side of the house. As usual I worked slower than Burghardt, and today he had a considerable head start. Soon he reached the end of the house and began working back toward me on my side of the aisle. As we moved nearer and nearer to each other, I kept stealing glances at him, hoping to determine his mood, but he appeared purposely to avoid my eye. The stench of chicken manure seemed especially pungent today, and the chronic chatter of the chickens grated on my nerves. When we were about fifteen feet from each other, Burghardt caught me glancing at him and said, "What are you looking at?"

I climbed down from the bucket. It didn't feel right to be standing up there higher than him and saying what I had to say. I tried to give him my sincerest face and said, "Burghardt, I know what really happened."

"What you talking about?" he said.

I meant to reassure him that I believed Granny Mays's story about the books, that I wasn't among any white folks who suspected her of lying or having some kind of spell. So I said, "I know for a fact they were stolen."

He returned to marking cards. "They weren't stolen," he said calmly. "I found them."

"You found them?" I said, astonished. "Where?"

"Somewhere," he said.

Was it possible that Al had somehow rescued the books and planted them in a place where Burghardt would find them? If so, why wouldn't Al have told me? And since he'd learned about the stolen books only an hour or so ago, when could he possibly have done it?

"I don't see how that's possible," I said. "But did you tell Granny Mays already?"

Now Burghardt turned and gave me a look so bitter and bewildered I understood that we'd embarked on a comedy of errors. My subject in this exchange was Granny Mays's books, his was the pornographic playing cards.

I sat on the inverted bucket and laughed. I said, "Burghardt, I'm talking about Granny Mays's books."

Comprehension crossed his face, but he didn't appear especially pleased by it. "Oh," he said, and returned again to his work. I allowed him to finish the few hens that remained between us. I guessed he'd been worrying through the night and day about the playing cards, my discovery of them, and what it would lead to. Maybe he'd been dreading seeing me. Apparently he was relieved now that I hadn't even been thinking about the cards, for he gave me a hint of his crooked grin. He stuck his black crayon in the pocket of his shorts. "They were old," he said. "Just a bunch of beat-up old books, not worth anything. Come on."

We left the henhouse through the opening at its middle and walked up the alley to the end of the next house. Grass and weeds grew between the houses, brown and yellow now, and the alley was marked by two bare troughs made by the wheels of Daddy's trucks. I walked in one of these, Burghardt in the other. I said, "But she was going to teach you out of them, Burghardt."

He only shrugged his shoulders, but when he entered the shade of the next house, he stopped and looked at me, thinking.

"What?" I said.

"Are they really gonna close those schools?" he asked. "For sure?"

These last few days, we'd moved beyond talk of "probably they won't really close," and "if they do close, you're lucky." Since the topic had last come up between Burghardt and me, I'd heard Al's opinions and Barrye Wall's convictions and witnessed the overwhelmingly successful first day of Library Week. I said, "Yeah, but my brother says they won't stay closed for long."

Burghardt nodded and moved on through the feed room and into the aisle between the cages. Now we were working together, near each other in the usual way. I climbed onto my bucket and marked five cards at a time before switching positions; he deliberately tarried a bit so as not to get too far ahead. After quite a long silence had passed, he said, "They must really hate us."

I hadn't followed his train of thought; I imagined for a second that *they* meant the chickens and *us* meant him and me. My back to the aisle, I said, "Who?"

I turned and looked at him over my shoulder. He drew his forearm across his brow but didn't look at me. He marked another card, then bent to reach his fingers up under the cage and free an egg trapped in the wire. The egg rolled down to the lip of the cage, and Burghardt moved on to the next chicken and the next. "They must hate us *real* bad," he said at last. "So bad they'd lock up the schools to keep us out."

Now he looked at me quickly and returned to marking the cards. He needed to see if what he'd said—far more candid than was customary—would pass muster with me. I moved my bucket along the aisle. All I could think to do was to elaborate on what I'd already told him. "They won't stay closed for long," I said. "My brother says the courts won't let them. He says the courts is the law and the law always has the last word. He predicts that in a while everybody'll be wondering what all this fuss was about."

Evidently Burghardt wasn't much persuaded or consoled, for after another long silence, he said, "Yessir, they must hate us *real* bad."

Al didn't stay for supper that evening, for which I was thankful, since Mother couldn't restrain herself from recounting our morning at the Presbyterian assembly hall, and I didn't want to have to be exchanging knowing glances with Al throughout the meal. Daddy said that old nigger woman didn't have no business going down there to that church and making a public scene, and Mother told a long story about her own mother and how she'd begun to show the first signs of senility at the young age of sixty-seven; the last time Mother had visited Grandmother Tutwiler in Richmond, shortly before her death (bless her sweet soul), the poor old thing had become completely convinced that she was living in the Fontainebleau Hotel and Mother was her chambermaid. Mother said it was just sad, sad, sad. Lainie, more forlorn even than usual, offered the opinion that Mother would've probably made a very good chambermaid at the Fontainebleau Hotel and that perhaps she'd missed her true calling, which opinion Mother received with an icy silence. I thought Daddy looked unwell, though I didn't at the time connect his poor appearance to his drinking of the night before. When Lainie asked him to please pass her the green beans, he asked her why she couldn't eat something close to her. Lainie left the table, but before going out the living room door, she turned to Daddy and said, "That 'old nigger woman' has just as much right to make a scene at the Presbyterian church as you do making one at Daddy Cary's birthday party last night, drunk as a lord."

I had never heard that expression before, "drunk as a lord," and I found it interesting, since the only lord I'd heard of was *the* Lord, whom I'd certainly never imagined drunk. The most intriguing picture of Jesus I'd ever seen was one in which he walked on water, appearing to Peter and the other disciples as their boat tossed about in a storm, and later, as I lay on my bed in my room, I envisioned Jesus staggering and weaving across the whitecaps, stewed to the gills. Suddenly the sea changed to milk, and Jesus opened the palm of his right hand, revealing a shiny silver dollar. I started, fully awake, thinking I felt wet fingers creeping up my leg.

My bedroom door opened and Lainie stuck her head inside and said, "Are you okay, Benny?"

I noticed that the room was unusually bright and that lines of moonlight framed the blinds closed over my windows. I told Lainie that I was fine, but she came over to the bed and put her hand on my forehead. "You feel a little hot," she said.

She wore her white pajamas with the blue piping and had braided her hair. It was the middle of the night. "You let out quite a squeal," she said.

"I did?"

"Bad dream?"

"I didn't even know I was asleep," I said. "You heard me all the way in your room?"

She touched my forehead again, then sat beside me on the bed. "I couldn't sleep," she said. "I was coming back from the kitchen and heard you. I bet that thing at the church this morning upset you, didn't it, Benny?"

I knew that if I told Lainie about the O'Bannon twins, she wouldn't hesitate to shout it from the rooftops. I said, "She was gonna teach Burghardt out of those books."

Lainie nodded and touched my forehead a third time. "You never did like to see anybody getting hurt," she said. She removed her hand, bent forward, and kissed me in the same spot; I recalled it as the location of the single eye of the Cyclops. As she drew away, I saw that her eyes were red, the skin around them splotchy. "Your eyes are all red," I said.

"Yeah," she said, wiping her nose with the back of her hand. "They usually are, this time of night."

"Do you miss Claud Wayne?" I asked.

She smiled and shook her head. "No," she said, "but I sure do wish I did."

"Oh," I said, as if I understood something I hadn't understood before, which I didn't, not entirely.

"Well," she said, "if you're sure you're all right, I'm going to give sleeping another try. You want to tell me your dream? Sometimes it helps."

"I don't remember it," I said, and when she'd left the room, I closed my eyes and my father's face rose up in the darkness. He sat big-eared across from me at the kitchen table, eating, eating, eating. I could tell, even though he appeared oblivious to the world, that his thoughts were full of butterflies and church weddings, pleasure books and beautiful sunrises, Christmas tinsel and the stars in the heavens. How grateful he was not to be interested in such sissy pursuits! He was free to concentrate on egg farming and keeping Burghardt and the other niggers out of the public schools. I could easily have told my sister about my dream and what it signified. Likewise, I could have told my mother and my brother. There was one and only one reason I didn't: They might have told my father.

9

NEITHER AL NOR I KNEW enough in 1959 to observe that the same courts he counted on to prevent the public schools from staying closed had taken four long years to contemplate how and when to implement the *Brown* ruling. During that period, fear of integration had combined with fear of communism and produced something very much like fear of extinction. Dwight Eisenhower carried Virginia in the 1956 presidential race, but in Prince Edward a states'-rights candidate by the name of T. Coleman Andrews won. And lately we'd heard that a Catholic was running for the Presidency, yet another indication that life as we knew it and valued it was under siege. Between '55 and '59, segregationists found a friend in a federal judge by the name of Sterling Hutcheson. My father believed Judge Hutcheson properly understood things because he was "one of us," a white Southside native. In truth, the judge was wary of bringing integration too fast to counties like Prince Edward, in which the Negro population just about equaled the white, and segregationists gave him an earful about the danger of violence should the NAACP succeed in rushing us. It was not only violence the judge hoped to avoid but also school closings, which he thought would hurt both races. He first ruled that we must desegregate our schools eventually, but specified no time. When that decision was remanded by an appellate court, he ruled that we could take until 1965 to integrate. This second decision was the one that a circuit court of appeals changed in 1959, declaring that we would have to open our doors to Negro students that very September, and sparked the summer frenzy of preparations for private schools.

During these early years of my boyhood, I had an exaggerated tendency to imbue adults with mythical traits and powers, especially adults I'd only heard of but never met. This tendency was attributable to my being the only child among four adults in my immediate family, a condition sharpened by my growing up on a farm, largely isolated from other children. (It also accounted, in part, for my attachment to Burghardt, though he would have stood out among any set of available friends.) Of course, plenty of adults imbued adults with mythical traits and powers as well. It did not escape me that *Life* magazine conferred upon a solitary Russian individual, Nikita Khrushchev, the power to start World War III; that my mother actually believed my father was possessed of the devil; that 140,000 Australians had flocked recently into Melbourne's Olympic Stadium to hear Billy Graham make his pitch for salvation; that four American presidents had so shocked history with their greatness that their likenesses had been carved into the side of Mount Rushmore. I never saw any photograph of Judge Sterling Hutcheson, but his name, sounded now and again at our supper table, created a mythical image in my mind. Enormous in his black robes, he stood fast on the steps of the Parthenon and wielded a mahogany gavel, his mane of silver hair swept backwards by something called the "winds of time." I didn't know precisely what the winds of time were or where I'd heard of them, but I imagined Sterling Hutcheson the kind of man to withstand them.

Another name sometimes spoken at our supper table was that of the Reverend L. Francis Griffin, the preacher at the Negro Baptist church in Farmville. Though it lacked the cachet of the name Sterling Hutcheson, my father's description of the preacher as having taken up the torch of dissatisfaction among the coloreds, and as the ringleader of everything wrong in Prince Edward County today, was sufficient to conjure a formidable black man in a top hat, brandishing a flaming torch in one hand and a whip in the other. (I'd confused *ringleader* with *ringmaster* here.) The names of these two men were linked because Sterling Hutcheson had done what he could to slow the designs of the NAACP, and Mr. Griffin was that heinous organization's representative in our county.

If anybody had paid their dues to remain a resident of Prince Edward, it was Mr. Griffin. After he'd reluctantly assumed his father's pulpit at the First Baptist Church, back in 1949, he soon became the embodiment of a change in attitude among the colored community: from that of older Negroes (typified by men like Julius Mays), who saw themselves dependent on the good graces of white folks, to that of younger Negroes (typified by NAACP lawyers like Oliver Hill and Spottswood Robinson), who were sick and tired of making do with white folks' leftovers. My father was right when he said that Mr. Griffin had come under the influence of the outspoken Vernon Johns. Mr. Johns, who'd preached in Darlington Heights when Francis Griffin was a boy, was in the habit of scolding his congregations for their lack of enterprise and for their complaisance in a social system that once held them in bondage and then continued to subjugate them with everything but actual shackles. As a young man, Mr. Griffin wasn't quick to choose the ministry, but when at last he did, he more closely followed in Mr. Johns's footsteps than in his own father's. He came to his decision during World War II, while serving in the first Negro tank battalion. He served for four years, some of it under General George Patton—a fact never mentioned by my father, who'd been stationed at a naval base in Puerto Rico for two years during the war and saw no combat. When Mr. Griffin returned home from the war he was twenty-eight, and one academic year shy of a high school diploma. He completed his senior year and enrolled at Shaw University, in Raleigh, North Carolina. While there, he fell in love, married, and started a family. When the elder Mr. Griffin died in October 1949, Francis was invited by the First Baptist Church to become its minister.

The church was home to the largest Negro congregation in the county and stood near the center of town, right across from Longwood College. (This prestigious location for a Negro church had surprised me as a boy; I later learned that the building had served a white congregation before the Civil War, but after it was taken over by the Yankee army and used as a hospital, it was considered forever tainted, suitable only for Negroes, and sold for a thousand dollars.) Francis Griffin hadn't envisioned a Southside life for his family, but he saw the pulpit of the red-brick church on Main Street as a place where his ideas might be of particular service. He'd already joined the NAACP while a student at Shaw. His theological disposition was pretty much formed, grounded in the social gospel. He believed the whole purpose of Christian principles was to inspire action in the here and now. "Religion ought to be lived up to," he said, "squared with economics, politics, all that."

The many white folks who thought Mr. Griffin had plotted the student strike led by Barbara Johns, back in 1951, never found any evidence of such; it was reprehensible enough that he praised and encouraged that kind of thing. After the NAACP got involved and transformed the student protest from a demand for better colored schools to a demand for integrated schools, Mr. Griffin got flak not only from whites but from some of his congregants as well. Before long, it appeared that his job might be in jeopardy. One July Sunday morning in '51, he endeavored to clear the air. In a forty-five-minute sermon, taking as his text the passage from Isaiah that begins, "Every valley shall be exalted, and every mountain and hill shall be made low," Mr. Griffin proclaimed that God didn't want segregation but wanted equality.

"When I see healthy colored babies, I think how God has brought them into the world properly and how the rotten system of the Southland will twist them into warped personalities, cringing cowards, unable to cope with the society into which they were unwillingly thrown and which they have a God-given right to enjoy. When I think of the years of economic exploitation made on my people by the white race, and the hatred thrown against us, I must, in all sincerity, fight against such inhumanity to man with every ounce of energy given to me by God. I would sacrifice my job, money, and any property for the principles of right. I offered my life for a decadent democracy, and I'm willing to die rather than let these children down." He ended the sermon with, "No one's going to scare me from my convictions by threatening my job," and asked for a show of hands of those who wanted him to stay on as head of the First Baptist Church. There was hardly a person whose hand didn't shoot up.

But in the years following the student strike, some of the white merchants of Farmville tightened the screws on Mr. Griffin, using the very economic means at their disposal he'd cited in his rousing sermon. Debts he'd incurred were suddenly called in. He was served warrants by some retailers and put on a cash-only basis with others. By 1955, the Griffins had five children, and when they went to local stores to buy clothing or food, they were denied credit. Fuel oil for heating the house had always been provided on credit—customers would generally pay off the debt over the course of the entire year—but now he could buy only the few gallons he had the cash for. The church, unable to provide an increase in salary, did allow him to preach elsewhere. He took on some rural posts in Cumberland County and on Sunday mornings rushed around from pulpit to pulpit, collecting his pay and hurrying back to town to buy food. He received threats by telephone and written note, inviting him to attend a necktie party in his own honor. White folks of the O'Bannon stripe yelled obscenities from passing cars. Shotgun shells were left at his door. A dud of a home-made bomb sputtered itself out on his front porch. Somebody tried to start a fire outside the parsonage. Mr. Griffin's wife sank into despair, suffered a breakdown, and had to be hospitalized. The children's grandmother took over their care, and Mr. Griffin gave notice to the church, hoping to find a better position elsewhere.

No such better position emerged, however, and the church board, who hadn't wanted to see Mr. Griffin go, asked him to stay on. The NAACP urged him to stay too, for they feared that the county's Negroes, lacking his leadership, would lose heart. And Mr. Griffin him-self hated to create the appearance of having got people stirred up only to abandon them. He decided to stick it out, come hell or high water. His wife remained outside the county for a time, the children remained under the care of their grandmother, and the Griffins' economic plight slowly improved.

All I knew of Mr. Griffin in 1959 were the narrow depictions from my father at the supper table, but I must have had the preacher pointed out to me at least once on the streets of Farmville; on a blis-tering day in August, at the end of Library Week, I was to encounter Mr. Griffin in the flesh, standing in Daddy Cary's cornfield, and though he wore no top hat and brandished neither torch nor whip, I recognized him immediately.

It was Friday, August 21. Library Week had exceeded everyone's expec-tations, with about three thousand volumes donated by the people of Prince Edward and another four thousand from other parts of the state. (These were estimates, as the librarians, even with volunteer help, had been unable to keep up with the torrent of books; Friday was the last official day of the drive, but donations would continue to arrive on a daily basis over the next few weeks, and by the end of the month, more than nine thousand books would have been collected.) I'd felt peaked for the first part of the week, and I believed myself genuinely sick and running a fever, but Mother said it was just the relentless hot weather and told me to stay out of the sun and to drink plenty of fluids. Any extra attention I might have got was eclipsed on Wednesday, when my father nearly cut his left thumb off on a jigsaw in Farmville and had to be taken to the hospital for nine stitches. He and Al had signed up to help a group of citizens make desks for the Foundation schools, outfitting ordinary metal folding chairs with homemade desktops, and Al told us afterward that Daddy's stubbornness had caused the accident. He'd been warned to leave the jigsawing to men who had jigsawing experience, but Daddy had said, "Why, there ain't nothing to it," and proceeded to run his thumb straight into the blade.

That night, Mother took a good dose of spirits of ammonia at bedtime and repeated what she'd said a dozen times already: It was a miracle Daddy hadn't lost that thumb entirely. Lainie told me privately there was nothing miraculous about it. She said it would have been a miracle if Daddy hadn't needed to play the big shot, had listened to reason, and stayed away from a machine he didn't know how to operate.

That same night, I was awakened in the wee hours by the sound of Lainie whimpering in her bedroom. Sleepily, I first thought she was crying because of Daddy's injured thumb, but then I recalled her persistent unhappiness, the nature and depth of which I didn't fully fathom. I'd imagined she would gradually get better, like someone with mumps or the common cold, but that night it occurred to me that some illnesses, like polio and cancer, didn't improve but steadily got worse.

When I considered what getting worse would mean in Lainie's case, I worried that she would eventually lie in bed and cry around the clock. After the baby was born it would lie next to her and cry. Soon Claud Wayne would come home from Wiesbaden and crawl in next to them in his military uniform and cry. Of course Daddy would kick them out of the house because he wouldn't be able to tolerate the noise, and where would they go? I'd heard of some very poor people who ended up living in their cars. Maybe Lainie and Claud Wayne and the baby would be reduced to living in the Willys, which was rather small. I resolved to swipe food from our refrigerator and take it to them, wherever they might be parked. I hoped they wouldn't park too far away and thought the junkyard in the woods where Granny Mays did her speaking might be a suitable place. It occurred to me that they might slowly become more and more drawn in by Granny Mays and that listening to her would somehow cure them. Then I fell back to sleep.

Unfortunately, the real future of Granny Mays's speaking was up in the air. Over the week, I'd stolen off three times down to the junkyard and waited for her to come along, but she never showed. I feared she'd been so done in by the theft of her books that she'd given up coming to the woods. Again and again, I kept seeing in my mind's eye the flight of her straw hat and kerchief, sailing into High Street, and I heard the *clackety-clack* of the other woman's gold sandals on the pavement. I was happy meanwhile that Burghardt and I had resumed normal relations in the henhouses; although I hoped to take up the mystery of the pornographic playing cards with him at some later date, for the present I was content to make sure it didn't come between us.

On Friday, the day on which I was to encounter the Reverend Griffin in Daddy Cary's cornfield, the temperature actually hit 100 degrees. Burghardt and I had finished our morning chores sooner than usual, as we'd made foot races of cleaning the waterers and feeding the cage birds. In the feeding category, he won every house—stronger than I, he could handle more feed in his bucket, which meant he needed to refill it fewer times. Speed and agility were the important factors with cleaning the waterers, and I beat him in four of the six houses. We were sweating and out of breath when we finished, and Burghardt pointed to the woods about fifty yards away across a field of weeds and suggested we find a place over there in the shade to rest our bones. Small wispy chicken feathers stuck to the sweat on our arms, and we picked these off as we walked through the field. Halfway across, the smell of the air changed, from chicken manure to pine sap. The sun beat down on our shoulders, and Burghardt removed his sleeveless T-shirt and wrapped it around his head so that it resembled an Arabian turban.

Granny Mays had cautioned him that morning not to get over-heated and had sent him off with a mason jar of drinking water and a few pinches of table salt in the pocket of his orange shorts. When we reached the shade of the pines and found a suitable spot to sit, leaning our backs against opposite sides of a tree, Burghardt unscrewed the lid of the mason jar, turned it up, swallowed four or five times, replaced the lid, and set the jar on the brown needle-strewn ground between us. He wiped his lips with the back of his hand and sighed noisily. He caught me eyeing the jar, but quickly averted his gaze. After about ten seconds, he suddenly stood and said, "I'm gonna step over there and take myself a leak." As he'd stood, he'd knocked over the jar of water with his foot—I thought it almost looked deliberate—and now he bent to right the jar and set it down a few inches closer to me than it had been before.

I turned and watched him stroll a good hundred feet through the trees. He paused to put his shirt back on, then ducked behind a stand of dogwoods. I quickly grabbed the mason jar, removed the lid, wiped the glass mouth with my T-shirt, and gulped the water. I was so parched I didn't care if I caught sickle cell disease or any other thing.

When Burghardt returned, he sat down and looked at the jar, which I'd all but drained. He glanced at me, and for a moment I thought he might say something about its diminished contents, but instead he asked me if I had ever passed out.

"Passed out?" I said. "You mean passed out like fainted?"

"Women faint," he said. "Men pass out."

"Oh."

"Well, did you?"

I took a moment to consider whether or not it was shameful not to have passing out as part of one's life experience, but decided to answer truthfully and say no.

"I did," he said. "Last Sunday."

"What was it like?"

"It was like life just went on without me," he said. "It was like I was gone but not gone, at the same time. You want to try it?"

"How?" I asked.

"This boy name of Moses that was at that barbecue over to Rice last Sunday, he showed me how to do it. You want to try?"

"I don't know," I said. "What do you have to do?"

Burghardt stood and stepped a few feet away from the tree. "All's you have to do is breathe," he said. "Here. You just stand up here in front of me."

I stood, and he turned me by the shoulders so that my back was to him; I noticed that as he did this he quickly surveyed our surroundings, as if he wanted to make sure nobody else was around. Surely this was why God had made the woods, as a place for secret things, for Granny Mays's speaking, for my sneaking a drink from a colored person's mason jar, and for whatever Burghardt and I were about to do now. From behind me, he reached beneath my arms, pulled me backward against himself, and clasped his hands over my chest. Where his forearms bore in against my ribs, I felt a damp heat through the fabric of my T-shirt. Burghardt's hands smelled of chicken feed, a pleasant mixture of corn and soybeans.

"Okay," he said. "Now just take ten real deep breaths, in and out through your mouth. And on the tenth breath, hold it in."

I took ten deep breaths through my mouth, then held the last one, at which point Burghardt squeezed me hard, pressing on my chest with his hands. In the next moment I found myself gazing up at him from a considerable distance, and there was something changed about his face. He looked as he had in my dream, in which we'd swum together in a river overarched by oaks with Spanish moss—he was giving me that crooked grin of his, and I could see beads of water on his brow. But most oddly, he appeared as he would in a photographic negative; his skin was ashen white, as were the pine boughs high up behind his head, while irregular, visible patches of sky were solid black. When Burghardt spoke, I could hear and understand him perfectly, yet he seemed to speak under water. "See what I mean?" he said, and I had a certain sensation of nodding, but with an equal certainty that I hadn't actually moved my head.

As I came to, heat suffused my body, and I noted that wherever I'd just gone, it had been pleasantly cool there. I lay on the ground at Burghardt's feet. He reached for my hand, then pulled me into a standing position. I saw a mason jar on the ground nearby and vaguely recalled that I'd broken some rule associated with it. Then I heard the sound of Burghardt's laughter. He was doubled over and slapping his thigh. Soon I began to laugh too, not sure what I was laughing at.

"I reckon it worked," he spluttered, as I moved back toward the pine tree and sat down.

He sat next to me and repeated the question he'd asked me before: "See what I mean?"

"How long was I out?" I said.

"Thirty seconds," he said.

"It seemed longer."

"I know it did," he said. "Wasn't it just what I said? Life went on without you, didn't it. You was *gone*, man. I put you *out*. Did you like it?"

"I don't know," I said. "It was kind of weird."

"Well, I sure liked it when that Moses put me out last Sunday," he said.

We sat silently for a minute or two. Then Burghardt said quietly, "Man, I think somebody done hit me with a sleepy stick."

"Me too," I said, and let my eyes close.

All I felt in my body was heat, which at the moment was pleasant enough. The incidental sounds that reached my ears—Burghardt's breathing, the buzz of a random insect, the cry of a jay, the distant murmur of the henhouses—melted into one deep and nameless drone, and when I opened my eyes I had a sure sense that our position had shifted, that the great tree we rested against had turned a few inches in the earth, and now we viewed the woods from a slightly different perspective.

Burghardt picked up a small hard pinecone from between his legs and angrily hurled it against the trunk of another tree. "Summer's almost over," he said.

"No," I said, "we still got a couple of weeks."

"That's what I mean," he said. "Almost over. Let's go. I'm hungry."

We walked out of the woods, through the field of weeds, and just before we parted ways and headed toward our separate dinners, he said, "You better not tell anybody about me putting you out. Your folks wouldn't like it."

Lainie wouldn't return from Dr. Shanks's office until around two-thirty, so it was just Mother, Daddy, Al, and me for dinner. Mother said the kitchen was simply too hot for human habitation and served bologna sandwiches, potato chips, and ice tea outside at the picnic table under the chinaberry tree. Daddy, Al, and I sat at the table with our shirts off, and I noticed that Al repeatedly glanced down at his own body and occasionally laid his palm against his stomach, testing its hardness. Mother wore khaki slacks and a white sleeveless blouse that allowed a view of her brassiere through the armholes. Al asked Daddy how Daddy's thumb was doing, and Daddy said, "I don't know, why don't we take a look and see."

Daddy began peeling away the adhesive tape on his hand, throwing Mother into a small panic. "Royalton," she cried, "don't you dare remove that bandage and don't you dare remove it at this picnic table."

This tickled both Daddy and Al, and Daddy slowly unwound the gauze with an impish grin on his face. Mother said that if he wanted to risk getting an infection, that was his business, but she was certainly not going to sit there and watch. As she got up from the table, she said, "Come on, Benjamin, you come with me."

Daddy told me to sit still. He said, "The boy just might be interested, Diane, and everybody don't have your weak stomach."

"It has nothing to do with weak stomachs," Mother said. "He just doesn't need to sit here and watch his father make a fool of himself."

"But maybe he wants to watch his father make a fool of hisself," Daddy said. "Did that ever occur to you?"

During this exchange Daddy never looked at Mother or me but concentrated entirely on unraveling the bandage. Mother glared at me as if I'd betrayed her in some way and then strode to the side of the house, where she kept a small patch of sweet william and some phlox, bordered with monkey grass and close to the water faucet. She knelt there in the shade, where the dirt was moist, and busied herself with some unnecessary weeding. I turned back to the table just in time to see all the blood drain from Al's face; he threw his forearm over his eyes and cried, "Oh, God, that's gross, don't look at it, Benny."

But of course I'd already seen. Daddy aimed the thumb at the sky, holding it perfectly still, viewing it from different angles. "Boy," he said, "I very nearly did lose that thumb."

What surprised me most was how extraordinarily fake it looked—a slightly swollen, pinkish-yellow, waxy-looking human thumb, horizontally crosscut near the base by a black line of stitches that pinched and gathered the nearly purple skin nearest the wound—a novelty from a joke shop.

"I think I'm gonna be sick," Al moaned, lowering his head to the table and covering his head with his arms.

"Yes, sir, I sure did very nearly lose it," Daddy said.

After a moment, I said, "What does it feel like?"

Al peered out from under his arms, not lifting his head from the table, and gave me a look that said, Are you crazy? And Daddy allowed his eyes to stray from his thumb for the first time, glancing briefly at me and smiling. It was the same collusive glance he sometimes cast me in the henhouse, if I was watching him perform exploratory surgery on a poor layer. Having wrung its neck and dropped it to the ground, where it flopped around in the shavings like something powered by springs, he waited for it to die, then tore away the breast feathers and opened the chest cavity with his penknife, reached in and pulled out the long tubular craw, split the craw, and fingered the olive-drab half-digested stuff inside it.

Now he touched the tip of his injured thumb with the index finger of his other hand. "It don't feel like nothing, Benbo," he said. "It's numb."

I thought, but didn't say, Numb thumb, and just then Mother called out my name from the house. As I went toward the stoop, where she stood holding a large brown book, I was fascinated by an idea that had popped into my head—because my father's thumb was real, I considered it fake-looking, but had it in fact been fake, I would have considered it remarkably real-looking.

The book Mother held was the *F* volume of *Compton's Encyclopedia*. "I want you to take this down to the tenant house," she said, "and give it to Ole Nezzie."

"You mean, you didn't give it to her yet?" I said.

"Well, Benjamin," she said, "I don't guess I would be standing here in the hot sun holding it in my hands if I'd given it to her already. I wanted to wait awhile. Give her time to forget about the whole thing and then surprise her with it."

What I thought was that Mother was the one who'd forgotten about it. "Well, what if she's not home?" I said.

"If she's not home, it will be fine to leave it on the porch," she said. "I want you to go real slow, walking down there. Try not to get too hot. Put your shirt back on so you won't get burned. And stop at the Big House and get yourself something cool to drink."

I put my shirt on and took the book from her. I didn't plan to get any something-cool at the Big House, but it wasn't necessary for Mother to know that.

Ten minutes later, I encountered the Reverend L. Francis Griffin at the edge of the dried-dirt lane that cut through Daddy Cary's corn-field, a bear of a man not unlike my father but with eyeglasses and a thick black mustache. The sight of him caught me by surprise, not only because it was unexpected but because he happened to be stand-ing around a blind curve. An old Buick with a dull blue finish sat idling just beyond him, and he appeared to have stopped the car and got out of it in order to view something up close in the corn at the edge of the lane. My initial fear, caused by stumbling onto a sizable Negro man unknown to me, evaporated, for I identified him as the preacher at the Negro Baptist church in Farmville, but it was immediately replaced by a less fleeting three-headed alarm: A preacher visiting the tenant house might mean somebody had died, most likely Granny Mays; based on what I'd been told about Mr. Griffin, I didn't anticipate for myself a friendly reception; and I suspected that my father wouldn't have knowingly allowed him onto the property, which meant I hadn't just stumbled onto him, I'd discovered him and felt some shadowy call of duty. I stopped dead in my tracks, about ten feet from where he stood. He pushed his glasses up on his nose and looked at me with half-closed eyes, perhaps himself startled. Then his gaze shifted to the large book cupped in my left hand, and something like recognition crossed his face. He began to smile, crinkling the flesh at the corners of his eyes. In a gravelly voice, he said, "Well, hello there."

He pulled a handkerchief from his hip pocket and patted his brow. When he'd folded the handkerchief and returned it to its pocket, he tugged on a button of his short-sleeved white dress shirt, rapidly pumping the fabric back and forth from his chest seven or eight times, saying, "Whew! And I thought it was hot in town!" He extended his hand toward me and added, "I'm Mr. Griffin, from the First Baptist Church. How do you do?" When I didn't budge, he let his hand drop to his side. He smiled again and said, "Are you on your way to see Mother Mays?"

This question implied an alliance between him and Granny Mays (though I'd never before heard her referred to as *Mother* Mays); it probably meant she was still alive, and it also recalled for me her proximity and my sense of purpose—all of which caused me to relax. I nodded my head.

"Me, too," he said. "I suppose you must live nearby, being as how you've come on foot."

I nodded again. "This here's my granddaddy's cornfield," I said.

This news failed to insinuate any occasion of trespassing but seemed to delight him instead. He arched his eyebrows and pointed to the corn at the edge of the lane. "Well, take a look at this," he said. "I'm no farmer, but I can tell you this corn's in trouble. Look at that, you know what they call that?"

I moved closer.

"You see how the leaves are turned in on themselves? They call that leaf-rolling. It's what the corn does when it's trying to protect itself from the heat. What it does when it doesn't have enough moisture. Yes, I imagine your granddaddy can expect about half his usual yield this year. Funny, isn't it. That's what we humans do when we're trying to keep *warm*, turn in on ourselves like that."

He demonstrated, crossing his arms over his chest, a man shivering for cold. "Thank the Lord for July, is all I can say," he said. "After the June drought and now this hot and dry August. Yes, it's a good thing He saw fit to send us some rain in July."

I told him we'd received 3.37 inches in July, pleased with myself for remembering the exact figure.

"Is that right?" said Mr. Griffin. "Well, it doesn't sound like much when you put a number to it like that. A smaller blessing than I'd supposed. I hope you won't mind if I ask you a question: Is that encyclopedia there in your hand a gift for Mother Mays?"

I didn't think it exactly a gift since it had belonged to her in the first place, so I said, "I'm just returning it to her."

"Oh," he said. "Well, you might find it interesting to take a peek over here into the backseat of my car, see what I'm bringing to her."

I moved to the dusty window of the old Buick and saw on the seat a wooden vegetable crate filled with ragtag books. They looked to be mostly old textbooks, generally banged up, some with covers missing. "You're giving her all these?" I asked.

"Not me," he answered. "I'm just the deliveryman. Word got around that somebody had broken into her house and stolen her books, and first thing you know folks started bringing books over to the church. Depositing them in my office. 'Wasn't it a shame what happened to Mother Mays, Reverend Griffin, and could you see that she gets this if you happen to be out her way?' I'm preacher by title only, you see. My real job is errand boy. I suppose I could have waited till Sunday, but I thought she would be right glad to receive them today."

"She had forty-one in all," I said, "not counting the Bible. I think they were afraid to take the Bible. How many books have you got in that crate?"

"There's only twenty-nine," he said. "But yours makes thirty."

"Maybe some of these books are bigger than the ones she had before," I said.

"That's a positive outlook," said Mr. Griffin. "I just hope she's half as happy to see them as you appear to be right now."

It hadn't occurred to me that I needed to conceal my happiness—I hadn't yet noticed that I was happy—and I didn't know why having it recognized embarrassed me. Mr. Griffin, as if he sensed my embarrassment, quickly said, "Well, I don't know about you, but I'm ready to get out of this sun. You want to ride with me the rest of the way?"

"No, thank you," I said. "It's not far."

"That's using your head," he said, moving to the Buick and opening the driver's door. "Don't get into cars with strangers. I shall see you at the house then."

As I walked the short distance the rest of the way to the tenant house, I thought how polite and intelligent Mr. Griffin had seemed, and I imagined he seemed all the more so because I'd expected him to be otherwise. Aloud, I whispered, "N-double A-C-P," which had always sounded to me like part of a football cheer. Overhead, a colossal gray cloud sailed in front of the sun. The sharp line of its shadow raced toward me straight down the dirt lane, enfolding the entire cornfield as it came, and the moment it fell over me was decidedly thrilling.

I found Mr. Griffin and Granny Mays on the porch. Dressed all in white—white dress, white kerchief—she sat in her rocker, fanning herself with a plain cardboard fan. A small wooden chair had been brought outside for Mr. Griffin, much too small for the appointed task, and the sight of him in it made me think of the Goldilocks story. The crate of books rested near Granny Mays's rocking chair.

In one hand, Mr. Griffin held a jelly glass of what looked like lemonade. "Here he is," he said, as I neared the porch.

Granny Mays said, "It's just who I said it was, Reverend Griffin. I

knew it from your description. Mr. Benjamin Rome. Of R. C. Egg
Farm up the road."

"Now, let me think," said Mr. Griffin, stroking his chin like an actor
in a silent movie. "I wonder what R. C. might stand for. Couldn't be
Royal Crown, because there's already a cola by that name. Could be
Recently Candled, I suppose, or Recently Cracked. Really Charming is
a possibility, but I don't imagine folks want their eggs to be really
charming unless it's Easter."

Granny Mays was quietly giggling and shaking her head at me as if
to say, Ain't he a caution! *Rabid Chicken* rested on the tip of my
tongue, but I was overcome by that special brand of shyness that
attaches to telling jokes. I moved to the edge of the porch, close to
Granny Mays's rocking chair, and handed her up the encyclopedia. I
couldn't help but notice a small feeling of having been outshone by
Mr. Griffin's greater surprise, but I didn't too much mind.

"Why, thank you, Mr. Ben," said Granny Mays, receiving the book
with apparent gladness but placing it immediately on top of the others, in Mr. Griffin's vegetable crate.

"Respectfully Cartoned?" said Mr. Griffin, and Granny Mays giggled
again and waved her hand at him. I'd expected her to ask me how I
came to have the encyclopedia, but she didn't. I meant to defend the
book's importance, however modest, so I said, "It's one of your own,
Granny. They let me and Mother bring it home for you last Monday
from the Presbyterian church."

She laid the fan down on the encyclopedia and looked at me
patiently, almost sypathetically, as if I'd failed to grasp something obvious about the volume of *Compton's*, but she didn't intend to judge me
for it. "Come on up here," she said. "I'm gonna get you a glass of
lemonade." As she entered the house through the screen door, she
said, "It's sweet, sweet, sweet, but I expect you'll like it."

I had just climbed the three worn and shiny wooden steps to the porch when she appeared behind the screen door, pushed it open, and handed me a jelly glass decorated with red and yellow flowers, identical to Mr. Griffin's. "Here you go," she said. "Now, I'll be right back. I got something I want to show both of y'all."

"Why don't you take this little chair, Benjamin," Mr. Griffin said. "I'm gonna move down here and dangle my legs."

I protested, saying I was fine, but he'd already moved, and then it would have seemed rude not to sit. He craned his neck forward and looked up at the sky. "Seems we've been granted a mild reprieve," he said, referring to the huge gray cloud that still blocked the sun.

The lemonade was not adequately cool, as it lacked ice, but it was good all the same. I finished it in four or five gulps and placed the glass on the floor beside my chair. Mr. Griffin drew in his head and said, "Do you know what happened today, Benjamin? We welcomed into the Union the state of Hawaii. Now there'll be fifty stars on the flag."

I was glad to hear this. Ever since Alaska had joined the Union, back in January, the American flag had endured an awkward zigzagged arrangement of forty-nine stars on its field of blue. Now I thought the stars would line up straight again, the way they'd been with forty-eight, but I couldn't think how. I saw immediately that ten rows of five would be too long and narrow.

"It was the Japanese bombing of Pearl Harbor that took us into World War Two," said Mr. Griffin.

And five rows of ten would be too short and wide. My continued silence prompted Mr. Griffin to look at me over his shoulder. "Pearl Harbor's in Hawaii," he said.

The screen door squeaked behind me, and Granny Mays came through it carrying a stack of about a dozen books, which she passed into my hands. I held the books on my lap as she reassumed the rocking chair.

Mr. Griffin turned sideways to the lip of the porch and said, "What are those, Mother Mays?"

"You won't believe me if I told you," she said. "Jerome Sellars brought those over here in his panel truck yesterday evening, and guess where he come by them? In the trash outside the Presbyterian church on Randolph Street. They's every one my own original books, thrown out by those librarians on account of being in too tattered a condition. Those books found their way home to me in just five days' time."

"Granny," I said. "there's eleven books here. That means with my one, and Mr. Griffin's twenty-nine, you have forty-one books again."

Granny Mays looked at me, stunned for a moment, then she leaned her head back against the top rail of the rocker and began to laugh. I didn't recall ever having seen her teeth before, which appeared to be smudged with chocolate or tobacco. After a moment, Mr. Griffin joined her, and it was quite a ruckus, to which I halfheartedly added my fake laugh.

Sooner than I should have, I asked where I might find Burghardt.

Granny Mays brought the rocker to a halt. "Oh, he run off back to the farm," she said, mildly indignant over Burghardt's bad manners. "Took no more than ten minutes to eat his dinner too." She lowered her voice and added, "Said your daddy cut his hand, Mr. Ben, is that true?"

I explained that Daddy and Al had gone into Farmville on Wednesday night to help make six hundred Masonite desktops for the Foundation schools, and that Daddy had nearly cut his thumb off on a jigsaw. Unintentionally, I'd introduced the subject of the school closings. In a distracted tone, Granny Mays said she hoped my daddy's thumb would heal up soon, and then a long silence ensued.

At last Mr. Griffin gave Granny Mays a portentous look and said, "You know we've had ourselves a regular exodus on our hands."

The meaning of this remark, as well as its connection to my father's thumb, eluded me, but Granny Mays nodded and said, "You talking about our teachers."

"Yes, ma'am," said Mr. Griffin. "I've been preaching hope all summer, because I felt it was my duty. But you can't fool the teachers. They'll be finding their hope in another county."

"That's right," said Granny Mays. "Or maybe even in some other state."

Suddenly, brilliant sunshine swamped the clearing around the house, and I said I guessed I better go hunt for Burghardt. I placed the stack of books on the porch floor, and when I said good-bye to Mr. Griffin, he looked at me quite seriously. "Are you and Burghardt good friends?" he asked.

I shrugged my shoulders and said, "I guess so."

He gazed past me. "Reminds me of when I was their age," he said, presumably to Granny Mays, though he faced straight ahead, into the cornfield. "I used to play with some white boys in the empty lot next to our house. Those boys were in and out of my mama's kitchen day and night. We had more fun than you could shake a stick at. And there wasn't any feeling of color between us whatsoever. Not one bit. That's how young we were."

Granny Mays started fanning herself and rocking again. Her eyes took on a distant look, familiar to me, but I didn't know whether she was viewing the past or the future. "Uh-hmm," was all she said, as if she knew exactly what Mr. Griffin meant.

I left the porch and took a few steps into the dirt yard, then turned and said, "Well, what happened?"

Mr. Griffin smiled and removed his eyeglasses, studied them for a moment, blew on one of the lenses, and put them back on. It appeared to me that his eyes had grown misty, but I thought I might have imagined it. "Oh," he said, "their mama came and had a talk with my— well, let's just say this: We all grew up."

Granny Mays repeated her cryptic "Uh-hmm."

"Well, thank you for the lemonade," I said, and headed for the mouth of the hard-packed lane through the cornfield. Granny Mays called out for me to be sure and thank my mother for the book, and I said I would.

Oatsie Montague flagged me down from the Big House, where she was sweeping the front porch. I couldn't imagine why she wasted her time sweeping, when it would be covered with dust again by evening. "Benjamin Rome," she called. "Bring yourself over here a minute."

As I approached the porch, she lifted a tumbler of ice tea from one of the nearby brick pedestals. "Do me a favor, please," she said, "and take this down to the barn for your granddaddy."

I told her I was sorry but I really couldn't spare the time. "I'm running late," I said.

"Late?" she said. "Late for what?"

"Late for work."

She stood up exaggeratedly straight, as if she'd found herself in the presence of royalty. "I *see*," she said. "Well, I guess you sure must be growing up to be a Southside Rome. They always did have their important work to do. No time for trivialities."

I didn't quite know what to make of this remark, though it seemed to stem from her position as Daddy Cary's domestic servant. Its tone brought to mind the ongoing conflict between my mother and my father over the question of whose work was more indispensable—his, running the egg farm, or hers, keeping the house and getting the meals. I noticed that Oatsie had rolled her thin white socks down to her ankles, probably due to the heat, and this made her feet look smaller. She peered into the tumbler of tea. "All the ice is practically melted anyway," she said. "I ought to make him a fresh glass. You want a drink of this one?"

I accepted the tumbler, drank some of the ice-cold watery tea, and thanked her.

"What brings you up here this time of day?" she asked.

"I was delivering something to the tenant house," I said.

She looked across the road at the cornfield. "Who did you see up there?" she asked.

"Granny Mays," I said, and she squinted at me as if she suspected me of lying, though technically my answer had been true.

"It seems like that old woman's been having a lot of company lately," she said. "I thought I heard another car turning up there a while ago."

I shrugged my shoulders. Before I passed the tumbler back to her, I wiped the moisture off it and rubbed my wet fingers over my face. Oatsie smiled at this, then stared at the tea again and shook her head. "Well," she said, "let me go fix him another one. I should've just sent this down to the barn with that little nigger boy, Bogie, when he passed by, but I didn't think I could trust him not to take a sip of it on his way."

She turned and went into the house through the screen porch.

A hundred feet up the road, I slipped into the shade of the apple orchard, for something from the direction of the milking barn had caught my eye—Burghardt coming out the front door. I watched him as he paused for a moment in the barnyard; he'd dropped something, now bent to pick it up, gazed at it in his palm, pocketed whatever it was, and then moved to the steps in the rock wall. I watched him walk up the slope behind the Big House and then angle toward the apple trees. He spotted me when he was about twenty feet away, and he didn't seem at all glad to see me. He kept walking, a pouty look on his face.

I followed him into the road and fell in beside him. "Hey," I said, and he said hey but wouldn't look me in the eye. After we'd walked in silence awhile, I said, "Man, you're sweating."

"So?" he said, as if I'd accused him of something. "It's a hundred degrees."

"It's hot, all right," I said. "What did you have to do in the barn?"

Now he scowled at me. "What were you doing hiding out under that apple tree?"

"I wasn't hiding," I said. "I just stopped a minute for some shade."

"Well, what are you doing down here anyway?"

I explained about the book, and then it occurred to me that he would be glad to know what book it was. "It's the encyclopedia with the flags of the world in it," I said.

"That's good," he said, but he sounded as if he didn't really care.

A car appeared in the road ahead, coming toward us, and we moved to opposite sides. The car slowed as it passed between us, and though I didn't recognize it or the driver, I waved at the man behind the wheel and Burghardt lowered his head, which was the country way. The driver waved back at me and never looked at Burghardt.

I desisted from asking Burghardt any more questions, as he clearly didn't welcome them, and we mostly had a normal afternoon getting our chores done, marking cards and pulling down eggs in the cage houses. If he was quieter than usual, that suited me, for the heat had made me dull and sluggish. Around four o'clock, I thought the day would start to cool down, but instead, it seemed that heat had stored itself in the earth and was now emanating back out. In the henhouses the odors of the soft-hot asphalt roofing and the creosote posts overwhelmed even the stink of chicken manure.

As we were finishing up in the last of the cage houses, Julius arrived with no evident purpose and followed us along in the aisle yammering about what a damaging effect this kind of heat had on egg production. When he reminded us to be sure to clean the waterers again in the ground-bird houses, Burghardt snapped, "We know what our chores is. You don't need to come around checking on us."

Julius, taken aback, said, "Nobody's checking on you, son. I'm just remind—"

"We don't need any reminding," Burghardt said.

"Well, all right, all right," said Julius. "You know, Mr. R.C. just—"

"Mr. R.C. just *what?*" snarled Burghardt.

"Pray tell what's eating on you, son?"

Burghardt gave Julius a look so cold it was almost as if he wanted him dead. Julius said, "Excuse us, Mr. Ben," and pointed up the aisle, indicating for Burghardt to march in that direction. As they moved away, I overheard Burghardt say, "I'm sick and tired of what Mr. R.C.—" and Julius gently pushed him forward with a finger in the middle of his back, then turned and looked briefly at me. I felt foolish, perched on my bucket and gaping, and resumed marking cards.

Julius escorted Burghardt to the break in the cages at the middle of the house. Burghardt stood silently, hands in his pockets, his weight shifted onto one foot, his head tilted to one side, barely tolerating what Julius had to say to him. When Julius was done, Burghardt spun around without a word and stalked back down the aisle toward me. Julius remained at the middle of the henhouse for a minute, staring at Burghardt's back, then removed his yellow baseball cap, wiped his head with his hand, and left.

All I could think was how hard my father would whip me if I spoke to him the way Burghardt had spoken to Julius, but I didn't think it beneficial to share my thoughts. Burghardt's impudence hadn't shocked me so much as Julius's tame response. I supposed that Julius had had the last word, in his own quiet way, but Burghardt's steely withdrawal had been a kind of last word too.

Burghardt worked silently, at top speed, finishing his side, then called out from the end of the aisle, "I'll meet you in House A."

I marked the remaining cards quickly and didn't take the time to pull down any eggs. Burghardt's curious behavior had aroused my spying instinct. I recalled lying on the bed during Daddy Cary's party, suddenly drawn by a glowing keyhole. Likewise now, I expected something interesting, if only I could get over to House A soon enough and quiet enough.

I walked as fast as possible without scaring the chickens. When I turned into the lane between the first two ground-bird houses, I slowed down and moved into the shade under the eaves of House A. When the feed room came into view, I crouched close to the ground, against the wire wall of the building. The little cagelike enclosure, seen this way through two meshes of chicken wire, was dusky, but I could make out, clearly enough, Burghardt inside it: He'd climbed onto the stacked burlap sacks of feed and stood with his back to me; he was reaching into one of the high recesses where the building's joists met the wooden frame of the feed room, into one of the small dark rectangular slots where I imagined rats nested. Either he'd just stowed something there or taken something away, for now he removed his hand, turned, stooped, and leaped down. I waited for a minute, crouched beneath the eaves, before I duck-waddled into the middle of the alley and pretended to shake a stone from my shoe.

At supper that evening, also served outdoors at the picnic table, Mother complained, with a pointed lack of energy, that we might have been dining in the air-conditioned comfort of our own living room if only a person could humanly eat while enduring the nasty odor of unwashed eggs. Al had gone home, to town, without staying for supper, but Lainie was reluctantly putting in an appearance. She wore the unflattering sack dress she'd worn to Daddy Cary's birthday party, and she had her hair in a ponytail, which she kept pulling over one shoulder and running her fingers through, as if it somehow comforted her to do so. Mother told her to stop that or she would end up with hair in her food. Supper was cold ham, slices of loaf bread smeared with margarine, and Mother's horrible version of slaw: lettuce and tomatoes mixed in mayonnaise. Lainie, who had no appetite, said the heat was actually making her ill, and Mother said Lainie could have taken refuge in the cool comfort of our own living room if it weren't overrun with baskets of stinking eggs. Mother sometimes got locked into a theme this way—Daddy had once said she liked to drive a stick into the ground and break it off, an analogy I grasped intuitively though I'd never seen anyone actually do that with a stick. Mother asked me if I'd taken Ole Nezzie her encyclopedia, and I said I had, calling to mind the Reverend Griffin resting on the tenant-house porch; I looked across the table at Daddy and felt a peculiar thrill over his not knowing that such an infamous black rascal had violated the Rome property. Daddy, hunched over his plate in a clean white undershirt, pointed out that there wasn't no sense in giving books to niggers since all they cared about was drinking and dancing, shooting pool and carrying on. "You know what they say," he said, smiling directly at Lainie. "Be a nigger on a Saturday night and you won't never want to be white agin." Lainie beamed a sugary sarcastic smile at Daddy but otherwise didn't respond. A minute later, as Daddy was rolling a slice of loaf bread into a little four-inch tube and inserting it whole into his mouth, I caught Lainie watching him with utter hopelessness, and Daddy suddenly looked at the new bandage on his hand and said, "This dressing you put on my thumb is too fat, Diane."

At that moment, Mother appeared to have wandered in her mind a bit too far to be fully retrieved. She stared absently at the road, her face turned away from Daddy, then said, "I'm sorry, Royalton," as if she'd added the bandaging to a checklist of her possible failings but would have to evaluate it at some later time.

I asked Lainie if she wanted to go swimming, and she looked at me wide-eyed. "Yes," she said, standing up from the table. "But can we go this very instant?"

"Sure," I said. "Let's go."

"Doesn't that sound like a good idea!" Mother said.

Lainie, who'd already taken a couple of steps away from the table, stopped. "Do you want to come, Mother?"

"Oh, no, thank you," said Mother. "I'll just stay here and clean up."

Lainie rolled her eyes. "You can come if you want to," she said. "We can clean up when we get back."

"No, no, no," Mother said. "Y'all go on and go. I wouldn't even know where to look for my suit. Just watch out for snakes this time of day down there. It wouldn't do for you to get bitten, Lainie."

Lainie said, "Fine," and began walking toward the house. I trotted to catch up to her. As we climbed the stoop side by side, she said, "She means I shouldn't let a snake bite me in my delicate condition. It's okay if one bites you, Ben. Since you're not pregnant."

Once we'd lost sight of the house, Lainie allowed me to drive the Willys the rest of the way to the creek. She placed our two folded towels on the seat to provide me a few extra inches in height—a tricky balance to strike, since the better my view over the dashboard, the poorer my contact with the foot pedals. It had been nearly a month since I'd last driven the Willys, but I did fairly well, stalling the car only once, on the way to the creek, and grinding the gears once between first and second. I balked at the bridge, though I knew it was plenty wide for the car and I had no trouble steering straight; the bridge lacked any railings and I dreaded the moment when the car seemed suspended in midair over the water. Lainie and I switched places again, and she took us over the bridge and parked the car on the other side.

The creek, so low we had to wade to the middle and bring our knees up to our shoulders in order to get fully wet, was warm but refreshing and less muddy than usual. Something about its being completely in shade this time of day—the absence of any contrasting patches of sun and shadow—made it seem more peaceful than usual, too. We found that by crouching in the water and anchoring ourselves in one spot, then facing upstream and closing our eyes, we could create the illusion of forward motion. After we'd done that for a minute or two, there was little else to do, and Lainie looked at me and shrugged her shoulders. I said, "It feels good," but we were both surprised at how quickly we were ready to get out.

We spread the towels on the gravel to one side of the bridge, and I sat and hugged my knees as Lainie stretched out flat on her back. I allowed my eyes briefly to roam her body, hoping for some sign of her pregnancy, but I saw only a slight bulge in her swimsuit just below her waist—less than irrefutable evidence. She drew one leg up, crooked at the knee, and shifted onto her side, facing me. "Ben," she said, "are you aware that I'm going completely out of my mind?"

Her eyes were closed, her face expressionless. The question made me uneasy, for it reminded me of my earlier vision of her and her new family living in the Willys, miserable, parked somewhere in the woods. I said, "Sort of, I guess."

She opened her eyes and smiled. "I'm sorry," she said. "I'm not going to think about that now. It's nice here. Maybe you and I could just stay and stay and not ever go home."

"They'd come find us," I said.

"Oh, I know they would," she said dreamily. After a minute, she said, "Wouldn't you know it—*now* I'm hungry."

"Daddy Cary let Burghardt fire his pistol from up there on the bridge," I said, not quite sure why I'd said it.

"Is that so?" Lainie said.

"I didn't want to shoot it," I said.

"I don't blame you."

"Do you think Burghardt's going away?"

Now Lainie raised up on one elbow. "What makes you ask that, Ben?"

"I don't know," I said. "Just a feeling."

"Has he said anything about going away?"

"No," I answered, "but I found out today that Granny Mays got her books back."

"Really," Lainie said. "How did that happen?"

I explained about people bringing books to the Baptist church, about the eleven that were found in the trash outside the Presbyterian assembly hall, and about the amazing fluke of her ending up with the same number she'd had before.

"She better keep a close eye on those books," said Lainie. "At least until this private school foolishness is over. We're talking real fanaticism here, Ben. If those scoundrels didn't feel any moral compunction about stealing a poor old colored woman's books once, they won't feel any about doing it twice. They'd see it as a good deed and go to church on Sunday thinking what model Christians they were."

I didn't believe Frank and Shelby O'Bannon thought themselves model Christians, but they did probably consider themselves to have done a good deed. I mentioned that Hawaii had become the fiftieth state today.

Lainie lowered her head again to the towel and closed her eyes. "I heard," she said. "Maybe we should go and live there."

"How do you think they'll fit fifty stars on the flag?" I asked.

"Five rows of six and four rows of five," she answered, bored and sleepy.

I did the necessary multiplication and saw that Lainie's answer did in fact add up to fifty. Distracted by the occasional leaf floating by in the creek, I struggled to picture in my mind the flag's new arrangement of stars, and soon I couldn't tell how much time had passed. Lainie appeared to be sleeping. After a while, sleepily, she said, "They're all so selfish."

It sounded like a pronouncement from a dream. Quietly, as if she'd truly spoken in her sleep and I didn't want to wake her, I said, "Who?"

She rolled onto her other side, now facing away from me. Once settled again, she whispered, "Everybody."

As she dozed, I stood guard, watching out for snakes, and some minutes later, unaware that any time had gone by, she sat up and said, "Hey, let's go, what do you say?"

I drove us home once we crossed the bridge but stopped fifty yards short of the house. Once Lainie had parked the Willys outside her private entrance under the pecan tree, she smiled and said, "Thanks, Benny boy." At first I couldn't think what she meant, but then I recalled that it had been my idea to go to the creek. I was barefoot and shirtless, wearing damp swim trunks, and, for the first time all day, cool.

Lainie paused on the little brick stoop outside her door. "Aren't you coming in?" she asked.

"I'm going to walk over to the henhouses for a minute," I said. "I need to check on something."

"Check on what?"

"I think I might have forgotten something."

"Forgotten what?"

"Just something," I said.

She looked at me suspiciously. "Ben," she said, "come here."

She sat on the stoop. I moved closer so our faces were at the same level. "You're worried about Bogie on account of the schools closing, aren't you?" she said. "That's why you had a feeling he might be going away."

I was immediately relieved to be asked this question, not because I'd been waiting for someone to ask it, not because it named the exact thing I was most worried about, but simply because it narrowed the vast field of my worries. It whittled my mountain to a molehill, and for a moment I thought, Yes, that's what I'm worried about! Before I answered, Lainie took my silence as consent. She said, "Worrying isn't going to change things, Benny. Just remember that the R. C. Romes of the world and the Al Romes—well, okay, let's leave Al out of it, give him the benefit of the doubt. The Barrye Walls and the Roy Pearsons and Robert Crawfords of the world . . . they won't always be in charge."

I nodded, though I couldn't see how this helped Burghardt any.

Lainie, satisfied that she'd offered a ray of hope where there had been only gloom, stood and turned to enter the house. As she opened the door, she must have had misgivings about her own slip into optimism. With her back to me, she said, "Just so long as we don't blow ourselves up first."

A universal glow of pale gold bathed the sky overhead, but by the time I reached House A, the interior lights had already turned themselves on in the henhouses. (The lights were set on automatic timers—scientific research had shown that extended "daylight" hours could increase egg production; they would turn themselves off around 10 P.M.) I opened the feed-room door and banged it a few times to scare away any early prowling rats. Inside, I found one of the toilet brushes we used for cleaning the waterers. This in hand, I climbed aboard the bulging sacks of feed. Before I began to explore the rafter above me with my bare hand, I knocked the wooden handle of the toilet brush against the frame. Tentatively, I ran my fingers along the edge of the rafter, producing no intelligence of any kind. I went up on tiptoe and put my hand into first one of the dark recesses and then another. In the first I found only cobwebs and dust. In the second, I found Burghardt's half deck of pornographic playing cards, bound with a green rubber band, and four silver dollars.

I didn't go through the cards, partly from fear of disordering them but mostly from the shame of my easy success. I put everything back, climbed down from the feed sacks, and left the henhouse.

On the way home, I paused at the top of a knoll, where the dirt path ran alongside a barbed-wire fence. I placed my hands on the wire, each palm over a barb, and pressed as hard as I dared, just to the point of pain. I faced an open field, overgrown with goldenrod and milkweed and clover. From here you could see where Rome Road cut across the property—there was a sudden rupture of low shrubs—but not the road itself. Then more open pasture, then woods. The orchard, the Big

House, Daddy Cary's cornfield, and the tenant house lay beyond, though none of these was visible, then more woods. The sun, having done its worst, had set some minutes before. An array of flat clouds rose from behind the farthest tree line, brown, and fiery on their undersides like half-burnt timbers. In a moment, a ribbed fan of white light opened over the sky, then faded away. I felt some of the cool sad distance I'd felt earlier in the day, when Burghardt had "put me out"; the walloping beauty of the sunset had squeezed my chest and I was gone but not gone, gripping a fence, a bit breathless, as life went on, hugely, grandly, without me.

10

THE NEXT DAY the mercury rose to 101, and I honestly believed I could feel that extra degree under my skin. In the afternoon, after dinner, I went to the woods with the intention of waiting for Granny Mays to make an appearance. I figured that if the theft of her books had caused a break in her speaking, she might resume it now that the books had in some fashion been restored. As I approached the spot, I saw through the trees that she'd already arrived. There was no chance of slipping into the rusty oil drum without her hearing me—it would have been too hot inside there anyway—so I detoured around the perimeter of the clearing and sneaked up on the other side of the abandoned Plymouth. I lay in the dirt and dry pine needles next to the car, which was comfortable enough, but since the Plymouth's flat decaying tires lifted it only five inches off the ground, my view was limited to Granny Mays's feet and ankles and the four legs of the chair she was sitting in. She wore the brown leather shoes she always wore and thin white socks, neatly cuffed. She continued to sit in silence for another minute or two, and when at last she spoke, she seemed to take up where she'd left off before I arrived. "Yes, sir," she said, "my mama's coming through loud and clear this hot afternoon. 'Child,' she says to me—I can hear her plain as day—'is that what you think? You think they sit around the breakfast table dreaming up ways to hurt you?' And she says to me, 'Sugar, you ain't on their mind at all, and that's a primary difference too, between us and them. Here we thinking about white folks sunup to sundown—what is it they like, and what is it they don't like, and what in the world is they gonna do next?—and they don't give us a single solitary thought. They don't have to think up ways to hurt you,' she says. 'Not when they can hurt you by not thinking at all.' That's what my dead mama says to me this afternoon while I'm sitting in this hard old chair in the woods. And she says, 'Don't fret, don't fly off the handle,' all that. 'Wash up, eat light, save your mind for what matters; a tree falls the way it leans.' All that."

Next I heard the sound of Granny Mays's laughter, and she added, "Yes, she is sure coming through this afternoon."

I saw both her feet shift to one side, as if she was rearranging herself in the chair, and then she crossed her ankles and grew perfectly still again. Now she remained silent for such a long time, I was on the brink of dozing off, and her next remark jolted me. "They never did like to spend the money," she said. "You know their heart wasn't in it from the start. 'Why waste the money when they gonna end up vocational anyway?' they'd say. 'And with all that on-the-farm training at their disposal? Why waste the money?' All right! This is how it's gonna be, no schools for a spell. It would not have been my chosen path; I don't mind saying it out loud, it would not have been my chosen path. But it's the one You done laid down. In Your wisdom, I suppose. It's how it's gonna be. I mean to do everything I can, my very best with him, rest assured. But You got to help keep him interested. You got to help keep himself applied. And You got to help me with Julius, too, and his wrong thinking. I got interference enough without that. And You got to keep me alive long enough and please please please remove from me my doubts. I would imagine that ought to be a right sight easier than parting the Red Sea. Remove from me my doubts and amen!"

Now she sighed deeply. I watched beneath the car as she uncrossed her ankles and planted her shoes firmly on the ground in front of the chair. Then suddenly the pair of feet turned and started to move in the direction of the Plymouth. All I could think to do was to close my eyes and pretend to be asleep, which I did for a moment; but immediately I feared she might take me for dead lying there on the ground and it might cause her to have a stroke. Hadn't I just heard her praying to be kept alive long enough to furnish Burghardt with his education? And now my foolish spying was to be the reason for her untimely death. I opened my eyes and saw with great relief that she'd turned again and was moving away. At first I could see more and more of her—the hem of a white skirt, the waist, the small of her back—and then she disappeared behind some trees.

I laid my head flat on the ground. "Amen," I whispered into the pine needles, "and now I'm gonna leave this off in my mind."

The evening before, when I'd felt a sting of shame over having so easily sniffed out Burghardt's cards and silver dollars in the feed room, I'd also met my first clear moral scruple with regards to spying. I'd imagined I might one day witness something truly important—meaning something adults would find useful—and thereby bring importance to myself. But part of me dreaded such an occasion too, the same part of me that sometimes imagined revealing myself to Granny Mays in the junkyard. For all its drawing power, the way of secret knowledge (and the methods of acquiring it) was a lonely business and needed constant watching over. I didn't honestly prefer it to a different way I'd known for a very short while some years earlier, a way I couldn't have named, for I'd never heard its name spoken: candor, whose root is found in the Latin verb *candere*, meaning to shine or to glow. When I crouched in shadows and pricked up my ears, when I glimpsed bits of human conduct bound by the curved margins of peepholes or key-holes, I surely felt a thrill of adventure. I even took pride at my evident God-given instinct for the avocation, but I wasn't sure I wanted to get especially good at it. And it was these conflicting feelings, rather than any simple fear of being discovered a snoop, that accounted for my racing heart as I lay in bed that last week of August and first began to picture myself hiding out in the hayloft of Daddy Cary's barn. It accounted also for my allowing a week and a half to pass before I actu-ally put myself in that position.

During those long continuously hot days, it seemed to me that Burghardt, withdrawn and cranky, was only going through the motions of his morning and afternoon chores. I had the impression from time to time that he was biting his tongue, both with me and with Julius, if Julius happened to be around. He stalled in his work as usual, so as not to get too far ahead of me, but now he did it without any cheer, as if stalling was just another of his chores. More than once I asked him what the matter was, but he looked at me as if the question had come from out of the blue and somehow offended him. "Nothing," he would say, indignantly.

On Tuesday the first of September, Al stayed to supper, which Mother served in the kitchen, since the temperature outdoors had dropped to a chilly 88 degrees. Al placed the window fan on top of the deep freeze and aimed it directly at the table, so we were obliged to cling to our napkins, and the pages of Daddy's *Herald* rattled in the wind. Mother was trying out a new dish on us, a casserole of chicken pieces, egg noodles, green peas, and Campbell's cream-of-mushroom soup. Repeatedly she solicited compliments from us on the dish, which meant that she herself didn't find it very appetizing. She would take a bite gingerly, then say, "M-m-m, I think that's pretty tasty, what do y'all think?" "Uh-oh, I think I might've got it too salty." "*H-m-m,* do y'all think it could've used more chicken and less noodles?"

It was understood that Mother's questions were not directed at Daddy, for he never responded to such things, and besides, Daddy happily ate most any food that was placed before him. But three or four times Al and I said the dish was good, even though I thought to myself that Mother had either added something or neglected to add something that caused the casserole to be gluey. Lainie said it was fine but that she was just not very hungry, then, at a moment when nobody was looking at her but me, she pantomimed an episode of severe gagging.

From the *Herald,* Daddy read to us a long excerpt of a speech that Senator Harry F. Byrd had made over the weekend at his annual Apple Orchard Picnic. Given my overabundance of experience with chickens and my disdain for them, I'd always found it amusing that people were actually named Byrd. It especially amused me that some poor soul had suffered through life with the name of "Hairy Bird," and I couldn't understand how he could have been elected to any significant office. But Daddy, along with J. Barrye Wall, Sr., was flattered that the senator had devoted the better part of his Apple Orchard Picnic speech to the goings-on in Prince Edward. Mr. Byrd summarized the history of the NAACP's effort to integrate our schools and called Sterling Hutcheson "the great and able Virginia judge." He praised white Prince Edward for establishing a system of private education that availed itself of not a single public facility, bus, or piece of equipment—which wasn't quite accurate, since buses and equipment both had been purchased from the public schools at cut rates. He said the NAACP had "deliberately and maliciously" forced Prince Edward to close its schools but then said in the next breath that "the action that Prince Edward has taken is courageous, and it was thoughtfully and well considered." I couldn't see how it was courageous to do something you were deliberately and maliciously forced to do. Senator Byrd ended his remarks about Prince Edward's heroes with "They are true to the faith of their fathers," borrowing some words from the famous church hymn and implying, as many had before him, that racial segregation was a Christian principle.

When Daddy finished reading, Al looked at me and said, "Hey, Ben, what's eating on your friend Bogie?"

I said I didn't know what Al meant. Daddy set the newspaper aside for a moment and inspected his thumb; he'd had the stitches out a few days before and now wore only a small bandage, which had got smudged black with ink.

"I mean," said Al, "that your friend is starting to adopt an attitude."

I said again that I didn't know what he meant.

Mother said, "I'm sure it's the heat, Al. If I was inclined to adopt attitudes I would certainly have adopted one these last few days. When it stays this hot this long, a lot of people just get plain irritable."

Lainie said she wondered what Mother was going to blame everything on come fall, when it cooled down, and Mother said that kind of remark was a perfect example of what she was talking about.

The glowing ceramic faces of the two Negro children on the wall behind Mother's stove—the pot-holder holders—caught my attention. I sometimes had the feeling that their wide-eyed perpetual happiness mocked what went on at our supper table. There was a sudden glint of light on their rosy cheeks, and I noticed that the windows behind the kitchen sink were unusually dark. In that same moment, Lainie said, "Was that *lightning*?"

We were up and out the back door in three seconds flat. There was a distant roll of thunder. It was raining.

Al began leaping around in the oyster-shell driveway, whooping like a wild man, which upset the dogs, and Lainie stood in one spot, her arms outstretched like Jesus on the cross, slowly turning, her face aimed at the sky. I pulled my T-shirt off, twirled it over my head, and then began sprinting in a figure eight that encircled Al and Lainie again and again. Mother came to the porch stoop, a section of the *Herald* tented over her head, and yelled for Lainie to come back inside this instant, she expected this kind of behavior from boys but not from a grown woman, and certainly not a grown woman who was with child. Soon the rain came down so hard and loud that it drowned out all but the general noise of Mother's complaint, a kind of high-pitched yelping that fit nicely with the racket the dogs were making. Lainie continued her slow ballerina turns, not even glancing in the direction of the stoop, and then Mother threw down the newspaper, marched out into the yard, and grabbed her by one arm. Al and I stopped to watch. Lainie, wet and slippery, easily yanked herself free of Mother's grip, but Mother, who looked immediately bedraggled in the rain, went for Lainie's other arm. Her hand slid briskly down Lainie's forearm to the wrist, and for a moment they appeared to be dancing. Lainie pried Mother's fingers from her wrist and took off running. Mother chased her, Lainie shrieking with laughter, and they made three full revolutions of the dog pen before Mother stalked back to the stoop and climbed the steps. Just before going through porch door, she turned a miserable face to us. She let the door slam behind her, and the three of us stood side by side in the rain, gazing silently at the stoop. Quietly, Lainie said, "Was she actually truly crying?" and Al did something I hadn't seen him do in a long time—he put his arm around Lainie.

"I think so," he said, "but I wouldn't worry too much about it." With his free hand he wiped rainwater from his eyes and added, "Nothing dries quicker than tears."

When we returned soggy to the kitchen, Mother was nowhere to be seen. Daddy sat at the table swirling the ice in his glass of tea and reading the *Herald*, apparently never having moved from his chair.

The weatherman measured the rainfall we received that first day of September at .63 inches. The next afternoon, while I was hiding out in the hayloft of Daddy Cary's barn, we got .22 inches more.

———

The trickiest part was getting into the barn undetected. I knew I couldn't simply walk up the road, stroll through the orchard, and enter the barn through the front door. I also had to get there early enough so as not to encounter Daddy Cary already inside. For three days, following dinner, I trudged through the woods the half mile to the pasture behind the barn, emerged with the barn itself blocking any view that might be had of me from the Big House, and sneaked in the back door by the manure pit. Once I'd climbed the stairs to the loft, I experimented with the gaps between the wide gray-veined planks until I found the position from which I could see the most. Still, what I could see below was awfully limited, and I knew that once I got settled I would have to stay that way; for fear of being heard I didn't dare risk moving from one spot to another. I lay prone, parallel to the planks in such a way that, by changing the angle of my head, I could view the stalls below through two different gaps. Through one gap I could see the central ridge of Dorothy Malone's spine and the full bellows of her stomach, hipbones, and tail; a joist interrupted my view of her head. Through the other, I could see the divider gate between the two stalls, a good part of the concrete floor on either side of the divider, and about half of Honey.

The first day, the sound of the rain on the barn's roof was so pleasant that I nearly fell asleep, and then I was drawn outdoors by it—I left before Daddy Cary ever showed up for the afternoon milking. I walked back home the way I'd come, through the piney woods; the rain was too gentle to penetrate the cover of the pines directly, but it collected in the needles overhead and fell in huge heavy drops that made splatter stains on the forest floor. At home, I noticed that the additional rain had put both Mother and Daddy into a good mood. Daddy, at his desk on the back porch, greeted me by sailing a paper airplane at my head, and Mother hugged me in the doorway to the kitchen. She asked me where I'd disappeared to in such a hurry after dinner, and I said I'd just taken a walk in the rain—an answer that caused Mother to smile but Daddy to snort through his nose, and I added walks in the rain to my list of unmanly pastimes. I'd noted Lainie's Willys parked at the side of the house, which meant she'd returned home from Dr. Shanks's office, so I wandered down the hallway to her room. I found her standing close to her window, leaning forward and resting her chin on the top rail of the inner sash, right next to the lock. When she heard me behind her, she drew her face away, and I saw that her breath had left its ghost on the glass, a pattern of twin shapes that resembled lungs. She turned and looked at me, and I could see that her window-pane thoughts had been low and troublesome.

Without a hint of surprise, she said, "Ben, can I ask you a question?"

"Sure," I said, and sat on the edge of her bed.

"Tell me the honest truth," she said. "Do you think I'm a bad person?"

"No," I said. "I think you're good."

"But what if I did something really bad?" she said. "Worse than anything I've ever done before."

"Like what?" I said.

"I don't know," she said, "something really selfish."

I thought this surely had to do with Claud Wayne and wondered if maybe she'd met somebody in town, a boy, and he'd asked her on a date. I said, "You're not selfish. What about the time you let Oatsie Montague have your favorite silk scarf after her sister died?"

Lainie gave me the kind of forgiving smile that meant that though she was making no headway here, she wouldn't hold it against me. She said, "Are you sitting on my bed with wet shorts on?"

The next day, I returned to the hayloft, remained there long enough for Daddy Cary to show up, and thoroughly regretted it. I had to stay perfectly still throughout the milking of both cows, my right leg fell asleep, and just when I thought things couldn't get any more uncomfortable, his cigar smoke drifted straight into the gap I was looking through and I had to bury my face in my arms and hold my breath to keep from coughing. Afterward I resolved not to return—I resolved to abandon the whole idea—but somehow, after dinner on Friday, I found myself creeping through the woods again. In my late-night musings about the hayloft, I'd pondered the moral unease of choosing unwisely, of pursuing actions against my better judgment, but I hadn't envisioned the practical aftermath of seeing what I expected to see. I had, however, entertained from time to time the fear of getting more than I bargained for—which was what happened on Friday.

Daddy Cary had already finished with Dorothy Malone and climbed the divider gate into the other stall. He'd reached over the front gate and slid the manger along the feed passage so it was available to Honey. He'd pulled the milking stool up alongside her and sat down when I heard the barn door open and everything was flooded with light and swallowed instantly in darkness, as if a flashbulb had gone off. For a moment I could see nothing through the gap but drifting, overlapping afterimages. Daddy Cary had stood up, and now he tossed the stub of his cigar to the floor of the stall and twisted it out with his boot, leaving a small brown star of tobacco on the concrete. Soft and high, he sang, "Bohhhhh-gie, Bogie, Bogie, Bogie," and put his hands into the pockets of his overalls. I heard a jingle of silver, and then he stepped forward toward the front of the stall, where my view was cut off by the joist below. I craned my neck in hopes of seeing beyond the joist, but the gap on the other side of it was only a hairline of gray light. I had to content myself with a long narrow rectangle in which I could see the milking stool, the right side of Honey's belly, her right ear, and the back of Daddy Cary's legs. Then even the legs disappeared, as he mounted the rungs of the gate and climbed out of the stall. I followed the shuffle of footsteps and determined that he'd moved into one of the gateless unused stalls on the other side of the feed passage. I lay still and tried to decide what to do. I imagined myself combat-crawling forward along the planks until I was above the other stalls, but whatever business was being conducted below, its lone symptom was a paralyzing silence—no word, no sigh, no audible inspiration of human breath—and I couldn't bring myself to move a muscle.

During this stillness, I thought of my fourth-grade classroom and its wall of windows, and how pupils who owned hula hoops had been allowed to bring them to school and store them on the levers that operated the windows—how beautiful the many colors of perfectly round hoops had looked, lit by daylight. I lamented the prospect of a fifth-grade year in Hubbard House, owned by, and located behind, the Baptist church; how could you have school in a *house*? Then the barn door flew open again, sunlight flashed through the gaps between the the loft planks and up the well of the stairs, I heard Julius say, "Lord Almighty, Mr. Rome, what—" and the door banged shut with a crack that sounded like the report of a rifle. As I swiftly moved on all fours toward the stairs, I heard Daddy Cary say, "Now git on out from here, Julius!"

On my belly, I eased myself forward over the lip of the opening in the loft floor where the stairs rose. Gripping the edge of the floor with both hands, I hung my head over, and the rest of what I witnessed was seen upside down: Burghardt raced along the feed passage, past Julius, and out the door, as Julius, his back to the passage, lifted the crossbar from Dorothy Malone's stall, the two-by-four that secured the gate; Daddy Cary moved toward Julius, saying, "I said git on out from here," and when Julius wheeled around, wielding the timber like a baseball bat, both men froze for a second; then Julius said, "I'm sorry, Mr. Rome, but I got to hit you," and swung away.

Of course I have seen this moment in my mind a hundred times, but I've never been entirely successful at turning it right side up. As Daddy Cary collapsed to the floor, he appeared to accordion into a concrete ceiling. Recalling the event, I never doubted that Julius meant to hit Daddy Cary with the two-by-four—he formally announced his intention—but I believe he swung for Daddy Cary's shoulder, or perhaps imagined that Daddy Cary would turn his back to the blow. But what Daddy Cary did instead was to duck, and the sharp edge of the timber caught him squarely on the upper left corner of his brow. Because Daddy Cary ducked, it appeared that his dropping to the floor was independent of the coincidental impact of the two-by-four. Shocked, Julius stared in disbelief at Daddy Cary on the concrete near his feet; he let the two-by-four drop to the floor and shifted his gaze to it, as if to see what could have caused such a thundering racket. Then he stepped backward three paces, turned, and hurried out the barn door, closing it noiselessly in his usual manner.

With one nudge of her head, Dorothy Malone pushed the unbarricaded stall gate over. She only meant to get to the hay in Honey's manger, but she had to step onto the fallen gate to get there, which now lay on Daddy Cary. As she moved, clumsy and frightened, over the teetering gate, trapping for an instant one hoof between the rungs, she pressed the breath out of Daddy Cary, and he expelled a raspy moan that contained a strange note of pleasure.

Somehow I got down the stairs into the feed passage. Somehow I made myself look at Daddy Cary—one side of his face rested on the nasty concrete next to the manure gutter—and in the next moment I was dashing through the barnyard, headed for the Big House and shouting, "Julius killed Daddy Cary! Julius killed Daddy Cary!" Any misgivings I might have had about incriminating somebody I liked, who'd ridded the world of somebody I hated, had been defeated by the sight of blood trickling down Daddy Cary's brow and pooling on the floor around his head.

Oatsie Montague met me in the yard and made me repeat "Julius killed Daddy Cary" five more times until she'd turned crystal white like salt and started waving her hands in the air over her head. Her feet twice left the ground, and then she told me to run inside the house and use the telephone. She said to call my daddy, that he would know what to do, and then she took off for the barn. Inside the living room, I found the phone and gave the operator our number. Mother answered, and I told her that Julius had killed Daddy Cary in the milking barn and that Oatsie Montague had said Daddy would know what to do. Mother told me to sit right there by the telephone and to stay put, which is what I did.

For about three or four minutes, before I heard the roar of automobile engines outside, it seemed to me that the colored race had fulfilled the lifelong promise I'd always been told it would—in the person of Julius Mays, it had risen up in violence against the white man—and briefly I welcomed this simpler, predictable world. But when I heard the screen door slam on the side porch and saw Al appear in the living room doorway, when my father loomed up behind him, shotgun in hand, the world quickly resumed its complicated nature. Over the next several hours, it would muddle in ways I couldn't have imagined, and by the end of the day, that very quality of life—that it was sometimes unimaginable—would feel oddly familiar.

Daddy Cary was not dead, that much was quickly determined. He'd suffered a serious blow to the head, however, and Daddy and Al put him into the backseat of Daddy's Impala and rushed him to the hospital. All the men were gone in a matter of five or ten minutes, so it was the women—Mother, Lainie, and Oatsie Montague—to whom I was required to give a detailed account of what had happened. They sat me down in a rattan chair on the screen porch and began to question me; my story, revised and expurgated, made almost no sense. First I said I'd gone to the barn to look for Al. Mother reminded me that Al had been sitting at the picnic table when I left the house after dinner. So I said I *meant* I'd gone to the barn to look for Burghardt. I said I'd climbed up into the hayloft to look for him, and while I was up there, Julius had come into the barn and hit Daddy Cary in the head with a two-by-four.

Mother said, "Why would he do such a thing? Did they have an argument?"

"Yes," I said. "A bad argument."

Lainie, still dressed in her white receptionist smock and slacks and nurse's shoes, said, "About what?"

"I don't remember."

"You don't remember?"

"Lainie," Mother said, "don't badger him. He's clearly had a shock."

Lainie said, "So Daddy Cary was already in the barn when you got there. You went up to the loft, and Julius came while you were up there and started an argument with Daddy Cary."

I nodded.

"Well, if you were in the hayloft, how did you see Julius hit him with the two-by-four?"

"I think I was on the stairs when he hit him," I said.

"So then Julius must know you saw it."

"No," I said. "He didn't see me."

"Ben," Lainie said, "how could you be on the stairs and Julius not see you? They're right out in the open."

"I don't remember exactly where I was."

Mother told Lainie that would be enough, to leave me alone, and Lainie said she was just trying to find out the truth of what happened. Mother said she was sure that things would get clearer in my head as the shock wore off, and in the meantime there was a lot of work to be done.

All the afternoon chores, including the collection of eggs, were carried out by Mother, Lainie, Oatsie Montague, and me. Mother wondered aloud what had happened to Burghardt, but she said she wasn't about to drive up to the tenant house to find out. Lainie, who wasn't allowed to do any lifting, came around with the flatbed close to sunset, and we loaded all the eggs onto it and brought them to the house. By the time we were done, the evening star had pierced the sky, and Mother, washing up at the outdoor faucet, looked worried and said to Oatsie that she'd surely expected to hear something by now. Oatsie offered to stay and help with getting supper, but Mother thanked her and told her to go on home, we could manage.

As Oatsie turned to leave, it occurred to Mother to say, "You're not afraid to be alone, are you, Oatsie?"

Oatsie paused and answered, "No, ma'am, I'm not afraid to be alone. That Julius ain't got any cause to hurt *me*."

Mother said, "I don't reckon he had any cause to hurt Cary either."

I observed an interesting hesitation here, in which both Mother and Oatsie seemed to be plunged into their own private consideration of what Mother had just suggested, after which Oatsie said, "Well, I guess that's true, that's true."

As soon as Oatsie was out of earshot, Mother added, under her breath, "Unless it was because he's never treated Julius like anything but dirt since the first day the man set foot on this farm."

Lainie smiled and said quietly, "Or because he just gave in to temptation. Julius isn't the first person who's felt like hitting Daddy Cary upside the head with a two-by-four."

Mother gave Lainie a naughty look, as if to say, Oh, you bad girl, and then they both burst out laughing. Mother bent down, turned the faucet back on, and threw some more water in her own face. "Mary Eleanor Rome!" she said. "We ought to be ashamed of ourselves!"

"I am, Mother," Lainie said, still laughing. "I am ashamed of myself."

"Well, I am too," Mother said. "I'm ashamed of myself too. Benjamin, you didn't hear a single word of this."

Lainie said she wanted to drive up to the tenant house to see what she could learn, but Mother said it was too dangerous. Lainie said, "What do you mean, too dangerous?"

"Well, what if they didn't catch him yet?" said Mother. "What if you go up there and surprise him while he's packing his bags?"

"Mother," said Lainie, "Julius is certainly not at the tenant house, not now. If they didn't catch him yet, he's miles from here."

But Mother still wouldn't permit her to go, so Lainie suggested we at least telephone the hospital where they'd taken Daddy Cary.

Inside, Mother tried the hospital but was told by the operator that the hospital's line was busy; she would keep trying and ring us when she got through. Mother said I should get bathed and changed for supper.

At the end of the hall, Lainie called my name as I passed her door. "Come in here and sit down a minute," she said.

She herself was seated on the bench in front of her dressing table, her back to the mirror. I paused in the doorway but told her Mother said I should get bathed.

"Ben," she said, emphatically, "come in here and sit down."

I moved to the corner of the bed and sat. "What do you want?" I said.

She leaned forward, folding her arms on her knees, and looked directly into my eyes. "*What* is going on?"

"I don't know what you mean."

"Yes, you do," she said. "I want to know what really happened this afternoon."

"I already told you," I said.

She narrowed her eyes. "Come on, Ben," she said. "You know you'll feel better if you tell me."

I dropped my chin to my chest and said, "I'm telling the truth."

After another brief silence, she said, "Well, if for any reason you're not telling the truth, Ben, I want you to carefully consider what the consequences for Julius might be. I thought you were fond of him."

"I am," I said. "I don't want to get him in trouble, but I'm telling the truth, I swear."

"Don't swear," she said.

"Okay, but I'm telling the truth."

"All right," she said, "all right"—clearly not satisfied—"go on and get your bath, then."

Afterward, Mother came to my room. I'd just closed my door, pulled on a fresh pair of boxer shorts, and lain down on the bed. She stuck her head inside the doorway and reported that she'd finally spoken to the hospital. Daddy Cary had a concussion and they'd had to put some stitches in his head. They intended to keep an eye on him for a day or two and take some X-rays. I should get dressed for supper. She was making pancakes. Daddy and Al were on their way home. We would eat as soon as they arrived. She closed the door, and I heard her down the hall repeating to Lainie everything she'd just told me.

I kept churning Lainie's words over and over: "consequences for Julius." I supposed Julius would go to prison, and what did that mean for Burghardt and Granny Mays? I didn't think Daddy Cary would let them continue to live in the tenant house. Of course I believed Daddy Cary had got what was coming to him, but I didn't imagine a judge or jury would feel that way. Even if I could somehow find the words to tell the whole truth, what had I actually seen between the planks of the hayloft floor? Nothing. And regardless of what provoked Julius, finally there was only one truth—a farmhand nigger had taken a two-by-four to a sixty-five-year-old white man and cracked his skull.

I dreaded Daddy and Al's arrival, for there would be more questions. Should I back out of my story, falsely confess that I'd been up in the loft for the duration, and hadn't witnessed any crime? I could say I just *thought* Julius had hit the old man, but I hadn't actually seen it. I had come down the stairs after the fact, I'd seen the blood, which scared the daylights out of me, I panicked, and I didn't know what I was saying. It was just what Mother had suggested—things had got clearer to me as the shock wore off—but what if the damage had already been done? What if they'd caught Julius and taken him out and lynched him? What if he'd resisted arrest, made a run for it, and they'd shot him? His death would be on my conscience, all because I'd chosen to hide in the hayloft and play the spy.

My room had grown completely dark now, my thoughts threatened to swamp me. For a moment, I felt drawn to the bullet hole high near the corner by my closet, and then I closed my eyes. A memory unfolded in my mind, from last year at school, when we'd staged a festival honoring the songwriter Stephen Foster. It was called "Stephen Foster in Living Pictures." Each class chose a song and prepared a presentation of it. Wearing costumes that reflected the lyrics, we performed the song onstage, and when the singing was done the curtains opened to reveal a life-size tableau within an enormous gold frame, a static scene that somehow illustrated the song. It was meant to look like a painting, but the people in the painting were real: elementary-school pupils, costumed, made up, and striking the required pose for about fifteen seconds while the audience applauded, oohed, and ahhed and then the curtains closed. My fourth-grade teacher, a towering auburn-haired woman named Miss Howell, had captured for our class the most coveted title, "Old Folks at Home." She oversaw every detail of our presentation. She chose the pupils who would appear in the "living picture" and designed the backdrop—a plantation scene with a white-columned mansion and cotton fields in the background, a weeping willow and the Swanee River in the foreground. On the riverbank a young man (teacher's pet Howie Austin) and a young woman (teacher's pet Madeleine Minor) would sit, idling the time away; the young man, wearing a sky-blue blazer and straw hat, would strum a banjo, his mouth open in song; the girl, moonstruck and wearing an antebellum gown, would be de-petaling a single daisy: he-loves-me, he-loves-me-not. Miss Howell assigned roles to each member of the class, a variety of characters comprising several southern belles in floor-length gowns, a preacher, many fishermen from different walks of life, the master and mistress of the plantation, and four unlucky pupils who were made to dress as what they already were, children. Because "old folks" figured so prominently in the song, I was surprised that Miss Howell had cast none; when I inquired about this, she laughed and said Mr. Foster hadn't literally meant *old* people, he'd meant "old" as in "old friends." She designated me as one of the fishermen, but at the end of the school day she called me to her desk. "Benjamin," she said, "it just occurred to me. We don't have a darky. What do you think? Would you like to be our darky?"

I didn't know what to think. She referred to the line in the song's chorus that went, "Oh, darkies, how my heart grows weary," but we had only just that day sung it for the first time, and I was unfamiliar with the antiquated word. I told Miss Howell I didn't know what a darky was.

She laughed and said, "A colored boy, Benjamin. Do you think your mama and daddy would let you dress up as a colored boy? You'll still be a fisherman, no need to change that, only now you'll be a colored fisherman."

I asked her how I could make myself colored, and she introduced me to the world of theatrical makeup and something called blackface that came in a tube just like toothpaste and could most likely be found in any good dime store. She said she would telephone my mother and ask her what she thought of the idea.

Mother was delighted. She went right out and found blackface and threw herself into preparing my costume.

The entertainment ran for two consecutive nights, a Friday and a Saturday. On the first night I appeared onstage barefooted, wearing a derby hat, a soiled long-sleeve shirt, and soiled dungarees; I held a bamboo fishing pole in my hands; a tin can for worms had been tied with string to one of my belt loops; the dungarees were rolled above my ankles, one leg higher than the other. Mother had applied black-face to every visible part of me—my hands, wrists, legs, ankles, and feet; my neck, face, and ears. The second night of "Stephen Foster in Living Pictures," I appeared in the same costume but without the blackface. Miss Howell had telephoned Mother on Saturday morning and explained that a parent in Friday night's audience, another mother, had been overly shocked when I walked onto the stage. The woman had thought for a moment that I was real, and it had so upset her she went to the principal of the school and complained. Everyone felt that under the circumstances it was best if I didn't appear in blackface again. Mother, relaying the conversation, introduced it with, "Well, Benny, your Miss Howell has got herself into some hot water."

I recalled that I'd enjoyed the special attention I'd received that first night. I recalled saying to Mother on Saturday morning, "But I'm *not* real!" Now it seemed to me peculiar that the parent had complained to the principal even after she knew the truth. She would certainly have complained if I'd been a real Negro onstage, but even when she knew I wasn't, she still complained, simply because she'd been fooled for a moment.

I rolled onto my stomach, thinking that it was as if the truth didn't matter, the truth didn't change anything, and then my father was gently shaking my shoulder. "Wake up, son," he said, "wake up."

He was sitting next to me on the bed. He said, "Now close your eyes for a minute, I'm gonna switch on your lamp."

When I opened my eyes, I was lying on my back, looking straight up at his face, starkly lit by my bedside light. He still wore his work clothes, and his beard had come in and darkened his chin. His breath smelled of whiskey. "We was gonna wake you up for supper," he said, "but your mother said to let you sleep."

"What time is it?"

"A little bit after nine," he said. "Time for you to tell me what the hell got into you this afternoon."

"What got into me?" I said.

"You heard me," he said. "Do you have any idear the kinda trouble you coulda got ole Julius into? That's not like you, Benny, to be telling lies like that."

"I didn't lie, Daddy," I said.

"All right now, Benny, you better listen to me. The only reason I'm sitting here talking instead of tearing you up good is I think there might be something wrong with you."

"Something wrong with me?"

"To make you do such a thing," he said. "Is that it, is there something wrong with you?"

Vague as it was, he'd given me my out. I said, "Yes, sir."

"Well, what is it then?"

"I don't know."

"You don't know?"

"No, sir."

"There's something wrong with you but you don't know what it is?"

"Yes, sir."

"Well, you better get it figured out, son. I ain't got the patience for this."

"Yes, sir."

"Now get up from there and get out to the kitchen. Your mother's got your supper, and I'm gonna let her talk to you."

"Yes, sir."

After he'd left the room, I put on some shorts and a T-shirt and went to the kitchen, where I found Mother at the range flipping a pancake in a black iron skillet as if it was the saddest thing she'd ever done. She'd turned off all the lights save the dim bulb over the stove, which reminded me of how Oatsie Montague's kitchen had looked at the three wakes she'd held at her house. Mother gave me a brief look, half angry, half mournful, and told to me to sit down. On the red Formica table there was a single place setting, and I had the feeling I was being served my last meal before execution. I took my seat at the table and said, "Mother, I—"

"Just don't say anything," she said. "I don't want to hear a word yet."

In a minute she brought the skillet to the table and slid four pancakes from it onto my plate. She returned the skillet to the stove and banged it down. She brought a tub of butter to the table and a bottle of syrup and banged those down, one after the other. She took the chair at the opposite end of the table and watched me as I buttered the pancakes. She continued watching as I poured the syrup. I took the first bite and swallowed, though it felt as if my throat had closed, and the swallowing was quite painful. I said, "Thank you. These are good."

She locked eyes with me. "Don't," she said.

"Don't what?" I asked, but apparently the question didn't merit an answer.

"All I want to know is why," she said. "Until you're ready to tell me that, I don't want to hear a word."

I didn't know what to say. I was lost, so I kept quiet.

After about half a minute had passed, she stood, walked to my end of the table, and removed my plate. She jerked the fork from my hand. "As a matter of fact," she said, "until you're ready, I don't even want to see you."

She took the plate and silverware to the sink, turned on the water, and put her back to me. Bewildered, I sat for another minute at the table. At last, I said, "Mother—" but she put her hand up in the air to stop me from speaking.

"Are you ready?" she snapped.

I gave her the only answer I could think of. I said, "No, ma'am."

Into the dishwater, she said, "Then kindly leave the kitchen."

Lainie was waiting for me in my room, dressed in her pajamas, sitting on my bed, and using an emery board next to my bedside lamp. She looked at me and said, "There you are. Close the door."

I closed it, and she patted the mattress next to her. After I sat, she said, "Let me see your hands."

She pulled them under the cone of light and examined my fingernails. "These are terrible," she said. "Do you work on a chicken farm or something?"

I didn't even begin to laugh.

"So how was it?" she said. "How was *she*?"

"She wouldn't let me speak," I said. "She took my plate away before I was finished eating."

Lainie laced her fingers between mine and looked at me with startling pity, as if I had a terminal illness. I felt a kind of wildness let loose in my mind. I said, "Did I really lie about Julius?"

She released my hands and folded her own in her lap. "Yes, Benny," she said, loving but firm. "Yes, you did."

I said, "How do you know?"

"How do I know?" she said. "They sewed up Daddy Cary's head, Benny, and asked him what happened."

"What did he say?"

"Well, he didn't say Julius hit him with a two-by-four," Lainie answered. "He said he was climbing out of the stall and fell."

11

LAINIE WENT ON TO EXPLAIN everything she'd learned, and Al told me a good bit more the next day. Just before Daddy and Al had left the Big House with Daddy Cary in the backseat of the car, Daddy had told Mother to telephone the county sheriff and report the incident, which she did. On the way to the hospital, Daddy Cary had been woozy and scared and mostly incoherent, but he did repeat more than once that the stall gate had fallen out from under him. At the hospital they gave him something for pain and Novocain around the wound. As they were closing the gash with stitches, the sheriff, a man Al described as "sweating like a pig," arrived at the treatment room. Daddy Cary, who appeared surprised to see the sheriff, also seemed surprised by every question the sheriff asked him. He said he'd been out to the barn for the afternoon milking, and when he'd climbed over the gate into the stall, he'd accidentally kicked the crossbar from one of its hooks; he then forgot all about it while he milked the cow, as his thoughts tended to wander onto many things when he milked cows;

after he was done, he went to climb out, and when he got up to the top of the gate and was about to swing his leg over to the other side, the thing just fell out from under him; he couldn't quite say what exactly he'd hit his head on, but he'd connected with something on the way down, most likely the divider gate to the adjacent stall. The sheriff told him they'd had a report that Daddy Cary's hired hand, Julius Mays, had given him that head wound. Daddy Cary said he didn't know where in the world the sheriff might've heard that from; he hadn't even seen Julius all day. Why in the world would Julius want to do something like that? he asked. He'd always got along just fine with Julius. He'd always taken good care of him, and his family too. There wasn't no reason for Julius to do something like that. He did add that Julius's mind seemed to be slipping lately. From time to time, Julius had been known to imagine things that didn't really happen. But he was still a good worker. Then Al, Daddy, and the sheriff stepped into the hallway, where Daddy apologized to the sheriff for his trouble. Of course the sheriff had already dispatched his men to look for Julius, but he now went directly to his car radio and called them off. As far as Al knew, nobody told Daddy Cary that I was the one who "made up the story." Al said Daddy wouldn't want to put me on Daddy Cary's bad side, as if Daddy Cary had any other kind.

When Daddy and Al returned to the farm, they'd gone straight up to the tenant house to look in on Julius, thinking Julius might have caught wind of my tall tale and might be scared into running away. They found Ole Nezzie on the front porch, who told them Julius wasn't home. She said she didn't know where he'd gone off to, but that her grandson Burghardt was sick and Julius most likely had got a friend to drive him into town for some medicine. Daddy asked her if one of the county sheriff's men had stopped by the tenant house, and she said one surely had. She said a handsome young man had come by in a police car, wanting to talk to Julius about something, he didn't say what. She'd told him she didn't know where Julius was, and then the man had talked on his radio to somebody. After that, he came back up to the porch and told her to never mind. Ole Nezzie said that "never mind" had put a fright into her, because it was all so mysterious—she was worried about her Julius. So the man explained that Mr. Cary Rome had suffered an accident in his barn, and they'd received a false report that Julius was responsible for it, but he wasn't. She needn't to worry anymore. He was innocent. She told Daddy and Al that she expected Julius would turn up before too much longer, and she sure hoped Mr. Cary Rome was going to be all right.

Daddy and Al had then returned to the house for Mother's pancake supper. When Al went to call me to the table, he found me sleeping. Mother—who "didn't exactly take it in stride," the news about my telling lies—said to just leave me be for a while. Daddy asked Mother what she thought could have made me do such a thing as that, and Mother went cold and silent as a stone. Lainie suggested to Mother that it wasn't the end of the world, and Mother told her to shut up. Al said he hadn't heard Mother speak to Lainie quite like that since Lainie had first got pregnant.

It was abundantly clear that the world needed me to have lied about Julius, and once I got used to the idea, I didn't mind. I could see that "admitting" the lie was best for everyone, especially for Julius. A thornier problem was the question of why I had lied. That first night, when Lainie brought me the fresh hard evidence of my duplicity and then filled me in on some details about what "really happened," she of course asked me why I'd done it. The next morning, Mother, who gave me the silent treatment at breakfast, didn't want to hear me or see me until I had an answer to that question. A bit later, when Al cornered me in the feed room of House B and fleshed out the story of the hospital, he concluded with, "So tell me, Ben—why'd you do it?" You would have thought it was the very heart of the matter.

With Lainie, I recalled a certain feeling of relief I'd had earlier, when my father woke me up, questioned me, and suggested that there might be something wrong with me. By improvisation and happenstance, I'd arrived at this bizarre station, proclaiming myself in a brand new way: There was something wrong with me, but I didn't know what it was. At first, it was merely the thing I'd reached for in desperation, something to try on in preference to nakedness, but once I'd donned it, I did notice a certain not-unpleasant whiff of its suitability. So when Lainie asked me why I'd lied about Julius a few minutes later, I tried it on again. I said, "I think there's something wrong with me, Lainie, but I don't know what it is."

She looked surprised, but then immediately and sadly resigned. She turned down the corners of her mouth and sighed. At last she met my answer with another question, this time rhetorical: "Well, how could anybody grow up in this crazy household," she said, "and not have something wrong with them?"

This felt like a success. I slept well. The next morning, I got through breakfast as best I could and then gave the same answer to Al in the feed room. He was thoughtful about it. After some silent reflection, he nodded and said, "Yeah, I've had that feeling too." He touched my nose with the tip of his index finger affectionately and added, "A *lot*."

So now it became my official truth, and what a satisfying raw quality it had. It was, by its nature, incontestable—or so I thought. Midday, I went to the kitchen early so I might catch Mother alone. She was at the stove, frying some slices of Spam for our sandwiches. Partly because of the odd circumstances, in which the confession of lying was a lie, I was having some trouble understanding Mother's extreme reaction. I recognized that the "lie" was a big one and, granted, lying was a sin. But I also knew that people everywhere lied on a regular basis and that there was, through Jesus, plenty of forgiveness available. My alleged transgression had seemed to cut Mother to the quick. When I went and stood next to her at the stove and dared to place my arm around her waist, she didn't look at me, only stared into the skillet. But she didn't shrug off my arm either. She spoke in a businesslike voice, slightly less brittle than it had been at breakfast. She said, "Are you ready?"

"Yes, ma'am," I said. "I am."

Now she turned, bent forward, and gave in to some expression of feeling. "Well, then, why?" she said. "Why, Benny, why?"

"I think there's something wrong with me," I said.

She snapped to attention, straight as a rail. "That's perfectly ridiculous," she said. "I'm sure I don't know what you mean. What could be wrong with you?"

"I don't know," I answered. "I know there's something wrong, but I don't know what it is."

"That's the silliest thing I ever heard," she said, really angry now, more angry than before. "It's nothing but an excuse, Benjamin, and a sorry one at that. Go to your room. When you father gets here he's going to give you a whipping."

And when Daddy took his belt off to me fifteen minutes later, he said the whipping was meant to help me figure out what was wrong with me. There was nothing unusual in Mother's prescribing the whipping—she always did—but I thought that today's whipping was meant to help me figure out that there *wasn't* anything wrong with me; she and Daddy didn't seem to be quite in accord on this matter. As was our ritual, he whipped me in their bedroom, while Mother stood by the door and watched. I did not cry, for the first time ever. I remained true to the vow I'd made myself some days earlier, on the lawn of the Big House after Al had wrestled me to the ground. This change, my not crying, made Daddy whip me longer and harder than ever before, but he didn't succeed at making me cry, though I did do a fair amount of tearless squealing. I hated everything about the belt—the clink of the buckle as he yanked it from his pants, the leather's snakelike thinness, its crack and sting. In the open area at the foot of their bed, he held my left hand with his left hand, as men sometimes do in certain folk dances, and he swung the belt with his right. Today he told me to "watch out" for his sore thumb, and as I carefully wrapped my hand around his fingers, I noticed his sad, chewed nails and split cuticles. It was our custom for me to move forward as he whipped me, and thus for us to inscribe a circle. Oddly, I moved on tiptoe, as if the floor were hot coals, and more oddly, I squeezed Daddy's hand, the center of our circle, throughout, as if for solace. My mother's blurred image passed in my peripheral vision again and again, a rhythmic reminder of her relentless neglect to save me. Today, surprising everyone, Al appeared at the bedroom door and spoke in a deep stern voice. "That's enough, Daddy," he said, and Daddy stopped. Al turned to go, but in leaving he stared a dagger through Mother and whispered, "Shame on you." She was already crying, which was also usual. It was her role, to watch and cry. And as usual, Daddy put his belt back on, moved toward her, took her in his arms, and comforted her, a moment that never failed to take my breath away, as it was the only display of affection I ever witnessed between them. As usual, I was sent to my room. As usual, in my room, I pulled down my shorts and inspected my injuries, the customary basketweave of bright red welts that reached as high as the small of my back and as low as the bend in my knees. A knock came at my door, and I quickly pulled up my shorts and hopped onto the bed. Al stuck his head inside and said, "Are you all right?"

"Yeah," I said. "But don't tell Lainie, okay?"

"Why not?"

"It would just upset her," I said.

"Okay, Benny," he said. "You want me to bring you a sandwich?"

"I'll get something later," I said, and when he closed the door, I stood up, to ease the pain of having sat down. I did, finally, shed a tear or two then, because I recalled my Mother's stricken angry face at the kitchen range, when I'd said there was something wrong with me but I didn't know what it was. For Mother, I couldn't have given a wronger answer. It wasn't her belief in my lying that had cut her so deeply, it was her fear that, if I'd told such a lie, there must indeed be something wrong with me.

I changed to long pants, so that when Lainie came home from the dentist office, she wouldn't see any stripes on my legs. I found a No. 1 pencil, SOFT, in the plastic tray on my card table. I went to the window of the room that looked out onto the camellia bush. I knelt on the floor so I could write on the window frame's wooden apron, close up under the stool, where no one would see it until the day, one day, when our house would be torn down: *Benjamin Rome lived here, 9-5-59.*

On Monday, Labor Day, we celebrated by laboring. Daddy thought this idea, of laboring on Labor Day, extremely funny and never failed to remind us that the chickens couldn't read the calendar. If we wanted the day off, he said, we needed to teach the chickens to read. I supposed that because he'd spent his entire life around animals, jokes in this vein appealed to him. Anytime we passed a DEER CROSSING sign on the road, he would say, "They can put up all the signs they want to, but the deers can't read. The deers are gonna cross where they want to cross."

Lainie had made some special plans for Labor Day, a secret adventure of some kind, and she'd invited me to go with her. She'd told me we could leave after I'd finished my morning work, and she would have me back in time for the afternoon chores. She swore me to secrecy, saying I couldn't mention to anyone that we were going anywhere. I deduced from her tone that whatever she had planned for us, it was something serious and possibly even dangerous.

Yesterday, Julius had shown up at the henhouses to substitute for the ailing Burghardt. Julius was, with me, exactly as he'd always been. I couldn't begin to tell whether or not he knew I'd accused him of hitting Daddy Cary. When I asked after Burghardt, he simply said, "Oh, he's gonna be fine, Mr. Ben, don't you worry," and I saw nothing in his eyes that hinted at a double meaning. Of course I could have said to Julius that I knew the truth about everything, but I didn't think he would take any comfort from it; on the contrary, I thought it would threaten him. The only moment I might have interpreted as any sort of tacit collusion between us came early in the morning, after we'd been working silently for about an hour. I felt uneasy with him, as I didn't know what he knew. I'd finished with the waterers in one of the ground-bird houses and gone into the feed room to shake out my brush. I suddenly looked up and found Julius standing just outside the little room, staring at me through the wire. He smiled and said, "I was wondering about something, Mr. Ben, I hope you don't mind. I was wondering what you plan to do?" My ears burned, for I thought he was boldly broaching the subject of the milking barn, but he quickly added, "You know, what you plan to do in life."

I shrugged my shoulders. "I don't know, Julius," I said. "I'm only ten."

"That's true," he said. "That's true, but if you was my boy—"

He stopped himself.

I said, "What?"

"Oh, nothing," he said, "nothing at all. Your daddy would have my hide if he heard me say it."

"Say what?"

He squinted as if he was trying to see me more clearly. At last he said, "I just can't see you egg farming, Mr. Ben. Ask me, you already know too much to waste it on these here dumb chickens."

That was as close as he came to acknowledging anything secret between us—if that had been his intention. I couldn't say for sure, but I did know this: He'd carefully chosen his words, and they'd risen from a spell of deep thinking; it was no idle remark.

Daddy Cary came home from the hospital midafternoon, having been issued a clean bill of health. Mother baked a pound cake after church and invited me to come to the Big House with her to deliver it. I politely declined, and she didn't force me to go. She seemed restored to her old self, as if nothing extraordinary had happened. At supper Sunday night, she reported the news from the Big House: Oatsie Montague had suggested to Daddy Cary that his recuperation would benefit from the purchase of his first television; Harris Electric was having a Labor Day sale on all their 1959 models, and Daddy Cary had told Oatsie to go ahead and order him one. Mother said Oatsie was the only living human being on earth who could have recommended that Daddy Cary spend money and him do it.

Burghardt still didn't return to work on Labor Day morning, and Julius would say only that he was "still not quite hisself" but I shouldn't worry about him. I tore through my chores, eager to meet Lainie at her private entrance, as we'd planned the night before. I'd been instructed to come directly to that side of the house where she parked the Willys and to knock very gently on her door.

She opened the door quietly and put her finger to her lips. She was dressed for the dentist office, and looked as if she'd been crying. She said, "Is it going to rain?"

I hadn't noticed before, but now that she mentioned it, there were some dark clouds gathering in the northwest part of the sky. I said, "Maybe. Are you all right?"

"Yes," she said. She turned to grab her brown leather purse and a khaki-colored trenchcoat from her bed and said, "Let's go."

As she silently pulled her door closed, I said, "Why are you dressed like that?"

"Sh-h-h," she said. "This way, if they catch us leaving, I can say I'm going in to Dr. Shanks's office. I can say I forgot that he wanted me to come in for a while today."

"But why would I be going with you?" I whispered.

Moving around to the driver's side of the Willys, she shrugged.

"Maybe I told you I'd teach you how to operate the sterilizer, I don't know. Now don't slam your door. Just pull it closed and we'll shut them tight once we're on the road."

She started the engine, backed up to turn the car toward the road, then let it coast down to the mouth of the driveway. She eased out onto the road, made the left turn toward the creek, pressed the accelerator, and said, "Okay, slam your door now."

Two bangs of the doors and we were on our way. I said, "All right, tell me where we're going."

"I have an appointment," she said. "Roll your window up some. I don't want all the dust."

"What kind of appointment?" I said.

She waited a few seconds before answering. "To tell you the honest truth, Ben, I don't know if I'm going to keep it. I just had to get out of the house today. Let's see what happens."

"Okay," I said, "but where are we going?"

I'd assumed that wherever we were going, it would be in town, but we bypassed Farmville by turning onto a narrow county road that ran west of the town. I didn't recall ever having been on this particular road. Judging from the bright spot in the sky where the sun was hidden by clouds, we were headed northwest, into the weather. In about ten or fifteen minutes, a soft drizzle began to light on the windshield. The road curved around a swamp where dead trees stood, their trunks suddenly wider where they met the stagnant water; then the pavement tunneled through a stretch of live oaks, and we emerged onto a dam that cut like a rail through an expanse of sky and water. "What's this?" I said.

"I don't know," said Lainie. "Some kind of reservoir, I think."

The water was impossibly still, a great slab of slate. I asked Lainie again where we were going, but she looked straight ahead and answered in a faraway voice that she hadn't decided yet. I was hungry and had begun to regret having come along. We were obviously in the middle of nowhere. I said, "Let me drive."

She leaned forward to get a look at the sky, then said, "I don't think so, Ben. I've got too much on my mind right now."

"So let me drive," I said. "Then you can think all you want to."

She ignored this reasoning but, after a moment, said, "Maybe on the way home."

I slid down into the seat and propped my feet on the dashboard, a ploy to pull Lainie back from whatever distant plane she'd drifted to, but she didn't seem to notice. At last I said, "Aren't you going to tell me to take my shoes off the dashboard?"

She glanced briefly at my shoes, which were the filthy sneakers I wore to work in the henhouses. "No," she said. "I don't care anymore."

"What do you mean you don't care?" I said. "They're dirty."

"Oh, what difference does it make, Ben?"

"What do you mean?"

"I mean, what difference does it make? It's only a car."

"Only a car?" I said, shocked. I thought she'd given me a glimpse into her thoughts. Only one thing could push her this far into hopelessness, in which she ceased to care about the Willys—she'd wandered off onto the prospect of nuclear holocaust. I did think there was something about the gray road and the gray reservoir and the gray sky that might call to mind total annihilation.

"Yes," she said, as we crossed the line into Buckingham County. "Only a car."

After twenty minutes more of silence, we passed an abandoned gas station. She suddenly stepped on the brakes and steered the car to the shoulder of the road. A blue jay flew out of a ditch by my door, and I sat up straight in the seat and looked at Lainie. She reached for her purse on the seat between us and took out a folded sheet of notebook paper. I noticed what appeared to be an impressive stack of ten-dollar bills in the inner side pocket of the purse. Lainie unfolded the sheet of paper and read what was written on it. I said, "What's that?"

She refolded the paper and returned it to the purse. She stretched her right arm out along the back of the seat, facing me. "I'm going to make a left turn up here after about another mile," she said. "You have to promise me something, Ben. I want you to promise me that everything that happens from now on is our secret, just between me and you. You can't tell anybody where we went. No matter what questions they ask you when we get home, you just have to say we went for a ride and that's all. Can you promise that?"

The night before, when—in hushed tones, in the privacy of her room—she'd first announced the plan, I hadn't been entirely sure I wanted the burden of yet another secret, but of course the prospect of something cloak-and-dagger was too hard to pass up. Now the reality seemed short on adventure and decidedly long on the burden of secrecy. And the earnestness with which Lainie was trying to extract further assurances made me suspect that she no longer thought me trustworthy. I supposed she'd invited me along because I'd proven myself a liar, so if lying was required at the other end of the thing, I was her man.

"Okay," I said, keeping my voice neutral, "but where are we going?"

"I'm just going to see some people out here," she said. "Way out here in the country. You don't know them. You can stay in the car while I'm inside."

"But who are they?" I asked.

"Never mind who they are," she said, looking doubtful. "It wasn't really fair of me to ask you to come, Ben, but I thought I might need you. I'm sorry."

"That's all right," I said. Her expression of possible need dispelled any hurt feelings or grudges that were forming, but I still felt a little tricked—lured by a promise of intrigue, only to learn that I was to sit in the car somewhere in the middle of nowhere. Thinking of the stack of bills I'd seen in her purse, I said, "Do you owe these people money?"

"No," she said, and almost smiled. "I don't owe anybody any money."

She faced forward, put the car in gear, and pulled it back onto the road. Once we were cruising along again at about fifty miles per hour, she said, "At least I don't owe anybody any money."

No name was painted on the mailbox at the edge of the unpaved road. The house, secluded by tall hedges of arborvitae at the end of a long driveway, had a small concrete porch with two brick columns; it was one story, painted white, rambling in a haphazard way but tidy-looking. Altogether we'd driven for about an hour and a half. Lainie parked the Willys behind a beige Volkswagen van, which sat facing what clearly used to be a garage but was now closed in for a sun porch. She told me to stay in the car. Reaching for her purse, she added, "Sorry, Ben. I won't be too long."

I watched through the rain-blurred windshield as Lainie stood on the porch and talked to a white-haired woman who'd answered the door. After a brief exchange, she disappeared into the house.

Ten minutes later—when I'd grown fully remorseful about having come, need or no need—the same white-haired woman reappeared and walked to the edge of the porch, where she signaled for me to join her.

"You might as well come inside," she said, as I stepped under the roof of the porch, out of the drizzle. "You must be bored to tears out there."

Rarely had I been so immediately understood, but I was distracted from this pleasure by the woman's hair, which was pulled into a single braid that fell to the middle of her spine. It struck me as a childish way for a grown woman to wear her hair, but somehow, because she was old, it looked elegant. (On Mother it would have looked like a Halloween version of Pocahontas.) "I suspect you're her brother," the woman said, holding open the door. "I'm glad to see you. We suggested she bring someone with her."

She was dressed in a black skirt made of some gauzy fabric with many pleats, and a white blouse with a white pattern of vines embroidered around its buttons. I noted that she wore gold sandals something like the ones I'd seen on the colored woman who'd chased down Granny Mays's hat and kerchief that day on High Street. The old woman asked my name; when I told her, she extended her hand. I believed it was the first time I'd shaken hands with a woman of any age.

We entered a large and rather dark room with bamboo furniture of a kind I'd seen only on porches and lawns. The walls were covered with something that looked as if it was made of dried grass, and a large white paper globe, a lamp, hung low from the ceiling above a round bamboo table in the center of the room. On the table, a crystal vase held a colorful bouquet of zinnias, which made me think it odd of my mother, with her love of flowers, not ever to have brought any into the house. Between two windows stood a grandfather clock with its pendulum swinging; it was about five minutes past one, and I regretted that I'd probably just missed hearing it chime. An entire wall of the room was lined by shelves full of books, and a gold corduroy-covered easy chair sat near the shelves, with its own small end table and gooseneck lamp; an open book rested on one of the chair's wide arms and, atop the book, a pair of eyeglasses. In my mind, I saw the old woman hearing Lainie's knock at the door and removing her glasses, putting down her book, and pushing herself up from the chair. The other walls of the room were decorated with many modern-looking paintings, all similar: thick gobs of paint, thrown or dripped onto the canvases, representing nothing recognizable. I detected a slightly medicinal odor in the room and thought maybe it came from the paintings. Lainie was nowhere to be seen.

"Well, Ben," the woman said, "please have yourself a seat. I'm making some hot tea for us now that we have a rainy afternoon. Are you hungry?"

"I'm ravishing," I said, which produced a surprising bolt of laughter from the old woman. She smiled and left the room.

I sat on the bamboo couch with cushions in a floral pattern, and it was then that I noticed, in the opposite corner of the room, a xylophone. I recognized it immediately as the thing learned about in first grade that began with x. Two small mallets lay crisscrossed atop the flat wooden bars. I suppressed the natural urge to go and experiment, but I heard in my mind what I thought would approximate its sound: I thought of soap bubbles bursting in the rain. Then I explored the chaos of the several paintings. I judged them to be amateur, and I found that when I viewed them with half-closed eyes, I could begin to see the shapes of things in them—a marlin, a watering pot, a tarantula.

The woman returned with a tray. "Let's sit over here," she said, placing the tray on the central table under the white globe. In addition to the tea there was a plate of small crustless sandwiches. I took a seat at the table and asked, "Is my sister coming soon?"

"Oh, yes," said the woman. "I expect she will before too much longer."

I recognized this as the kind of answer that was meant to pacify me, to ward off any further questions. She poured tea from a pot into two matching cups and said, "Lemon or milk, Ben?"

I'd never drunk hot tea before, and I arbitrarily chose lemon.

"There's the sugar," she said. "Please help yourself. I hope you like pineapple sandwiches."

It turned out I did. I discovered that day that I adored pineapple sandwiches.

"You must be a nice boy," said the woman, smiling sadly. "Coming out here with her. A very good brother. The poor thing . . . all this to go through when she ought to be going to dances and—"

She set down her teacup and waved her hands in the air, searching for what else Lainie ought to have been going to. "And ball games," she said at last.

At that moment, an electrical humming noise came from another room inside the house—a machine had switched on somewhere—and the woman pushed the plate of sandwiches toward me and said, "Won't you have another, Ben? I guess you'll be starting school in another three days."

I said, "Yes, ma'am," and the humming noise from within the house stopped. It had been on for so short a time, I expected it to start up again, but it didn't.

"What grade will you be in?" she asked.

"Fifth," I said, which seemed to delight her.

"Fifth," she said. "That's a good year. What subjects do you enjoy?"

I shrugged my shoulders, my usual response to the various versions of this question. Then I heard myself say, "Everything, I guess."

"Everything?" she said. "That's wonderful. Hold on to that, Ben. That's a gift that will see you through many a long day or night. I suppose you must like to read."

Because of my experience with Mr. Wall at Daddy Cary's birthday party, I decided to stay closemouthed in this area. I said, "A little," hoping that would hold her at bay.

"It's such a terrible thing, what we've done," said the woman. "Closing the schools. This is all about the grown-ups, Ben, never mind the children. I'm afraid we've failed our children dreadfully, especially our Negro children. It's the children who'll have to pay the price for our lack of foresight, isn't it. For our refusal to change with the times. Don't you agree, Ben?"

I said, "Yes, ma'am," letting my eyes stray to the doubtful paintings on the walls, and she caught me at it.

She said, "Mine. Do you like them?" She gazed around the room herself, and as she did this, she reached a hand inside the collar of her blouse and pulled out a single strand of pearls, pensively.

I thought it kind of the woman to have invited me inside and kinder still to have made the sandwiches. Without any hesitation, I said, "Yes, ma'am, I really do."

She coiled the pearls around her index finger and gave me a look that suggested she didn't believe me. "I'm so glad you do," she said. "I bet you have an artist's eye yourself."

I was perfectly at ease with this most innocent exchange of fibs and flattery—it was child's play compared to what I'd just come through—and I felt well prepared to show this old woman, or anyone else, a thing or two about lying.

She poured more tea into her own cup, glancing at mine and finding it still full. She smiled the same sad smile as before and said, "I know they're not very good. But I keep trying, and my sweet husband lets me hang any old thing on the walls. It takes my mind off the world when the world gets to be too much. Which is often enough, don't you find?"

"Yes, ma'am," I said again, but I didn't want to have to talk about the paintings anymore and, restlessly, I stood up and began walking around the room, taking a sandwich with me. I had of course been taught better manners than this, but somehow I thought the woman wouldn't disapprove. Seeing that I'd reached the musical instrument in the corner of the room, she said, "Do you know what that is, Ben?"

"A xylophone," I answered.

"Very close," she said. "It's a marimba."

The error, or her correction of it, made me absurdly unhappy. I wanted, in this strange place where so much was new, to be exactly right about something. I wanted everything to seem less strange and new than it was. I went to touch one of the longest bars, near the wide end of the marimba, when the woman said, "My husband's first love, I think," and I withdrew my hand. Smiling at the marimba, as if it were a living thing, she appeared to drift into a reverie. I noticed that the room had grown considerably darker. I looked out the front windows and saw that rain was pouring down outside, and now that I'd seen it, I could hear its hissing sound on the roof of the house. I wandered to the wall of books. I said, "This is like a library."

"Well, it *is* a library, Ben," said the woman. She came and stood next to me, gazing up at the books. "It's my library," she said. "My collection of books. Mine and my husband's."

Now she sat in the easy chair, where she lifted the book from the arm and held it in her lap. It appeared that she wished to return to her reading, and I moved to the windows on the front of the house and looked out at the rain and the tall arborvitae bushes, whose lacy fronds drooped and wagged in the weather. From behind me I heard the old woman's voice. "Would you like to hear something beautiful?" she asked.

"Yes, ma'am," I said, and turned and rested my backside against the windowsill.

She already wore her reading glasses, and now she switched on the gooseneck lamp, which spilled light over the book and the woman's hands and caused me to notice for the first time that she wore several rings on the fingers of both hands, like a Gypsy in a sideshow at the state fair. By way of introduction, she said, "This is a poem," and then began to read.

"There's a certain Slant of light,
Winter Afternoons—
That oppresses, like the Heft
Of Cathedral Tunes—

"Heavenly Hurt, it gives us—
We can find no scar,
But internal difference,
Where the Meanings, are—

"None may teach it—Any—
'Tis the Seal Despair—
An imperial affliction
Sent us of the Air—

"When it comes, the landscape listens—
Shadows—hold their breath—
When it goes, 'tis like the Distance
On the look of Death—"

When she'd finished, she said, "Isn't that remarkable, Ben? Isn't that truly remarkable?"

I had no doubt that it was remarkable. I returned to the bamboo table, where I sat down. I thought Granny Mays occasionally strung together words in the woods in such a way that the sound was like music without melody, and I knew that what had just occurred here had also occurred in English, my native tongue. Apart from that, I knew only that I had to sit, for the sound had stirred me in an unfamiliar way, as if something terrible had befallen me, but something that was really the opposite of terrible. I remembered "heavenly hurt" and "shadows hold their breath," for these had lodged in my skin as a dozen other sharp things scratched by barely heeded. The woman brought the book to the table and set it down before me, pointing to the poem, then sat silently as I read it to myself. When I was done, I looked at her and said, in a voice comical in its degree of awe, "What does it mean?"

She glanced at the grandfather clock and said, "Well, we don't have enough time, Ben—not to go through it line by line—but tell me what it made you think of."

"A sunset?" I said.

"That's absolutely right," she said. "I had you pegged correctly. Now let me ask you a question. Did you ever stand somewhere and see a sunset, and it was so beautiful it almost hurt? So beautiful you couldn't possibly love it any more, and yet it made you feel strangely sad and a little lonely?"

"Yes, ma'am," I said, and the minute I said it I knew I'd gone farther than I wanted to go with this stranger in this strange place, and I felt the kind of all-over derangement you feel when you've stood up too quickly or too quickly drunk ice water. I said, "Thank you, but I better go back to the car now. I think—"

"Oh, no, Ben," she said, reaching for my hand. "I've overwhelmed you, haven't I. I do that, I'm afraid, though I don't mean to." She released my hand suddenly, as if she'd thought better of holding it so tightly. "Please stay here where it's dry," she said. She glanced again at the clock and added, "I'm going to have to leave you alone now for a few minutes anyway. Read some more poems if you like. Or anything else you find."

Just then a door opened, behind my left shoulder, and an old man, also white-haired, entered the room. He was small and neat, in a light blue sport shirt and brown trousers. The woman had already stood, and now I did too.

"Her brother," the woman said to the man. "Ben."

The man said he was pleased to meet me and shook my hand. He then drew the woman aside and spoke to her quietly as he slowly escorted her toward the door he'd come out of. At last the woman turned to me, smiled, and said, "I'm going to see to your sister, Ben. It won't be long now."

"Some rain!" said the man, as soon as she'd left.

"Yes, sir," I said.

"Did you ever see one of these before?" he asked, indicating the nearby marimba.

"No, sir," I said, "but I've seen a xylophone."

"Would you like to hear it?"

I said I would, though I'd not quite let go of the idea of running for the solitude of the Willys. The man pointed to the couch, and as soon as I was seated he began to play a song I'd never heard. I thought whatever it was wasn't well suited to the instrument, but the athletic way he played and the obvious delight he took from it were interesting to watch. There was, after all, something delicate and bubbly about the sound. It turned into quite a long song, with many repetitive passages, and when he was done, he stared down at the marimba thoughtfully and began a second piece, also unknown to me. I could see that I would weary of this before he did, and I was challenged by having to make my face respond to the man's occasional smiles in my direction whenever he did something with the mallets that especially pleased him. He began to play yet a third piece, which I recognized as "Smoke Gets in Your Eyes." I made up my mind to ask him where Lainie was the minute he struck the last chord, but I didn't have to, for the door to the other room opened before he was finished.

He stopped and quickly crisscrossed the mallets on the marimba. Lainie appeared in the doorway, her face registering shock at seeing me there on the bamboo couch. She turned to the old woman behind her, who made some assuring, dismissive gestures with her hands and whispered something to Lainie I couldn't quite hear.

The man said, "You better have a seat there next to your brother for a minute."

Lainie sat next to me. I searched her face for an explanation, but all I found was the extreme paleness of her skin and dry eyes that appeared to be further from tears than I'd seen them in a while. The man came to the couch and took Lainie's wrist between his thumb and fingers, looking carefully into her face, as if he too was looking for an explanation. He smiled at Lainie and said, "You're just fine, young lady, and pretty as a picture." He turned to the old woman and said, "Isn't she pretty, Louise?"

The woman said, "She's beautiful. And going to be more beautiful as she ages. She's got that kind of skin."

Lainie smiled, and some color came back into her face. She whispered, "Thank you," and looked at me apologetically, genuinely embarrassed.

The man said, "Better just let me have a quick listen to your heart, sweetheart, and you'll be on your way." He took a shiny silver and black stethoscope from the hip pocket of his trousers, uncoiled it, and rigged it to his ears.

We were not quite out the drive. The sky was even darker now, and rain still came down. "What does it matter, Ben?" said Lainie, gripping the steering wheel.

"Well, they had to be somebody," I said. "Was he a doctor?"

"Yes," she said.

"Why didn't you go to your regular doctor?"

"Ben, I'll explain later."

"Explain now," I said.

She turned onto the dirt road that led to the narrow county road we'd come by. Lainie stopped the car, shifted into neutral, and raised the emergency brake. "Ben," she said. "It's female."

"Oh," I said, for nothing had the power to shut me up quite so finally as that.

Lainie said, "Do you think you could drive part of the way home?"

It struck me that she was having to make an effort to keep her voice steady. "Sure," I said. "But—"

"I'm just going to lie down in the backseat," she said, already opening her door.

I made a cushion of Lainie's raincoat, slid over behind the wheel, and released the brake. When she was situated in back, I said, "Are you sick?"

"I'll be fine," she said. "This is better. Just go straight until you come to the pavement. Then turn right and it's one road all the way past town. And go slow."

I put the car in gear and moved forward, pleased at how smoothly I'd executed this first start. I looked into the rearview mirror and saw rain streaming down the dark blue oval of the back window. Lainie told me to switch on the headlights, which I did. I'd driven only on sunny days and dry roads before. The rain made it difficult to see out the windshield, and I was distracted by the wild flapping of the wipers, but I was grateful that the bad weather would make it harder for a state trooper to spot me as an underage driver. "Are you sick?" I asked Lainie again.

After a moment, I heard her voice, quiet and flat, as if she were talking in her sleep. "I'll explain later, Ben," she said. "It feels better lying down. Thank you."

"You're welcome," I said, and suddenly I had a vision of running the car off the road into a ditch. The muscles in my shoulders tightened, and after another few minutes of silence, I began to worry that I would go too far, drive right past our turn on the other side of town. I passed the abandoned gas station about a mile from the dirt road. I recalled the words from the poem, "the landscape listens, shadows hold their breath," and I repeated them over and over in my mind, as if to anchor my mind inside my head, to keep it inside the car, behind the wheel, on the road and out of any ditches.

Coming, we'd met only three or four cars. Going back, I hadn't yet met any. After a while, Lainie fell asleep—or at least appeared to—so I drove and didn't speak. I was in no danger of falling asleep myself. I couldn't recall a time when I'd felt more wide awake.

After a long indeterminate time had passed, I heard Lainie's voice again from the backseat. "Where are we now?" she asked.

"On the road," I said.

"I know that," she said. "I mean, where on the road?"

"There aren't a lot of milestones," I said. "We crossed the county line awhile back. Are you all right?"

She laughed quietly and said, "I just want to be in my own bed, in my own room."

Soon we gained the reservoir, now a dark charcoal. The Willys bounced over the metal seams of the dam, and Lainie groaned, "Oh, oh, oh, Ben, slow down."

I slowed the car and glanced in the rearview mirror, where I saw a red pinpoint of light blinking far behind us on the road. As the red flashing light drew closer—really fast—and burned larger and brighter, I couldn't quite bring myself to speak. I heard no siren. I sat up straight behind the steering wheel, tried to will myself bigger and older, and then there was a moment when the interior of the Willys was bathed in red light, and Lainie cried, "Oh my God, what's that?"

I held my breath as the patrol car passed us, doing eighty easily in the other lane. With the confidence of a veteran explorer, I said, "Nothing, Lainie. Just a state trooper chasing after somebody. Not us."

At the farm, we'd not got a drop, only the dark clouds, which still glided over our land slowly toward the line, a few miles from here, where they would begin to release their rain. We'd driven out of the drizzle shortly after crossing the reservoir. For the first time ever, I'd taken the Willys over the bridge at the creek. I'd been so relieved to find a dry bridge rather than a wet one, the task had seemed easy. I stopped the Willys a hundred yards from our driveway and told Lainie she'd better take the wheel.

"Oh, hell," she said, still horizontal in the back. "Just take us on in, Ben. Who cares?"

"Are you sure?" I said.

"Yeah. What can they do, arrest us?"

I pulled into the drive, around the corner of the house, and parked under the pecan tree by Lainie's private entrance. As she started to push herself up from the seat, she moaned and grabbed her stomach, doubling over for a moment, but whatever pain she'd suffered was passing. "Just a little cramp," she said and sat up. She reached over the front seat and placed her hands on either side of my head, pulling me backward and planting a big long kiss on my right cheek. "Brother Ben," she said, "you are my prince of peace."

"That's sacrilegious," I said, wiping my cheek.

We'd been away from the farm for a little more than four hours, and I was, as promised, back in plenty of time for my afternoon chores. At supper that night, Mother asked me where Lainie and I had disappeared to in the middle of the day. I said we'd just taken a ride, and Mother gave me the fish-eye and said, "A ride? It must've been a long ride. Y'all didn't eat anything unusual, did you?"

This question alluded to Lainie's not coming to the supper table, complaining that she didn't feel well. Of course I thought of the pineapple sandwiches the white-haired woman had served, but Lainie hadn't eaten any of those, and all I said was, "No, ma'am."

The next morning, Lainie phoned in sick to Dr. Shanks's office and stayed in bed. Mother persisted in her suspicion that we'd gone somewhere the day before and eaten something we shouldn't have. She made Lainie take Pepto-Bismol and said that if she wasn't feeling better by tomorrow she was to phone the doctor. She didn't want any ifs, ands, or buts. You couldn't take chances, she said, when you were expecting.

On Wednesday, Lainie showed up for breakfast dressed for work. The only clear change in her was her hearty appetite, which pleased Mother. Lainie had scrambled eggs, two pieces of toast with apple butter, and two slices of bacon. When I reported for duty to the henhouses, I again found Julius instead of Burghardt. I asked Julius when he thought Burghardt was going to get well, and Julius said, "Oh, he's improving a little bit every day, Mr. Ben. Don't you be worrying about him."

I resolved to visit the tenant house immediately after dinner. At around one o'clock in the afternoon, as I was walking up Rome Road in that direction, a delivery truck from Harris Electric roared past me with a two-short-toots-of-its-horn hello. I was eager to see Daddy Cary's new TV set; I assumed it would be bigger and more modern than ours, and there was even a chance that, unlike ours, it would have sound and a legible picture. But I hadn't yet been anywhere near the Big House since the events of last Friday, and I still didn't feel ready. My plan today had been to climb over the fence into the cornfield before I reached the Big House, and approach the tenant house under cover of the corn; despite my curiosity about Daddy Cary's new TV, I decided to stick to that plan.

I found Granny Mays on the porch, sewing some heavy gold drapes and pumping her foot treadle with such vigorous ease, she and the old Singer appeared to be one thing, one machine. She'd spread a bed-sheet on the floor behind the sewing machine, a clean spot for the drape fabric to collect and not get dirty. I didn't climb the porch steps but went and stood next to her, on the ground. She continued with the long seam she was running under the needle, never allowing her eyes to stray. I said hello and asked her how Burghardt was doing. She pushed the gold fabric forward with her hands on either side of the needle bar and said, "He's doing just fine, Mr. Ben. I'm letting him sleep this afternoon."

"He's not well enough for chores yet?" I asked. I meant, When am I going to see him again? but it came out sounding like the boss's boy questioning a hired hand's absence, which I regretted. I regretted it so much I said the next thing that popped into my head: "I miss him, Granny."

She reached the end of the seam and clipped the thread with a pair of shears. I expected her to begin gathering up the fabric from the floor where it lay crumpled on the sheet, but she let the last of it fall there behind the treadle. She placed the shears in her lap, her elbows on the surface of the machine desk, and laced her fingers together; she bowed her head slightly, as if she was composing her thoughts. Either she reached the end of what she was thinking or she gave up on it—I couldn't tell which—but she turned her knees toward me and placed her hands in her lap. She smiled, both warmly and sadly, and said, "I thought you'd be in school today, Mr. Ben."

"It starts tomorrow," I said. "Opening day at the State Theatre. A big hoopla."

"Oh, I thought that was today," said Granny Mays. "I've got my days all confused."

We continued looking at each other in silence. She'd dodged my question about Burghardt, but she hadn't managed to divert either of our minds from him. At last she said, "My Burghardt's gonna be all right, Mr. Ben. Did you know I was the one who named him? I'm the only mother he's ever known. You know, Julius is a good man, was always a good boy growing up, not a mean bone in his body. As sweet and kind as he could be, but oh, what a time he's had finding his way in the world! I used to think it was his own daddy's untimely death that did it. But I come to think Julius just had some wayward blood from his daddy's side of the family. Always meant to do good, but struggled to tell a good idea from a bad one."

I couldn't see what this had to do with Burghardt. Midway through it, she'd raised her eyes above my head and aimed her voice at the corn a few feet behind me. I didn't know how much she knew about the milking barn, and I didn't know whether she'd heard about my "lying," but I wondered if that wasn't the reason she was talking about Julius's being good. I squatted in the spot where I was standing, and it suddenly occurred to me—probably it was proximity to the ground that did it—that Granny Mays was doing her speaking. She wasn't in the woods, and I wasn't hiding in the old oil drum, but that was what she was doing, speaking, and both of us right out in the open.

"Wandered off down to the Carolinas," she continued, "doing I-don't-know-what. And after a good long time passed, came back home with a baby in his arms. I said, 'Whose is that?' and he says, 'It's mine, Mama. It's a little boy.' I said, 'Well, where is its mama, Julius?' and he says, 'Ain't got no mama.' I said, "Well, what's its name, son?' and he says, 'Ain't got no name yet neither.' He had that baby wrapped up in an old flannel shirt—I still got that shirt in my suitcase where I keep my memories. And feeding it Carnation evaporated milk. I thought to myself, 'Uh-hmm, humble origins, I seem to recollect some right good examples of that.' Kings, prophets, and scholars, some right good examples. And so I named it after a great thinker whose book had lately come into my possession."

Her gaze shifted and I heard the sound of a car rolling up behind me. Granny Mays whispered, "Oh, Lord," and I turned and sat on the lip of the porch. A gleaming-white 1960 Pontiac Bonneville had pulled into the clearing and stopped. A blond woman not much older than Lainie stepped out of it, placed her hand flat above her brow and glared at us for a moment. She wore a sleeveless blouse, pedal pushers, and red lipstick. She cried out, "Helloooo," as if we weren't sitting right there in front of her, and then adjusted the strap of her purse, which hung over one forearm. "Hi, there," she called from about ten feet away, "Are you Ole Nezzie Mays? Have I come to the right place?" She gave the tenant house a quick once-over, doubtful.

Granny Mays said, "You've come to the right place," nodding throughout, and this appeared to frighten the woman a little, but she stepped forward into the shade of the house.

"Well, good," she said. "I'm Mrs. Philip Boselle. Of Farmville? My friend Samantha Glenn told me I could get you to make me some slip-covers for my living room couch. She said you did good work and that you were very fair in your pricing. Is that right?"

I wandered over to admire the car, which sat idling with its windows up and its air conditioner running. The woman turned and smiled at me.

"White leather," I said. "Nice."

"Thank you," she said. "It's brand new."

"I know," I said. "It must be fresh out of the showroom."

The woman giggled and said, "It is. As of Labor Day afternoon."

Customarily, anyone who wanted Granny Mays's slipcovers would come out to the farm and drive her to their home, where Granny Mays would take measurements of the furniture that needed covering; then they would bring her back, and she would give them a price and a pickup date. But today she said, "I'm sorry, Miz Boselle, but I can't be going anywhere at the moment—I can't leave my house. Can you come back on Friday?"

"Well, I guess I *can*, Granny," said the woman, "but it's not very convenient. I already drove all the way out here. It's not a very big couch. I don't think it would take you more than a few minutes to measure it."

Granny Mays said, "My grandson's home sick today. I'll be glad to come with you on Friday."

"Well, I'm surprised there's not somebody else who can stay with him for a short while, Granny. Or can't you just bring him with you?"

"No, ma'am," said Granny Mays.

"Well, what's wrong with tomorrow?" asked the woman.

"I can't do it tomorrow," said Granny Mays. "I can get to it on Friday, though."

The woman said she was very disappointed but that she guessed she would be back on *Friday* then. She sure hoped Granny Mays would be ready, because she didn't want to have to drive way out here to kingdom come a third time. I stepped away from the Bonneville, trying to act casual, for during this exchange I'd seen Burghardt peeking around the frame of the screen door. Broadly, he'd pointed three times over his shoulder, indicating that I should meet him in the cornfield, behind the house.

When the woman left, Granny Mays asked me if I would be kind enough to collect that drapery panel on the floor behind the machine and give it to her. Once she'd gathered the fabric from my arms into her lap, she said, "Thank you, Mr. Ben. I expect Burghardt to be well enough tomorrow. You'll have a short day of school. You just look for him first thing when you get home."

"Okay," I said. "Just tell him I hope he feels better."

"I'll tell him you said so," said Granny Mays, but I thought she said it despondently, as if Burghardt's getting well soon was unlikely. Then she seemed to catch herself, and added, "He's gonna be fine."

I departed down the dirt lane, but as soon as I was out of sight, I entered the corn and cut around the clearing in a wide arc to the back of the house. We had some trouble finding each other in the corn, because we couldn't call out or whistle. I didn't know how deep he might've gone into the field, so I started fairly close to the edge of the clearing and worked my way outward. Soon I heard his quiet but sharp "*Pssst, pssst*" and found him crouched on the ground about twenty rows out.

"Hey," he said, and gave me his crooked grin. "What were y'all talking about before that woman showed up?"

I sat beside him in the dirt and tore off a blade of corn that was dangling in my face. "Oh, just stuff," I said. "Are you really sick?"

"Kinda," he said. "But I feel fine. What stuff?"

"She was talking about when you were born," I said. "How Julius brought you home and said you didn't have a mama and she named you."

"Oh, that," he said.

He asked me if I'd done anything special for Labor Day and I told him I'd labored, which he thought was funny. I said I'd gone somewhere with my sister, out in Buckingham County, where we'd visited some people who had a xylophone.

"A xylophone?" said Burghardt. "I thought that was just a make-believe thing. Something in a fairy tale."

"What fairy tale has a xylophone in it?" I asked.

"None's I know of," he said, "but you know what I mean."

Then I remembered two things: it had been a marimba, not a xylophone, and Lainie had told me not to tell anyone where we'd gone. I said, "Actually it was a marimba, but it looked like a xylophone, except it was made out of wood, but don't tell anybody, okay? It's a secret."

Burghardt looked at me sideways. "What in the world are you talking about?" he said.

"Listen, Burghardt," I said. "Are you sure you're not sick? You didn't get hurt or anything, did you?"

"Hurt doing what?" he said.

"I don't know," I said. "Hurt doing anything."

"Only one I heard about getting hurt around here was your granddaddy," Burghardt said, with something almost like pride. "Heard he took a fall and cracked his head."

I said, "Burghardt, are you coming back to work?"

"I don't think so," he said. "But you'll be in school anyhow starting tomorrow."

"But I get out every day at one-thirty," I said. "We'd still have the afternoon chores."

"I don't think so," he said. "Granny's got some plans for my education."

"Well, try to come back," I said. "You want to, don't you?"

"I don't know," he said. "It was fun, but summer's over."

"But we've got a lot more warm weather ahead," I said. "Try to get them to let you do the afternoon chores."

"Shoot," he said. "Did you see that Pontiac?"

"It was nice," I said. "But I would've bought a red one."

"Red's nice," he said, "but mine would be midnight blue."

I told him about the white leather interior, and he said he thought that might be too much white in one car. He stood and brushed dirt off his knees. "She's gonna notice I'm gone," he said. "You want a hand up?"

I let him pull me up from the ground, and then we were facing each other. He appeared taller than usual, and I noticed that I stood in the deep part of the furrow while he was a little on the rise. He said, "Put your hands like this," and flattened his hands vertically in front of his chest, as if to say, Stop.

When I'd done it, he balled up his fists, feinted like a boxer, and punched one of my palms and then the other. It was a method he'd concocted for saying good-bye, I supposed, for he said, "Gotta go," and hurried away through the corn. I whispered loudly, "Try to get them to let you, okay?" but I guessed he couldn't hear me.

I went back the way I'd come, in a wide arc around the clearing, and eventually found the better part of the dirt lane that led to our road. I thought I would venture a peek at the Big House and maybe catch from a distance the delivery men unloading the new TV. In my heart I knew I was too late for that, but I might glimpse the cardboard box sitting outside and learn something about it. I heard hammering coming from the Big House, and when I was a few feet shy of the road, I ducked into the corn so as to take a look without being seen. I stooped close to the ground and looked across the road through the ragged archway between two rows of corn. The delivery truck had come and gone, and I saw no cardboard box in the yard, but I did see a wooden ladder leaning against the eaves of the screen porch, and my father standing on the roof, next to where the roof met the second story of the house. He was banging a hammer low against the exterior wall. Beside the ladder, a television antenna rested on a long metal pole, which extended several feet above the edge of the roof. Now Daddy stopped hammering, reached for something in his hip pocket—a small metal bracket of some kind—held it against the wall, and started hammering again.

A door slammed on the back of the house and Daddy Cary emerged from around the corner of the screen porch. He was wearing what looked like a new pair of overalls, and his head was wrapped all the way around with a wide white bandage. He stepped backward a few paces away from the house so he could see who was up on the roof. "What in hell is all that racket about?" he yelled. "What in hell are you doing up there?"

Daddy stopped what he was doing and walked to the edge of the roof, hammer in hand. "I'm putting up your TV antenna, Daddy," he said, "so you can start watching."

"I don't remember asking anybody to put up any goddamned TV antenna," said Daddy Cary. "Now kindly git down off of my roof and give me little peace and goddamned quiet."

He stalked back to the house and disappeared around the corner of the porch. I heard the door slam again. Daddy wiped his forehead with the back of his wrist, then hurled the hammer like a tomahawk to the ground, right where Daddy Cary had been standing. He turned around backward to the edge of the roof and climbed down the ladder. On the ground, he fetched the hammer and anchored it in his hip pocket, where its wooden handle waved around at odd angles with each step he took. He pulled the ladder away from the eaves of the porch, lowering it one rung at a time above his head. When he reached the middle rung, he lifted the feet of the ladder from the ground and began carrying it over his head toward the barnyard. I quickly moved through the corn a few rows to the right, came out behind the smokehouse, and continued watching him from around its opposite corner. He went down the stone steps into the barnyard and on to the old tractor shed. He stopped beside the shed and rotated the ladder 90 degrees above his head like the blade of a helicopter. He reared back and heaved it against the gray shed wall with such force that the corner post of the shed broke loose and moved inward half a foot, causing the tin roof to sag. Daddy yanked at the hammer, trying to free it from his hip pocket, and at last its claw ripped the material of his pants, tearing open a flap that hung down and exposed a triangle of white underwear. He hurled the hammer at the shed wall. The impact moved the loosened post farther in, and the roof sagged a few inches more. He stepped forward, retrieved the hammer, and hurled it at the wall again, and the roof sagged a bit more. Finally, he moved close to the shed, lifted his leg high, and planted the heel of his boot against the wall, again and again and again, until the wall of boards caved in against the big rear wheel of the John Deere. The shed roof cantilevered out over the top of the wall. Daddy went to give the shed one last kick but lost his footing, swung around, and fell against the wall, sliding down it to the ground. And there he stayed, hanging his head.

I stepped into the road. I meant to go to him, though I imagined he wouldn't like it. I was afraid the roof of the tractor shed might come crashing down on his head. What stopped me was that as soon as I got to the other side of the road, I saw Daddy Cary standing on the back stoop of the screen porch, facing the barnyard and calmly smoking a cigar. And just as I'd stopped dead in my tracks at the edge of the grass, Oatsie Montague came out the porch's front door. She stood there on the concrete and stared straight at me, giving me a look she might have reserved for the Devil himself, except it had no fear in it. I guessed she was mad at me for the big lie I told her about Julius killing Daddy Cary. For a moment, the look she gave me was open plain-faced hatred, then it was oh-I-really-don't-have-the-time. She turned without a word and went back inside.

Late in the day, the alternator belt on Al's Fairlane snapped. He bathed and changed at our house and stayed to supper, but he had to phone Jeannette to come pick him up and take him home to Farm-ville. He planned to buy the required belt in town the next morning and get Shelby or Frank O'Bannon to give him a lift to the farm. At the supper table, Lainie appeared physically exhausted and only pushed around a few wheels of fried squash on her plate. I noticed that Mother, who'd served hamburger steaks tonight, monitored Lainie's every move, more eaglelike than usual, and both she and Lainie were laconic throughout the meal. Mother told me to choose what I wanted to wear tomorrow for the opening day ceremonies in the State Theatre and to lay it out before I went to bed. She lamented the fact that parents had been asked not to accompany their children to the cere-monies. Al said it was too bad, but the State Theatre wasn't big enough to hold everybody, students and teachers and administrators, as well as all the newspeople who were going to show up to cover the event. He said some serious history was being made tomorrow, as it would be the opening of the nation's first countywide private school system. Daddy had come to supper still in his work clothes, unbathed, unshaved, and his hair uncombed. He'd brought a glass of whiskey with him, too, something he rarely did, for Mother refused to speak to him or in any other way acknowledge his presence as long as whiskey was on the table. I had no doubt that his loose condition was con-nected to the scene at the tractor shed, and I suspected that the whiskey on the table was not his first of the afternoon. I credited it with transforming him—there was no lingering evidence of his former rage. Because of the Labor Day holiday, there had been no Tuesday *Herald*, but Daddy recalled for us that last Friday's paper had said that Farmville was going to be swarming with reporters tomorrow morning. He said they expected fifty or more newsmen, from different parts of Virginia, from other states, from up north, and all over. "Radio and tel-evision too," he said. He lifted his whiskey glass, as if to propose a toast, and said, "The eyes of the nation will be watching us again." He looked directly at me and said, "You behave yourself tomorrow, Benbo.

If a reporter stops you on the sidewalk and asks you a question, you just be polite and tell the truth."

Al laughed and said I should probably avoid the subject of two-by-fours.

Lainie said, "That's not even close to being funny, Al," and Al said, "I'm sorry"—unable to suppress a smile—"it just slipped out."

Before Mother had served her dessert of canned peaches and vanilla ice cream, a horn sounded outside. Al jumped up, knocking his chair to the floor. Lainie said, "Goodness!" and Al righted the chair and slid it under his end of the table.

"That's her," he said. "Gotta run."

Immediately, the dogs started barking, and I decided to go out and try to quiet them. Lainie slipped me her untouched hamburger steak, but Mother only rolled her eyes, hopelessly.

Jeannette, in her father's black-and-white Chevy station wagon, was backing out the drive. I waved, but only Al returned the wave, as Jeannette had her head turned. I broke the meat patty in two, passed pieces through the wire to Lady and Bullet, and the dogs fell into single-minded chomping at opposite sides of their wooden kennel. From the road, Al called out my name. Jeannette had fully executed her turnaround and had stopped the car on the far side of the road; this meant she was nearer me, and Al had leaned across the front seat and called to me through her window. "I forgot something, Benny," he said.

Jeannette, her head resting in the rear bottom corner of the window, smiled sleepily and said, "Hi, Benny."

Al was reaching into his pants pocket, and after a brief struggle he produced a long, flat, rectangular box. He passed this to me through Jeannette's window. He said, "I almost forgot. For your first day of school."

The box opened on a hinge, and inside it was the most beautiful fountain pen I'd ever seen. It was marbled burgundy, trimmed in gold. "Wow," I said, and exhumed it from its little pen casket. Jeannette said, "Al *Rome*, that is an expensive fountain pen! Where did you get it?"

"Somewhere," he said. He leaned forward and said to me, "You like it?"

"Like it?" I said. I quickly stuck the box in the pocket of my shorts and removed the cap from the pen. "Look at it."

"The nib is real gold," Al said. "You take good care of it, Benny. And keep a good eye on it, too. It's just the kind of thing somebody might try to steal."

"I bet it is," said Jeannette, smiling at me again.

I didn't know what a nib was, but I assumed it to be the point of the pen, for it was indeed gold. "Thank you," I said.

Al said, "You're welcome. Good luck tomorrow."

Jeannette turned to Al and said, "Well, I think I'm just a tiny bit jealous."

Al kissed her and said, "Now, what makes you think I don't have a present for you, too?"

"Do you?" she said.

"Maybe," he said, "but you're just gonna have to wait and see."

She pushed him away, then turned back to me and said, "Good luck tomorrow, Benny."

I said thank you again, and they drove away. I stood in the middle of the road and watched them go. The car stirred the bushes and weeds along the right side of the road and disappeared behind the first hill. A single leaf, tinged with yellow, fell from a persimmon tree at the edge of the road and zigzagged down into the dirt. A blackbird swooped from the tree, landed beside the leaf, and pecked at it twice, then flew back up into the shelter of the branches.

At bedtime, I laid out my clothes and put my new fountain pen on my lamp table, turning it once or twice to achieve the best angle for its proper display. As with many exceptional gifts, it came with built-in delayed gratification—I would have to wait until tomorrow to buy ink. I wasn't in the habit of saying bedtime prayers, but tonight, after I was under the covers, I closed my eyes and silently raced through the Lord's Prayer. Lainie knocked on my door and came in to say good night. She would take me to the State Theatre tomorrow, as the eight-thirty starting time coincided with hers at the dentist's office. She would also bring me home, for I was to be out around lunchtime and could kill an hour or so until she quit work. She sat next to me on the edge of the bed. Most surprisingly, she asked me if I had said my prayers. I said I had, and she said she hoped I would forgive her her trespasses.

"What trespasses?" I asked.

"I shouldn't have taken you with me on Monday," she said. "It wasn't right."

"But I wanted to come," I said.

"You weren't sorry?"

"No," I said. "I liked it."

She asked me if I was ready to have my lamp switched off, and I said okay. She hesitated for a moment, glancing at the fountain pen, and said, "You know that's ill-gotten gain, don't you, Ben?"

"You think he stole it?"

"What do you think?"

"Probably."

"Yeah, probably," she said, and switched off the lamp.

She sat still, in the dark, and after a few seconds, I could begin to make out the bluish-gray features of her face. "Trouble is," she said, "I don't know what I'm going to do now, about Mother and Daddy. I think Mother already knows something's changed."

I thought it was a curious thing, how you could know something but not know you knew it. I said, "You mean about the baby?"

She nodded.

I said, "Did you stop being pregnant?"

This time she didn't nod but rose from the bed and walked to the window. She pulled one side of the blind two inches from the frame and peered through the crack. At last she said, "I don't love him, Ben."

"What?" I said, though I'd heard her perfectly well.

"I don't love him," she repeated. "I think I hate him."

"Well, if you hated him," I said, "why'd you marry him?"

She released the blind and returned to the bed. She found my toes and squeezed them through the covers. I jerked my feet away. "I think it didn't occur to me not to marry him," she said. "He *loved* me. Quee-nie. Fattygrub. He loved me."

"You're not fat," I said.

"Yes, well, not anymore, I'm not going to be," she said, and turned for the door.

"Lainie," I whispered. "Do you think Mother and Daddy love each other?"

"No, Ben," she said. "Whatever you do, don't confuse what they have together with love."

"Okay," I said, easily assured on this question. "See you in the morning."

My dreams were replete with deep hard-edged shadows, low-flying beams of orange sunlight, and Southside landscapes: rolling hills, dirt roads that cut through fields of corn and tobacco, the dome of a pasture strewn with butter and eggs, muddy streams, stands of white oak and Virginia pine. I drifted up through layers of sleep and found myself in my own bed, in my own room. I heard female voices, agitated and distraught. Lainie's crying. Mother's crying. Long fierce silences. Shrill skirmishes in the dead of night. Then my father's voice joined the two others, providing a bass line, a complaint of a different color, and I resumed my dreaming. From my place on the bed, I could see straight through the roof of the house to the black sky, where some dark-green clouds composed of pine boughs coursed east to west at breakneck speed. My family's brawling went on and on, but now and again a sudden hole opened in the mad flurry of the clouds, and the smart spark of a star dropped through with a watery, marimbalike *ping*.

12

AT THE STATE THEATRE, the house lights typically went up at the end of movies, but the auditorium was never meant to be so brightly lit as it was on the morning of September 10, and certainly never meant to suffer the glare of television lights. The walls, as well as the curtain that had been drawn over the movie screen, were dingy-looking, the blood-red carpet in the aisles threadbare in patches and spotted with spill stains and chewing gum. At the front of the theater, a table, covered with a gleaming white cloth and adorned with a large arrangement of white chrysanthemums, had been set up to accommodate four chairs and a wooden lectern rigged with five different microphones. An American flag brought in for the occasion hung limp on a mahogany pole to the left of the table. There were not enough seats for everyone, and a hierarchy had been established, with teachers and school administrators occupying the seats closest to the front and the youngest of us, the fifth-graders, obliged to stand against the theater's back wall. (Kindergartners and grades one through four had not been invited to the ceremony, since it was felt that children under the age of ten lacked the maturity to benefit from it; they reported directly to their classrooms instead, which were scattered about at various locations throughout the town.)

The general air of the occasion was a mixture of solemnity and high excitement, an ambiguity sharpened by a lingering aroma of popcorn. The important men who would lead the assembly, dressed in their Sunday finest, gathered at a speakers' table flanked by murals of Charlie Chaplin and Mickey Mouse. The spots-before-your-eyes experience, caused by all the flashbulbs that constantly went off in the theater, created more than the usual amount of giddiness in us kids on our first day of school. And there was a fair amount of waiting to be done, as we were asked to arrive at eight-thirty so the ceremony could begin promptly at nine. Some of the time could be taken up with observing summer metamorphoses in classmates: Phyllis Banks now wore bangs, JoJo Cram a butch-waxed flattop; formerly fat Karen McAllister had lost about twenty pounds; Lester Gaston had got eyeglasses. But soon there was not enough to keep my mind from straying to the morning I'd already had.

At home, Mother hadn't emerged from her bedroom to make breakfast or to see me off on my first day of fifth grade. When I'd dressed and gone to the kitchen, I'd found it empty, though the electric coffee percolator was plugged in and warm. I went to Lainie's room to inquire, passing Mother's closed door along the way. Lainie, dressed for work, sat applying her makeup at the vanity mirror. When I asked her what had happened to Mother, she simply glanced briefly at my reflection in the mirror and said I should get myself a bowl of cornflakes. A minute later, as I was taking a bottle of milk from the refrigerator, Daddy came in from the back porch dangling an empty cup from his index finger; he said hey and poured himself some fresh coffee. He appeared to be in a hurry, so I quickly asked him if he knew what was wrong with Mother. He harrumphed, said, "You better talk to your sister about that," and left through the porch door the way he'd come.

Five minutes after that, Lainie opened the door between the kitchen and the living room and said, "Come on, Ben, we're going to be late." We left the house by way of her private entrance and drove into town in the Willys. The day was overcast. Lainie, quiet and tired, would say only that she and Mother had "had it out" last night, and I recalled the nocturnal clamor that had accompanied my dreams. Once we'd turned onto Main Street, she told me that after school was over, I should walk to Dr. Shanks's office and we would get a bite to eat somewhere before going home. She pulled the Willys to the curb in front of the State Theatre, where hordes of people were filing through the double doors and the marquee read:

THE MUMMY
AND
CURSE OF THE VNDEAD

"I guess they ran out of Us," Lanie said.

I looked up at the marquee but didn't say anything.

She said, "Benny, don't worry. Everything's going to be all right. If anyone does something Mother doesn't like, she always acts like they did it to *her*. But she'll get over it." She faced forward, gripped the steering wheel, sighed, and said, "And life will go on."

"You're not going to leave home again, are you?" I said.

"I don't have any plans to, Benny. You better get on in there. And prepare yourself for a lot of 'The future is in your hands.'"

Inside the State Theatre, a hush fell over the crowd when the first speaker approached the lectern. It was Dr. C. Lloyd Arehart, the Presbyterian pastor who'd taken up the pulpit relinquished by the scorned and exiled Reverend Kennedy. He now asked us to bow our heads for the invocation, and when he was done Roy Pearson stepped to the lectern and announced the official opening of the eight private schools throughout the county that had enrolled some fifteen hundred white students and formed the Prince Edward School Foundation.

Mr. Pearson's declaration was greeted with great cheering and applause, which was quickly squelched in an effort to impress the media with our seriousness and our disinclination to gloat. Mr. Pearson said, "The hopes of several hundred thousands will be kindled if you make this year an outstanding one." Our current mayor, W. F. Watkins, Jr., took over the lectern and told us we should attend our new school with dignity and diligence and as ladies and gentlemen, so we could be a credit to ourselves, our families, our country, and our God. On its face it seemed a tall order, but I imagined that everyone, stirred by the weight of the moment, felt entirely equal to it. Mayor Watkins, who wore a light-colored sport coat and a snazzy bow tie, said we should be aware of the enormous sacrifices that had been made on our behalf by parents, teachers, and the Foundation. "Success from now on depends on you," he said. "You must take full advantage of all opportunities. You must, in short, assume the responsibility of being mature citizens."

The Foundation president, B. Blanton Hanbury, also called on us to exercise our maturity as we adapted to our new facilities, which we might find lacking in some respects compared to what we were used to. And Mr. Pearson returned to the lectern to sing the praises of the new schools at some length and in some detail. We (and the press) should understand that the Foundation schools would offer virtually everything in course work that had been offered in the public schools, and certainly there was no need to compare our private school teachers to those we'd had in public school, since they were one and the same. He reminded us again of the sacrifices made by people like J. Barrye Wall (of the *Herald*) and James J. Kilpatrick (of the Richmond *News Leader*), who, among other things, had helped us amass a library of about nine thousand volumes. Then Mr. Pearson asked us a question: "What will be your response to these sacrifices by those who love and cherish you in this county and those numerous other supporters throughout the state and country?" And provided us the answer: "You should be more studious and more determined to improve your level of work. You should be model guests in the buildings made available, in the same manner you expect a guest of yours in your home to treat your prized possessions. The churches you will be in represent investments made by generations of members, and accordingly, the buildings and everything in them made available for your use are just as dear to them as your personal possessions are to you. You should be more thoughtful of and helpful to the teachers and other students. Your behavior should be above reproach. We expect your full cooperation from the disciplinary angle. We will be just and fair, but I will emphasize most strongly that our schools will not be baby-sitters. In summary, you should be ladies and gentlemen, with a serious purpose to better yourselves to the maximum."

The last remarks of the morning were made by Robert C. Gilmer, the football coach who'd stood up at the 1955 mass meeting in Jarman Hall and said that if someone would feed him, he would look after the county's children without being paid a dime. Now he addressed us in his new role as headmaster of the upper school of Prince Edward Academy. He said, "I know what you can do. I say again what I've said many times in the past: Our community is fortunate in the caliber of its young people, and I know you intend to continue it so."

Then about a million people were introduced and recognized for their support, including all the officers of the Foundation, businessmen and civic leaders, and representatives of the churches who had donated space or made other contributions. At last we were told the locations of our specific classrooms and dismissed to report to them, where we would be given our assignments for the weekend. The formal school year was to begin the following Monday. We filed out class by class, and the assembly leaders remained at the theater to hold a news conference.

Hubbard House, where the fifth grade was to meet, stood behind the Farmville Baptist Church, about a block away. JoJo Cram raced up the stairs to the second floor, stomping for utmost noise production, and Madeleine Minor reminded him at the top landing that his behavior was not that of a model guest. Our young teacher, Miss Brandywine, had jet-black hair like Al's Jeannette, a beauty spot on her left cheek, and a tiny voice that commanded a more thorough quiet of us than usual, in order that we might hear her instructions. She said the first thing we needed to concentrate on was making our new classroom attractive and conducive to learning. So we would spend a good part of our first week making colonial and Confederate flags from construction paper, which we would use to create a colorful frieze around the room. Across the top of a large freestanding bulletin board, Miss Brandywine had already thumbtacked some cutout letters: BIRDS OF THE SOUTH. She'd mimeographed drawings of eight different birds for us. We were to select one to take home, color it with crayon, and bring it to class on Monday for this month's Theme Board. I considered this third- or fourth-grade work, but I loved the smell of the mimeographed drawings. All the blue jays and cardinals went fast, and I ended up with a mockingbird. We were done with our first day by about eleven-thirty.

I concluded that Hubbard House was not so bad, and I appreciated the fact that we would be sharing it with the kindergartners. They would occupy the first floor, and I expected them to be loud and disruptive on a regular basis. As we fifth-graders, about fifty in all, spilled onto Main Street, I took note of something I hadn't seen earlier—not when we'd filed into the State Theatre, and not when we'd walked from the assembly to Hubbard House: Colored folks on the sidewalks, children among them, stopped to stare. Now I saw a boy about my age, who had Burghardt's long lanky limbs, pause on the opposite side of Main Street, watching us with apparent neutrality; he was with his mother, who took the top of his head in her hand and swiveled it forward, away from us, and then prodded him along with a finger between his shoulder blades.

At the dentist's office, I found Lainie behind a desk in the waiting room, which was dark and frigid with air-conditioning. A framed needle-point sampler hung on the wall behind her desk: IGNORE YOUR TEETH AND THEY'LL GO AWAY. Lainie was supposed to stay until noon, but Dr. Shanks's last patient of the morning was already in the chair, and there wouldn't be another until one o'clock, at which time Mrs. Shanks took over the reception desk. Lainie got permission to leave a few minutes early, and we walked to J. J. Newberry's, where I hoped to find ink for my new fountain pen.

As I stood in the stationery aisle reading the labels on ink bottles— Blue, Dark Blue, Blue-Black, Black—Lainie approached me with a folded piece of turquoise oilcloth. "Do you think Mother would use this on the kitchen table?" she asked.

"Are you kidding?" I said. "It's aqua!"

We had Cokes and burgers and fries at Kelly's Main Street Diner, and I filled Lainie in on the State Theatre proceedings and Miss Brandywine. I splattered some catsup on my mockingbird, and it left a stain even after I'd wiped it off, but Lainie said it wouldn't show once the drawing had been colored in. She said she recalled a certain Imogene Brandywine from high school, who'd been a senior when Lainie was a freshman and who had a reputation as a slut. She said the girl had black hair, a mole on one cheek, a tiny little voice, and the nickname "Anytime Brandywine." I said I doubted if it was the same person.

After we left the diner, we walked up Main Street and encountered, several doors down from the State Theatre, a huddle of about a dozen men in suits and ties. Apparently, some reporters had not been satis-fied with the news conference inside the theater and had carried a few more questions out to the sidewalk. Lainie and I stopped for a minute to listen. Mr. Hanbury, the president of the Foundation, was saying, "There's absolutely no reason why the Negro people couldn't establish a system similar to ours."

At his side, Mr. Wall added, "All it takes is two or three easy steps. You form a corporation under Virginia law. You establish a school accredited by the Virginia Department of Education. You apply for scholarship grants from the state. And you acquire buildings for school use."

Lainie nudged me and we moved on. When we turned the corner up High Street where she'd parked the Willys, Lainie said, "Now ain't that Mr. Wall just plumb full of good ideas."

As we were passing Oatsie Montague's house I shouted, "Slow down, Oatsie washed her hair!"

Lainie laughed, braked the Willys, and we inched by, gawking at the house, where Oatsie Montague sat daydreaming in the porch swing, eyes closed. With one toe, she kept the swing rocking gently, and the black curtain of her hair hung down over the back of it, swaying to and fro, so long it grazed the floor. This was Oatsie's method of drying her hair, and she would be at it for an hour or more.

At home, Daddy sorted through the week's receipts at his desk on the back porch and operated the noisy adding machine. Mother, in a flowered apron, turned from the kitchen sink where she was peeling potatoes for salad and gave me a hug. She said she was sorry to have missed seeing me off to school that morning. With no obvious resentment, she said she'd been up half the night with Lainie, as if Lainie had been sick and Mother was required to nurse her. She asked me how the first day had gone, and I said fine.

Then Lainie said, "Look what we brought you," and unfurled the aqua oilcloth from Newberry's. While Mother watched in silence, Lainie and I removed the praying-hands napkin holder and the salt and pepper shakers from the red Formica table and then spread and smoothed the oilcloth over it. We all stood back from the table for a few seconds, considering the change, and Lainie glanced at Mother, waiting for her verdict. Mother went to the table, pulled out a chair, sat down, and passed the palms of her hands over the oilcloth meditatively, like a medium at a séance. The kitchen filled with the oilcloth's vinegary scent, and at last Mother said, "It's nice, Lainie, so nice." She turned and extended one hand to Lainie, who took it and sat at the table next to her. I left them like that and went to my room.

The bottle of blue-black ink had a small shallow well just inside its rim; you could fill it by tilting the bottle to one side. On the barrel of the fountain pen there was a little gold lever, which I pulled down; then I dipped the point of the pen into the well and slowly released the lever, drawing up ink from the well. At my card table, I opened a spiral notebook to a blank page and made a few curlicues, elated by the ease with which the pen glided over the paper. I quickly changed into my work clothes. I'd intended to take the new pen to the henhouses, hoping to see Burghardt and show it to him, but at the last minute, before leaving, I changed my mind, because I suspected it would put him out of sorts.

I found Julius in House A, cleaning waterers, and hailed him through the wire from outside the building. "Where's Burghardt?" I called. "He's not still sick, is he?"

Julius moved slowly to where I stood, a troubled look on his face. He held a toilet brush in one hand and hooked the fingers of his other hand in the chicken wire. He said, "No, Mr. Ben, Burghardt ain't still sick. He's about on his way up to Philadelphia, Pennsylvania. Gone to live up there with a cousin of mine and his family, where he can go to school."

"Philadelphia?" I said. At first I couldn't quite think what the word meant.

"I done said my good-byes to him," Julius added. "I liked to keep it short and sweet on account of my deep feelings. If I let it, Mr. Ben, it would tear me up inside."

"Philadelphia?" I said again.

"You can most likely still catch him if you run up to the house," he said. "I expect he'd appreciate seeing you."

As I turned and sprinted down the alley between the buildings, the chickens on either side bolted in every direction, flew about, and squawked. At the corner of the building, Al was just turning the pickup truck into the alley, back from deliveries. I passed him without a pause and heard him yell behind me, "Hey, where's the fire?"

When I stumbled breathless into the clearing at the tenant house, I saw no one on its porch, but I recognized the car idling in front, the dull-blue Buick belonging to the Reverend Mr. Griffin. He sat behind the steering wheel, talking with a teenage colored girl on the passenger side of the front seat. He spotted me as I approached his window and said, "Well, hello, Benjamin. What's wrong, son?"

I supposed I must have looked anguished, bright red from running. "Is Burghardt still here?" I asked.

"He is," said Mr. Griffin, and glanced at this wristwatch. "And I'm hoping he's going to come out of that house in a minute or we're liable to be late."

"Is he really going to Philadelphia?"

Mr. Griffin took a long careful look at me. "Well, yes, he is, Benjamin." His tone was slightly incredulous, as if I'd failed to grasp something obvious. "Burghardt's on his way up north to live with relatives," he said. "He doesn't have any school to go to here in Prince Edward County."

At that moment, Burghardt and Granny Mays emerged from the screen door onto the porch, and I eased along the length of the Buick to its taillight. Burghardt, dressed for church, carried a small gold-colored suitcase, bound with a leather belt. He set it down on the porch floor, bent his knees, and wrapped his arms around Granny Mays's waist. She clasped him so hard she could hold her own elbows in her hands behind his back. She lowered her cheek to the top of his head and rested it there. When at last they released each other, Burghardt lifted the suitcase by its handle and came down the wooden steps into the yard. Granny Mays stayed put, squinting at the Buick, then adjusted the pink kerchief she was wearing and crossed her arms over her chest.

Burghardt opened the rear door of the car and threw the suitcase onto the seat. "Hey," he said to me, looking a little afraid.

"When you coming back?" I said.

He shrugged his shoulders. "Soon," he said, then got in and pulled shut the heavy door.

I stepped away from the car, and Mr. Griffin backed it up a few feet before angling it at the dirt lane into the cornfield. He stopped when he'd come alongside me again. "Don't hold it against me, son," he said, smiling. "I'm just the deliveryman, driving him to the bus station. I'll tell you like I've been telling my Negro friends these many years. It's just one of those things. You may have to bear it, but you don't have to grin."

He steered the Buick forward, out of the clearing, while I stood and watched it go. The brake lights blinked once, and just before the car disappeared around the bend in the lane, Burghardt turned and waved at me from the back window. I hesitated but got my hand up in the nick of time, and then they were gone.

I sauntered to the edge of the porch, where Granny Mays still hadn't budged. She looked down at me, somber, but didn't speak.

I said, "I didn't know he was going," but even as I said it I wondered if it was entirely true.

"It was kinda last-minute, Mr. Ben," she said. "It's the best thing for him. My nephew's got a fine family. Burghardt's gonna get himself finished up, a real education. He's gonna be just fine, don't you worry."

I sat on the steps, rested my elbows on my knees, and stared dumbly into the mouth of the dirt lane. Soon Granny Mays said, "I reckon you can sit there for a while if you want to, Mr. Ben, but I've got to go inside the house now. I've got some things to do. And a right much reading, too, what with all these new books of mine."

I heard the screen door open and close behind me. I stood, walked out of the clearing, and started down the lane. As I reached the bend, I heard a sound from inside the tenant house that made me stop in my tracks. I returned to the edge of the clearing and hid in the corn where I had a good angle on the porch. The high wailing that was coming from the house frightened and repelled me, but I felt a positive obligation to stay. Granny Mays's weeping rose and fell like the howl of a terrible wind, long heartbreaking troughs of silence between each swell, and I knelt on the ground and listened to it. A breeze churned the morning glory vines that climbed the kite string tacked to the side of the house; the heart-shaped leaves nodded emphatically, then seemed to recant and shudder. Higher up, dirt daubers scribbled around the gable vent, darting in and out of the louvers, and meanwhile Mr. Griffin's Buick rolled down Rome Road—past the henhouses, where Julius was initiating Al into the hushed world of poultry hypnosis, a sport in which Al would someday outshine him; past our house, where Daddy studied a column of figures on a slip of adding-machine paper, reaching for the brown pint bottle hidden in the bottom drawer of his desk; and where Mother and Lainie, deadlocked at the kitchen table, pondered Lainie's future and the peril of her immortal soul; past Oatsie Montague's and the spectacle of her unbridled hair, swaying behind the porch swing—and finally thumped across the bridge at the creek, where Burghardt had fired Daddy Cary's pistol once, twice, once again, and yelped with glee.

Now the noise from the tenant house ceased—the bleached flour-sack curtains on the two front windows drew inward, faded from view, then smashed white and creased against the screens—and it was as if the whole cornfield gasped. I imagined the little wooden shack under its rusty tin roof coming unmoored from its cinder blocks, heaving through the field on wheels, a swath of doubled-over stalks in its wake. The screen door squeaked, and Inez Awilda Washington Mays appeared, a wine-colored book in hand. She did not gaze out from the porch, she did not peer into the sudden dogleg of the lane, but took up the rocking chair, where she sat, opened her book, and began to read.

Epilogue

THE PUBLIC SCHOOLS STAYED CLOSED for five full academic years. The legal question raised by our county supervisors—Could a judge, any judge, compel Prince Edward to levy taxes for the purpose of operating schools?—tied up the courts for four and a half years. Though Kittrell College, an A.M.E.-sponsored school in North Carolina, extended reduced tuition and scholarships to some of our oldest Negro students; though the American Friends Service Committee came to the county with volunteer tutors and also made arrangements to send kids to live with families in Ohio, where they could finish high school; though another handful, including Burghardt Mays, were sent to live with relatives; and though Reverend Griffin worked with the local community to set up activity centers to keep some of the children busy during the daytime, about fifteen hundred Negro children were deprived of any form of education besides what their parents might provide at home.

Many colored folks thought the Foundation schools would fail, but they were so successful that hundreds of visitors came to Prince Edward to study our methods, and Roy Pearson sat down and wrote a manual for those who wished to outsmart the Supreme Court the way we had. *Setting Up Private Schools*, he called it, and he did a fair amount of traveling around the South, speaking to large assemblies, including the Georgia legislature. Many white people, like my brother Al, had expected the private schools to be short-lived, but when it became clear that the Foundation intended a permanent abandonment of public education, some white Prince Edwardians began to hold secret meetings, at which they discussed what the long-term economic and social consequences might be. Foundation leaders caught wind of this potential opposition and sent spies to the meetings. Transcripts of what was said, along with the names of everyone who attended, were published in the *Herald*, and that pretty much put an end to any such attempts to question the Foundation's desires. People whose names appeared in the *Herald* were ostracized—some were stripped of their civic and church posts, and they were snubbed in stores and on the golf course, their children bullied at school, their businesses boycotted. After this, white folks were afraid to voice the mildest complaint for fear of social reprisals. At home, I couldn't so much as complain about homework without Daddy reminding me that I was lucky not to be going to school with niggers.

But the cost of sending children to the private schools rose with each year, and it took a considerable leap in 1961, when a federal judge dealt the Foundation a setback: he ruled that the state and local tuition grants white families had been enjoying were illegal as long as the county had no public schools. (Negro taxpayers in Prince Edward, while their own children were denied public education, had been helping to pay for the private education of white taxpayers' children.) When I entered the upper school in 1961, the tuition was $265—this in a county where the average yearly income was just a little more than $3,000 per family—and even Daddy said he was glad he had only one child left to educate. The children of families who couldn't pay their tuition bills were barred from classrooms, and poor families, already neck-deep in debt, were told that the Foundation would be happy to arrange a bank note for them.

Eventually, the Justice Department took an interest in what was happening in our county. In a 1963 speech celebrating the centennial of the Emancipation Proclamation, Robert Kennedy said that "outside of Africa south of the Sahara, the only places on earth known not to provide free public education are Communist China, North Vietnam, Sarawak, British Honduras, and Prince Edward County." In May of 1964, a full ten years after *Brown v. Board of Education*, the Supreme Court ordered Prince Edward to open desegregated schools, and in September, some fifteen hundred students, all Negro save eight, enrolled in the county's public schools. Students were grouped according to ability rather than age, but many of the older kids from 1959 never returned. They didn't much relish sitting in a seventh-grade classroom at the age of seventeen, or in a sophomore class at the age of twenty, and many had already moved on with their lives, into such work as was available to people without a high school diploma. Four young colored men in this category found a job on my father's egg farm, where they worked from 6 A.M. till 7 P.M. for three dollars a day.

One cold early morning in February 1960, Oatsie Montague walked up Rome Road to the Big House, as she did every day except Sunday. Normally, Daddy Cary would not have returned from milking the cows yet, and Oatsie would proceed to the kitchen to start breakfast. But as she passed the living room door, she spotted Daddy Cary in his green leather recliner, apparently asleep, though she would say later that she hadn't much cared for the pallor of his skin. She would say also that once she'd drawn closer, she hadn't needed to touch him—she'd looked at the face of death three times already and was fully acquainted with it. Our country doctor determined Daddy Cary's cause of death to be heart attack, but everybody said Daddy Cary had never been the same after taking that fall and hitting his head. It was true that he'd changed after the incident in the barn. I'd noticed, for example, that he was very different around Julius. He continued to give Julius orders, but often he seemed absentminded as he did so. Julius had changed too—I observed that Julius pretty much did as he pleased, regardless of Daddy Cary's orders—but most oddly, Daddy Cary would simply walk away when Julius did that, without protest. The other change in Daddy Cary came to be known as his "lapses." Because unresponsiveness had always been one of his central personality traits, these lapses were difficult to interpret at first. If he didn't acknowledge you when you spoke, if he didn't answer a question you asked him, there was nothing unusual in that. And he'd recently turned sixty-five; certain declines were to be expected. But Oatsie Montague began to worry when she would find him staring at the test pattern on the new TV; or randomly sleeping past eight in the morning, often fully dressed from the day before; or moving to the screen porch when she called him to the kitchen; or daydreaming in his recliner as the telephone rang. He complained of headaches and shortness of breath for the first time in his life, and he often stumbled dizzily when getting out of the Oldsmobile. Daddy Cary's heart had stopped that February morning, for sure, but most likely what had stopped it was a subdural hematoma, causing pressure on the brain—a consequence of the blow to the head Julius delivered back in August.

In his will, Daddy Cary left the Big House and all its contents to Mother and Daddy, but the rest of the farm was to be divided among all five of the children. Daddy quickly arranged with his brothers and sisters to buy their shares from them over the next fifteen years, and in Mother's view that made us "debtors for the rest of our lives." A month after Daddy Cary was laid in his grave, Mother took down the painting of the Saint Bernard that hung behind the couch in the living room of the Big House. She thought she'd figured out a way to pay off

Daddy's brothers and sisters sooner rather than later, and she wrapped the painting in an old quilt, had Al strap it to the top of the Impala, and drove it to Richmond, where she had it appraised. The painting, purported to have been Dutch and in the Rome family for generations and worth a fortune, turned out to be a copy. The appraiser, a man Mother considered honest, put its value at around forty dollars, but he said he knew somebody who would probably give her a hundred for the gilt frame it was in. Mother brought the painting back to the Big House and got me to help her hang it in its old spot. She moved a few steps backward away from the couch, stood in the middle of the living room, and glared at the painting; at last she sighed and said that if God had given her the talent to paint like that, she sure wouldn't have wasted it on painting no dogs.

Claud Wayne Rivers returned from Germany in April, but he never lived with his bride, Lainie, who remained with us until she left for Tennessee the following autumn. She and Claud Wayne were divorced in the shortest time allowed by Virginia law. Lainie had applied for and received a scholarship to Southwestern at Memphis. Something I had long suspected about her turned out to be true: She was smart. When she graduated from Southwestern four years later, she was the first member of the Rome family ever to receive a college diploma. During her fourth year, she married a classmate, Jack Jackson, of Chattanooga, and they settled outside Memphis, where they both landed jobs teaching in the public elementary schools.

In July 1963, my brother Al was arrested in Charlottesville, caught trying to steal a jukebox from a warehouse. He and the jukebox had been standing on the warehouse loading dock when the police arrived. Since Al had no visible means of transporting the jukebox (or himself, for that matter) away from the scene, it was obvious to the police—and later to a judge and jury—that Al had at least one accomplice. The police interrogated Al's Farmville housemates, Frank and Shelby O'Bannon, and clearly suspected them, but they lacked any evidence that definitely put either of the twins at the warehouse the night of Al's arrest. Al invented some cock-and-bull story about hitchhiking to Charlottesville, getting drunk in a bar whose name he couldn't remember, and meeting a man who'd offered to pay Al ten dollars to help him pick up a jukebox the man had bought; Al didn't know the man's name and he couldn't remember how he'd ended up stranded on the loading dock. He was convicted of statutory burglary. Because of his refusal to reveal the identity of any accomplice, he was handed a rather stiff sentence, despite its being his first conviction—three years in the state penitentiary. Ever afterward, Mother wouldn't allow either of the O'Bannon boys to set foot on our property; when Al was paroled after serving two years of his sentence, Jeannette had married a man she knew from Harrisonburg, moved there, and already had a baby girl.

After I completed ninth grade at the Prince Edward Academy, Lainie and her husband invited me to come live with them in Memphis. By then, Mother, Daddy, and I had moved into the Big House, and our old house sat empty, though it was intended for Al and Jeannette, as it had been assumed they'd be married eventually. Daddy's egg business had continued to thrive; he had a dozen hired hands, and for the past two years I'd been required to work on the farm only during the summer months. Daddy said that if I went to live with Lainie in Memphis, I could kiss a career as an egg farmer good-bye, but that he wouldn't stop me. Mother said that if it was what I really wanted, she wouldn't stand in my way either, but it was going to be awfully lonely for her, rattling around in that great big old barn of a house. I moved to Memphis in July 1964, two months before the Prince Edward public schools reopened.

After Daddy Cary's death, Oatsie Montague had gone to work in our egg room, candling eggs four mornings a week, and Julius and Granny Mays had stayed on in the tenant house. Burghardt had returned home in June of 1960, after completing his first year at his new school up north. I'd thought he would spend the summer on the farm, but he stayed only a week and then returned to Philadelphia, where, he said, he could earn twice as much money doing half as much work. Over the next four years, while I still lived at home, Burghardt paid the farm three more short visits, two in summer, one at Christmas. With each visit, we seemed to have less to say to each other, which corresponded to an ever-widening physical gap between us; he'd always been bigger, but while I grew at a reasonable rate proportionate with my size, Burghardt, in Granny Mays's words, "shot up like a weed." When I saw him in June, shortly before I left for Tennessee, he'd grown to a height of 6 feet 5 inches. He was taller than Julius, taller than my father, taller than my Uncle Dillon Halliday, taller than any adult man I knew personally, and the loss of Burghardt's friendship would always feel to me, at least in part, like a biological event.

Paisley Chatham, the boy who sang for his supper at Daddy Cary's sixty-fifth birthday party, and his two brothers, were three of the eight white students who attended the public school when it reopened in Farmville. I'd already left for Memphis, but I heard some years later that Paisley had made a name for himself as a soloist with the high school chorus. He stayed in school as long as it took to make up his lost years and eventually graduated. Then he fell from sight. Mother heard a rumor at church that he'd disappeared somewhere up north to study music.

After I was living with Lainie, my visits home didn't coincide with Burghardt's, and all I could ever get out of Julius or Granny Mays was that Burghardt was "doing just fine." Around Eastertime 1967, near the end of my senior year of high school, I phoned home and asked Mother whether she'd heard anything about what Burghardt's plans were once school was out, and was he aiming to come back to the farm in June?

"I haven't heard a thing in the world," said Mother.

"Well, if you run into Julius," I said, "would you please ask him?"

"Oh, honey," she said, "Julius isn't with us anymore, I thought you knew that."

"What do you mean, not with you?"

"Well, he just up and left," she said. "He might've told your daddy where he was going but I can't recall."

"I don't understand, Mother," I said. "What about Granny Mays?"

"You mean Ole Nezzie?" she said. "Ole Nezzie died before Christmas last year, Benjamin. I know I mentioned it to you."

I told her I'd been accepted at Southwestern and, like Lainie, had received some scholarship money; then I hung up. The Mayses had been our neighbors for fifteen years, and it came down to *Ole Nezzie died, Julius up and left, haven't heard a word about Burghardt.*

I went home for a week in August before I was to start college. The milking barn stood empty, as Daddy hadn't kept the cows. The old tenant house stood empty too, stark in its now-fallow field, as Daddy didn't grow corn or any other crop. One afternoon as I lay napping on a quilt in the apple orchard, a panel truck pulled to the side of the road and stopped about ten feet from where I lay. I'd been dreaming that the tenant house had burned to the ground, reduced to charred ruins putting out gray-white vines of smoke that climbed high into the sky. When the sound of the panel truck awakened me and a young black man came ambling around its front bumper, I thought for a moment that he emerged from a cloud of smoke. It was Burghardt, in the county visiting Julius, who now lived in Rice, not more than ten miles away. I could see immediately that Burghardt had changed somehow, for he looked me in the eye when he spoke, and he spoke very quietly. He was dressed in grown-up clothes, navy cotton dress pants, a white short-sleeved shirt, black leather shoes; two pens stuck out of his shirt pocket, and he wore a gold Timex on his wrist. We walked through the shade of the orchard, where Burghardt had to watch his head and frequently duck. He asked me if I had a girlfriend, and I told him there'd been somebody for about six months, but we were about to part as we went to our separate colleges. Burghardt said he had the exact same situation in Philadelphia. His girl was staying in Pennsylvania, but when he was done visiting Julius he was off to Howard University. I didn't know where Howard University was, but I thought I should know, so I didn't ask. Burghardt said he wanted to be a lawyer and asked me what I wanted to be. I only shrugged, for I'd started writing poetry but wasn't ready to tell anybody about it yet.

We stopped at the end of the orchard, by an old falling-down split-rail fence, and I caught him gazing out across the defunct cornfield at the tenant house. I said, "You want to go see it?"

"Yeah," he said, and we moved along the fence toward the road. Once we'd left the orchard, we crossed the road and climbed a briary embankment on the other side. We approached the tenant house in a straight line, at an angle of about 45 degrees to the old dirt lane that had been the Mayses' driveway. The sun beat down on our heads, and once we'd reached the house, we sought the shade of the front porch. Granny Mays's rocking chair, inert and weathered, had somehow traveled to the very end of the porch. Burghardt pulled it away from the edge and offered it to me. I said, "No, you take it," and sat on the top step. After he was seated in the rocker, I had to look over my shoulder in order to see him. Not looking at him, I said, "Don't you want to go inside?"

"I thought I did," he said, "but maybe not."

He said it with such solemnity I turned and looked at him. "You want me to leave you alone out here for a while?"

"No, thanks," he said. "I'm happy enough, just sitting here."

So we sat in silence for a while, and this time, this last time I was to see him, the silence between us felt friendly, as if we'd agreed to it and shaken hands to seal the deal. I imagined something important had happened in Philadelphia, something with tragic trimmings, that had matured him in this solemn way; I was never to know if I was right about this, but in time I came to understand that no tragic thing in Philadelphia was necessary.

At a certain moment, I thought I heard him speak and I turned to him again. I saw that he hadn't spoken, but now he looked me in the eye and said, "Benjamin Rome."

It was the first time he'd ever called me by my name, which took me aback, but I said "Burghardt Mays," then added, "Attorney at law," and we both laughed.

A month later, when I started college, I befriended during fraternity pledge week one of the two black students at Southwestern, a freshman from Alabama named Ernest, who reminded me of the tall solemn Burghardt I'd said good-bye to on the tenant-house porch. Ernest and I each wanted to be rushed by ATO, and if they had rushed him, he would have been the chapter's first black pledge. But ATO did not rush him, nor did any other fraternity on campus. ATO did rush me, and after I'd pledged, I sat with Ernest for a half hour in his dorm room as he tried to express his anger and disappointment without crying. That was on a Friday. The following Monday I quit the fraternity, not because they'd rejected Ernest but because I learned that I would be required, on a nightly basis, to polish the shoes of senior members. Ernest and I didn't remain friends after that—I found him cold—and eventually I came to think it was because I'd handily discarded something he'd wanted and been denied.

Just before Thanksgiving that year, while doing some reading about the American Revolution, I came across a reference to King George III's younger brother Edward, Prince of York. I recalled from a high school civics course that our county in Virginia had been named for this Edward, and that he'd been described as "otherwise uncelebrated." I went digging in the Southwestern library and found that Edward, only a year younger than George, had shared almost every minute with his brother during boyhood. He studied the same subjects under the same tutors and was in every way George's equal except that their mother, as well as their father, Frederick, the Prince of Wales, clearly favored Edward. Despite all that, Edward would never wear the crown, for having been born a few months too late. (Their father Frederick wouldn't either, for he would die while his own father George II still held the throne.) Edward grew up to become a libertine, frivolous, selfish, and hungry for a kind of power that was not rightfully his, undistinguished in any way, and forgotten by history save as a footnote to the biography of his brother, America's last king.

Author's Note

Prince Edward is a work of fiction, but I've set the Rome family's story against a backdrop of actual events, in a specific time and place. For the sake of narrative convenience, I've occasionally altered some particulars, but none that substantially distort the record. Two examples:

1. In order to illustrate that the children of some of Prince Edward's poorest white families were deprived of an education during the years of the school closings, the story asserts that Paisley Chatham's father couldn't afford Prince Edward Academy's tuition of $15 per pupil; in reality, the cost of tuition during the Academy's first year of operation was financed by the generous contributions of people who wished to support the cause of segregated schools, and Senator Byrd used his influence with the IRS to ensure that such contributions were tax-deductible; during the second year, state and local tuition grants, later determined to be illegal (since such grants availed themselves of African Americans' tax dollars while effectively depriving African Americans of public schools), covered all but about $15 of tuition

costs; by the third year, parents had to foot the entire bill themselves, $240 in the lower school, and $265 in the upper school.

2. In order to dramatize the Foundation schools' opening-day events, the story places Benjamin Rome in the State Theatre on September 10, 1959; in reality, a child his age would not have attended the assembly there, as only upper-school students were invited.

My decision to use the real names of some of the key players of the time was rooted primarily in a desire to credit those individuals, like Barbara Johns and L. Francis Griffin, whose courage deserves a permanent place in the history of the civil rights movement in the South and particularly in the dangerous struggle to overturn the specious contentions of the separate-but-equal doctrine in public education. It would have been idiosyncratic to credit these individuals by using their real names and then to change the names of other players, on whom history has taken a dimmer view. This felt to me especially evident when considering the roles of such men as Roy Pearson, Robert Crawford, and J. Barrye Wall, Sr., who enjoyed (along with others in similar positions) a kind of oligarchy fully recognizable today—formed of economic, political, and public-opinion constituents. The closing of public schools was not uncommon in the South as an early response to the slow implementation of *Brown*, but nowhere else did schools remain closed as they did in Prince Edward. Every account I found of these events suggests that the extraordinary outcomes in Prince Edward were predicated on the collaboration of business, control over the organs of government, and the tenacious regulation of public dialogue exercised by the Farmville *Herald*.

Of course I have imagined these real people into the lives of the fictitious Romes. In doing so, I've made an effort to characterize them according to what I learned about them from the historical writings I consulted. When I've given them words to say, they are usually based on actual remarks made by them at other occasions or in other venues.

The remarks made by Mr. Wall at Daddy Cary's birthday party, for example, were gleaned from Mr. Wall's editorials in the *Herald*.

Granny Mays's practice of "saying justice" in the woods is borrowed from Barbara Johns's real-life grandmother, Mary Croner, as reported in her own words in R. C. Smith's study of Prince Edward County, *They Closed Their Schools*. In no other way is Granny Mays meant to resemble Mrs. Croner.

Prince Edward offers only a glimpse of the fascinating and instructive events of the fifties and sixties in Southside, Virginia. For readers interested in learning more about this time, I refer them to the exhaustive study of the road to *Brown* by Richard Kluger, *Simple Justice: The History of Brown v. Board of Education and Black America's Struggle for Equality*; to *They Closed Their Schools: Prince Edward County, Virginia, 1951-1964* by journalist R. C. Smith, who took up residence in the county during the period of the school closings and rendered a detailed, thoughtful account of what happened; and to "The 'Impossible' Prince Edward Case," a thoroughgoing summary of these events by Ann Murrell, collected and edited by Matthew D. Lassiter and Andrew B. Lewis in *The Moderates' Dilemma: Massive Resistance to Desegregation in Virginia*. In creating the historical backdrop for my novel I have relied on these writers, on newspaper accounts of the time, and on the work of Edward H. Peeples, Jr., Donald P. Baker, George Gilliam, and Vernon Johns. Anything in my novel that might be considered to be in error historically reflects not the work of these writers but either a mistake on my part or the kind of deliberate alteration of fact mentioned earlier.

Finally, I express my gratitude to a number of people I'm fortunate to know and who helped me more than I can say: to Peter Bryant, Lisa deLima, Michael Downing, Thom Harrigan, Gail Hochman, Richard Hoffman, Mike Lew, Debra Nystrom, Kent Olson, Matt Penney, and David Savitz, whose many contributions were indispensable; to

Jennifer Barth, Frances Kiernan, and Janet Baker for their splendid editing of the manuscript; to my wife, Michelle Blake, who gave with her usual kindness and insight both to *Prince Edward* and to me, as I tried to sort out my many dilemmas; and to Linda Mizell, who not only offered many useful suggestions as I worked on the book but who proposed I write it in the first place.

About the Author

DENNIS McFARLAND is the bestselling author of *Singing Boy, The Music Room, A Face at the Window,* and *School for the Blind.* His fiction has appeared in *Prize Stories: The O. Henry Awards, Best American Short Stories,* and *The New Yorker.* He lives with his family in Massachusetts.